Tom Holt was born in 1961, a sullen podgy child, much given to brooding on the Infinite. He studied at Westminster School, Wadham College, Oxford, and the College of Law. He produced his first book, *Poems by Tom Holt*, at the age of thirteen, and was immediately hailed as an infant prodigy, to his horror. At Oxford, Holt discovered bar billiards and at once changed from poetry to comic fiction, beginning with two sequels to E.F. Benson's *Lucia* series, and continuing with his own distinctive brand of comic fantasy in *Expecting Someone Taller*, *Who's Afraid of Beowulf?*, *Flying Dutch*, *Ye Gods!*, *Overtime*, *Here Comes the Sun*, *Grailblazers*, *Faust Among Equals* and *Odds and Gods*. He has also written two historical novels set in the fifth century BC, the well-received *Goatsong* and *The Walled Orchard*, and has collaborated with Steve Nallon on *I, Margaret*, the (unauthorised) autobiography of Margaret Thatcher. Thinner and more cheerful than in his youth, Tom Holt is now married, and lives in Somerset.

Praise for Tom Holt:

'Literate; light fiction, an under-appreciated genre of which Tom Holt has made himself a modern master.'
Washington Post

'A rival to the comic throne'
Starburst

FAUST
AMONG
EQUALS

Tom Holt

ORBIT

An *Orbit* Book

First published in Great Britain in 1994 by Orbit
This edition published in Great Britain in 1995 by Orbit

A CIP catalogue record for this book
is available from the British Library.

ISBN 1 85723 265 8

Printed in England by Clays Ltd, St Ives plc

Inside Front Cover:
The Garden of Earthly Delights: Hell
Prado, Madrid
by Hieronymus Bosch (c 1450–1516)

Orbit
A Division of
Little, Brown and Company (UK)
Brettenham House
Lancaster Place
London WC2E 7EN

For

KEN FUNNELL

and

Mike Hughes, Dave Little, Peter Wolf, Arthur Harvey,
Ed Howard et al.

And all charcoal burners, everywhere

CHAPTER ONE

THE Laughing Cod in downtown Hlidarend is rated as one of north-east Iceland's premier restaurants. Or one of north-east Iceland's restaurants. In practice, it amounts to the same thing.

On the three hundred and sixty-four days each year when the Laughing Cod isn't being a restaurant, you can still walk in to the bar and order a coffee; and this is precisely what the Most Wanted Man in History did.

Six of the seven regulars turned and stared at him as he did so; the seventh, Wall-Eyed Bjorn, just carried on complaining about herring quotas.

Torsten Christianssen, the ever-popular proprietor of the Cod, poured the coffee, waited for it to settle, and leant back against the cash register, soaking in the thrill of a new experience.

'Just passing through, are you?' he asked after a while.

The newcomer looked up. 'You could say that,' he replied, with only the very faintest trace of an unfamiliar accent. 'Could you fix me a toasted sandwich, while you're at it?'

'Sure,' Torsten said. 'Coming right up.' He withdrew into the kitchen, wondering what the hell he was doing. It was theoretically possible to get a toasted sandwich in the Cod, but

1

you needed references from two doctors and a justice of the peace before your application could even be considered.

When the stranger had eaten his sandwich, drunk his coffee and spent about forty-five seconds studying the framed photograph of Einar Sigfussen's record grayling on the wall opposite, he stood up and asked for the bill.

'The what?'

'The bill,' repeated the stranger. 'Please.'

'Oh, yes, right. Coming right up. Anybody here got a pencil or something?'

There was a brief, stunned silence, which was resolved when the stranger unclipped one from his top pocket and handed it over. Torsten took it as if it was red hot, and tentatively pressed the top.

'How do you spell coffee?' he asked.

The stranger told him; then took the paper from his hands, glanced at it, and fished a banknote out of his shirt pocket. A ten-thousand kroner note.

'Hey,' said Torsten, when God's marvellous gift of speech had been restored to him. 'You got anything smaller?'

The stranger looked at him, took back the note and put it down on the counter. Then he smiled at it.

It began to shrink.

You couldn't say how it did it; it just gradually occupied less and less space, until eventually it was about the size of a postage stamp. The stranger picked it up, blew on it, and passed it back across the counter.

'Is that better?' he asked.

On the other side of Death, there is a tunnel, leading to an archway. Then the road forks, and this is the point at which you find out whether the ethical system you've been following all these years was the right one after all.

If you've backed the Betamax version, you'll come at last to a rather impressive black stone gateway. There is no name or street number, but the chances are that you'll have guessed where you are anyway. However, by way of a heavy hint, the gateway bears the celebrated inscription:

ABANDON HOPE ALL YE WHO ENTER HERE

– or so your Michelin Guide would have you believe. It's very possible that it still does, but you can no longer see for yourself, because the whole of the architrave of the gateway is now covered with a huge banner, on which is painted the legend:

UNDER NEW MANAGEMENT

– and when you get up really close, you can see that it actually says:

UNDER / *entirely* NEW MANAGEMENT

– just to ram the point well and truly home. At this juncture, you will be met by your guide, who will escort you to the ticket office (where you can also purchase guide books, souvenir pencils and locally-made coconut ice). The Michelin Guide doesn't mention that; but if you think about it, how would they know, anyway?

Once you've passed the ticket office, your tour will take you all round the justly celebrated architectural gems that comprise the inner courtyard, with the exception of the Council Chamber, which is not yet open to the public. This is a pity because apart from the Michelangelo floor (remember where we are) the Chamber houses three late Veroneses, a rather fine set of Dürer engravings and, naturally, the finest collection of works by Hieronymus Bosch in the universe. They are, of course, all portraits, such as may be found in the boardroom of any long-established corporate body.

On the day in question, the Council was in session, and had been for sixteen hours. The Council members (or Board of Directors, as we must call them now) each sat under his, her or its respective portrait, each one looking just the same as he/she/it had when Ronnie Bosch had painted them six hundred years previously; except that they were all wearing, somewhat self-consciously, identical red T-shirts with the words:

HAVIN' A DAMNED GOOD TIME

printed on them in big white letters.

'I still reckon we haven't thought this thing through properly,' said the Production Director stubbornly. He'd opposed the whole idea of a management buy-out from the start, and had only come in with the rest of the consortium under considerable pressure.

'Listen, Harry,' replied the Sales Director, lashing his tail irritably. 'We know what you think, so you stick to keeping the ovens going and we'll all get along just fine. You leave the management side to the grown-ups, okay?' For the record, he'd been the one applying the pressure, with a pitchfork, in the small of the Production Director's back.

'Actually,' interrupted the Admin Director wearily, 'Harry has got a point there, of sorts. I mean, it's one thing getting the blasted franchise. Keeping it's a different crock of entrails entirely.'

The Sales Director scowled, displaying a wide selection of unlikely components. 'All you can do is make problems,' he complained. 'We're running a *business* now, people. I suggest we all remember that, okay?'

'Sure.' The Finance Director nodded what, for the sake of argument, we shall call his head. 'We all know that, Steve, you've told us often enough. I'd just like to remind you that if those bloody inspectors catch us breaking the terms of the franchise, they'll have us out of here like the proverbial pea through a trumpet. Is that what you want?'

The Sales Director groaned theatrically and paused for a moment to scratch his nose (the one growing up out of his navel, not the one sprouting between his eyebrows). 'Look, Norman,' he said, 'there's ways round all that stuff, you know that as well as I do. All it takes is a little . . .'

The Finance Director shook what he had recently nodded. 'And there's such a thing as being too bloody clever for your own good, Steve. You'd do well to remember that.' He rubbed the bridge of his beak with a thoughtful claw, and continued; 'If they think we're not fulfilling the public service part of the deal . . .'

'But we are.'

'I'm not so sure.'

'Neither am I,' interrupted the Production Director. 'Take the perjury business, for instance. We could have got in serious schtuck with that.'

'I hadn't heard about any perjury stuff,' murmured the Finance Director, tapping the edge of the table with his offside front wing. 'Sounds interesting.'

The Production Director grinned unpleasantly, even for him. 'I'll bet,' he said. 'Look, in the franchise agreement it says, clause nine, sub-para three, all perjurers shall be broken on the wheel, right?'

'Right,' agreed the Finance Director. 'Standard procedure, it's what we've been doing for years. So?'

'So this dangerous clown here only had the whole department cleared out and fifty roulette tables put in. If I hadn't found out about three days before the last random check . . .'

'I still don't know what you're getting so uptight about,' growled the Sales Director. 'A wheel's a wheel, right? And I can guarantee the whole lot of them were broke by the time . . .'

He subsided under the glare of the Finance Director's six

beady red eyes, and took a sudden interest in the pencil on the table in front of him.

'That,' said the Finance Director, 'is definitely going too far. As,' he added sharply, 'is this idea of changing the name of the place to Netherglades Theme Park. How the hell am I meant to explain that to the inspectors, Steve? A smear campaign by the printers?'

The Sales Director sniffed – quite an achievement, considering. 'Come on,' he said. 'Even a bunch of blinkered, concrete-brained civil servants is going to realise the importance of image in a business like this. You honestly believe the punters are going to be able to relate to the image we've got at the moment? I mean, would you fork out good money if you thought you were going to get your lungs ripped out with a blunt meathook?'

'But that's the business we're in, Steve.'

The Sales Director waved an impatient talon. 'So are an awful lot of people, Harry, that's not the point. The point is, you can torture the punters and roast them alive and coop them up in confined spaces indefinitely and flay them on spits and they'll still fall over themselves to give you money, just so long as you can convince them it's fun. That's what the holiday industry's all about, Harry. Just so long as your image is okay . . .'

'I think we'll have to agree to disagree on this one for the time being,' said the Finance Director smoothly. 'I mean, there's obviously good arguments on both sides. Yes, we have to watch our backs as far as the inspectors are concerned. On the other hand, we've got a bloody good compliance record as far as everything else is concerned. Like, you know, waiting lists cut, catering costs reduced by half, maintenance schedules improved, security as good as ever . . .'

There was a soft cough from his left. If the Head of Security had had a head, he'd have shaken it.

'To a certain extent, yes,' he muttered.

The Finance Director turned round sharply, and his horns twitched; a sure sign of impending trouble.

'What do you mean, a certain extent?' he demanded. 'Look, either nobody's escaped or . . .'

'I was coming to that.'

As the echo of the report died away, a faint breeze dissipated the remaining wisps of smoke, revealing that (against all the odds) the Vampire King was still on his feet.

'Hmm,' he croaked. 'I'm not sure how many points you score for that.'

On the other side of the valley, Kurt 'Mad Dog' Lundqvist blinked, swore quietly under his breath, and reached into his top pocket for another silver bullet. Nothing. Just a compass, a pearl-handled switchblade and a roll of peppermints.

'Oh-*kay*,' he called out. 'You want to do this the hard way, that's fine by me.'

A few minutes later they were facing each other, *mano a mano* in the sand. Lundqvist could see that the Vampire King was sweating now, his face more than usually drawn, his teeth protruding just a telltale smidgen more. All the King could see was the flash of the noon sun on Lundqvist's mirror Ray-Bans.

'Not like you to miss the heart at four hundred yards, Kurt,' muttered the King. It was intended as a taunt, but Lundqvist accepted it as a statement of fact; which, of course, it was.

'It's this goddamn awful rifle,' he replied. 'Comes of trying to do two jobs at once, I guess. You ready?'

The King backed away. 'How do you mean, two jobs, exactly?'

'I promised the guys at *Terminator Monthly* I'd do a write-up on the new McMillan .30. Nothing like actually testing the bugger in the field, I always say. Ready yet?'

The Vampire King looked round. He was six hundred years old, completely invulnerable to anything except silver bullets and fire-hardened yew, with the strength in his hideously attenuated body of nine rogue elephants. He was also shit scared.

'We don't have to do this, you know,' he mumbled. 'We can just walk away, and . . .'

Lundqvist shook his head; a tiny, precise movement. The peak of his cap came up level with the King's third nipple. He tested the balance of the mallet in his right hand.

'Sorry, Vlad,' he said. 'A contract's a contract. Nothing personal.'

Maybe the King's mistake was to try and rush him, or maybe he didn't make a mistake at all. When you've met your match, that's it; no shame, no dishonour, just the natural course of events. In any case, there was a short blur of activity, a thud, the hollow sound of mallet-head on stake. And that was that.

As six vindictive centuries caught up with the Vampire King, he raised his head one last time and tried to give Lundqvist the stare. All that happened was that he got the stare back, with interest.

'Just tell me, Kurt,' he croaked with the last of his breath. 'Why the hell do you do it?'

'The money, Vlad. So long.'

When it was all finally over, Lundqvist got to his feet, wiped the stake off on a patch of couch grass and stuck it back in his belt. There were times, he realised, when the job did get to him, although he found it hard to admit it to himself. Not the danger, of course, or the incessant conflict with hideous and unnatural monsters, or the mind-bending horrors he came face to face with every day of his life. Certainly not the killing. When a man is tired of killing, he's tired of life.

No, Lundqvist said to himself as he tucked the vampire's severed head under his arm, shouldered the rifle and started the long walk back to the jeep, I guess what really bothers me most is the lack of excitement.

* * *

The Most Wanted Man in History, wishing to get from Iceland to Holland and having no transport of his own, had hitched a lift. Nothing unusual in that, except that he'd hitched it off an airliner.

Since there's virtually nowhere in Iceland where you can put down a 747 without breaking bits off it, the fugitive had left it hovering about four feet off the ground, on a cushion of pink cloud. With a little grunt of effort, he jumped up, caught the pilot's door, wrenched it open and swung inside the cabin.

'Hi,' he said cheerfully. 'Thanks for stopping.'

The pilot looked at him, eyes rimed over with incredulous terror. What he wanted to say was, Who are you, what's happening, have you the faintest idea what's going to happen to me when the federal aviation boys found out I dumped my plane in a volcanic desert just because some guy stuck his thumb out. What actually came out was, 'I can take you as far as Schiphol if that's any good to you.'

'Schiphol's fine,' replied the fugitive, dropping his rucksack on the floor and flopping into the wireless operator's chair. 'Thanks a lot.'

Without the pilot's having to do anything, the engines roared, the idiot lights on the console flickered into angry, bewildered life, and the pink cloud slowly floated up to around about ten thousand feet. Normal service will be resumed as soon as possible.

The wireless operator and the co-pilot took an early lunch.

'Going far?' the pilot asked, as the plane resumed its flight. He was dimly aware of a heavy, oppressive force lying across large areas of his mind like a sleeping cat on the knees of an impatient visitor, blanking off those parts of his brain that might want to raise such issues as what in God's name is going on here. Dimly aware, however, butters no parsnips.

'Just bumming around, really,' the fugitive replied. 'And

Amsterdam's as good a place as any for that, as far as I'm concerned.'

Another thought that was hammering vainly on the locked door of the pilot's consciousness was, Hang on, why am I taking this nerd to Amsterdam when this flight's supposed to be going to Geneva? It hammered and hammered and hammered, and nobody came.

'Very much a fun place, Amsterdam, from what I've heard,' the pilot's voice agreed. 'Not that I've been there for, oh, fifteen years, I suppose. Not to stop, anyway. Been travelling long?'

Flight AR675, Flight AR675, come in please, urgent, come in, please, yammered the radio. Sundry captives in the coal cellar of the pilot's mind tried using a big chunk of basic survival instinct as a battering ram, but all they did was hurt their shoulders.

'I move about,' replied the fugitive, looking out of the window at the North Sea. 'Born under a wandering star, that sort of thing.'

Flight AR675, Flight AR675, what the fuck do you think you're doing up there? Are your instruments shot, or what?

The pilot turned to his passenger. 'Should I answer that, do you think? They seem rather uptight about something.'

'I shouldn't bother,' the fugitive replied. 'They'll call back later if it's important.'

'I guess so.' The pilot leant forward and twiddled a dial on the console. The voice of Oslo air traffic control was abruptly replaced by Radio Oseberg's Music Through The Night. By virtue of some sort of ghastly air bubble in the stream of probability, they were playing 'Riders In The Sky'.

'Do you know,' said the pilot after a while, 'something tells me that if we carry on this course much longer we'll be violating Swedish airspace. Do you think they'll mind?'

'I don't think so,' replied the fugitive firmly. 'Nice people, the Swedes.'

– At which point, two massively-armed Saab Viggens were scrambled out of Birka and screamed like stainless steel banshees north-east on a direct interception course –

'Very expensive country, though,' the pilot was saying. 'I had to buy a pair of shoes there once, and do you know how much they cost? Just ordinary black lace-up walking shoes, nothing fancy . . .'

'You don't say.'

'And coffee's absolutely astronomical, of course. Not so bad in the little back-street cafes and things, of course, but in the hotels . . .'

Ernidentified ercraft, ernidentified ercraft, here is calling the Svensk er force. Turn beck immediately or down you will be shot. Repeat, down you will be . . .

'Would you like me to talk to them?' suggested the fugitive.

'Gosh, would you mind? That's extremely kind of you.'

'No problem.'

The pilot of Gamma Delta Alpha Five Three Nine set his jaw, repeated the message one last time for luck, and programmed the weapons systems. First, a five-round burst from the twin twenty-mil Oerlikons, then a couple of heat-seekers, and then back home in time for a quick beer before the press conferences.

Calling Gamma Delta Alpha Five Three Nine, come in please.

The pilot was a relatively humane man, but he couldn't help just the tiniest twinge of disappointment, deep down in the nastier bits of his repressed psyche. *Receiving you, ernidentified ercraft. Turn beck immediately or . . .*

The radio crackled. *Yes, thanks,* it said. *Do you know your flies are undone?*

Proof, if proof were needed, that technology has outgrown the ability of Mankind to control it. At the end of the day, even a really first-class piece of state-of-the-art hardware needs a human to steer it, and that human must inevitably be subject to fundamental human instinctive behaviour; such as, for example, quickly glancing down to check his zip. But in the third of a second that takes, a modern class one fighter bomber can get seriously out of hand . . .

'Good Lord,' exclaimed the pilot of the 747, 'that fighter nearly crashed into that other fighter. Whoops!'

'Butterfingers,' agreed the fugitive.

'I do hope they'll be all right.'

'I expect so. Marvellous things, ejector seats.'

'You wouldn't get me in one of those things without one.'

The fugitive craned his neck slightly to look at the sea. 'Expensive pieces of kit, these modern warplanes, I expect.'

'Very.'

'Waterproof?'

'I assume so.'

'That's all right, then.'

Lundqvist strode into the tiny branch sheriff's office in Las Monedas and banged the bell until it broke. Then he shouted.

The deputy on duty doubled as the postmaster, the trading standards officer, the funeral director, one of the town's two chartered accountants and the blacksmith's assistant. It was therefore several minutes before he was able to answer.

'The reward on these two,' snapped Lundqvist. 'In cash. And I want a receipt.'

The deputy looked up at the two severed heads and quickly ran a mental scan through his various portfolios to ascertain which one was relevant. It was easy enough to narrow the field down to two alternatives; and relatives bringing loved ones to the Las Monedas funeral parlour generally tended to have rather more of the bits.

'Hold on,' he said. From under the desk he produced a receipt book and a blue cap with red facings marked *FEDER-ALES*. It was entirely the wrong uniform, of course, but this was the sticks. You had to make do with what you could get.

'Vampires,' said Lundqvist, patiently (by his standards, at least). 'This one's Vlad the Indefinitely Respawned, and this one' – he broke off and glanced at the label hanging from the left ear – 'this one here is Count Bors Vilassanyi. I've got the ISBN* details somewhere, if that's any help.'

'Just a moment,' replied the deputy, thumbing through a loose-leaf binder. 'Vlad, Vlad – there's a lot of Vlads isn't there? – ah, right, here you go. Vlad the Indefinitely Respawned. Hey, Category Three, not bad. What did you say the other one was?'

'Count Bors Vilassanyi. Two 's's in Vilassanyi.'

'Sorry, doesn't seem to be here.'

'Try the supplement.'

'Yes, right. No, not in here either.'

'Okay, try looking under zombies.'

'Right – yes, here we are. Category Four A.' The deputy frowned. 'Sorry,' he said, 'but we don't keep that much cash in the office.'

'Bank's still open.'

'Or the country, come to that. You could try America, just up the road and turn left; they might be able to help.'

Lundqvist sighed. 'Fuck that,' he said. 'I guess I'll just have to take a cheque.'

'I'll need to see your licence and some proof of identity.'

Lundqvist growled ominously. 'Here's the licence.'

'Thanks, that all seems to be in order. How about this proof of identity?'

With no apparent exertion whatsoever, Lundqvist picked the deputy up one-handed by the lapels, held him about two inches from the tip of his nose and treated him to a long, special stare.

---

*International Supernatural Beings Number

'Is that okay?'

'That'll do nicely, Mr Lundqvist.'

There was a brief interval while the deputy laboriously wrote out a cheque, during which time Lundqvist amused himself by shuffling through the file of Wanted posters on the desk. Since they were a trifle behind the times at Las Monedas, the file read more like Lundqvist's curriculum vitae. Sorry. Curriculum mortis.

Theodore 'Fangs' Lupo – March 1992, Guatemala. Trouble getting his pelt over the border, Lundqvist recalled, because of the endangered species by-products regulations. Ironic, since it was largely due to his efforts that werewolves were endangered in the first place.

Rameses IV – July 1992, Cairo. One of the few contracts that had given any real degree of job satisfaction. Amazing what these new hi-tech wallpaper pastes could do with three-thousand-year-old papyrus bandages.

Aldazor, Lord High Marshal of the Infernal Hosts – August 1992, Akron, Ohio. A miserable job, that, and he was still getting letters from the Vatican legal department about infringement of copyright. Copyright bullshit. Show me a priest who uses bell, book and 20mm recoilless rifle, and then sue me.

With a sigh, Lundqvist flicked through the rest of the file. Nothing but the commonplace, the routine, the uninspiring, the run-of-the-mill. For a man who had got into this line of work purely for the adrenaline rush of living on the edge, he was spending far too much time pottering about in the epicentre.

And then . . .

He stopped.

He turned back.

Wow!

'Hey,' he said. 'How long's this one been out? Don't remember seeing it before.'

The deputy looked up over the rims of his spectacles. They had belonged to his great-grandfather, and it was a moot point as to whether the myopia that ran in his family was cause or effect.

'Oh, that one,' he replied. 'That's new. A man delivered it specially.'

'When?'

The deputy thought for a moment. 'Three days ago,' he said. 'Maybe four. It was the day Little Pepe's mule cast a shoe and Miguel sent the telegram to San Felipe.'

'Thanks.' With a swift movement, Lundqvist snapped open the file, removed the flyer, and snapped the file shut. 'I think I'll just borrow this for a while,' he said. 'You don't mind, do you?'

Before the deputy could answer, Lundqvist had folded the flyer away, snatched his cheque and hurried out.

In the cantina, over a triple hot chilli and a jug of coarse red, Lundqvist studied the flyer in detail.

WANTED

and then a space; and in big, old-fashioned letters:

PAST OR
PRESENT

(they keep that typeface specially for wanted posters); and then a blurred photograph; but the face was already familiar. More than that; it had been an unshiftable grape-pip behind the dental plate of Lundqvist's professional pride for more years than he cared to remember. And then the name, and the aliases. The Most Wanted Man in History.

And then the reward. There were so many noughts it looked like the string of bubbles left behind by a swimming otter.

Lundqvist nodded gravely, finished his chilli and lit a cigar.

Yes, the challenge. Yes, the adrenaline rush. Yes, the chance to settle a really big old score.

And yes – yes, indeed – the money.

CHAPTER TWO

'THAT'S fine,' said the fugitive. 'You can drop me here.'

The pilot looked at him.

'Thanks,' added the fugitive significantly, 'for the lift. I'll be seeing you. Goodbye.'

The airliner obligingly stopped. Around its wingtips, the wind howled. Below, the sea groped for the plane's belly with ephemeral talons of spray. Two seagulls flew straight into the tailplane and knocked themselves out cold.

'It was a pleasure,' replied the pilot. 'See you around.'

The cabin door opened – it shouldn't have; it was pressurised, and if it opened under pressure the entire contents of the cabin would be sucked up and spat out – and the fugitive picked up his rucksack, waved politely, and walked down a flight of nothing into thin air.

The fugitive watched the airliner fade into a dot on the horizon, then strolled across the wavetops to the fishing boat which he'd selected as the best way to make an inconspicuous entry into Holland.

'Hi,' he said in fluent Dutch as two fishermen came running with lifebelts. 'If we crack on a bit we can be home by nightfall.'

You can feel a right fool, frozen in the act of throwing a

lifebelt to a perfectly dry stranger in chinos, sleeveless shirt and straw hat. The fishermen paused, searching their sparse but functional vocabulary for something appropriate.

'We haven't finished fishing yet.'

The fugitive smiled. 'Don't you believe it,' he said.

He clicked his fingers, and the mechanical net-winders began to purr. As the nets cleared the water, there was a distressing sound of groaning hemp. A couple of rivets popped in the crane.

'That ought to do for one day,' the fugitive went on, indicating the painfully overladen nets. 'Right then. Chop chop, busy busy.'

The elder fisherman, who had seen some pretty weird things in his time and been told about a hell of a lot more, removed his cap, turned it round and put it back on his head. It was the first time he'd removed it in thirty-two years, funerals included.

'How did you do that?' he asked.

'Entropy.'

The fisherman's old, shrewd eyes met the fugitive's and for a moment there was a flicker of recognition; not of the man, but of the phenomenon. Forty years at sea and you learn the wisdom of taking the other man's word for it.

'Fair enough,' he said. 'Thanks. Where do you want to go?'

'Amsterdam.'

'I can take you to Ijmuiden,' replied the fisherman, 'and then you can get the bus.'

'That's fine.'

The fugitive wandered astern, lay down on a coil of rope, tilted his hat over his eyes and went to sleep.

The younger fisherman turned to his colleague.

'Dad,' he said.

'Yes,' replied his father. 'I know. Don't worry about it.'

'But you don't know what I was going to—'

'I can guess, son.' The elder fisherman prodded a heaving

net with the toe of his boot. He was old, even for a fisherman, but not so old that he could remember the last time a Vollendam trawler had come home laden down to the bows with a record catch of coelacanth.

Coelacanth. An extinct species. You could name your own price. In fact, given the quantity now slopping about on the deck wondering where all the water had suddenly gone, you could cut out the middleman and open an international chain of Vollendam Fried Coelacanth restaurants.

According to the latest edition of the *Red Guide to Hell*, finding suitable accommodation during your stay should not present a problem.

For business travellers and those tourists who can afford the prices, the Hell Sheraton, the Inn on the Pit and the Hellton all offer the usual five-star facilities and enjoy a convenient central location. Tourists of more modest means can expect a warm welcome and high standards of cleanliness and service at the Mephisto, the Casa 666 and the Elysium Palace. Students and others on a fixed budget are recommended to try one of the many friendly, family-run *auberges* and guest-houses outside the old town of Los Diablos, particularly in the suburbs of Beverley Hells and Hellywood.

There is, however, one thing that all these fine establishments have in common. To put it as nicely as possible, they don't provide you with a late key. Or an early key, for that matter.

Getting out of Hell is a bit like successfully defrauding the Revenue; many people will tell you they know someone who's managed it, but the name somehow eludes them. In practice, it's never happened.

Until . . .

'It's amazing,' said the Finance Director.

'Yes,' replied the Head of Security. 'Clever little sod,' he added.

They were standing in the doorway of a room on the third floor of the Hotel Dante. It was empty, except for a bed with no sheets, a hacksaw and the Visitors' Book.

'Where he got the hacksaw from,' the Head of Security said, 'I have no idea.'

He picked up the instrument in question, which promptly sniggered at him and vanished. At the same time, the rope of sheets hanging from the stump of the severed bar in the window frame retracted itself, shrugged off its knots and slipped back on to the bed. The Finance Director examined them.

'Ironed, too,' he observed. 'I call that class, don't you?'

The Head of Security scratched the back of his head. 'I still don't get it,' he remarked. 'I mean, hacksaws don't just appear, and sheets don't just tie themselves into knots. I think they called it physics when I was at school.'

The Finance Director sighed. 'If you look at the file,' he said patiently, 'you'll see he was in here for sorcery, necromancy and dabbling in the Black Arts.'

'Was he? Well I—'

'In which case,' continued the Finance Director remorselessly, 'perhaps it wasn't the most sensible idea in the history of the cosmos to set him to work in the machine shop.'

'But—'

'Bearing in mind,' the Finance Director concluded, 'that in the machine shop he'd have access to pentangles, tetragrammata, Vernier mandalas . . .'

'They're under strict orders to keep all that stuff locked away—'

'. . . Eccentric-drive sabbats, adjustable familiars, coven wrenches and all the string he could possibly want. Let's face it, we goofed.' He closed his eyes, sighed again and thought for a while. Two of the principal skills of the high-class manager are damage limitation and positive thinking.

'We'll just have to get him back, that's all,' he said. 'Which shouldn't be difficult. I've had posters sent out and we can pay the reward out of the repairs and maintenance budget. It's more a question of time.'

They left the Dante and walked slowly back up towards the Mouth via the attractive and unspoilt Usurer's Quarter, pausing only to buy some locally-produced candy floss from one of the many picturesque stalls.

It comes in three flavours: sulphur, brimstone and strawberry.

'Why?' asked the Head of Security.

'Because,' replied the Finance Director through a mouthful of sticky yellow froth, 'he was a Purchase, and we've got the auditors in next month.'

'Sorry?'

The Finance Director wiped his mouth on his sleeve, which smoked. 'A Purchase,' he repeated. 'Sold his soul to the ... to the previous administration. There was a lot of it went on in the old days. Sort of like subsidies. Bloody awful way to run a railway in my opinion, but what the, um, thing, it was just public money, so nobody cared. Anyway, we've got stuck with the aftermath. From an accountancy point of view, it's an absolute nightmare.'

He stopped, while the Head of Security, who had foolishly chosen the strawberry, was violently sick.

'It's all a question of book-keeping, you see,' he went on, when the retching had subsided. 'Purchased souls go in the balance sheet under Fixed Assets. Subject to straight-line depreciation and writing down allowance, of course, but you've got to account for them at the end of the day. If they go missing, you're in real trouble, believe me. Since miladdo's only been here, what, five hundred years, he's still got about eighty-five per cent of his original value after allowances. That's one heck of a shortfall.'

The Head of Security frowned. Books in his experience were not things you kept so much as threw at persistent offenders. He groped under the sink of his memory.

'Can't you write him off?' he suggested.

The Finance Director scowled. 'Against what? Good debts? No, we've just got to get the bastard back again. It's as simple as that.'

'Right,' said the Head of Security. 'So you'll be wanting me to get a squad together and—'

'No.' The Finance Director shook his head, nearly slicing the Head of Security's scalp off in the process. 'Out of our hands now, I'm delighted to say.'

'So what are we doing about it?'

For the first time that day, there was a faint glint of pleasure in the Finance Director's voice, and his third eye positively sparkled. 'I've hired a bounty hunter,' he replied. 'The best.'

He smiled, set light to the rest of his candy floss, and ran up the steps to his office.

There are three immutable laws in the Universe. Only three.

Two of them concern death and taxes, and they have been waived on occasions. Not so the third, which states:

NOBODY GETS TO SEE
MR VAN APPIN
WITHOUT AN APPOINTMENT.

Having played fast and loose with the other two in his time, the fugitive (now dressed in a lightweight grey suit, smart light tan brogues and a dove-grey tie) is going to have a crack at the third.

'Excuse me,' said the receptionist, 'but do you have an appointment?'

The fugitive turned round slowly and looked at her.

'That depends,' he said.

'I doubt that, sir,' the receptionist replied. If you left her tone of voice outside in the rain overnight, it'd have rust on it come morning. 'Do you have an appointment or not?'

'That depends,' said the fugitive, 'on which way round you like your Time. I personally like it arse-about-face, so I make all my appointments retrospectively. Come back about five minutes ago and I'll have got it sorted for you.'

'I'm sorry,' said the receptionist. 'Nobody sees Mr Van Appin without an—'

'He'll see me.'

'With respect, sir . . .'

The fugitive smiled, and vanished.

Almost simultaneously, he rematerialised in Mr Van Appin's office, sat down in the large leather armchair and started linking paperclips together.

'Morning, George,' said Mr Van Appin, without looking up. 'I'll be with you in two shakes.'

Although his face did not betray the fact, the fugitive was impressed. It's not everyone who's cool enough to take the sudden materialisation of an escaped soul in torment so totally in his stride.

'That's okay,' he replied. 'No hurry.'

Mr Van Appin finished annotating the document he had been studying, put it in his out tray, steepled his fingers and leant back in his chair.

'Long time no see, George,' he said, 'if you'll pardon the expression.'

'Good of you to fit me in at such short notice,' the fugitive replied. 'Look, I'm in a bit of a jam, I wondered if you could help me get it sorted out.'

The cigar box on Mr Van Appin's desk floated across the room and opened itself under the fugitive's nose. He shook his head slightly.

'I'll do my best,' Mr Van Appin said. 'Tell me all about it.'

The fugitive grinned. 'Starting where, Pete?'

Mr Van Appin considered. 'Well,' he said. 'I think we can take all the In-the-beginning-was-the-Word stuff as read and pick up the story where you'd sold your soul to the Very Bad Person and he'd taken delivery. To be honest with you, George, I took that as being a suitable juncture to close my file and send in my bill.' Mr Van Appin frowned. 'Did you ever pay it, by the way?'

'By return,' George replied. 'Or rather, my executors did. I saw to that well in advance, believe me. I may have been facing eternal damnation, but I didn't want to get into *real* trouble.'

'Ah yes.' Mr Van Appin's brow cleared. 'I remember now. Anyway, to get back to what we were saying just now, I'd rather assumed that that was it, as far as you were concerned. Terribly sorry to lose you as a client and all that, but these things happen. In fact, the term "banged to rights" did float across my mind more than once in connection with your affairs. Nobody followed you here, did they?'

'Unlikely,' said the fugitive. 'As far as I can see they haven't the faintest idea when I am, let alone where. Listen, Peter, I want to fight this one.'

Mr Van Appin raised an eyebrow. 'Fight it, George?'

'Yeah.' The fugitive nodded. 'Call it a matter of principle.'

Mr Van Appin frowned again. 'That's expensive talk, George.'

'I've got the money.'

Mr Van Appin shrugged. 'I don't doubt that you do. Even then, I can't really hold out much prospect of success. Those soul-and-purchase contracts are the nearest things you'll ever get to watertight.'

The fugitive looked amused. 'Are they really.'

'Fraid so, George,' replied Mr Van Appin. 'I drafted them myself. And,' he added, with a wisp of nostalgia, 'I was good then. Just starting up, I was, anxious to make a name for myself. Landing a client like that, I wanted to make a good impression.'

'So you don't think it's possible?'

'I think it'll be very, very difficult,' Mr Van Appin replied.

'Mind you, I'm looking at the worst possible scenario here, you understand.'

'Playing devil's advocate, in fact.'

Mr Van Appin smiled without amusement. 'You could say that,' he said. 'Actually, I don't act for them any more. All their work's done in-house these days.'

'Really?'

Mr Van Appin nodded. 'Makes sense,' he said. 'After all, they get their pick of the entire profession down there, sooner or later.'

'Except you, Pete.'

A faint pinkness experimented with crossing Mr Van Appin's cheeks. 'Flattery will get you nowhere,' he said. 'I'm not saying it's impossible, George. Nothing's impossible. I just can't see how, that's all. Maybe I'm getting old or something.' He stopped, tapped his teeth with a pencil, and considered for a moment. 'That's a thought, actually,' he said. 'A hundred years ago I'd have accepted like a shot. Why don't you try our office then?'

(As a result of the unique nature of his practice, Mr Van Appin found it convenient to have a main branch office in every century, with sub-offices at thirty-year intervals to take over his practice each time he retired. Because of his equally unique skills, he had never been able to find a worthy partner or associate, with the result that he ran all his offices simultaneously, thereby taking the concept of overwork into a whole new dimension.)

The fugitive shook his head. 'Nah,' he said. 'I've got other business to attend to in this decade, Pete, I couldn't find the time.'

There was a long silence.

'It'll cost you, mind,' said Mr Van Appin.

'Like I said,' the fugitive replied. 'No worries.'

Mr Van Appin grinned. 'In that case,' he said, 'I'll need a copy of the original agreement, a signed affidavit from the

Holy Ghost and fifty billion guilders on account.'

'I thought you'd say that,' replied the fugitive. He passed over the attaché case he'd brought in with him. Mr Van Appin raised the lid and nodded.

'Where can I call you?' he said. 'I imagine you'll need to be hard to find for a while.'

'I'll call you,' the fugitive replied. 'Better that way.'

When he'd gone, Mr Van Appin swivelled round in his chair a couple of times, chewing the end of his pencil and humming. Then he reached for the dictating machine.

'Please open a new file, Miss Duisberg,' he said. 'Client profile C, client name, Faust, that's F-A-U-S for sugar -T, George Michael. Re ...' He paused, wound the tape back, wound it forward again. 'Re, dispute with Hell Holdings plc.'

Faust wasn't, of course, his real name.

Faust was just the German abbreviation of Faustus, which was the nickname he'd picked up as an undergraduate at Wittenberg. It means 'Lucky'.

Only goes to show how wrong you can be, doesn't it?

Out of a particularly ill-fated year (his contemporaries included Martin Luther, Matthias Corvinus and Hamlet, Prince of Denmark) Lucky George was the student people remembered as having come to the most spectacularly sticky end. So devastating was the ensuing scandal that the university authorities promptly dropped Black Arts from the University curriculum; replacing it, seamlessly, with economics. A wave of hysteria swept across Europe, and for the next two centuries, witchcraft and sorcery remained (so to speak) a burning issue on the agenda of the known world. Even Lucky George's mother stopped talking about her son, the doctor, and transferred the picture of him in his matriculation robes from the mantelpiece to the coalshed.

Lucky George was not, however, such a misnomer as all that. Nobody could deny that he had more luck than any other hundred people put together. It's just that luck comes in two varieties.

Call them flavours, if it makes it any easier.

The other scoop in George's cone, in his opinion at least, more than adequately made up for the slight downside effect he'd experienced over the soul business. All that had been a means to an end, and a very nice end it was, too. Make no mistake; Lucky George had got value for money.

Ronnie Bosch sat in his studio, stared long and hard at his drawing board, and groaned.

It was, they'd told him, all part of a concept which was definitely going to be The Future as far as Hell Holdings was concerned.

For reasons he couldn't quite grasp, but which he couldn't help but find mildly flattering, they were going to call it EuroBosch.

Visit, they had postulated, a land of wonder and enchantment. Meet your favourite characters from the repertoire of Europe's most imaginative artist face to ... Take a ride through spectacular landscapes to see sights you'll never see anywhere else.

Sounded good, in theory; but Ronnie, faced with the prospect of creating seven hundred thousand different appropriate latex masks in time for the Grand Celebrity Opening, was asking himself whether they'd really thought it through properly before committing the funding.

For a start, he muttered to himself, scowling at a recalcitrant design and then turning it upside down (much better that way), masks really weren't going to be enough, not for some of the more *outré* designs. We're talking body suits here, and quite probably bodies as well. Dammit, about forty per cent of his best work was anatomically impossible. Which meant starting from scratch.

Yuk.

A stray pellet of inspiration struck home, and he reached for a pencil.

A mouse, he thought. A seven-foot, grinning, anthropomorphic mouse, with perky little front fangs and big hands which . . .

He shook his head, as if trying to dislodge the very idea. Broad-minded he most certainly was, but there are limits. The mere thought of it gave him the willies.

What he'd really always wanted to do, of course, was design helicopters. And parachutes, and telescopes, and wonderful ships powered by paddles driven by treadmills turned by oxen. And siege engines, and washing machines, and refrigerators, and combination tin-openers and potato-peelers, and space-saving compact disc racks, and ironing-boards that ingeniously fold away into nests of coffee tables. He would have been good at it, too. In fact, he'd invented the Swiss Army Knife before the Swiss even had an army.

Unfortunately, he'd been too successful as a commercial artist and illustrator, at a time when what the public wanted was spare-part-surgery demons and hideously teeming egg-shells. It was a bit like being a fashionable book-jacket artist, only not quite so well paid.

And then it had started coming rather too easily. Even when he shut his eyes. Particularly when he shut his eyes. Like now, for example.

How about an enormous mutant duck, with huge oval eyes and a beak the size of a tennis racket, and a hideous sort of hungry leer which made you think it was about to . . . ?

Quickly, he opened his eyes, rubbed them with the knuckles of his fists, and swallowed a heaped handful of librium.

He started to draw a cow.

Drawn-faced, travel-sore and ever so slightly out of his head with fatigue, Lundqvist pushed open the door of the American bookstore in Paris and leant both elbows heavily on the counter.

'Goethe,' he said.

'Pardon me?'

'You deaf or something? I said Goethe.'

The girl behind the counter adjusted her spectacles. 'You want a book by Goethe?' she hazarded.

'You got it.'

The girl considered. 'I think we've got one somewhere,' she said. 'We used to have, anyway. I haven't been here long.'

'Fetch.'

The girl went away; shortly afterwards she came back.

'You're sure the book you wanted was by Goethe?'

'Yes.'

'We've got this one.' She handed over a dusty paperback with the air of someone who's been asked for some pretty daffy things in their time but is still just occasionally capable of surprise. 'Is this the ...?'

Lundqvist glanced down at the spine. *Faust*. Parts One and Two. Complete and unabridged. A Mentor Classic. 'Yeah,' Lundqvist growled. 'Marlowe.'

The girl took a look at his hard-worn trenchcoat and the bulge under his left arm. 'That's your name, right?'

'Christopher Marlowe,' replied Lundqvist, suggesting that his patience was not unlimited. 'British sixteenth-century dramatist. Complete works. Move it.'

The girl went away again, and again came back.

'We've only got Volume One in the NEL edition,' she said. 'I can order ...'

Lundqvist took the book, flipped it open at the list of contents and nodded. 'That's fine,' he said. 'No problem. Keep the change.'

On a bench beside the Seine, Lundqvist ripped open the paper bag in which the girl had insisted on wrapping the books, selected the Complete Works of Christopher Marlowe, and began to read.

He found it hard going. His usual reading matter tended to

be terser and less flowery ('Step three; wire up the timing device to the detonator') and he knew for a fact that large parts of Marlowe's version were heavily embroidered, fanciful or just plain wrong.

He wondered why. For a start, the jerk he'd known all these years had his faults, God knows, but even he didn't go around talking poetry all the time, like some goddamn faggot.

Eventually, however, he found what he was looking for. Having underlined it heavily in yellow marker pen and noted down the page number in his notebook, he opened the Goethe version and, after a great deal of tedious slogging through, found the passage that corroborated exactly what he'd found out in the Marlowe. Fine.

He stuck the books in his pocket and went off to buy a 55mm recoilless rifle.

The Company Secretary looked up, his hand over the mouthpiece of the receiver.

'It's *him*,' he hissed. 'What do I do?'

The Finance Director frowned. 'I'll take the call,' he said. 'You get Security to see if they can get a trace on the line.'

He lifted the telephone in front of him, took a deep breath, and said, 'Yes?'

'Hi.'

The Finance Director thought for a moment. 'It's a terribly bad line,' he said. 'You'll have to speak up.'

'Listen,' replied the voice at the other end. 'I'm giving you fair warning. No doubt you've got people on my trail. Call them off. Otherwise, you'll regret it. Got that?'

The Finance Director smiled. 'I think so,' he said. 'You're saying that unless we leave you alone, something *bad* is going to happen to us.' He paused, for effect. 'Hasn't it crossed your mind that every conceivable bad thing there is has probably happened to us already? Bearing in mind—'

The line went dead.

'No luck,' said Security. 'Not enough time. Somewhere in Europe, probably late twentieth, early twenty-first century. Otherwise . . .'

'It doesn't matter,' the Finance Director replied with a sigh. 'The chances of him doing anything silly and giving himself away are a snowflake's chance in . . . Anyway,' he went on, 'at least we're in communication. Of a sort. We'll have him, don't you worry.'

The Company Secretary stroked his chin, causing sparks. 'Excuse me if I'm barking up the wrong tree here,' he said, but wasn't that a threat he just came out with? *Otherwise, you'll regret it*, something like that?'

The Finance Director shrugged. 'Bluster,' he said.

'Ah,' replied the Company Secretary. 'For a moment there I thought it was a threat.'

'Same thing. Bluster is a threat you make when you're backed up against a wall facing certain death at the hands of overwhelmingly superior forces.'

'Ah. Like, Bluster's last stand, sort of thing?'

The Finance Director gave him a look, and he grinned sheepishly. They both knew what the Company Secretary had originally been sent down for; and it wasn't simony or stealing sheep. You'd have thought he'd have learnt his lesson by now.

'Don't worry,' the Finance Director said. 'There's no threat he can possibly pose to anyone. He's got nothing up his sleeve except his arm, take it from me.'

CHAPTER
THREE

NOT long afterwards, Lucky George started his reign of terror.

That's overstating the case somewhat. More a series of brisk showers of extreme aggravation.

Historians have, after exhaustive research, pinpointed what you might term the Sarajevo or Harper's Ferry of Lucky George's war against humanity. It was half past six on a Friday; the place, the centre of Amiens. The victim, a young insurance salesman whose name is not recorded. As a result, the annual wreaths are laid at the Tomb of the Unknown Soldier, although soldier is probably pushing it a bit.

The victim, hurrying to catch his bus, pauses for a moment outside a branch of the Credit Lyonnais. He fumbles in his wallet until he finds his cash dispenser card. He inserts it. He waits.

After five seconds or so (which is a long time when you're standing out in the street, painfully conscious of the ebb and flow of the French provincial bus service passing you by) the cash dispenser makes a noise. Par for the course, sure; but this isn't part of its usual repertoire.

It burps.

The victim frowns. He presses the button marked *Cancel Transaction*, and waits.

The lights flicker. The machine spells out a message.

YOUR CARD HAS BEEN RETAINED

it says. Then it flickers again.

OR RATHER, EATEN

The victim raises an eyebrow. Some last smear of the basic survival instinct spattered across the back of his mind prompts him to take a step back. The lights dance.

RATHER SALTY, I THOUGHT

This time, the victim can actually smell the danger, but it's too late. The machine is looking directly at him. In fact, it's smiling.

AND YOU CAN'T HAVE IT BACK, SO THERE

There is a fundamental and rather dangerous urge in all of us to try and cling to the jagged edge of normality, even when it's blindingly obvious that the longer you hold on, the further you're going to fall when your grip finally fails. The victim presses *Cancel Transaction* again. Bad move.

LOOK, FOUR-EYES

The victim tries to back away, but the machine is doing a very good mongoose impression. It seems to have a direct line to the victim's feet.

NOBODY TRIES TO CANCEL ME AND GETS AWAY WITH IT. YOU GOT THAT?

The victim's first thought is to apologise, but the dead hand of normality is gripping the scruff of his neck. You can't talk to these machines, he's thinking, they're just machines, they can't . . .

A stream of banknotes, glued together to form something disquietingly like a tongue, lashes out of the cash slot, flails horribly in the air, and lands on the victim's tie. Then it retracts.

TWO CAN PLAY AT THAT GAME, BUSTER

Just as the victim's nose is pressed up against the perspex screen, his chin flattened against the diagram showing the Right Way Up, the tortured fibres of the tie give way, leaving the tongue wrapped round three inches of terylene, and the victim flat on his back in the gutter. But not for long.

He scrambles to his feet. He runs. In his haste to get away, he fails to notice the patrolling gendarme and collides with him heavily. There's a short interlude, while the gendarme brushes the insurance salesman off his lapels.

'Monsieur!' There's a wildness in his eyes that commands attention, and fair enough. When a Frenchman is palpably more afraid of something that he's recently seen than a gendarme he's just knocked over, there's got to be something badly the matter. 'Monsieur, the bank just tried to kill me. It swallowed my card, and then it ate my tie.'

The gendarme has summed up the victim as mentally disturbed and is just about to render psychiatric first-aid with his truncheon when he catches sight of the banknote tongue, still thrashing about, trying to feed three inches of tie in through the cash slot. He stares.

The machine stares back. Then – there's no other way to put this – it sticks its tongue out at the policeman.

The gendarme stiffens. There are certain things you just don't do, no matter how many branches and wholly-owned subsidiary companies you've got.

It only takes him a fraction of a second to bark out the obligatory warning. The tongue extends further and waggles about. In fact, it connects with the gendarme's kepi, twists it round a couple of times, and stuffs it into the cash slot. There is another burp. A button lands on the pavement and rolls drunkenly away.

The rest is most definitely not silence. Out comes the gendarme's 9mm service automatic. Three cracks, like the breaking of a giant's leg bones. The machine goes on grinning.

It displays a derogatory message on its screen.

All this is well known, of course; you'll find it in any history book, in one version or another. What isn't so well recorded – probably because it's so very unnerving, and mankind can only take so much reality before it starts demanding that something be done about it – is the fact that when the gendarme in question received his bank statement at the end of the month, he was disturbed to find an entry recording three rounds of 125-grain full metal jacket 9mm Parabellum credited to his account on the day in question.

With interest. And, of course, basic rate tax deducted at source.

Shortly after the first reports of this contretemps had reached the Hot Seat and were dismissed as being a rather offbeat practical joke, a fax machine in Toronto grabbed a secretary by the wrist as she was feeding paper into it, hurled her across the ionosphere and dumped her down in Winnipeg, in the front office of a highly respected firm of water diviners.

To make matters worse, it was a wrong number.

Microwaves the length and breadth of Florida burst simultaneously into song until switched off, while a team of firemen in Tokyo fought for two hours to release a chat-show host from the interior of a portable television set. When the unfortunate man was eventually freed, he was found to have broken several small bones in his wrists while hammering on the inside of the glass.

In Novosibirsk, an entire warehouseful of retractable ball-point pens was destroyed by long-range artillery fire after turning into small but incredibly agile yellow snakes. The President of Venezuela appeared on national television to appeal for calm after all the office dictating machines in the country started answering back. Large parts of the centre of Perth were sealed off, leaving a handful of bemused Marines to watch the stately dance of the traffic lights over the sights of their machine-guns. In London, all the telephones refused to speak to each other for three hours, but nobody noticed. Workers on a People's Farm at an undisclosed location in Shantung province were frightened out of their wits when they reported for work only to find that the newly planted rice-paddy had spontaneously landscaped itself into an eighteen-hole golf course, complete with electric carts, clubhouse and conference facilities.

Absolutely nothing peculiar happened in Ireland at all, which was perhaps the most disconcerting part of it. No statues of the Virgin Mary moved their arms or were seen to weep tears for a period calculated to have been in excess of three hours.

In Paris, the Mona Lisa giggled.

'Okay,' said the Finance Director. 'You win. We're withdrawing our agents.'

'And about time too,' replied Lucky George. He fumbled in his pocket for a coin to feed the phone box, but could only find a small, bent washer. He smiled at it. 'Just count yourselves extremely lucky I'm a bit out of practice.'

'You won't get away with it, you know. You can hide, but you can't run.'

'Shouldn't that be the other—'

'Think about it.'

Lucky George thought about it and decided he didn't like the Finance Director's tone, with the result that back in the hastily prepared emergency rooms at Pandaemonium, the receiver gave the Finance Director's ear a big, wet kiss. The Finance Director wound his handkerchief round the earpiece and went on:

'Tell you what we'll do, George. Give yourself up, come quietly, we'll forget all about it. You can even have your old job back in the ... We'll give you a nice cushy job in the kitchens. Now I can't say fairer than—'

The mouthpiece of the telephone popped an apple neatly into the Finance Director's mouth, and the line went dead. Lucky George hung up, smiled the phone booth back out of existence, and crossed the road to a cafe, where he ordered a beer and a toasted sandwich.

Withdrawing all their agents. Like hell they were.

He sat for a while and smoked (a process which in his case did not involve tobacco) and then reached for his glass, upended it on the table, and began a seance.

In order to conjure the spirits of the dead, you need to link up at least three pairs of hands. Although he was alone, Lucky George didn't seem to find this a problem.

'You there, Bull?'

The saucer with Lucky George's unpaid bill in it rocked backwards and forwards a couple of times. Lucky George grinned and slipped a coin under the rim ...

Oh. You thought it was the *waiter* who took it. Sorry to have disillusioned you.

... Whereupon a cloud of ectoplasm materialised above the table and hovered there, refracting light. A man in a bow tie and a black waistcoat hurried up, and took its order for coffee and a slice of cheesecake.

How.

'Sheer bloody-mindedness, mostly,' replied Lucky George. 'And you?'

Not so dusty, replied the shade of Sitting Bull. *They've recently transferred me to a job in Administration.*

'Administration?' Lucky George raised an eyebrow. 'Why was that, Bully?'

Search me. The only reason I could come up with was that my name fitted. Like, you do a lot of sitting and—'

'Quite so,' Lucky George replied. 'Anyway, to business. I seem to remember you owe me a favour, Bully.'

The ectoplasm shook its head violently, causing a fortuitous rainbow.

Don't make me laugh, paleface. Your people stole our lands. They wiped out the buffalo. They raped our hunting-grounds with the telegraph and the iron horse. They massacred us when we tried to fight and drove us into reservations. They destroyed our unique and vital cultural traditions and poisoned our youth with fire water and flame-grilled spicy bisonburgers. I don't seem to recall owing any favours to anyone with skin that particularly revolting shade of pinky-apricot.

Lucky George frowned. 'Short memory you've got, Bully,' he said. 'I'm amazed you've forgotten who it was advised you to invest heavily in railroad bonds and Wells Fargo Unsecured Loan Stock back in the early 1870s. Maybe I'm thinking of somebody else.'

The ectoplasm quivered slightly, like a fluorescent jelly.

Point taken. All right, what do you want?

Lucky George paused while the waiter brought the coffee. They shared the cheesecake.

'To tell you the truth, Bully,' said Lucky George, 'I find myself in a bit of a jam.'

You don't say.

'Leave heavy irony to the living, Bully, they've got a flair for it. The point is, I need a spot of help. From someone on the inside on the Other Side, if you follow me.'

You want jam on it, you do.

'Do I?' George replied mildly. He smiled at the remains of

the cheesecake, rendering it inedible under two centimetres of damson preserve. 'It's not a lot to ask. Of course, if you want the entire Sioux nation to find out about your career in bond-washing . . .'

All right, there's no need to get nasty. They've called off all their agents, just like they said.

George raised both eyebrows. 'You surprise me, Bully, you really do.'

Freelances, on the other hand, are not covered by the term 'agent'. In contract law, as no doubt you recall, no contract of agency subsists in the case of a unilateral, open-ended contract (such as the offer of a public reward) until the contracting party signifies his acceptance of the offer by actually performing the contract. The leading authority on this point is the old case of Carlill versus the Carbolic Smoke Ball Company, in which—

'I beg your pardon?'

I'm taking law at night school. No way I'm going to be just another dumb Injun all my life. I'm allergic to sun-dried buffalo and wampum gives me eczema.

'Good for you, Bully. Any particular freelance you have in mind?'

The ectoplasm began to laugh; and laughed so violently that it shook its fragile manifestation out of existence and vanished, absent-mindedly taking the rest of the cheesecake with it. Lucky George sighed.

'Oh,' he said. '*Him.* I might have guessed.'

Ask any detective, and he'll tell you that getting the initial lead is the difficult part. Once you've got something, however slight, to go on, it's just a matter of inspired perseverance. The problem is getting that initial lucky break.

Ask Kurt Lundqvist, and he'll tell you that the only way to get a break is to hit something hard. Or someone.

'Now, then,' he said, wrapping his belt round his fist. 'We could do this the hard way, or . . .'

He paused and reflected. Nah. Why confuse the issue by introducing alternatives?

'We'll do this the hard way,' he said.

Possession of a warrant card valid in all jurisdictions, temporal as well as geographical, meant that it was no problem whatsoever for Lundqvist to nip backwards and forwards in Time in the pursuit of his enquiries. This was a great help. For one thing, if a suspect sneakily died under interrogation, he could rewind back to the deceased's last lucid moment and start all over again . . .

'I've never heard of him,' whimpered the interviewee. 'Honest.'

'Listen.' Lundqvist laid aside the belt and put an arm round the subject's shoulders. 'Co-operate, why don't you? Do yourself a favour.' He paused and grinned. 'I have to say that, you know, it's in the rules. Personally, the less you talk, the more I like it.' He picked up the belt again and waggled it meaningfully under the subject's nose.

'No, but really,' the subject said. 'I honestly have never heard that name in my life before. How can I have, for Christ's sake? He won't even be born for another seven years . . .'

Nostradamus paused; and bit his lip.

'Oh shit,' he said.

'Precisely,' Lundqvist replied. 'Don't mind me, though. If you want to persist in fruitless denials for an hour or so, that's absolutely fine by me.'

Nostradamus passed the tip of his tongue across his bone-dry lips. 'All right,' he said. 'All right, I admit, I've heard of him. Doesn't mean to say I know where he is. I mean, I've heard of all sorts of people, I've heard of Elvis Presley. Doesn't follow that I know where he's hiding out.'

Lundqvist raised an eyebrow. 'Who's Elvis Presley?' he asked.

Nostradamus shrugged. 'After your time, I suppose,' he said. 'Or before. It gets a bit confusing, sometimes.'

'Yeah.' Lundqvist smiled, or at least he drew back his lips to exhibit his teeth, and clenched his fist round the belt. 'You know, it's really nice of you to be so brave about this. Most guys just crack up and start talking the moment I've tied them to the chair.' He patted his knuckles against the palm of his other hand. 'Say this for you, Nos, you've got balls. For now, anyway.'

'Hold on!' Nostradamus closed his eyes tightly, clenched his eyebrows together and grimaced alarmingly. 'Something's coming through, right now.'

'There's a coincidence.'

'I can see . . .' The prophet began to rock the chair he was tied to backwards and forwards. 'I can see a man.'

'Good start.'

'He's beating up this other man. He's got a belt round his knuckles. He's punching – Ouch!'

Lundqvist grinned sardonically. 'Yes?'

'The man's just broken his hand,' Nostradamus replied. 'God, he's in real agony, poor devil, rolling about on the floor. Hey, that really does hurt. If only I could see who it is, maybe I could warn . . .'

He stopped. Lundqvist had taken hold of his ear and was trying to unscrew it.

'Thanks for the tip,' he said. 'Now, try again.'

Well, Lundqvist decided as he washed his hands, it was a start. It was something.

He examined himself in the mirror, and then stopped for a moment to remove a last splash of something nasty from his left cuff.

A date, in the late twentieth century. Some rather peculiar events, which could only be explained by reference to (a) the supernatural, (b) the considerably aggrieved, and (c) the extremely childish. Could be; or was it just coincidence?

Not that Nostradamus was in fact the greatest seer the world had ever known, he reminded himself, as he opened the door and walked out of the washroom. If he'd been any good at all, it was a safe bet that he'd have made bloody sure he spent Thursday March 16th, 1498 in a locked stone-walled room surrounded by armed guards.

It had been a long time since Lundqvist had last been in Amsterdam, or almost. In fact, he'd been here the previous week – May 9th to 16th, 1995 – but that was seven years ago . . .

He tried to remember if there were any warrants out for his arrest. Or was that next month? Probably, he decided with a grin, that was after he'd done whatever it was he'd come here to do.

Lucky George.

George and Lundqvist went way back (and forwards, of course). Not that he'd ever had a failure, exactly; at the end of the day, he'd served the warrant, collected the subject and delivered him, in accordance with the terms of the retainer. But even he had to admit that Lucky George hadn't come quietly. In fact, he'd come very noisily indeed, and nearly taken a substantial tranche of the fabric of reality with him. There had been moments – April 1563, for example, and December 1749, not to mention February 1255 and August 2014 – when he'd been sure that the bastard was slipping through his fingers. Likewise, just as the thing any cop dreads most of all is having his own gun used against him, he particularly resented the way George had made him look a fool in the final showdown. Even bounty-hunters have their feelings, and nobody likes being chased round the centre of a densely populated city by a seven-foot-tall scale replica of himself, brandishing an array of hopelessly anachronistic weapons and calling out for all to hear, 'Look at me, I'm a pillock!'

And they'd let him escape! The idiots!

Outside the airport he found a telephone booth with a

directory in it. He opened it until he found what he was looking for.

TROY, H.O.

Relieved, he made a note of the address, fed the machine some money and dialled the number.

The lady in question was, just then, having a bit of a problem at the port of Rotterdam.

She'd got as far as 'I name this ship . . .', and then dried. Buggery!

Trying not to appear conspicuous, she glanced out the corner of her eye at the big letters painted on the side. That wasn't much help; they called ships some pretty weird things these days, but even so she had a feeling that *Passengers are not allowed beyond this point* probably wasn't the damn thing's name. She'd have to mumble.

'I name this ship rhubarbrhubarbrhubarb,' she therefore said, 'and God bless all who sail in her.' Then she smiled. That was okay.

I needn't have worried, she told herself later, on her way home. The chances of anybody listening to what Miss World actually says are pretty minimal. In fact, it's reasonably safe to say that nobody takes any notice of Miss World at all, except in a fairly superficial way. Otherwise, how come she'd held the title forty-seven times under various assumed names, and nobody had ever noticed? The number of people who look at her *face* is, after all, limited; the number who remember it, more limited still.

Which was, she reflected, a pity, for them. It was a nice face, besides having been extremely useful over the years to the shipbuilding industry.

For the time being, Home was a flat in one of the terribly old, terribly beautiful houses beside the Kaisergracht. It was hellishly expensive and the stairs half killed her unless she took her heels off and walked up them in her stocking feet, but that's the price you have to pay for being sentimental. For it was in this very room, in this very building, that she and George . . . She blushed.

The building had been new then; in fact, not completely and one hundred per cent finished. No roof, for one thing. But they'd been young, and in love, and it's nice to be able to lie in each other's arms and look up at the stars. They'd been on a day trip to the seventeenth century, and had been so wrapped up in each other (literally as well as figuratively) that they'd missed the last time-warp home. Not that they'd minded terribly much about that. It had been, she remembered with a slight shudder, about four months before George's year ran out, and even then they'd both spent an awfully large proportion of the time Not Thinking About It.

Having paid off her taxi, she let herself in, slipped off her shoes, and trotted up the stairs. As she reached the second-floor landing, she started to feel that faint prickling down the back of the neck that means either a premonition of terrible danger or too little fabric softener. Since she was wearing a backless dress, she decided it was probably danger.

Unfortunately, she had a very bad attitude towards danger, mainly because when she was around, it tended to be something that happened to other people. Ninja-silent in her shoelessness, she crept along the landing and pushed the door of her flat with the tip of one finger.

It swung open.

She swore.

At first sight, it looked like the aftermath of a visit from an incredibly conscientious burglar – you know, one of those dreadfully pernickety perfectionist types who insist on knifing the cushions for concealed pearls and ransacking the shelves for hollowed-out books. Unless, however, he had also been an extraordinarily picky burglar, brought up on only the finest aristocratic country houses and the hunting lodges of minor royalty, it would only be reasonable to expect him to have taken something; and he hadn't.

Or rather he had. And that was something of a bitch, because it was the one thing she would really rather not have parted with, given that it was genuinely irreplaceable. A framed portrait, early sixteenth century.

She made sure that the intruder had gone, and then sat down on all that was mortal of the bed and had a good swear. While she was doing this (and doing it ever so well) a thought struck her like a Mack truck and she froze in mid-oath.

If they'd come here just to steal his picture . . .

Why would they want to steal his picture?

And who the hell were they, anyway?

From the epicentre of the mess she extracted a suitcase, a few changes of clothing and a big, heavy, silver candlestick. Then she left the flat and caught a taxi.

CHAPTER FOUR

HAVING concluded his interview with Lucky George, Sitting Bull had a wash, brushed his teeth and put on his body.

For someone who'd been dead for over a century, his wardrobe was extensive and reasonably fashionable; a credit to his good taste and the lucky fact that he could put on a lot of noble savage/oppressed ethnic minority chic without actually trying. He selected one of his favourite outfits – the Mexican/ Chicano adolescent streetfighter with designer scars and matching paranoid psychosis – and took the elevator down to his grave.

Not so much a grave; more a sort of pied-à-terre. It was perhaps the only grave in the entire United States that had remote-control operated hydraulic car-port doors.

Down at the Silver Dollar on Whitier Boulevard, heart of the *barrio*, is one of the best places to pick up anything that's new on the street in downtown LA; at least, that's what they say in the brochure for the Los Angeles package tour offered by Mob 18-30, the holiday company specialising in tours for militant activists. When Sitting Bull wandered in and ordered a beer, the place was empty except for two old men playing dominoes and the brewery rep. And a strangely obscure figure, sitting on a bar stool by the juke-box drinking a pineapple juice.

'Hiya, Jack,' said Sitting Bull. 'How's it going?'

'I got a cold,' replied Don Juan, heavily.

'Too bad. You want to play some pool?'

They strolled over to the pool table, and Don Juan racked up.

'How's business?' Sitting Bull asked, chalking his cue and examining it for straightness. Don Juan shrugged.

'Not so good,' he replied, 'not so bad. Still, I think maybe I did wrong to change my career direction. As a philanderer I was good. This I don't do so well.'

Sitting Bull tossed a coin and called heads, accurately. 'Maybe,' he said. 'Then again, maybe not. The way I see it, Jack, informing is good, steady work. Philandering, you're only ever as good as your last job.' He drew back his arm and shot the white against the pack with a satisfying crack. Nothing went down. 'Is there much about right now?'

'Pretty quiet, Bull, pretty quiet.' Don Juan crouched down over the table, examining the lie of the cue ball. 'You know how it is. All the guys are out of town right now. Nobody who's anybody sticks around this dumb century for June these days.' He executed a tiny, stabbing movement that sent the white ball spiralling across the cloth like a vertiginous comet. 'Things'll pick up again in July, probably. I'm okay,' he added, straightening up and noting the position of the balls with approval. 'I had a good May, so I'm not complaining.'

'Anything special?'

Don Juan nodded. 'I turned in the captain of the *Marie Celeste*,' he said. 'There's some guys in the insurance business in London who want to see him real bad, you know?' He chuckled without humour. 'This time I have the feeling he's going to disappear *completely*. Your shot.'

Sitting Bull examined the table, calculating angles of incidence and refraction. He liked his new lifestyle (deathstyle, whatever). It was lower profile, but it was worth it simply for not having to shave every day. The hair and the fingernails were a nuisance, of course, but you can't have everything.

'I heard,' he said, perhaps trying a little too hard to sound as if he was just making conversation, 'that there's something really big going down in your line right now.'

'Maybe.'

Sitting Bull addressed the cue ball, made the shot and chalked his cue. 'Yeah,' he said. 'I heard Lucky George is back on the street.'

'That's interesting.'

'I heard,' Sitting Bull continued, sizing up the chances of cannoning off the back cushion to bring the cue ball back for the seven, 'that there's a nice long price waiting for anyone with good information.'

'Could be.'

'Wish I could get me a piece of that,' said Sitting Bull to the cue ball. 'Just because you're dead doesn't mean you can't take it with you.'

He watched the cue ball drift down the baize, clip the lip of the middle pocket and run with a clatter into the remains of the pack. Too much goddamn left hand side. Don Juan clicked his tongue sympathetically and sank four balls in quick succession.

'You got anything, then?' he asked.

'Who, me?' Sitting Bull drank some beer. 'I was just interested, that's all. Just in case I did hear anything, that's all.'

'I wouldn't bother,' Don Juan replied. 'The latest is, they've called off all agents, what with the trouble and everything. Pity about that,' he added sideways. 'If you had got anything, I mean.'

He took his shot, but misjudged it by about an eighth of an inch. The ball quivered in the jaws of the pocket and stayed put.

'Hey,' Sitting Bull said. 'Just as well I don't, or I'd be disappointed.' He walked round the table a few times, remembering some very good advice he'd received from the

Great Sky Spirit, way back in the old days. Never shoot pool with a spic, the Great Sky Spirit had said, or at least not for money. 'What would the trouble be, Jack?'

'A lot of very heavy things, Bull,' Don Juan replied, stroking his chin. 'Well, maybe not heavy. More making the administration look a complete asshole without actually breaking anything. Neat touch the man's got, you've got to hand it to him.' He looked up, his eyes catching Sitting Bull's attention like, say, a sawn-off shotgun placed two inches from one's nose. 'I like Lucky George, Bull,' he said. 'A really regular guy.'

'Absolutely.'

'Got me out of a jam more than once. I hope he makes it all the way.'

'Yeah, me too.'

'That's good.' Don Juan bent his back and cleared the rest of the table in successive shots. 'You know, maybe I am in the wrong business, Bull. Maybe I should try your line, huh?'

'What, being dead?'

Don Juan shrugged. 'It's a living,' he said. 'And you don't have to sell nobody down the river, either. I feel bad about it sometimes, Bull, I really do. Basically I'm a very sensitive person.'

'Me too. I was misunderstood.'

'You want another game?'

'Thanks, but I've gotta move.' He put his cue back in the rack. 'It's been good seeing you, Jack.'

'Yeah, you too.' Don Juan smiled thinly. 'And remember,' he added, 'if you do get to hear anything about Lucky George, nobody wants to know, right? You got that, Bull?'

'I got that, Jack. Be seeing you.'

After Sitting Bull had left the Silver Dollar, Don Juan sat for a while, staring at the dregs of his pineapple juice and ignoring the obvious glances of the barmaid. It's a wonderful thing, being retired.

Some time later, he got up and went over to the payphone.

* * *

A trapdoor opened, and four shadowy forms emerged.

So shadowy were they that the driver of the car didn't see them till too late. It would have been a nasty accident if the shadowy form actually hit by the car hadn't simply dematerialised.

'Brilliant,' muttered the leading shadowy form under his breath, as the three survivors paused in a shop doorway to regroup. 'What bloody genius put the hatch in the middle of a main road?'

They looked back at the scene of the tragedy, which was faintly illuminated by the edge of a streetlamp's penumbra.

'Stone me,' growled the Number Two form. 'It's a perishing manhole cover. How cheapskate can you get?'

'I thought I could thmell thomething while we were coming up.'

The leader shrugged. 'Ours not to reason why,' he said, with a certain deficiency of conviction. 'Right, here's what we do. We slip in, we ransack the place, we slip out again, we go home. All clear?'

'Yes.'

'Yeth.'

Try as he might, the leader couldn't help but find Number Three's speech impediment tiresome in the extreme. Sheer bias on his part, he knew; spectral warriors are considered fit for active service if they pass a number of physical and mental tests, painstakingly designed after extensive research to ascertain whether the subject is up to the demanding tasks likely to be encountered by Hell's commandos in the field. None of these tasks involved the correct pronunciation of sibilants, and quite right, too. Nevertheless . . .

'Okay,' the leader sighed. 'Synchronise your watches, people. Now . . .'

'I make it nine forty-three.'

'Nine thorty-*thickth*.'

'No, you're wrong there, Vern. I checked with the speaking clock before we left, and—'

'Now,' repeated the leader, 'according to the street map, we're in Silver Street, so King's College should be . . .'

'Your watch mutht be thatht. Hey, thkip . . .'

The leader turned slowly round. 'Yes?'

'What do you make the time, thkip? Only my watch theth—'

'Yes, but I checked it before . . .'

The leader winced. 'It doesn't matter,' he said. 'Just synchronise them, okay?'

'Yeth, but thkip, mine theth nine thorty-thickth and hith theth—'

'Yeah, skip. What does yours say?'

With a gesture of suffering fools, the leader looked at his wrist, only to see the sleeve of a black pullover and nothing else. Dammit, he'd forgotten his watch.

'Nine forty-five,' he said. 'Now, can we please get on with it?'

The brief: break into King's College, Cambridge and comb the archives to see if there was anything there which might shed some light on where Christopher Marlowe, sixteenth-century dramatist and graduate of said college, had got his information from. It was, the leader decided, absolutely typical of the bloody stupid, pointless . . .

'Shit,' observed Number Two, looking up at the gatehouse. 'It's like a damn fortress. How are we supposed to get into *that*?'

'Through the door,' replied the leader, mercilessly. 'They haven't locked up for the night yet.'

'Oh. Right.'

'That's the whole idea. We go in, we hide till everyone's gone to bed, we frisk the place and bugger off. Now, when you've quite finished . . .'

'Hey thkip, that'th pretty neat thinking.'

'Thanks, Vernon. Come on, follow me.'

Hiding till nightfall in a Cambridge college during termtime is easier said than done. Particularly if you're distinctively dressed in black trousers and pullover, black balaclava and black face-paint. Acting natural and inconspicuous takes just that bit more effort than usual. Stanislavski could have managed it, but not first time out.

'Thuck thith for a game of tholdierth,' observed Number Three eventually, after they'd been politely requested to leave the boiler room for the third time. 'I thought you thaid—'

'Well I didn't,' the leader replied. 'Just count yourselves lucky this is a university. Here, the weird is commonplace, so we should be okay. Let's go and have a drink in the bar.'

'Have they got a bar, skip?'

'They'd bloody well better have.'

They did. Huddled in a corner of the Junior Common Room over three pints of Abbot Ale, just under the dartboard, they looked totally inconspicuous.

'Real bummer, Howard getting run other like that,' observed Number Three, wiping froth from the mouthhole of his balaclava.

'Yes.'

'You'd have thought they'd have warned uth.'

'Yes.'

'Maketh you thick, thometimeth.'

'You are already, Vernon.'

'What, thick?'

'Yes.'

Number Three considered. 'No I'm not,' he replied, puzzled. 'I had a headache thith morning, but . . .'

The leader cleared his throat with a semblance of authority, before the whole bloody thing degenerated into farce. 'According to the plan,' he said, 'the library is up the stairs on our left as we came in, keeping the hall doorway to our right. Got that?'

'Sure thing, skip.' Number Two finished the last of the salted peanuts. 'What is it we're looking for, exactly?'

'A lead,' replied his commanding officer, with wasted irony.

'What thort of a lead?'

'Any sort of a lead.'

'Only,' Number Three continued, 'there'th a lead coming out of the back of thith computer game thing, if that'th any help. It goeth right acroth the wall and back into the—'

'A clue. Something to go on. A material fact.'

'What sort of a material fact, skip?'

One of the minor tragedies about being a spectral warrior is the fact that, being inhuman, they can't settle down and have children. Just now, the leader felt, he had an inkling of what he was missing.

'All right,' he said. 'Listen carefully. There's this bloke called George Faustus, right?'

'You mean Lucky George.'

'You got it. Now, shortly after he was arrested – very shortly, in fact, this nerd of a playwright called Christopher Marlowe wrote a play all about him. Lots of details in it that he couldn't possibly have known unless he was privy to some pretty restricted stuff. Marlowe was a student here at the time. The idea is, perhaps there's some papers or diaries of his lying about here somewhere which might put us in the right direction. Understood?'

Number Two considered the proposition, and clearly found it counter-intuitive. 'Hey,' he said, 'that was years ago. Unless they're really, you know, untidy . . .'

'My couthin Thimon'th very untidy. He keepth all hith old electrithity billth and gath billth and water billth and—'

'Not for over four hundred years he doesn't, I bet.'

'That'th becauth he'th only thirty-thickth. Give him a chanthe.'

'No, listen,' interrupted the leader, slightly desperate. 'Marlowe's a great playwright. When you're a great playwright, they keep all your letters and papers and things. It's called research.'

'My couthin Thimon'th not a playwright.'

'Vernon.'

'Yeth?'

'Shut up.'

At twenty to twelve, the bar steward turned them out and they wandered about in the night air for a while, waiting for the college to go to sleep. At half past one, they crept noiselessly, or relatively noiselessly, to the library door, and the leader fumbled for his skeleton key.

'Keith.'

'Yes, skip?'

'Whose turn was it to bring the key?'

'Yours, skip.'

'Kick the door in, Keith.'

'Okay, skip.'

It was, they realised, a big library. Big as in huge. There were, as Number Three perceptively remarked, books everywhere.

'All right,' the leader said, raising his voice to a whimper. 'Let's make a start, anyway. Those shelves over there.'

They hadn't been at it for more than an hour, scrabbling aimlessly by the light of small dark torches, when all the lights suddenly went on. They turned, to see a small, bald man in a dressing gown bearing down on them.

'Thkip.'

'What is it now?'

'Can we do the thilent killing, thkip? It'th my turn to do the thilent killing, and you promithed.'

'It's not really appropriate right now, Vern. Next time, I give you my word.' The leader then straightened his back, smiled and said, 'Can I help you?'

The bald man stopped in his tracks for a moment. 'Who the hell are you?' he asked.

The leader thought quickly. 'Interloan,' he replied. 'We got here late, your librarian's gone home for the night, we're in a bit of a hurry, so . . .'

The words dribbled away like a test-tube of water into the Gobi desert. The bald man shook his head.

'I know who you are all right,' he said.

'Oh.' The leader frowned. 'I don't want to sound facetious, but you don't seem terribly frightened, in that case.'

The bald man snorted. 'Frightened?' he replied. 'Frightened of you? Don't make me laugh. It'd take more than a cack-handed attempt at academic espionage to frighten me.'

The leader felt a nudge at his elbow. 'What'th academic ethpio—?'

'Well,' the bald man went on, 'you can jolly well think again, because it's not here. I suppose that rat Amesbury sent you, didn't he?'

Why not? 'That's about it,' the leader said. 'Mind, we're only obeying ord—'

'Appalling! Going about trying to steal another man's research papers and you call yourselves scholars! Where's your ethics?'

'Hang on, I know that. It'th the one between Kent and Thutholk, ithn't it?'

The bald man blinked twice. 'What?'

'Ethekth.'

Just for once, the leader was glad he had Vernon along. Someone capable of saying something so completely disconcerting at a time like this was worth his weight in gold. He decided to press home the advantage.

'Right,' he said. It was his favourite word. Positive without meaning anything. 'That's enough out of you, Grandad. You tell us where it is, or it'll be the worse for you.'

'I beg your pardon?'

'He thaid . . .'

Time to get moderately heavy, the leader decided. From

behind his back he produced a heavy black metal object that glinted unpleasantly in the fluorescent light of the library. It was, in fact, the remote control for opening the trapdoor, and likely to break or come loose if you so much as breathed on it, but not enough people knew that for it to be a problem. 'Show me where it is or you'll get it, understand?'

There was a pause, just long enough to set the leader wondering what he was going to do when the old man said *What are you pointing that remote control key at me for?* Then he started to back away. About bloody time too.

'You won't get away with this.'

'That's our business. Come on, move.'

Slowly, and with deadly hatred written all over him, the bald man opened a cupboard and produced a folder.

'I'll make you pay for this,' he said.

'Hey, thkip, that'th not right. I thought thith wath a library. You can take thingth out for free from a library, that'th the whole—'

'Okay,' the leader snapped, 'that'll do. Come on, move it out. Now.'

It was a close-run thing, at that. Eluding the porter and his wife's Yorkshire terrier wasn't a problem, and neither was the Yale lock on the main gate. What they hadn't bargained for was the Rugby Club, celebrating defeat at the hands of a superior Magdalene Fifteen.

'Hey skip,' Number Two panted as they fled along the High Street, hotly pursued. 'You know back there, when you said, Show me where it is or you'll get it.'

'I know.'

'But,' Number Two persisted, 'if he knew where it was, surely he'd got it already.'

The leader pulled up short, too breathless to run any further. The pack was about forty yards behind, and closing.

'Stone me, Keith, I never thought of that. Right, lads, going down.'

The trapdoor opened, just in the nick of time. For the reasons stated above, the manuscript, when it eventually reached the Hot Seat, was soggy, curled at the edges and just a little smelly. But nobody noticed.

It was Professor Ambermere's long-awaited disclosure of his researches into new material on the life and works of Christopher Marlowe, based on recently discovered manuscripts.

The so-called Amsterdam Archive.

CHAPTER FIVE

THANKS to research carried out in the last twenty-odd years, it is now tolerably well known that once they reach the stage of being able to make articulate sounds, all babies, regardless of nationality, ethnic grouping or environment, make virtually the same noises.

Far from being meaningless gurgles, these noises are the only words human beings ever get to speak in their own basic, unpolluted, indigenous language, of which the myriad tongues of Mankind are mere vulgar and corrupt dialects. Within weeks of finding their voices, human infants begin the long process of soaking up the stimuli of their immediate surroundings, and by the time they reach five months old, the Old Language has been supplanted in their centres of speech by the variant they will usually speak and think in for the rest of their lives.

What they are saying, in those initial weeks of vocalisation; is, 'You *bastards*! Get me back up there *immediately*!'

The Old Language is, of course, not confined to the newly born; it is also the lingua franca of the dead, the immortal and the ineffable. And magicians, necromancers and conjurors also speak it, albeit with an accent that makes them sound like the Germans in war films. For the convenience of our readers we shall ignore this and translate simultaneously as we proceed.

'Ronnie, old mate,' said Lucky George. 'Wonderful to hear from you. How in buggery did you get my number?'

In his office in Pandaemonium, Hieronymus Bosch glanced furtively about him and cupped his hand tight round the receiver.

'Shut up and listen,' he hissed. 'I'm only doing this because I owe you one, right? Remember that. If they catch me, my life won't be worth ...' He hesitated. 'Sorry, Freudian slip. Anyway, they'll bloody well crucify me. Look, George, they're on to you.'

'They are?'

'Believe it. I got this number from your dossier, okay? That suggests they're pretty well informed about your whereabouts, doesn't it? They got it all from your diary.'

'My diary? I've never ...'

George stopped, blinked and then winced.

'Sod it,' he said. 'That's really aggravating, that is.'

Everyone, at some stage of their lives, keeps a diary. Now, the usual reason for doing so is to help you remember, years later, what you did in the past.

Trust Lucky George to be different from everybody else.

'Where was it?' he asked.

'Long story,' Bosch replied. 'To cut it short, though, it showed up in Amsterdam, about twenty years ago. I think you left it on a tram or something.'

'Did I?'

'Not did. Will. I think. Did you ever read it, by the way?'

'What, and find out my future? No fear. I wouldn't be able to sleep nights.'

Bosch shrugged. 'Anyway,' he said, 'never mind all that. It's showed up at last, some of our boys from the Spooks department raided some university somewhere and got hold of a copy. The rest is history, if you'll pardon the expression.'

George frowned. 'Thanks,' he said. 'Now I owe you one. Has Lundqvist seen it yet, do you know?'

'It's a reasonably safe bet,' Bosch replied. 'Of course, they've undertaken to you to call off all their people from persecuting you, so they couldn't have shown him openly. I did hear, though, that once they'd read it, they deposited it in the maximum security vault of the Credit Infernale, with fifteen armed guards and a hi-tech laser-assisted alarm system. Where Lundqvist's concerned, that's the next best thing to pinning it on the notice board in the staff canteen. He's bound to have seen it. It's also on the database, of course, which is what I'm looking at, but Lundqvist's computer-illiterate.' Bosch raised his head, glanced round once more and added, 'I have an idea they also know about Nellie, so maybe you'd better . . .'

George shook his head. 'Nah,' he said, 'that's all right, Nellie can look after herself. Well, thanks a lot, Ronnie. I won't say *Be seeing you*, but take care, be good.'

'Don't worry about it, George. Oh, George.'

'Yes'

'You didn't mind me reversing the charges, did you? Only they check the phone bills now, and—'

'No problem, Ronnie. Ciao.'

History, most aggravating of the Nine Muses, has forgotten what the favour was that Lucky George did Hieronymus Bosch all those years ago, when they were students at Wittemberg together. History's other infuriating habit, apart from forgetting things, is using all the sugar in the communal kitchen and never replacing it.

The first thing George did after replacing the receiver was to turn round, very slowly. Nothing untoward happened. Good.

Next on the agenda was getting the hell out of town, but there were a couple of things he had to see to first. First Van Appin, then Nellie. Or maybe the other way round.

He was trying to make a decision on this point on his way

downtown when a choice became unnecessary. A girl on a bicycle drew up beside him with a screech of brakes, walloped him on the back and said, 'Hello, George.'

Now then. We want this to be a civilised book. There are some authors, prurient types with the morality of paparazzi, who stoop so low as to eavesdrop on their characters' most private and personal moments and then print the whole lot, verbatim. Well, not quite; they do leave some bits out. In all the works of D.H. Lawrence, for example, the girl never once says to the man, 'Hold on a minute, my arm's gone to sleep.' Nevertheless, standards in this respect are deplorably low. It's time something was done about it.

We therefore rejoin the narrative at the moment when Helen of Troy and Lucky George have got over the emotional side of meeting again for the first time in over four hundred years, and are discussing what they should do next over coffee and pancakes.

'It's looking hairy,' George said. 'Apparently that toad Lundqvist is after me.'

Helen clicked her tongue sympathetically. 'Poor lamb,' she said, 'what a bore. Is that what all the stuff with the credit cards and the biros and the golf courses was about?'

George nodded. 'Actually,' he added, 'I quite enjoyed all that. It's been a long time, you know.'

'You always did have a childish streak.'

'Maybe.' He shrugged. 'Comes in handy. Anyway, it didn't do a blind bit of good. Sure, all the hobgoblins and so on were pulled off the street, but that's neither here nor there. The day I can't sort out a few idiots with pitchforks . . .'

Helen frowned. 'Be that as it may,' she said. 'Had you got something in mind?'

'Not really. I was thinking of keeping my head down until the lawyer's ready, playing it by the book, that sort of thing. There's no point looking for trouble, after all; I don't want to start a fight if I don't have to.'

Helen considered this as she finished her pancake. 'Somehow I don't think it's going to be as easy as that,' she said. 'Besides, if turning all the traffic lights in Milan into sunflowers isn't starting a fight, it'll probably do to be going on with. That's always been your trouble, George,' she added sternly. 'Too much of this silly artistic integrity stuff.'

By way of reply, George simply grinned. 'All this,' he said, changing the subject, 'may look to you like aggravation, but to me it's more like . . . What's the word I'm looking for?'

Helen of Troy applied her mind in the search for the appropriate word. 'Extreme danger?' she hazarded.

George shook his head. 'Fun. That's the word I'm looking for.'

'Fun?'

'Fun.'

Helen broke off a corner of bread to mop up the last of the maple syrup. 'Breaking out of Hell,' she said. 'Being hunted across the face of the earth by the most deadly contract killer history has ever known, who incidentally has a personal grudge against you. If that's your idea of the meaning of fun, I suggest you sue the compilers of your dictionary.'

George shrugged. 'I get what you're driving at,' he replied, 'in a way. On the other hand,' he said, smiling at the empty coffee pot, 'compared to what I've been doing for the last four hundred years, it's absolutely bloody hysterical.'

Helen gave him what, in a poor light, could have been mistaken for a serious look.

'And what have you been doing, George?' she demanded.

'Time.'

Funny old stuff, Time.

There is, notoriously, a lot of it about. But it is, of course, a finite resource.

This could have been a problem. Back in the dark ages, pre-ecology, the powers that be had the curious notion that they could go on pumping the stuff out indefinitely. 'Plenty more where this came from,' they reassured themselves, as they gaily sank new bore-holes and erected giant new rigs.

But they were wrong. Time, like everything else, is running out.

Not that you'd know it if you went by the commodities markets. Just now, for example, over-production has led to a serious glut. The price has, accordingly, tumbled. They're practically giving the stuff away, with free wineglasses.

This state of affairs can't last, of course, and the wiser heads are already planning for the day when the wells run dry. They're also at last grasping the nettle of what to do with all the enormous dumps of used Time which litter up the underprivileged back lots of the Sixth Dimension, slowly rotting their half-lives away and doing awful things to the environment.

This stuff, they say, can be recycled. All we need is a little more research, one tiny breakthrough.

Which is rather like saying that Death can be cured just as soon as we can find a way of making people live for ever.

'I'm sorry,' the receptionist said. 'Nobody can see Mr Van Appin without an appointment.'

The mirror sunglasses stared back at her, and she wriggled slightly.

'That's okay,' said the man in the shades. 'Seeing him is not essential. Just so long as I can kick his liver out through his ears, I'll pass up on the visual contact.'

Before she could press the panic button, Lundqvist leant over, ripped the wires out with a tiny flick of the wrist, wrapped them round a couple of pencils, and presented them to her, corsage-fashion. Then he kicked in the door.

'Kurt,' said Mr Van Appin, not looking up, 'great to see you, take a seat, I'll be with you in just a . . .'

Shit, Lundqvist thought, I'm getting slow. He'd managed to

get the drawer open two millimetres before I grabbed him.

'Help yourself to a revolver,' Mr Van Appin said. 'I usually have one myself about this time.'

Lundqvist smiled without humour, removed the revolver from the drawer and pocketed it. Then he leant forward, thrusting his chin under Van Appin's nose.

'So,' Mr Van Appin said, 'what can I do for you? Thinking of making a will, perhaps?'

Lundqvist shook his head.

'You should,' Van Appin said. 'Dodgy business like yours, I'd have said it was a very sensible precaution. Thinking of buying a house, then?'

This time, Lundqvist didn't shake his head. For variety, he shook Mr Van Appin's.

'Shall I take that,' remarked Mr Van Appin, spitting out the syllables like a boxer spitting teeth, 'as a negative?'

'Where is he?'

'Who?'

'Faust.'

Mr Van Appin smiled, his professional smile which does not mean, 'Hello, I like you, shall we be friends?' Quite the opposite, in fact.

'I'm sorry,' he said. 'Mr Faust is my client, and I cannot disclose confidential information. And,' he continued quickly, 'just in case you were contemplating being so ill-mannered as to threaten me with bodily injury, may I just remind you that I practise the law in all the major centuries simultaneously, and I include your present employers among my most valued clients. One false move out of you, and I'll have an injunction out to stop you ever having been born before you can say "chronological dysfunction."' He paused, and gave Lundqvist a patronising grin. 'In your case,' he added, 'that's probably being over-ambitious. Do you think you could manage "Jack Robinson"?'

There was a long pause.

'You think you're really smart, don't you?'

Mr Van Appin looked modest. 'In the same way that I think cold is the opposite of hot and that water is wet, yes, I do.'

'Fine.' The telephone at Mr Van Appin's elbow rang. 'Answer it, it's for you.'

For a moment, the lawyer hesitated; then he picked up the phone.

'Yes,' he said, 'Van Appin here.'

Likewise. This is Van Appin of Van Appin (Fifteenth Century) and Company. Hiya, partner, how's things your end?

Mr Van Appin blinked twice. 'Fine,' he said. 'We're doing okay. A bit different from your day, of course, we're doing more in the commercial property line and not so much of the witchcraft trials, but we make a living. What can I do for you?'

It's like this, partner. I'm speaking to you from the maternity ward here in AD 1449, where Mr Kurt Lundqvist is just about to be born.

If Mr Van Appin was thrown by this remark, he didn't let it show. 'It's a small world,' he remarked.

You can say that again, because I have Mr Kurt Lundqvist with me right now. I've tried explaining to him that he's risking setting off a really serious temporal paradox just by being here, but it's hampering me having this cheesewire round my throat, you know?

Mr Van Appin (twentieth century) nodded slowly. 'I can relate to that,' he said. 'I would most strongly advocate not making any sudden movements.'

I was working along the same lines myself. I'd also appreciate it a whole lot if you told Mr Lundqvist what he wants to know.

Mr Van Appin frowned. 'I hear what you say,' he replied. 'I'm just wondering how that would leave us from a professional ethics viewpoint.'

There was a gurgling noise from the telephone, and for a brief moment, Mr Van Appin was aware of a most curious sensation; that of vaguely remembering that he didn't in fact exist, having died many years previously. *I think we're just going to have to take a view on that one, really. Like, I think we have a serious conflict of interests situation here, and maybe it's time we took a more flexible approach vis-à-vis the strict interpretation . . .*

There was a particularly vivid flashback, which made Mr Van Appin wince sharply. It wasn't so much the physical pain, or the fear, or the horror; it was the thought of the catastrophic effects that having been unwittingly dead for five hundred years while continuing to trade would have on his tax position that decided him.

'What you're saying,' he therefore gurgled into the receiver, 'is that maybe this is an instance where we should interpret the statute in its wider sense, having regard to all the circumstances and implications of the case.'

Absolutely, partner. I would also recommend doing it quickly, because otherwise . . .

The sentence was not completed. Mr Van Appin, tearing himself away from a rather fascinating recollection of his own funeral, nodded sharply three or four times.

'Okay,' he said, 'you got it. I'll tell him right away. Oh, and by the way.'

Yes.

'You'll never guess who didn't even bother sending a wreath or anything.'

The line went dead; and, by dint of some rapid talking, Mr Van Appin narrowly avoided the sincerest form of flattery.

Lucky George came out of the phone booth, stopped, turned back and smiled at the coin slot, which promptly disgorged slightly more loose change than he'd originally fed into it. Slightly more, only because there's a limit to the amount of coins one man can conveniently carry, or one government can comfortably produce.

'Right,' he said, 'that's got that sorted. What do you fancy doing the rest of the day? If you like, we could go to the Rijksmuseum and wake up some of the paintings . . .'

Helen frowned. 'Hold on,' she said. 'When you say that's sorted . . .'

'I mean,' George replied, 'I've taken care of things. For now, anyway. Some friends of mine owe me a few favours. Things'll be okay, you'll see.'

'In that case,' Helen said, 'let's go eat. I'm hungry.'

One of George's telephone calls had been made to a small family-run Italian restaurant in Brooklyn.

Mrs Loredano had taken the call.

'Hey, Lorenzo,' she called, over the rumble of simmering pans, 'it's for you. Some guy called Buonaventura.'

There was a crash, as Mr Loredano dropped four helpings of osso bucco, two garlic breads and a side salad.

'Giorgio Buonaventura?'

'Yeah. You know him?'

'Give me the phone.'

Mrs Loredano shrugged, handed over the receiver and went for the broom.

'Larry?'

'George,' replied Mr Loredano, with slightly too much emphasis on the ecstatic happiness. 'Hey, it's been a long time. What you doing out?'

'I absconded, Larry. I got bored. How's things?'

'Fine, George, fine. Couldn't be better.'

'Business okay?'

'Well, you know, times are hard, not much money about, and then there's the overhead . . .'

'Sure.' The voice on the other end of the line hardened slightly, like a carbon deposit suddenly subjected to billions of tons of top pressure. 'Listen, Larry, I need a favour. Can you drop everything?'

'I just did.'

'Sorry?'

'Nothing. I'm just taking off my apron, George, I'll be right with you.'

'That's wonderful, Larry. Mike there too?'

'Sure,' Mr Loredano replied. 'I'll tell him to come too. Where are you?'

As George explained, Mr Loredano made notes on his order pad. After a few more cordial exchanges he replaced the phone, removed his apron and called his wife.

'Honey,' he said, 'me and Mike, we gotta go out for a while. Business.'

Mrs Loredano expressed herself, stating her opinion of this suggestion. Her husband stopped her.

'I know,' he said. 'Sure. That was George on the line.'

The penny dropped.

'We'll be back as soon as we can,' Mr Loredano assured her. 'Don't give any credit while we're away.'

He then found his business partner and explained, whereupon both men retired to the back office and changed for the journey.

'You ready, Mike?'

'Ready as I'll ever be.'

'Window open?'

'Yeah.'

'See you there, then.'

The two proprietors of La Veneziana then spread their wings, squawked a few times, and flitted out of the window. Ten minutes later they were midway across the Atlantic, slowed down by a strong headwind and driving rain from the south-east. Not bad going, nevertheless, for a pair of superficially ordinary herring gulls, particularly when you bear in mind that they'd been out of practice for four hundred years.

Mrs Loredano, meanwhile, was explaining to Mrs Steno why their respective husbands had abandoned the restaurant at the height of the mid-day rush. She knew all about it, having been let in on the secret some years ago; and besides, she believed that a good marriage is built on mutual trust. Mrs Steno, who believed that a good marriage is built on unilateral terrorism, hadn't been favoured with her husband's confidence in this regard.

Mrs Loredano explained that many years ago, before they went into the restaurant business, Larry and Mike had worked for this guy back in the old country. What as? Well, as familiars. No, not that, that's a valet, familiars are those guys who help out sorcerers and magicians. Yeah, hand them the top hat and get sawn in half, that sort of thing. And other things, too, of course. Yeah, usually it's some bimbo with no clothes on, but sometimes it's men as well. And sometimes – here Mrs Loredano took a deep breath – it's seagulls.

Seagulls? You mean like performing animals?

Yeah, only more than that, sometimes.

She explained further.

It took Mrs Steno some time to recover.

You mean, she said, Mike and Larry are *seagulls*? Yes, well, *were* seagulls, but when the guy they were working for, (pause for thought), when he *retired*, he turned them into human beings, regular guys. Even set them up in the restaurant business. A very thoughtful man, by all accounts, the guy really knew how to look after his employees.

Seagulls!

Catholic seagulls, Rosa, I absolutely guarantee that. Almost the first thing they did after getting their human bodies, they went out and got baptised. You've got absolutely nothing to worry about on that score.

Anyway, part of the deal was that if ever this Mr Buonaventura needed them again for anything, anything in the familiaring line, then of course they'd be only too pleased. A matter of honour. You've got to have respect in this life, or what have you got?

Yes, but seagulls . . .

At which, Mrs Loredano became slightly affronted. No offence intended, but she hoped Mrs Steno wasn't prejudiced in any way, because that wasn't a very nice thing to be. After all, everybody's something, if you go back far enough: Italian, Jewish, Irish, German, Chinese, seagull, Greek, whatever. Bring us your huddled masses. Had Mrs Steno taken a look at the Statue of Liberty lately, by the way?

There was a long silence.

'Sorry, Maria,' said Mrs Steno.

'That's okay, Rosa,' replied Mrs Loredano. 'Just forget it, okay?'

They went and tossed the salad.

CHAPTER
SIX

A fortuitous tail wind and a lift hitched from a passing anticyclone helped Larry and Mike make up time, and they swooped down on the Oosterdok just on two and a half hours after leaving Brooklyn.

They were only just in time.

Not that they were to know that, of course. They circled for a while, making kawk-kawk noises and generally getting used to being seagulls again. Oddly enough, what both of them found strangest was being without their watches.

'It's like riding a bicycle,' Larry observed.

'Bloody uncomfortable, yeah.'

'No, I meant—'

'And cold. And very, very tiring.'

Mike tilted his wingtips and dropped down a hundred feet or so. 'Right,' he said, 'we'd better report in, I guess. Where's the map?'

Larry looked at him. 'What map?'

'The street map.'

'I thought you had it.'

'Don't be dumb. How can I carry a goddamn street map in a seagull outfit? You think I've got pockets in the wings or something?'

Larry made no reply. He'd been putting up with Mike's logic for approximately twice as long as America had been an independent nation, and although it still occasionally had the power to make him want to scream, he had built up a sort of immunity to it; apparently, you can do the same thing with arsenic, if you take a microscopic amount each day. 'What was the address again?' he asked.

'Intersection of Keisergracht and Hartenstraat,' Mike replied. 'I guess we just fly around until we see the street names, or . . .'

He broke off and craned his head down under his wing.

'Hey,' he remarked. 'Maybe we won't have to, at that. Look.'

'That's him all right,' said Lucky George. 'I'd know him anywhere. Come on, time we weren't here.'

From their window they could see a man in mirror sunglasses and a green jacket strolling along the canal bank, with a long brown paper parcel under his arm. At a respectful distance of maybe five yards, there followed a troop of assorted demons, all unexpected heads, misplaced organs and unfashionable colours, wheeling handcarts. The carts were piled high with some very impressive-looking machinery, the specific uses of which you couldn't hope to guess if you didn't actually know (although you'd have no trouble coming up with the general idea). For the record, they were a set of the latest state-of-the-art magical effect suppressors, together with generators, transformers and other ancillary hardware, capable of neutralising supernatural forces up to thirty kilo-grails within a six-hundred-yard radius.

Nobody seemed to be taking the slightest bit of notice, probably because the entire procession was theoretically invisible; a wonderful new effect produced by photoelectric mimesis. Put simply, the process works by making the subject closely resemble the viewer's most boring relative or acquaintance. The viewer is then so preoccupied with getting past without being noticed himself that he doesn't stop to look twice at the subject. The only living person in the cosmos who can't be taken in by theoretical invisibility is, of course, Lucky George; all of whose relatives have been dead for centuries, and none of whose friends are boring.

'Where?' Helen asked, hopping towards the window with one leg in and one leg out of a pair of Ann Klein slacks. 'I can't see . . .' She froze. 'Hey, that's not possible.'

George grinned. 'I know. Personally, I can see my aunt Hilda, my cousin Norman, my cousin Norman's second wife's brothers and what looks like seven enormous cappuccino machines. You make a break for it down the back stairs while I try and hold them off with a few . . .'

He stopped in mid-sentence, his face a picture of absolute bewilderment. Then he swore.

'Suppressors,' he muttered. 'Nuts. All right, we'll just have to run for it. Come on.'

(Meanwhile, the magical effect which he'd launched by way of a ranging shot and which had ricocheted off the suppressor field sang away into the upper air, bounced off a TV satellite and was broadcast into millions of homes worldwide in the form of a seven-hour-long subtitled Japanese art movie about a day in the life of a portable typewriter.)

Lundqvist looked up sharply and raised his hand.

'In there,' he snapped.

As posses went, he reckoned, they were no worse than being trapped in a lift with an independent financial adviser; second-rate press-ganged local evil spirits, reluctant to get involved and anxiously awaiting any pretext for slipping quietly away to a bar somewhere. He could handle them.

'You,' he said to the tallest demon present, 'rig up the kit and give me maximum power. The rest of you, fan out, don't let anyone or anything leave the building. And,' he added, 'remember, I've got all your serial numbers, and anyone who's not here when I get back is going to find himself in an oil lamp granting wishes so fast his hooves won't touch.'

He hitched up his trousers, unwrapped the flame-thrower, and strode towards the house.

His hand was on the doorknob when something white, wet and smelly hit him smack in the eye.

'Shot!'

Larry shrugged modestly. 'It's a gift,' he said. 'Either you got it or you haven't. Your turn.'

By this time, Lundqvist had wiped his eye carefully with his handkerchief, turned round and stared long and hard at a goat-headed electrician who'd sniggered, and put on his hat. Bugger the doorknob, he was thinking. In fact, bugger the door. He turned the dial on the back of the fuel tank to one-quarter power, pressed the pilot light switch, and . . .

And a passing seagull swooped down, gave him a nasty nip on the left index finger, and rocketed off into the sky. Lundqvist swore, dropped the flame-gun and sucked the wound.

While he was thus occupied, a second passing seagull flapped up behind him, caught the fuel throttle awkwardly in its beak and twisted it on to maximum.

The flame-gun at his feet at once erupted, making Lundqvist jump about three feet in the air and dislodge his sunglasses. By some quirk of gravity, they reached the pavement before he did (although they had quite some way further to go), just in time to be under his feet when he landed. There was a crunch, like a lorry crossing gravel.

Two seagulls met in mid-air.

'That'd better do for now,' said Larry. 'Otherwise he might start to suspect . . .'

He didn't finish what he was saying, his attention having been distracted by a fifty-foot jet of fire passing within twenty centimetres of his tail. With more speed than dignity, the seagulls withdrew.

* * *

Outside the back gate, meanwhile, a demon stood guard.

He had the head of a dog, the nose of a gryphon, broad bat-like red wings, a pitchfork, four feet of tail and a stammer. He was the diabolical equivalent of sixteen and a half years old, and this was the first time he'd ever done anything like this. The reason why he'd been assigned this spot was because the was too junior to be able to refuse.

'Excuse me.'

He looked up. Despite his poor eyesight (he was short-sighted, glasses made him feel self-conscious and, although he had contact-lenses, such was his biochemistry that they melted as soon as he put them in) he could see that the back door had opened and a female head had appeared round it. He swallowed hard, and tried to remember his lines.

'Huhalt,' he said, in a high, quavering voice. 'Whogugugu-goesthere, friendorfufufufufufoe?'

'Sorry, what was the choice again?'

'Fufufuf . . .'

'Friend.'

'That's all right then.' He lowered the pitchfork and stepped forward, and five seconds later was lying on his beak wondering how come the house had fallen on him. Helen of Troy, for her part, was looking at a slightly bent silver candlestick and sighing.

'Okay?'

She nodded. 'George,' she said, as he came out of the house and locked the door, 'we are friends, aren't we? I mean, you and me.'

'I guess so,' he replied. 'Why?'

Helen stepped over the demon. 'I'd hate to think I'd told a lie, that's all. Which way now?'

George shrugged. 'Doesn't really matter, so long as it's generally north-east. All I really need is a phone box. Ah, there they are. About time too,' he said, as two seagulls flopped down on to his outstretched wrist. 'What kept you?'

'We came as fast as we could,' replied Larry, wounded.

'Like hell you did,' George replied. 'What were you doing, waiting for the exchange rate to swing in your favour? Follow me.'

By dint of reckless trespassing in the gardens of perfect strangers, they came out by the Westerkirk, where George flung himself into a telephone booth, grabbed the receiver and rattled his pockets for change. Helen sat on a bench and took out her powder compact. The seagulls ate a discarded ice-cream cone.

'Right,' said George, stepping out of the booth and not bothering to gather the cascade of change that was flooding out of the coin box, 'that's all settled. Lunch?'

Larry raised his head. 'Settled, chief?'

'Settled. What we need,' he went on, leading the way, 'is either somewhere with a garden or somewhere they don't mind pets. Otherwise, you two'll have to hover overhead with a bottle of lemonade and a packet of crisps.'

Helen of Troy gave him a look. 'Settled exactly how, George? Not that I'm doubting you for a minute, of course, but . . .'

George grinned. 'I phoned a couple of old friends of mine,' he said. 'They're on their way.' He glanced up at the sky, smiled and nodded. 'My only regret is, we'll miss all the fun.'

The ability to make friends easily is a gift you're either born with or you aren't. If you've got the knack, cultivate it. It's worth having.

People who have the gift do tend to find life rather easier than the rest of us. If they want a new solenoid for the car, they get on to their friend who works in a garage. If they fancy a holiday in Portugal, they stay in the villa which belongs to a couple of friends who only go there for three weeks in July. The houses of the friends of builders tend to sprout porches and extensions like a flourishing tree.

Lucky George is to the likes of these as the Sargasso Sea is to nine square inches of pondweed.

'I can see that,' Lundqvist observed. There was a certain icy quality in his voice which would have started an Eskimo property developer rubbing his hands and applying for planning permission.

The demon who had just remarked that the fugitives would appear to have escaped shrank back and tried to look inconspicuous, something he frankly wasn't cut out for. He was unsuccessful.

'Okay,' Lundqvist went on, 'you're such a goddamn expert, go find them.' The bounty hunter growled irritably. He should, he knew, have been exercising his uniquely incisive mind on what the fugitives were likely to do next, but try as he might his thoughts kept straying off in the direction of seagulls, bird-snaring and new and savage advances in the ancient art of taxidermy. 'Jump to it,' he snapped, breaking free from his reverie. 'The trail shouldn't be hard to follow.'

With a soft whimper, the demon in question looked round and prepared to do his best. Fortunately for him, he was about eighty-five per cent nose, having been custom-designed for the torment throughout eternity of a cocaine dealer. He sniffed.

'Thad way,' he said. 'Foddow me.'

Now then.

Given the choice, a good storyteller tries to keep the early stages of his narrative relatively plain and simple – clarity begins a tome, as the old saw has it. Sometimes, though, with the best will in the world, this option just isn't available. If confusing things happen, with people dashing about hither and yon and tripping over each other's feet, the narrator has to do the best he can. At least let him try and bring the participants on stage in some vestige of order.

In possession of the field, then, Lundqvist and his highly trained and motivated associates.

Somewhere off and circling, two seagulls.

In a taxi bowling down the Leidsestraat, sincerely wishing he was somewhere else but remembering to keep a careful note of time engaged so as to facilitate drawing up his bill of costs at the end of the day, Mr Van Appin.

In another taxi speeding up the Stadholderskade, completely at a loss as to what was going on but chuffed to little mint balls at being allowed on dry land three years ahead of schedule, and looking forward to seeing his old college chum Lucky George again after all this time, one Julius Vanderdecker, otherwise known as the Flying Dutchman.

Sharing the taxi with him, two other fellow students from those dear old Wittemberg days (an inventor of parachutes and a shabbily dressed Dane with a habit of muttering to himself) and a TV reporter*, who'd asked if he could share their taxi as he had to be at an important meeting at the Anne Frank House in twenty minutes.

Down below somewhere, the management of Hell Holdings plc, roughing out the publicity campaign for Fryathon '95 and blissfully unaware of what was just around the corner.

In the gods, God.

Two seagulls swoop Stuka-like on to a traffic jam by the Stadsschouwburg and peck frantically on the window of a taxi.

'Hello, Mike, long time no see,' exclaims the designer of parachutes, winding down the window. 'What are you two doing in these . . .?'

'Use your brains, Lenny,' mutters the Dane.

'Gee, sorry. Of course, you're from . . .' the parachute

---

*Guess who

designer lowers his voice to a conspiratorial whisper they could still probably hear in Leiden '... From you know who. Any orders from the big guy?'

'Quark, quark,' replies the seagull patiently. 'Quark. You got that?'

'You bet, Mike,' says the parachute boffin, grinning. 'Just leave it to us. Ciao.'

Two seagulls perch, a few seconds later, on the window-sill of a taxi a hundred yards further up the same jam.

'Larry, Mike, good to see you,' exclaims Mr Van Appin. 'This is really opportune, you know, 'cos I was going through the accounts and you guys still owe me for doing the lease of the restaurant.'

'Quark,' interrupts a seagull quickly. 'Quark quark quark.'

'Quark,' confirms the other seagull.

Mr Van Appin shrugs. On the one hand, he's simply not the running-about type, every minute out of the office is costing him thousands of guilders in lost fees and the course of action to which his client has apparently committed himself is extremely hazardous and liable, if it goes wrong, to have disastrous consequences both for himself and his professional advisers. On the other hand, it's a poor heart that never rejoices.

'Okay,' he says. 'Go for it.'

'Helen.'

'Mmmm?'

'Pass the maple syrup, there's a love.'

Cleaving the air like two postgraduate smart missiles, two seagulls flash down out of the sun on an increasingly ragged procession hacking its way through the back gardens of the Keisergracht.

Lundqvist sees them; and just as the penny drops and he realises that these are no ordinary herring-gulls, they bank in mid-air over the handcarts, snip lengths of wire off the suppressor machines with surgical precision in their sharp beaks, and beat it.

No point even trying a shot at this range. With a snarl, he holsters his .475 Wildey, scowls horribly at his skilled assistants, and returns to the task of cleaving a path through someone's begonias with his machete.

Three old college chums standing rather self-consciously on the banks of the Prinsengracht, wondering what they've let themselves in for.

'You ever done anything like this before, Jule?'

'Nah. What about you, Lenny?'

The designer of parachutes stroked his beard. 'Depends,' he replied. 'In 1499 I designed a contrivance for harnessing the power of the winds and the tides to operate a small, left-hand-thread ratchet screwdriver, not that there was any demand, bloody Luddites. Does that count?'

The Dane and the Dutchman looked at each other.

'Frankly,' said the Dane, 'no. Oh well, I suppose we'll all just have to learn together.'

Two seagulls flapped wearily over the rooftops and perched on the Dutchman's head.

'Quark,' they said in chorus.

'We're on, then,' said the designer of parachutes. 'Over the top, and all that.'

'You can say that again.'

'Right,' the parachute man continued, 'let the dog see the rabbit. Which one of us do you think ought to say the magic words and so forth? Any volunteers?'

The Dane mole-wrenched his mind back from recollecting what a right pain in the arse Lenny had been in the old days, and locked it back on course. 'Tell you what, Lenny,' he said, 'why don't you do it?'

'If you're sure.'

'I'm sure.'

'Jule? How about you"

'Just get on with it, Lenny, please. And could you possibly manage to be a tiny bit less cheerful about everything, because you're giving me a migraine.'

'You always were a gloomy old sod, weren't you? All right then, here we go.'

Three old college chums, plus two seagulls, vanished.

Lundqvist lowered his field glasses, licked his lips and smiled. He didn't speak, but his lips framed the word *Gotcha!*

He was standing in a large, rather mangled gap in the front wall of a fine late seventeenth-century merchant's house facing on to the Prinsengracht – when serious guys take short cuts they don't muck about – and observing the rather awkward progress towards him of three giant, self-propelled windmills. Show-off, he said to himself.

'You,' he called to an assistant demon, 'full power to the suppressors, now.'

The demon scurried away and pulled a lever. Nothing happened.

'Excude me,' the demon said in a small, terrified voice, 'only I think sud of the wired are mithing frod the machide.'

Lundqvist stared at him for a moment, as if the demon had just leant forward and extracted all his teeth. Seagulls, he was thinking, oh *shit*.

'Try the others,' he yelled. 'Move it, quickly.'

The demons, however, were backing away, muttering. As if by telepathy, they had all suddenly started thinking, Yeah, sure, we're demons, but this is *spooky*. A few seconds later and they'd gone.

The windmills continued to advance. They were swinging their sails. Little puffs of superfluous flour drifted out on the wind and scattered like mist.

You can disconcert Kurt Lundqvist, but you can't frighten

him. It took him about a third of a second to get his head together, lose his temper, draw his gun and start firing. Bullets whistled through the sails of the windmills, melted and dropped into the canal.

Never mind, there was still the flame-thrower. A few deft twists on the fuel tap, and a billowing, wind-blown rose of red flame swept across the street and licked the brickwork of the windmills.

Complete waste of time. Goddamn, the Dutch pioneered fire regulations.

He could feel the backdraught from the sails now, as the three shadows fell across him. Time to withdraw and re-group. What would Napoleon have done under the circumstances?

Swish!

Okay, Napoleon would most probably have curled up in a ball and screamed, and likewise Hannibal and Irwin Rommel. Alexander the Great, however, would have jumped back into a shop doorway, grabbed the first thing that came to hand – in this case, a long wooden pole with a hook on the end, used for raising and lowering shutters – and *attacked*, by golly. And what was good enough for Alexander was good enough for Kurt Lundqvist.

He tucked the pole under his arm, lowered his head, and charged.

A taxi drew up at the intersection of Radhuisstraat and Prinsengracht, and a man got out. He was late for a college reunion.

'*How* much?' he demanded, shocked.

The taxi driver said it again. Muttering darkly about inflation, the passenger paid him and looked down the street.

Because, like the other Old Wittembergers present that day, he was dead and buried, the theoretical invisibility effect cut no ice with him. He therefore saw, in the distance, a man running frantically backwards and forwards, trying to prod three windmills with what looked like a spear.

'Damn,' muttered Don Quixote de la Mancha. 'Buggers have started without me.'

Okay, thought Lundqvist, as a sail whistled past his ear and cut off a button from his sleeve, that's what Alexander would have done. Any other suggestions?

He thrust hard with the shutter pole, and had the satisfaction of connecting with a bit of winding mechanism. The pole broke.

Ulysses S. Grant. A really savvy guy. He'd have dropped the pole and run like buggery.

Also Belisarius, Cortes and the Duke of Marlborough.

The edge of a sail whirled past his head as he ran, parting his hair down the middle and making him look like a nineteenth-century curate. As he sprinted past the now useless suppressors his subconscious mind was thinking, *About three feet of ordinary insulated cable and I'll have you yet, you bastard.* His conscious mind was saying, *Help, help*, very loudly.

Lundqvist was a good runner. Usually, of course, he ran after people, not away from them, but the principle is pretty well the same. On the corner of Prinsengracht and Berenstraat he was able to stop, lean heavily against a wall and catch up on his breathing, secure in the knowledge that the windmills were a long way behind.

He looked up.

Those windmills, sure. The three animated monsters advancing towards him, sails slicing the air like so much salami, were probably entirely different windmills, or else the same windmills, cheating. Did it really matter? He picked up his feet and ran.

Not noticing that overhead, two seagulls were floating on a thermal, in their claws two string bags. Simultaneously they let go their payloads, said 'Quark!' and banked off.

The bags hit the pavement and burst, scattering bulbs everywhere. Ordinary everyday tulip bulbs, only recently snatched up from a stall in the flower market.

They started to grow.

Fortunately, Lundqvist still had his machete with him, and by hacking away for all he was worth, he was able to clear a path through the thicket before the horrible snapping flowers could reach down and wrap their petals round him. Gasping for air and soaked from head to foot in sticky green sap, he staggered out, only to find himself surrounded by furiously sprouting daffodils. Meanwhile, two seagulls were hovering in the still air, string bags clutched in their talons . . .

The windmills were closing. The tulips were opening a path for them, letting them through . . .

The key thing to do in situations like these is to keep your head, Lundqvist remembered, as a sail-edge grazed his collarbone. He ducked down on his hands and knees, machete between his teeth, and crawled. The sails couldn't reach him down here, neither could the carnivorous flowers. If he met an ant, at least it would be hand-to-mandible fighting, he'd have a chance.

Behind him, he heard a rumbling sound, like thunder, and the nauseating squeaking of living tissue being crushed. He cast a quick glance over his shoulder, and saw . . .

. . . A huge yellow wheel, at least twelve feet high at top dead centre, flattening a squishy path straight at him. Not a wheel. A cheese.

Lundqvist stood up. He'd had enough.

'You bastard!' he screamed. 'You fucking bastard! Can't you take *anything* seriously?'

Then he threw himself at the cheese, tripping over tulip-roots, dodging the murderous sails, soaked in sap and three-quarters blinded with pollen. As the leading edge of the cheese rushed towards him he hurled himself sideways, cannoning into a tulip stem, bouncing off the rubbery surface, being hurled like a baseball at the mountainous flank of the cheese. He thrust the machete out in front of him and screamed . . .

And found himself sitting in the gutter, a bent machete in one hand, a large slice of Edam in the other, surrounded by a crowd of bemused onlookers and wearing a baseball cap inscribed with

I ♥ AMSTERDAM

Five minutes later, a police car came and picked him up. He was later charged with obstructing the highway, disorderly conduct and fourteen breaches of the street trading regulations.

CHAPTER
SEVEN

THERE was, of course, only one course of action open to Lucky George after the battle of Amsterdam: retribution. Immediate, savage and on a sufficient scale to convey the magnitude of his displeasure.

Not that he minded. Not one little bit.

As soon as he had thanked his old college chums, therefore, and caught the first available flight to his next port of call, he settled down and worked all the details out in his mind. Then...

The first intimation that the members of all the governments of all the nations of the earth had been turned overnight into farmyard animals came from the BBC radio news, with its crack-of-dawn summary of yesterday's proceedings in Parliament. Being a radio broadcast, there was no visual confirmation; and at first the grunts, squeals, clucks, squeaks, miaows and moos were interpreted as the combined effect of atmospheric disturbance, a fault on the line somewhere and the full and free exchange of views in the most highly respected democratic forum in the world. It was only when the breakfast television pictures started to come through that anyone was able to bring himself to put a more logical interpretation on the data.

Toast-crunching news addicts were greeted with footage of the pleasant green lawn-cum-verge outside the House of Commons, where the House was dividing on the third reading of the Finance Bill. The doors opened, and what can only be described as a flock shambled out, led by an extremely old, indifferent-looking sheepdog in a full wig.

The flock divided; the goats wandering into one lobby, the sheep into the other. After the tellers had done their work with their customary speed and efficiency, the sheepdog sat up on its hind paws, waggled its tail, and proclaimed that the meeeehs had it.

Simultaneously, in Washington DC, an old grey mule opened the day's proceedings of the Senate by eating the order papers and kicking the Barker of the House with his offside rear hoof. In the Knesset building the rows of seats were empty, and the elected representatives present wheeled and banked under the ceiling as the hawks tried to catch up with the swifter but less agile doves. This was at about the time when the German parliament adjourned for Swill, oblivious of the fact that across the border in France, the nation's leaders had abandoned a crucial debate on the economy to chase a catnip mouse round the boiler room. The Japanese legislature twice narrowly missed complete annihilation; first when somebody spilt a kettle of boiling water down a crack in the floor, and second when the Peruvian foreign minister arrived in the building for a top-level meeting and nearly swept the whole lot of them up with one lick of his long, sticky tongue. The Belgian government buried the contents of the Exchequer under a tree, curled up in little nests of scraped-together leaves and went to sleep for the winter.

Perhaps the most startling manifestation of all was in Iraq, where the entire government were changed overnight into human beings.

'I suppose we ought to, really,' admitted the Marketing

Director, wistfully. 'Seems a shame, though.'

'We've got to,' replied the Production Director, stifling a giggle. On the TV screen in front of him were satellite pictures of the emergency debate in the European Parliament, meeting for the first time in that august body's history on the summit of a steep cliff outside Ostend. 'I mean,' he went on, 'fun's fun, but ...' He broke off and stuffed his tie in his mouth as a cascade of small, scuttling, furry-bodied politicians streamed off the edge of the cliff into the waves below. Further out to sea, the Council of Ministers were leaving a sinking ship.

'Not,' commented the Finance Director, with more feeling than originality, 'for the first time.' He stopped, and forcibly returned his mind to the issue in hand. 'Look,' he said, 'this has got to stop. Get the tiresome little man on the phone, somebody, and tell him to turn them back this instant.' He hesitated, turned his head back towards the screen, and caught a glimpse of the Parliament's select committee on agriculture scurrying frantically backwards and forwards to avoid a flock of ecstatic gannets. 'Well, pretty soon, anyway,' he said, his eyes glued to a close-up of the President of the Council playing hide-and-seek with a cormorant. 'By mid-day tomorrow at the very latest.'

'That's easy enough to say,' grumbled the Marketing Director. 'Got to find the blighter first. I don't suppose he's going to be all that easy to find ...'

A telephone rang at his elbow and he picked it up.

'Got someone called Van Appin on the line,' he said a moment later, 'claims to be George's legal adviser. Anyone want to—'

The Finance Director grabbed the receiver. 'Hello, Pete?' he barked. 'What the bloody he-heliotrope does he think he's playing at? Tell him to get this mess sorted out immediately, or he's going to be in real trouble.'

At his desk, Mr Van Appin smiled. 'Excuse me,' he said, 'but I thought he was already. I mean, excuse my ignorance, but I thought everlastingly damned was about as in trouble as you could possibly get without actually working in advertising.'

The Finance Director waved his hand feebly. 'You know what I mean, Pete,' he replied. 'For pity's sake, this is going too far.' As he spoke, the image on the television screen changed, and he found himself staring at a huge, distended anaconda which had apparently just imposed one-party rule in the small South American state of Necesidad by swallowing the Social Democrats. 'All right,' he muttered wearily. 'Tell me what he wants and I'll see what I can do.'

There was a pause, then Van Appin said, 'You know what he wants, Norman. He wants to be left alone. Call off your people, leave the kid in peace.'

The Finance Director growled petulantly. 'I already did that, Pete,' he said. 'All agents returned to base, no further action. You want me to swear an affidavit or something?'

'Lundqvist.'

The Finance Director shuddered slightly. 'Not our man,' he said, as casually as he could. 'Nothing to do with us. Entirely freelance, you know that. I'll withdraw the reward if you like but that's the best I can—'

Van Appin shook his head. 'Don't act simple, Steve,' he replied irritably. 'After yesterday's little performance, I don't suppose the money's really at the forefront of his mind.'

'Not my fault. Serves your client right for teasing him. Anyway, nothing we can do about it, so if you'll just—'

'No.' Van Appin took the phone away from his ear, covered up the earpiece with the palm of his hand, and counted to ten.

'You still there, Steve?' he asked.

'Yes, still here.'

'This,' said Van Appin, 'is the deal. You give me your formal undertaking to do everything you can to get Lundqvist off my client's case, we'll let you have your politicians back. And that's our last offer.'

There was a long silence.

'And now,' burbled the television set, 'we're going over live to Danny Bennett at the United Nations building in New York, where . . .'

'Switch that bloody thing off!' shouted the Finance Director. 'Hello, Pete? Look, I'm making no promises but we'll do our very best. Now, tell your man to stop mucking about.'

'And you'll stop Lundqvist?'

'I'll put my best demons on it, Pete, right away.'

'You'd better,' Van Appin retorted. 'Remember, germs are also animals, of a sort. You want the civilised nations of the world led into the twenty-first century by a bad cold, all you have to do is try and be clever.'

The line went dead. With a long, chilly sigh the Finance Director straightened his back and turned to his colleagues.

'Get me the Captain of Spectral Warriors,' he said.

'What did you say it was called?' asked Lucky George, looking round at the thronged piazza, the buzzing crowds of cosmopolitan citizens, the emerald blue of the bay and, in the background, the dazzling white masonry of the eighth wonder of the world.

'Australia,' replied Helen. 'Have a crisp.'

'No, thank you.' Lucky George considered. 'Don't think we had it in my day,' he said. 'I suppose you're going to tell me it's Progress.'

'Well, isn't it?'

Lucky George thought for a moment. 'That or entropy,' he decided. 'You know, the older I get, the harder I find it to tell 'em apart. I still say we managed perfectly well without it, but there we are, what's done is done.' He sat down on the steps and focused on the sails of the yachts in the distance.

'This,' Helen continued, crunching, 'is Sydney.'

'I thought you said it was—'

'Sydney, Australia.'

'Ah. Sydney's its Christian name.'

'Don't be tiresome, George. You'll like it here.'

'Will I? Why?'

Helen sneezed. 'Because nobody will ever think of looking for you here, that's why.'

'Figures,' George said. 'I wouldn't, certainly. Wouldn't be seen dead, in fact.'

'Well, there you are, then.'

'Yes,' George replied thoughtfully, 'here I am. Indeed. Do they have food in Australia?'

Helen nodded. 'Absolutely. Tons of it.'

'Ah. That's something, I suppose. Let's go and investigate.'

Over the coffee, George expanded on his proposed course of action.

'The only real problem,' he said, 'is Lundqvist. The rest of them we can probably handle. By the way, did you know that this country you're so fond of is governed entirely by warthogs?'

Helen frowned. 'You're going to have to change them all back sooner or later, George. I mean, you've made your point. There's nothing to be gained by ramming it into the ground.'

'If,' George said, changing the subject, 'we could find some way of getting rid of Lundqvist once and for all, then I'd be prepared to try and negotiate. A few concessions here and there, it oughtn't to be a problem. But while that nutcase is on the loose, I really don't fancy it. Pass the ashtray.'

'I think you've got a complex about Lundqvist,' Helen replied. 'You saw how easy it was to deal with him in Amsterdam. We made him look a complete idiot. I expect he'll go back to chivvying the undead and leave us in peace.'

'Don't you believe it.' George shook his head, accidentally turning the cash register into a bottomless purse. 'In retrospect, I don't think I handled that particular encounter quite right. All we've achieved so far is to get so far up his nose that we're practically coming out of his ears. Not sensible.'

'But surely,' Helen said over the rim of her coffee cup, 'once they withdraw the reward, surely he'll just go away. I mean, he's a professional bounty-hunter, he doesn't do it for fun. If he's not going to get paid . . .'

George gave her an indulgent look. 'Bless the child,' he said, 'for her naivety and purity of spirit. If Lundqvist succeeds in delivering yours truly, I've little doubt they'll come across with the money. He knows that perfectly well. Besides, he'd carry on regardless, money or not. He doesn't like being made a fool of. Probably,' he added, 'an ingrained dislike of gilding the lily.'

'So?' Helen said. 'Any bright ideas?'

George nodded. 'Sure,' he said. 'That's why we're here. Although,' he added, looking round, 'when I said find me the most desolate, godforsaken place in the Universe, I didn't actually *mean* the most desolate, godforsaken . . .'

'Don't be silly, George. There are far worse places than this.'

'Name me one.'

'Adelaide.'

'Ah.' George raised an eyebrow. 'I take it she's Sydney's sister.'

'No, that's Victoria. You think we can just hide out, then, and wait for him to biodegrade or something?'

George shook his head. 'No such luck. No, what I had in mind was something quite different.'

He leant back in his chair, waiting for her to ask him what he had in mind. She, however, folded her arms and started telling him all about the First Fleet, Ned Kelly and Aussie Rules football. 'What I had in mind,' said George, raising his hand for silence, 'was going on the offensive. A pre-emptive strike, in fact.'

Helen picked up a crystal of coffee sugar and bit on it. 'And how are we going to do that from here, may I ask?'

A grin spread across George's face like a late-summer

sunset; or, if you prefer, an oil slick. 'We're not,' he replied. 'However, there's this bloke I know owes me a favour . . .'

Two seagulls, circling in the first light of dawn.

'Maybe,' screamed one above the hissing of the wind, 'I should just call them, check they've delivered the canned tomatoes.'

'Cool it, Mike,' screeched Larry. 'They're perfectly capable of running the joint for a few weeks without any help from us. We've just gotta concentrate on the job in hand, okay?'

Mike stared down through the quickening light at a wet green landscape. In the distance there was a hill, curiously man-made in appearance, crowned by what looked like a church tower without the church. At its foot, like a spilt plate of seafood risotto, sprawled a small, untidy town, coagulated around the ruins of a monastery.

'You're sure he's in?'

Larry turned his head and tried to endow his windlashed eyes with a look of contempt. 'He's been in his grave for a thousand years, Mike. Dead guys don't just slip out for a pizza.'

They waited for a suitable downdraught, adjusted their wing angles and swooped.

It used to say:

HIC IACET ARCTURUS
ANGLIE
REX QUONDAM REX FUTURUS

in rather wobbly capitals on a piece of broken millstone. In 1259, however, a passing blacksmith in need of a bit of something to sharpen scythes on removed the original memorial, and the spot remained unmarked until the middle of the twentieth century, when the appropriate government department replaced it with a large concrete slab bearing the suitable inscription:

NO DOGS

which is, considered all in all, perhaps the finest obituary a man can ask for.

Two seagulls dropped awkwardly out of a thermal and flumped on to a concrete slab.

'You do it,' whispered Mike. 'I'm sick of always having to be the one who gets landed with all the talking.'

'All right,' Larry said irritably. 'What do I do now?'

The seagulls looked around, and then at each other. 'Search me,' said Mike. 'Knock. Ring the bell.'

Larry thought about it for a moment, and then addressed the side of the slab with his beak. He rapped three times, and waited.

Piss off. We gave already.

The seagulls looked at each other again. The voice hadn't come from anywhere; nor, strictly speaking, had it been a voice. If it resembled anything at all from the realms of conventional experience, it was a vague recollection of hearsay.

'We aren't collecting,' Mike replied. 'We've got a message. From George Faustus.'

Never heard of the schmuck. Go mug a buzzard, there's people trying to sleep.

This time, however, the recollection was of a statement that had turned out, on closer inspection, not to have been true. A false rumour, perhaps, which proves impossible to pin down to any specific source.

'Mr Faustus says,' Larry went on, 'that if you've never heard of him, then you can't ever have lent him the fifty thousand marks, which means he doesn't have to pay you back, and sorry to have—'

All right. All right. You wait there, I'm coming.

* * *

'Really?' said Helen, impressed in spite of herself. 'He's a friend of yours too?'

George made a slight face. 'Friend is maybe an over-statement,' he said. 'We did some business together, I owe him money, he owes me a few favours. No, I guess friend is okay, on reflection, just so long as you leave out the affection side of things.'

'Gosh.' Helen dabbed powder on her nose and put the compact away. 'And did he really have a round table full of knights and a magic sword and a Holy Grail and all that?'

George nodded. 'Sure thing,' he said. 'Brilliant camou-flage,' he added.

Helen looked up at him sharply. 'Camouflage?'

'Naturally. What else?' An idea struck him. 'You didn't think all that stuff was for real, did you?'

Helen nodded. 'Insofar as I believed he existed,' she added.

George laughed. 'Strictly for the customers, all that,' he said. 'Sure, Arthur was the best king Albion ever had, absolutely marvellous administrator, had the rivers running on time, that sort of thing. But you don't manage that just because you've got a few hundred idiots in steel long johns on the payroll.'

'You don't?'

''Course not.' He turned his head and smiled. Immediately, the waiter brought him the bill, which shows just how unimaginably powerful George's magical powers were. 'Think about it. If you want to conquer inflation, revitalise the moribund standing stone circle industry, eliminate racial tension between the Wee Folk and the Nixies in the Inner Toadstools and stabilise the magic ring against the deutsch-mark, what you need is sound fiscal policies, not a bunch of brainless pillocks on horses and an overgrown letter-opener that glows in the dark. Dammit, you don't drag a whole nation kicking and screaming into the Dark Ages without a firm grasp of the principles of revenue management, and that's what Arthur had. That,' he added, with an unwonted tang of respect in his voice, 'is why they called him the Once and Future Accountant. A reputation like that, it's something you've got to earn, believe me.'

'Oh.' There was just the tiniest hint of disappointment, disillusionment even, in Helen's voice. 'An accountant. How unspeakably romantic.'

'Yes,' George replied. 'And that's why he's just the man we need.'

Say what you like about accountants . . .

Finished?

Good.

Say what you like about accountants, for clarity of thought and an ability to get to the heart of the matter, they have few rivals. Accordingly, it took the greatest accountant in history roughly the same amount of time to grasp the proposition and reach a decision as, say, the shutter of a Leica is open when taking a picture of a moving object on a very bright day.

'Sure,' said King Arthur. 'No problem. It worked with Al Capone, so why not with this Lundqvist? Now we talk about money.'

Larry ruffled his feathers with his beak. 'I thought we just were.'

'Remuneration,' King Arthur replies. 'This sort of work I don't do for the good of my health. Especially,' he added, 'now I'm dead. Now then, I charge for my work on a time basis, with a basic hourly rate of—'

'Expense no object,' Mike interrupted with his mouth full. One good thing about being in a grave, he was thinking, always plenty of worms. Even (he reflected queazily) if you don't know where they've been.

'Expense no object,' King Arthur repeated. 'The fink owes me fifty thousand marks already, he says expense no object.

He's probably planning to pay me with my own goddamn money.'

Mike swallowed the rest of his mouthful, fearful lest he'd said the wrong thing. 'But you will do it?' he said. 'Only I'm sure—'

'Of course I'll do it,' grumbled the Once and Future King. 'Son of a bitch owes me fifty grand, naturally I'll do it, or when will I ever see my money again. That George, he sure understands economics. He's got a lawyer?'

'Van Appin of Amsterdam,' said Larry.

'Oy,' said King Arthur, impressed. 'That's one very expensive lawyer, the boy has taste. A good man, Van Appin, he acted for my Uncle Joe when he first came to this country from Arimathea. Artie, he said to me on his deathbed, if ever you're in trouble with the law, see Van Appin. A goy but a good lawyer. All right, this is what we've gotta do . . .'

It's bad enough having to do something you know is pointless, dangerous and doomed to failure. Having to order your subordinates to do it with you, when they're pointing out forcefully just how pointless, dangerous and doomed to failure it is, makes being eaten alive by ants seem like the height of Sybaritic luxury.

'It'll be a piece of cake,' muttered the Captain of Spectral Warriors, keeping his voice down. 'We go in, we nick him, we leave. No problem.'

Two pairs of coal-red eyes glowed their hostility at him in the pitch darkness of the sewer.

'You said that,' remarked Number Two, 'the last time.'

'And the time bethore.'

The Captain winced. 'That was different,' he said. 'Freak accident, that was. Nobody could've known . . .'

Somewhere in the darkness, water dripped. There are many, many strange and unexplained noises in a sewer; and Number Two, who had seen all the Mutant Turtle films, was more than usually edgy. 'Happened, though, dinnit? So, it could happen again.'

All three sat in silence, recollecting the image of that horror. It should have been a routine job – take possession of a human body (the owner having failed to keep up the payments) and terrorise the local community with acts of demonic, hellish horror. It had, however, gone quite flamboyantly wrong . . .

'I mean,' said Number Two, breaking the silence like a rock thrown into a stagnant, scummy pool, '*double booked.* Never again, I said, not if they offered me a seat on the Board. I was *terrified.*'

'I keep telling you,' the Captain snapped, 'they weren't real devils. The people were making a film, it was all special effects . . .'

'I know they weren't real devils,' replied Number Two with venom. 'Real devils, we'd have been all right with *real* devils, they'd have been in the Union. Those bastards in there, it was *horrible,* I've never seen the like.'

'All right, we needn't go into all that—'

'Screamin' and hauntin' and rushin' about with hideous worm-eaten faces and all that stuff. I had to sleep with the light on for weeks afterwards.'

'Well,' said the Captain firmly, 'there's no chance of that happening this time, is there? The worst that can happen to us—'

'Go and arrest Kurt Lundqvist,' Number Two interrupted relentlessly. 'Yeah. Worst that can happen to us is, they scoop us up and take us home in a jam jar. Well, you can tell whoever it is who—'

'Quiet!' The Captain sat on his heels, straining for the slightest sound. It came; the signal, three knocks. 'Right, move it out. I'll go first. Stay right behind me.'

He poked his head up into the mouth of the pipe, took a deep breath (being a spectral warrior he had no lungs, but somehow it always made him feel better) and started to wriggle his way up. His two henchmen followed, grumbling on the threshold of sound as they squirmed.

A few minutes later, the Captain's head popped up through the sink trap in Kurt Lundqvist's kitchen. Having paused to make sure the coast was clear and lever a squashed pea and a horribly limp tube of macaroni out of his path with the shaft of his ice axe, he scrambled out, looked round and hissed, 'All clear. Come on, we haven't got all damn night.'

'It'th really *yuk* down there,' snarled Number Three, hauling himself out and wiping himself against a pair of rubber gloves beside the plate rack. 'And they didn't ithue uth with protective clothing or anything. If we catch anything nathty, we could thue.'

They abseiled down from the sink to the floor. It was a long way, and en route Number Two was at pains to point out to his companions that he suffered from vertigo. By an error of judgement they all landed up in a saucer of milk left out for the cat.

'He's got a cat?' said Number Two, as he lay gasping on the rim of the saucer. 'Wouldn't have thought he's the type, somehow.'

'Wasn't in the briefing,' admitted the Captain. 'Now then, who's got the transformer? Better get ourselves back to our proper size quick, before the bloody cat wakes up.'

Pause.

'I said, who's got the transformer?'

Long pause. During this pause, if the perceived length of time passing correlates in any way to objective criteria – time as recorded by a clock, for instance – you could have built the pyramids and watched them fall down.

'Fine,' said the Captain, 'we've forgotten the transformer. Never mind. We'll just have to cope. Follow me.'

It was probably the noise made by Number Three walking into the foot of the vegetable rack and dislodging a potato that woke up the cat, either that or Number Two tripping over a grain of spilt sugar. Details are not important. What is germane to the issue is that the cat woke up, pricked up its ears and jumped out of its basket. Its tail lashed. For a cat, it had a highly developed sense of cultural integrity, and as a rule there were no mice in the house. This led to frustration, self-doubt, crises of identity and long periods of black depression, when it would sit motionless at the top of the stairs waiting to be sent to the newsagents to collect the paper in its mouth. Now at last, it seemed, the mice had arrived. Destiny called.

'Thkip.'

'Shuttup, Vern.'

'Yeth, but thkip, there'th thomething big and horrible over there watching uth.'

'It's just your imagination, Vern. Now shut up and—'

The cat sprang. It was not a classic spring; the head a trifle too low, perhaps, the forepaws not completely extended, the back not quite unflexing like a longbow at the moment of release. But it was the best the cat could do at such short notice, being out of practice and more than a little overweight, and it reckoned it would probably do. There was a thump and a squeak . . .

'Hold on, Vern, I'm coming.' The Captain drew his revolver and sprinted back, to be confronted with a nightmare mass of convulsed fur, a waking horror of green eyes and teeth like ploughshares. He stopped, raised his arms and fired three times.

Shrink a revolver, even a Smith & Wesson 686, down to 1/72 scale, and the noise it makes on firing is slightly less deafening than a grain of rice falling two inches on to a cushion. Its effect on a healthy cat is of the same order of magnitude. Chances are it didn't even notice.

Number Three was, however, making a pretty good fight of it. By virtue of his being about the size of a small spider and reasonably agile, he wasn't the easiest thing in the world to catch hold of with non-prehensile paws. Attempts to swat him

were foiled by the rapidity and random nature of his movements. The deciding factor, however, was the fact that he kept
yelling out blood-curdling threats in cat-language (which all
demons speak fluently), which the cat couldn't help but be
intimidated by.

This pantomime had been going on for quite a while when
suddenly the kitchen was flooded with light, and a slipper the
size of the Flatiron Building planted itself within a few
millimetres of where the Captain stood, rooted to the spot.

'Fluffles,' boomed a voice high up in infinity. 'You goddamn
crazy cat, what d'you think you're playing at? Gitoutavit!'

Fluffles froze in mid-swipe, horribly self-conscious, as if
he'd been discovered at an all-night catnip party without his
collar on. He tried to explain, but his vocal chords jammed and
all that came out was, 'Mew.'

'You dumb bastard,' the boom went on, 'you've knocked
over your milk. Here, it's back in your basket for you.'

A hand like the Hand of God scooped up the cat and
vanished with it. The three spectral warriors crawled into the
gap between the bottom of the fridge and the floor and lay
there, shattered. The light went out.

'Okay,' said the Captain, five minutes or so later. 'I thought
we'd had it there, lads, didn't you? Narrow scrape, I thought.
Still, you've got to laugh, haven't you, or where would we
all—?'

'That wath him, wathn't it?'

'Maybe,' replied the Captain. 'I'm not committing myself
till we get a closer look, but provisionally . . .'

'You want *uth* to arretht *him*.'

'There may be some unforeseen technical glitches, but . . .'

'Thorgetit. I'm going home. Now.'

With which, Number Three drew himself up to his full
height and walked away. Unfortunately, he went in the wrong
direction.

He didn't realise this until he bumped into something,

which happened to be the back of the electric plug.

A word of explanation. Lundqvist's flat was last rewired many years ago, and in places the wiring is a bit dicky. Thus, when Number Three bumped into the back of the plug, he came into contact with four millimetres of uninsulated, live, wire.

Zappo.

The immediately perceptible effect was the fridge falling over on its side, crushing the kitchen table. It did this because a six-foot-four man had suddenly materialised underneath it.

'There,' said the Captain, slightly unnerved but triumphant. 'Told you we'd cope and we did. All we had to do was bodge up a substitute transformer, and . . .'

The rest of his remarks were lost as he instantaneously went from twenty-five millimetres to six foot seven, landing up lying heavily across the remains of the pedal bin. Number Two joined them a moment later and came to rest on top of the cooker.

'Fluffles, you scumbag, what the fuck do you think you're . . .?' The light flicked on, and the three spectral warriors turned to see Lundqvist, in a tartan wool dressing gown and slippers, standing in the doorway.

The Captain reacted well. The revolver was out of his holster and in his hand before Lundqvist could move.

'Put 'em up and keep 'em where I can see 'em. That's the way. Right, Kurt Lundqvist, I have here a warrant for your arrest, you are not obliged—'

'Thkip . . .'

'Not *now*.'

'Yeth, but I've got the warrant, it'th here in my . . . Oh, no, that'th not the warrant, that'th the tranththorm—'

'*Don't touch* . . .'

Lundqvist stood for a moment, puzzled. One moment there had been three spectral warriors draped all over his kitchen. The next moment, nothing. The cat, meanwhile, was staring reproachfully at him from over the rim of its basket with an I-told-you-but-you-wouldn't-listen expression on its face. It was as bad as being married.

Then the penny dropped.

'Okay, Fluffles,' he said, shutting the door firmly. 'This is your show now. Kill.'

It took the spectral warriors three days to escape, but in the end they made it. Their story is one of the most moving documents of courage, endurance and sheer dogged refusal to lie down and die since the escape from Colditz.

The movie rights are, incidentally, still available.

It was the Captain's idea to try and make it to the rubbish bin. Rubbish, he argued, gets chucked out sooner or later, and in the meantime there were a thousand and one places in a black plastic sack full of decaying kitchen refuse where they could hide.

The only problem, of course, was that the rubbish bin was, to all intents and purposes, a hundred and fifty stories high. King Kong might just have climbed it, with oxygen, on a good day.

Despair, gangrene of the soul, was just about to set in when Number Two noticed the onion. With a voice quivering with emotion, he explained his plan. They listened. It was a long shot, they decided, but there wasn't really any choice.

With Fluffles wandering around like a resentful tyrannosaurus, making a move from under the cooker to the vegetable rack in daylight was out of the question. As soon as night fell, however, they scrambled out, hoisted themselves up into the rack and set to work hacking a secure chamber in the side of the mouldy onion. It took them a little over eight hours, working in shifts, with nothing but their combat knives and belt-buckles to dig with. Once it was done, all they could do was climb in and wait for the onion to be noticed and thrown away.

Two days deep inside an onion is a long, long time.

Even then, it was touch and go. The hunt was still on, and despite the masking smell of the onion, Fluffles paused in his relentless prowl round the kitchen and sniffed horribly every time he passed the vegetable rack. On the evening of the second day, Lundqvist came home at a quarter to one in the morning and started to make himself a Spanish omelette. He had picked up their onion and raised the knife before he noticed anything wrong with it; and he'd stood staring at their entrance tunnel for a full two seconds before throwing the onion in the bin and selecting another one. For years afterwards, the Captain was wont to swear blind that Lundqvist must have noticed something. He could only conclude that the bounty-hunter's mind was elsewhere.

Which, in fact, it was. At that precise moment, he'd forgotten all about the spectral warriors and everything else, and was pottering around the kitchen in a stunned daze.

So would you if, returning from a hard day's work, you found lying on the mat a demand from the Revenue for over five hundred years' back taxes.

CHAPTER EIGHT

THERE are few experiences quite as nerve-frayingly horrible as being investigated by the Revenue. Hell (especially now that the new management team have taken over) is mild by comparison. For all his faults, the Prince of Darkness is a gentleman, or so Shakespeare would have us believe. The Inspector of Taxes, on the other hand, is an unmitigated bastard.

A week after receiving the assessment, Lundqvist was dragged out of his well-earned sleep at three in the morning by five carloads of weazel-faced young men and women in grey suits, who walked straight past him as if he wasn't there and impounded his files, records, books and bank statements. When he tried to scare them off with a 20" Remington Wingmaster they impounded that too, murmuring something about discrepancies in his claims for writing-down allowance on plant and machinery. Then they gave him a receipt and left.

When they'd gone he sat down and pulled himself together. As soon as he'd managed to overcome the feeling of having all his teeth simultaneously extracted by an army of hamsters, he got on the phone to the Duty Officer at Pandaemonium and demanded to know what they were going to do about it.

'Pardon me?' said the Duty Officer.

'Don't give me none of that crap,' Lundqvist roared. 'Get these guys off my back. Do you realise they've taken all my records back to 1456?'

'I'm terribly sorry,' the Duty Officer replied, 'but it's completely out of our hands. They're an entirely separate agency, you see. There's absolutely no way we can interfere with ...'

Lundqvist managed to keep his temper remarkably well. Apart from formally requesting that Hell use its good offices to have the investigation suspended and formally undertaking to pull the Duty Officer's kidneys out through his nose if his papers weren't returned by five past nine the next day, he accepted the situation with a good grace and hung up. Then he burst into tears.

Business, he decided next morning, as usual. The programme for the day was to visit the Delphic Oracle and sweat out of her details of where Faust was hiding. To do this, he needed to get to the airport. Since he was short of ready cash for taxi-fares, he popped down to the cash dispenser on the corner, which took his card, informed him that his account had been frozen, and referred him to Head Office.

Ten minutes with a Sykes-Fairburn fighting-knife and the piggy-bank he kept the gas money in produced enough loose change to get him as far as the airport, where he waved his credit card at the check-in girl and demanded a seat on the first flight to Athens. The girl smiled politely and asked him to wait just a moment while she ran the routine checks on his card ...

Fine, he thought, as he slouched disconsolate and ticketless away from the desk. I can't buy a ticket, I'll have to hijack a plane. No worries.

He was strolling up and down the observation area, casting his eye over the various airliners and deciding which one he liked the look of, when a discreet cough at his elbow made him turn.

'Excuse me, sir,' said a weazel-faced man in a grey suit, 'but if you were thinking of leaving the country, I'm afraid that's out of the question. Not until the investigation is completed, sir. We'll get a court order if necessary.'

Under normal circumstances, the next that anyone would have seen of the young man would have been his head, separated from his body, on some railings somewhere. So demoralising, however, is the cumulative effect of having the taxman after you that Lundqvist simply whimpered and walked away in the opposite direction. He found he had just enough change left for the bus-fare home.

Okay, so he couldn't leave the country. Nothing to stop him leaving the century. He phoned his usual firm of timetravel agents and asked for a reservation for the fifth century BC, first-class, non-smoking, not too near the engine.

'I'm terribly sorry, Mr Lundqvist, but we've had instructions. No credit till further notice.'

'But I've got an *account*,' Lundqvist screamed. 'Dammit, I've been travelling with you since five hundred years before you first set up in business. I've got a goddamn gold card. Doesn't loyalty count for *anything*?'

'I'm afraid your account has been suspended, sir. Court order. Injunction. Terribly sorry, but we can only help you if you can make it cash in advance.'

'Tell you what,' Lundqvist was physically shaking with rage by this point, hardly able to hold on to the receiver. 'Take me back to last Thursday and I'll pay you anything you like. My credit rating'll be fine then, I give you my word. Only for Chrissakes get me out of here.'

'Sorry, sir, but I've got my orders. If you'd care to come round to our offices with the money, we'd be only too pleased . . .'

He slammed down the phone and snarled impotently. Then he pulled open his desk drawer, slipped something under his shoulder and walked out.

He couldn't withdraw anything from the bank, huh? We'll soon see about that.

'Stick 'em up,' he hissed across the counter. 'This is a forty-five automatic and I don't care if I use it. Fives and tens, and take it real easy.'

'Certainly, sir,' replied the cool and efficient girl behind the till. 'Please bear with me a moment while I get your money for you.' She leant back and called to someone behind the scenes. 'Yvonne, could you bring me some more fives, please? Gentleman robbing the bank.' An unseen hand passed her a wad of currency notes, which she dropped into the little perspex shuttle thing and passed over. 'Thank you for calling,' she said. 'While you're here, can I perhaps interest you in our new range of personal equity plans, specially tailored to meet your individual investment requirements and help you plan for a secure and prosperous future?'

Lundqvist had got through the door and had his hand on the door-handle of the getaway car when a discreet cough at his elbow made him freeze in his tracks.

'Excuse me, sir,' said a weazel-faced man in a grey suit, 'but I trust you're going to declare all that? Let me see.' He took the money from Lundqvist's unresisting fingers, counted it and handed it back. 'I make that fifty thousand dollars which, seeing as how it's the profits of a crime, malfeasance or illegal enterprise, is taxable at your highest applicable rates under Schedule Nine Case Six. Plus, of course, grossing up to allow for notional basic rate tax deducted at source, leaves you with . . .' The young man produced a calculator from thin air, pecked at it with a moist fingertip and nodded sagely. 'I make that a deficit of two hundred and sixty-three dollars, sir. If you'd just sign here, please.'

Dazed, Lundqvist signed the receipt, allowed himself to be relieved of the money, and fell limply into his car, where he sat for about twenty seconds until the police arrived and he had to drive like buggery to shake them off. By the time he'd done that, he'd used up all his remaining petrol and had precisely one dollar and two cents to his name.

He dumped the car and walked home.

'That's all very well,' said Lucky George, 'but I'm buggered if I'm staying here. I mean, *look* at it.'

He waved his arm in an histrionic gesture and scowled.

'I think it's very nice,' said Helen. 'A bit suburban, maybe, but—'

'Suburban!' George turned up the malignity in his scowl. 'For pity's sake, woman, the only difference between this and where I've just come from is you don't have to die to get a visa.' He threw himself into a chair and grabbed a can of beer out of the coolbag. Helen gave him a disapproving look.

'You're exaggerating a little, I think,' she said coolly. 'No little men with pitchforks, for a start. No roaring flames. No—'

'You're wrong there,' George interrupted. 'Except here they shove bits of raw meat in front of them and call it a barbie. When I was a boy in Nurnberg we had a thing, I think it was called an *oven*. Wonder if the patent's expired, because you could make an absolute fortune . . .'

'George.' In this light, George thought, with her hair curling like that in the evening breeze and exactly that tone of voice, she's just like my mother. And no, I will *not* eat up my nice parsnips. 'It's only temporary,' she went on. 'Until—'

'Temporary.' George grinned. 'I don't think so, love. This is one case where you can't simply outlive the bastards. You know what that pompous little toad of a Finance Director told me the other day? You can hide but you can't run. He was right. And,' he added, draining the last of the beer and crumpling the can in his fist, 'there's no percentage in hiding, none whatsoever. It's exactly the same porridge, only with a slightly different tin.'

Helen sighed. 'That's just culture shock, George,' she said.

'We don't have to stay in Sydney, you know. It's a huge country. There's bits of it not even properly explored yet. We could go anywhere.'

'Marvellous.' George rubbed his eyes wearily. 'We can go and live in the middle of the bloody desert. Hell may not be all fun and games, but at least they've got hot and cold running water.' He considered for a moment. 'Hot water, anyway. All the hot water you can use, free. Bit like an Aga.'

'Give it a try.'

'What, go straight, you mean?'

Helen nodded enthusiastically. 'That's right,' she said. 'We could start a sheep farm or something. It'd be fun, George, really it would. No more magic and being chased about, just you and me and—'

'A sheep farm.'

Helen frowned. 'Yes,' she said. 'For my sake, George, please.'

'You're serious?'

'Yes.'

He shrugged. 'I've heard some pretty daffy suggestions in my time,' he said, 'but this has got to be one of the daffiest. You're really saying we should set up a—'

'Yes.'

'Okay, then.' He stood up, closed his eyes for a moment, and then smiled. Positively beamed.

When he opened his eyes again, they were standing in the middle of a huge, fenceless, featureless wasteland; a wasteland covered in white, seething bodies. From the air it would have looked just like a big, manky, sheepskin rug.

'You got it,' said George. 'Now, what precisely do you *do* with the little buggers to make them grow?'

It was three months later.

Australia is an old country; very old. At a time when Paris was a soggy fen and Rome herself little more than a select new development of starter homes for Sabine commuters, the sun-bleached immensity of the Outback was already cross-hatched with a hundred thousand intricate songlines, scored on the folk memory and linking the Dreamtime to the nebulous future as directly and reliably as fibre-optic cable.

Stare at this brain-curdling immensity long enough and your eyes will play tricks on you. You'll start to imagine that, just at the destruction-test limit of vision, you can make out a tiny black dot, moving as slowly as an hourly-paid glacier, dawdling across the infinite. You might even take it for a human being.

Which it is. This is Tjakamarra, humming and mouthing his way along the line with the precision of a wire-guided missile and the sense of urgency of a holiday postcard. Around him the Ancestors, perceptible to all the senses except five, crowded in a happy, shuffling mass, passing him on from hand to hand like a parcel.

The song takes him across the flank of a long, low escarpment and to the crest of a ridge overlooking a few thousand acres of dead ground . . .

'Stone the flaming crows,' said Tjakamarra under his breath.

In front of him was . . . Well, now. Yes.

A man on a quad-bike roared up out of the shadow of the crest and stopped, leaning on his handlebars.

'Can I help you?' he said. Tjakamarra stared at him.

'Sorry, mate,' he replied. 'I think we got a crossed line.'

The man with the bike raised an eyebrow. 'Really?' he said.

'Too bloody right,' Tjakamarra answered. 'How long's this lot been here?'

The man grinned. 'Not long,' he said. 'Oh, that reminds me. Is your name . . .' He dug a scrap of paper out of his pocket and consulted it. '. . . Tjakamarra?'

Tjakamarra nodded.

'Carpet Snake clan?'

'Yeah. How did you know . . . ?'

Lucky George nodded. 'Message for you from the Ancestors. It says, "Temporary interference with reception, please do not adjust your reception, we apologise for any inconvenience, C sharp minor, F natural, A sharp with a dot, rest, G natural." That make any sense to you?'

Tjakamarra nodded, relieved. 'Yup,' he said. 'It means, turn left at the gully and watch out for low-flying aircraft.' He paused, wondering how to phrase his next question tactfully. 'What the fuckin' hell are you *doing*, anyway?'

George shrugged. 'Earning a living,' he replied.

'Any money in it?'

'It's early days yet,' George replied. 'Once it catches on we'll be laughing, you wait and see.'

Tjakamarra pursed his lips. 'Best of luck, mate,' he said guardedly. 'Well, I gotta be making tracks. You sure it was C sharp minor?'

'Pretty sure. Is it important?'

'You bet. One wrong note, I could find myself in bloody Tasmania. Much obliged.' He waved solemnly and continued on his way . . .

. . . Through a shallow valley full of sheep. And each sheep was tethered to a post, from which hung a scale and a pair of scissors. And in the middle of the valley was a big, brightly-painted notice, which said:

GEORGE'S SHEEP FARM
SHEAR YOUR OWN

The one comforting thing about Hell is knowing that it can't get any worse. Once you're there, you can't actually get in more trouble.

Unless, of course, you run the place.

'It wasn't,' grumbled the senior accounts clerk, 'like this in the old days.' He tucked three overfilled box files under his arm and scurried off down the corridor. His assistant followed on with a heavily laden trolley.

'Sodding auditors,' the senior clerk went on. 'In the old days, all we had to put up with was the Bursar. And he was one of us. You knew where you stood.'

'Better the devil you know, huh?' hazarded his assistant.

'Yeah.' The senior clerk stopped to adjust his grip on a file and plunged on. 'What they want with this lot beats me. It's just old lost souls registers.'

'We should put all this on computer,' mused his assistant. 'Then they'd be *really* lost.'

'Shut up and wheel the bloody trolley.'

It had been a long day in the suite of offices assigned to the visiting audit team, but they were damned if they were going to let anyone see it. Mr Price, Mr Vincetti, Ms Khan, Mr Kowalski and Ms Gould of Messrs Moss Berwick Flintlock had worked long and hard to secure the second most impressive prestige client in all accountancy, and they were determined to do the best job they possibly could.

'Thanks,' said Mr Kowalski. He hadn't removed his jacket, let alone loosened his tie, and he had a shrewd suspicion that his feet had melted and were seeping out through the eyes of his shoes. 'Just put them on the table over there and bring us the green purgatory chits for the last twenty-five years. There's a few anomalies here we'd better get to grips with.'

The senior clerk shuffled his feet. 'Actually,' he said.

'Yes?' Mr Kowalski raised his head. 'Any problems?'

'Might be tricky,' replied the senior clerk. 'For the whole period, like. I mean,' he added wretchedly, 'we just don't have the storage, and . . .'

'Yes?'

'It's the economy drive,' the clerk confessed. 'I mean, the furnaces have got to run on *something*, so when they said—'

'You've destroyed them?'

A look of panic flitted across the clerk's eyes. 'Some of them. I mean, I'm not sure precisely which, it's just . . .'

Mr Kowalski gave him a nasty look. Although he didn't know it, he was running a severe risk of being the first man ever to be chucked out of Hell on the grounds of excessive unpleasantness. 'Don't worry,' he said. 'Mr Price will come with you and look for himself. I'm sure we'll find the ones we're looking for.'

Sure enough, he did. How the files in question had found their way into the roofspace, buried at the bottom of a disused sulphur tank and guarded by a fire-breathing dragon and a triple-headed dog, the senior clerk was at a loss to explain, although he mumbled something about Health and Safety and storage of bulk inflammable materials. The fire-breathing dragon didn't quite ring true there, but Mr Price was too polite to say anything. Instead he looked down about half a mile of nose and snickered.

As they trudged back to the file store, the senior clerk stopped from time to time to bang his head against the wall. 'I knew we should've shredded them,' he said. 'Bloody liability. It just goes against the grain, that's all, shredding files after all these years. I mean, this *is* Hell, it's about the only place in the sodding universe where they actually respect paperwork.'

'Hooky, was it?' enquired his assistant. 'Someone been cooking the books or something?'

The senior clerk grimaced. 'Worse than that, son,' he grunted. 'That's all the Lucky George stuff they've just asked for. If they spot that and cross-reference to the Visitor's Book, the sods'll realise he's flitted and then where'll we be?'

His assistant glanced round. From each of the dingy cells leading off the corridor came the muffled souls in various ingenious but cost-effective permutations of everlasting torment.

'Sorry,' he said. 'I thought we already were.'

His superior sniffed. 'Son,' he muttered, 'don't you believe it. That's just the stuff they give the customers.'

The third dustbin contained the end of a stale loaf, a sardine tin with a little grimy oil left in it, a rotten tomato and the carcases of two smoked mackerel. Lundqvist sighed with relief and made himself a sandwich. The neighbourhood alley-cat gave him a poisonous look, but he ignored it.

Nobody loves you when you're down and out. Admittedly, nobody had loved Lundqvist when he was absolutely loaded, but at least he'd been able to raise the price of a hamburger whenever he felt his ribs prodding their way out of his shirt-front. Not that he was a luxurious person by any means; but there is a subtle difference between surviving on roots and grubs because you're under deep cover five hundred miles behind enemy lines, and pigging it because the Revenue have garnished every last cent you own.

The bailiffs had even seized his entire collection of Ninja throwing-knives and death-stars, despite his objection that they were tools of the trade and therefore exempt. The most lethal object left to him was a toothbrush. When you're Kurt Lundqvist, however, a toothbrush will do nicely. It's all a matter of knowing how to use it.

Once he'd finished his meal, therefore, he walked the five miles to the private airstrip on the outskirts of the city and wandered into the first helicopter charter establishment he came across.

'Hi,' he said to the youth behind the desk. 'I want a chopper, now.'

The youth looked at him, observing the dusty jacket, the slept-in trousers. 'You want a helicopter,' he said. 'Fancy.'

Before he could go on, Lundqvist had vaulted the desk, landed beside him and thrust the toothbrush handle hard into the small hollow just below the lobe of his ear.

'Yeah,' he said. 'Is that a problem?'

The youth made a low, guttural noise, like a man gargling

with custard; then he raised one shaking hand and pointed.

'Keys in the ignition?'

'Yug.'

'Much obliged to you.' He hopped back over the desk and strode quickly across the tarmac to the helicopter indicated. Nobody even tried to stop him. He jumped in and slammed the door.

A moment later he opened it again.

'Hey, you,' he shouted to a cowering mechanic. 'Which one of these goddamned levers is the handbrake?'

As he flew, Lundqvist rationalised. He'd found an ancient bar of fruit and nut chocolate in the glove box – a bit grey and fluffy, but the sudden surge in his blood sugar level made his brain roar like the engine of a drag-racer on the starting line.

If I was Lucky George, he asked himself, where would I go?

Yes, well, if I actually *was* Lucky George, I'd cut my own throat this minute, because I'd know Kurt Lundqvist was on my trail, and it's only a matter of time, and I don't want to be sentient when he finds me. That guy is completely something else . . .

So, I'd go somewhere he'd never dream of looking. Three alternatives:

(a) Somewhere with lots of people, where I'd melt away into the crowd.

(b) Somewhere so far away and godforsaken, nobody even knows it exists.

(c) I'd stay exactly where I am.

Yes. Well, (a) was a non-starter, because wherever Lucky George went, the one thing he could never be was inconspicuous. His habit of turning things into other things saw to that.

Likewise, (c). The Amsterdam authorities are famous for their ability to look the other way when expedient, but even they would have trouble overlooking armies of marauding windmills and giant attack-cheeses.

Which left (b), and very good thinking it was, too, because the chances of finding him by guesswork were very remote indeed.

He was just coming to these conclusions when the radio crackled and addressed him; peculiar in itself, since it wasn't switched on.

Hey, Kurt, my man, gimme some skin.

Lundqvist groaned. He really wasn't in the mood.

'Piss off, Bull,' he said. 'And switch that thing off before you go.'

Don't be like that, man. There's something really heavy going down, and . . .

'Later, Bull, okay? I'm busy. And besides, I still owe you a kicking for that last tip-off you gave me. Remember?'

The radio crackled nervously. *Hey, man, that wasn't my fault. How was I supposed to know . . .?*

'Rule number one, Bull, nobody grasses·up the Antichrist, even if he is moonlighting. He wasn't pleased, Bull. We had him down at the station five hours before he told us who he was. I nearly got my licence pulled over that one.'

Yeah, well, nobody's perfect. This time, I got what you want. I got George for you.

Lundqvist jammed a wedge in his adrenaline and raised an eyebrow. 'Sure, Bull,' he said. 'You and every other cheap informer between here and Delphi. Go hustle somebody else.'

No, man, I'm serious. I know where he is. Or at least, where the girl is.

'How?'

How.

'No, you clown, how do you know where the girl is? Is it just pure intuition, or have you actually seen her?'

Let's talk money first.

Lundqvist snarled. Then he took off his tie, jury-rigged the joystick and put his hands palm-downwards on the console.

What you doing, man?

'Holding a seance, Bull. And when you materialise, I'm gonna kick your ectoplasm up through your ears, okay? Now then, have you seen her or not?'

Okay, okay, cool it. The Ancestors told me.

'I'm losing patience here, Bull. If you don't come clean before I count to five, it's gonna be one sadistic beating for yes, two sadistic beatings for no . . .'

I'm telling the truth, man, I heard it from the Ancestors. Like in Australia, okay? There's all these wild dudes out there who run the songlines, and they're all in the same union with me. As soon as I heard, I thought of you, I thought . . .

'Australia?'

You got it. Place called Maralinga. They don't call it that, of course, they call it D sharp minor, F natural, B natural, G flat, but I looked it up on a map and . . .

Lundqvist grinned and untied the joystick. 'Thanks, Bull,' he said. 'I'll check it out. And maybe I'll let you off with exorcism when I see you next. And maybe not.'

The radio switched off.

CHAPTER NINE

DANNY Bennett knew for a fact that he had a Destiny, just as a dog knows it has fleas.

It was written in the stars that one day, Danny Bennett would unmask the most staggering conspiracy, lay bare the most Machiavellian cover-up, make the ultimate documentary, win the ultimate award, make the once and future awards ceremony speech. The trouble with the stars is that sometimes they can't read their own handwriting. Either that, or there was another Daniel Woodward Bernstein Bennett out there somewhere who got all his namesake's mail by mistake.

In any event, his latest staggering exposé of corruption and intrigue in the Foodstuffs Colouring and Preservatives Directorate, engagingly titled 'Offal You Can't Refuse', had made such an impression that here he was, covering the Round-Australia Land-Yacht Race for one of the top forty satellite TV companies. Promotion, you could say, if you're happy with the concept of being promoted downwards.

Media analysts tended to observe that if Isaac Newton had followed Danny's career over the last five years, the apple would have been entirely superfluous.

He pulled in, stared blankly at five miles of featureless, arrow-straight road in front of him, and consulted the map.

Even with the map held the wrong way up, the only possible conclusion was that he'd come the wrong way, and that there was nothing for it but to turn round and drive the eighty-seven miles back into Arrampagatta. The fact that by the time he got to where he was supposed to be, the race would be across the state line and heading north was tempered by the certainty that Danny wouldn't be able to recognise a land-yacht if one ran up his backside.

Which is what one promptly did.

Glancing in his rear-view mirror, all Danny could see was a whacking great sail, flolloped untidily across the back window. He frowned, opened the door and got out.

'Excuse me,' he said. He couldn't help noticing something that looked uncomfortably like a sailing ship on wheels, which seemed for all the world as if it was trying to get into the boot of his car.

'Why the hell,' said a voice from somewhere inside the canvas, 'don't you look where you're bloody well going?'

'I wasn't going,' Danny replied. 'I was parked. What is that thing?'

Out from behind the sail came about seven feet of man, topped with flashing Ray-Ban mirror sunglasses and idly passing a toothbrush from hand to hand. 'Is that your car?' he said.

'It's a hire car,' Danny replied. 'What's . . .?'

He became aware that the handle of the toothbrush was level with his heart. Somehow, this frightened him.

'I need a lift.'

'Right,' Danny said. 'That's fine. I'm going back to Arrampagatta, that's about ninety miles that way, but you're welcome to—'

'No. I need to go this way. Get in and drive.'

The stranger emphasised these words by drawing the bristles of the toothbrush against the pile across the palm of his hand, and some sort of atavistic survival instinct told Danny that this was a really good opportunity to practise being scared shitless. He complied.

As he shut the door and turned the key in the ignition, he realised why. He knew the guy.

'So you're in the race,' he said, by way of a diversion.

'What race?'

'The land-yacht race,' Danny replied, looking straight ahead. 'That is a land-yacht you were riding, wasn't it?'

'Yes.'

Lundqvist! It had to be Lundqvist.

Excellence is its own best advertisement, in the covert assassination and dirty tricks business as in everything else. Build a better mantrap and the world will beat a path to your door. As a result, Lundqvist's identity and professional reputation were tolerably well known among certain circles, although nobody with a penchant for waking up two mornings in a row would ever have dreamt of trying to make any sort of fuss about it.

Now Danny had a talent; a quite staggering intuitive ability, which enabled him to see just under half the story in a blinding flash of inspiration. Once the speck of insight had found its way into his brain, he then proceeded to coat it with innumerable layers of his own brand of imaginative gibberish, but that was by the way. His most recent researches had led him to the plain fact that wherever something significant, mysterious and horrible had happened in the last fifteen years, one Kurt Lundqvist had been somewhere in the vicinity at the time – visiting his aunt, seeing his dentist, attending a conference on early church music perhaps, but *there*, nevertheless. Once you'd seen that common factor, the conclusion was obvious.

Danny Bennett knew, instinctively but conclusively, that Lundqvist was the number one torpedo for the Milk Marketing Board. And here he was, in Danny's car, toothbrushed up and twitching with raw adrenaline, out in the middle of the Australian Outback.

'Um,' Danny said. 'Where was it you wanted to go, exactly?'

'George's Sheep Farm. Carry on along this road another seventy miles, it should be the first turning on your left. Got that?'

Danny nodded, his brain teeming all the while.

Sheep farm! What the hell would the Milk Marketing Board want with a sheep farm? Either the MMB bosses were running a covert dairy operation using cows with cotton wool stuck all over their backs, or else the whole thing was a front for something even more sinister. Part of his flesh crawled with feverish excitement. The rest just crawled.

'Funny thing,' Danny said. 'I'd got the idea the race didn't go anywhere near here.'

He didn't look round, but he could sense the lenses of the Ray-Bans scorching the side of his head. 'I'm taking a short cut,' Lundqvist said.

'A short cut. In a race.'

'Yeah.'

'Fine.'

The next hour seemed to pass very slowly. There was Lundqvist in the passenger seat, grimly munching his way through a roll of peppermints he'd found in the glove box, and there was Danny, desperately trying to suss it all out and find the little stray clue that would tie in a New South Wales sheepranch, the Watergate break-in and the Banco Ambrosiano. It was there, he knew it; just a matter of isolating one little wisp of a connection . . .

'We're here.'

Danny stood on the brake, slewing the car half round. His eyes met Lundqvist's, in roughly the same manner as a hedgehog meets an eighteen-wheel Mack truck.

'So,' Danny said. 'This is where you get out, then.'

'Yeah.' The door opened, Lundqvist grabbed his rucksack off the back seat and extracted the grotesque lengths of knee and elbow from which he appeared to be largely constructed. He slammed the door and started to walk up the long dirt track.

Discretion is the better part of valour, as the saying goes. By the same author, but not perhaps so well known, are such equally profound saws as, 'Aspirin is the spice of geography,' and, 'You can lead a horse to water but never double on three no trumps.' Danny drove on, decided to count to ten, got to seven and backed up. Then he drove on down the narrow track. On the seat beside him there now rested a loaded video camera.

Lundqvist froze in the doorway.

That statement is rather ambiguous. Since it was something like ninety in the shade, and there was enough moisture gathering in the armpits of his shirt to hold a tall ships race on, Lundqvist was by no means frozen. He was, rather, still.

Inside the big shed thing (Lundqvist was a bit vague about the proper names of agricultural buildings) a girl was counting sheep.

'Seventy-six, seventy-seven, seventy-eight, seventy-*nine* – come on, Hilda, up you get – eighty . . .'

The shear-your-own idea, Helen admitted to herself, hadn't been the tearaway spectacular success she'd hoped for. In the back of her mind, she had the notion that you needed just a bit more passing trade for a venture of that kind, and perhaps she should have realised that earlier. Still, no use crying over spilt milk (Danny Bennett would have disputed that remark, and it's as well he wasn't on hand to do so); what she did have on the credit side of the ledger was many, many sheep, and it surely wasn't beyond the wit of man to find some way of exploiting the resource.

She paused, hands on hips, and frowned. Then she cracked the small whip she held and shouted.

'Come *on*, Doris, you aren't even trying.'

Doris gave her a blank stare, said, 'Baaa,' and trotted grimly round the jump. The rest of the flock, however, did as they were told, and jumped. The face that launched a thousand sheeps, and all that jazz.

Not a bad wheeze, though she said it herself. What do you give the insomniac who's got everything? Trained performing sheep, of course.

Meanwhile, in the doorway, Lundqvist was motionless, listening. Where Helen was, it stood to reason, George couldn't be far away. All he needed to do was wait, like a cat at a mousehole, and the idiot would walk straight into his arms.

Well yes. Quite.

On the one hand, Lundqvist said to himself, quite apart from his virtually infinite resources of supernatural special effects, Lucky George has the reputation of being a crack shot, naturally gifted all-in wrestler and ex-Wittemberg fencing blue. On the other hand, I have a toothbrush.

Had a toothbrush.

A few seconds of frantic pocket-searching followed, at the end of which Lundqvist moaned softly and bumped his head three or four times against the doorpost. He'd come all this way – stolen a helicopter, hijacked an airliner, taken a series of cars and lorries without permission and finally mugged a sailplane pilot – only to leave his toothbrush somewhere between here and the entrance of the driveway. And Lucky George liable to turn up at any minute . . .

'Excuse me,' called the girl from the interior of the shed. 'Can I help you or something?'

Lundqvist stood upright. A stray pellet of inspiration had lodged in the back of his brain.

'Yes,' he said. 'I think you can.'

By the time Danny Bennett had climbed up on to the rail of the silage clamp to get a better view and got the camera in his shoulder and found the thing you pressed to make it go and the other thing you twiddled to get it in focus, he'd missed some of the best bits. He'd missed Lundqvist running like a hare out of the shed, with a flock of ravening sheep snapping at his heels and the current Miss World bringing up the rear cracking a whip and shouting, 'Go on, Doris, kill!' He'd missed Lundqvist's quite spectacular leap up into the hayloft, and the lead ewe's frantic efforts to jump up and bite his throat out. He'd missed the really good bit, where the girl had brought up a ladder and the sheep had gone swarming up it like firemen on piecework, followed by Lundqvist jumping out the other side and landing in the water butt.

What he had got, though, was Lundqvist grabbing the girl, bundling her under his arm and running like fun back up the drive, while seventeen livid sheep stood on the hay platform realising that learning to come *down* the ladder had been pencilled on the timetable for the week after next.

He hadn't the faintest idea of what was going on, of course, but that was so close to normality that it was comforting rather than otherwise. What he did recognise was bloody good television.

Familiarity is, indeed, the most powerful anaesthetic of all. To Helen of Troy, bumping about under Lundqvist's arm and trying to write *Been kidnapped. Dinner in fridge. Love, Helen xxx* on the back of a feed bill with an eyebrow pencil, being abducted was just like old times. It was, after all, what she was best at.

'You,' screamed Lundqvist, 'start the goddamn car!'

Danny, recognising that the remark was addressed to himself, started to climb down from his eyrie and then checked himself. Yes, sure, a good journalist's first duty is to cover the story, but did that involve assisting in the abduction of beauty queens by known hit-men?

'Start the fucking car,' Lundqvist reiterated, as if somehow conscious of Danny's internal debate, 'or I'll rip your nuts off with a plastic fork!'

Yes, Danny decided, it probably did. Without releasing his hold on the camera, he fumbled in his trouser pocket for the car keys.

You know how it is with keys. Shy, elusive creatures, the trouser pocket is their natural habitat and they are masters of the arts of camouflage and concealment. Their favourite ploy is to snuggle down into the folds of a crumpled pocket handkerchief and stop up the mouth of the burrow with any loose change that might be lying about. Failing that, they find a loose thread in the seam to snag themselves on, and cling like limpets. Danny's keys did both.

'Just a minute,' he called out, jiggling furiously. 'I won't keep you, I've just got to . . .'

He jiggled too hard and dropped the camera.

Five minutes of the best action sequence he'd ever been privileged to witness, spinning and twirling through the air on its way to obliteration on the rock-hard ground, twenty feet below. In that split second when he realised what had happened, Danny felt the most devastatingly acute feeling of loss that any human being could conceivably register without the top of his head coming unscrewed. It had had everything – sex, violence, action, comedy and white fluffy animals – and in one and a half seconds' time it was going to hit the deck and go splat. He launched himself into the air, stretched out a frantic arm like Michelangelo's Adam, and just managed to get the tips of his fingers round the carrying handle.

His last thought, before he hit the deck and went *splat!*, was *Phew, that was close.*

When he opened his eyes, it was dark. Then someone slowly turned up the lights.

It was just like being at the cinema.

The faint glow was coming from directly in front of him. As he stared, it seemed to resolve itself into shapes. Patterns. Letters.

YOU ARE DEAD

Danny started violently; or rather, he didn't. It was like trying to rub your eyes with a hand that's just been amputated; the brain ordered a spasm of movement, and the space where the nerves had once been sent back the message that spasms are off.

SORRY

Gosh, Danny couldn't help thinking, it's nice of them to say that. Perhaps it wasn't a hundred per cent sincere, no more than *We apologise for any delay* notices at the head of a twelve-mile tailback, but the fact that they bothered at all was reassuring, in a way. It implied that there was someone, or perhaps Someone, you could write to and complain.

DEATH IS PERFECTLY NORMAL.
PLEASE DON'T WORRY

The letters flickered and faded, and it was dark again; but there was no immediate impulse towards terror, because they were playing piped music. Airport music. Supermarket music. Please-hold-the-line music. Now everybody knows that when this sort of music plays, the only possible emotion is passive boredom; and it's impossible to be passively bored and shit-scared at the same time. Danny sighed and allowed his mind to wander.

Well, I'm dead. What a bloody nuisance, here I am dead and no camera. My first really *big* scoop and there's absolutely nothing I can do about it.

Then it occurred to him that death is hardly a scoop for any journalist. It's the one story that everyone covers and nobody gets to phone in. Danny opened where his mouth had been and screamed.

Noiselessly.

And then the lights flickered again, this time resolving themselves into a ten-foot-high neon questionnaire.

PLEASE HELP US
TO HELP YOU
BY COMPLETING THIS SIMPLE FORM

Put like that, it would be churlish to refuse.

Full name: Daniel Woodward Bernstein Bennett.

Date of birth: December 14th, 1959

Nationality: British

Smoking or non-smoking: non-smoking

Evening meal?

And so on. The form scrolled forward – breakfast is served in the dining area between 7.00 and 9.00, the fire escapes are situated at the end of the corridor, if you have managed to take it with you, please deposit it in the safety deposit box in the front office – and as it did so, Danny realised something.

A common factor. A link. New South Wales, a sheep station, Kurt Lundqvist.

Me!

Lundqvist! Bloody hell fire, I've been hit by a hit-man!

Danny's spiritual remains sat bolt upright, and where his eyes had once been shone with ecstatic joy. For, in a moment of transcendent knowledge such as one tends to associate with the Great Transition, Danny had suddenly realised that all his life, everything he'd fought and worked and sweated and been humiliated for, must have been worthwhile.

'Hey!' he yelled, 'this is great! I've been silenced! I must have known too much!'

And then the reaction, deadening and crushing as a pile-driver. Absolute Sunday-morning-and-no-milk-left despair.

Yes, obviously he'd known too much. Obviously he'd been put out of the way, by Them, by the unseen conspirators . . .

(All rooms must be vacated by 12 noon on Judgement Day. Please do not place objects down the toilet bowl. If you would like your past life to flash before you, please dial your credit card number down to the front desk and select channel 12 on your remote control handset . . .)

Unfortunately, he hadn't the faintest idea what it was he'd known too much about.

CHAPTER
TEN

GEORGE frowned. This, he couldn't help feeling, was a trifle disturbing.

Your dinner, the kidnap note had said, is in the fridge. Upon inspection, however, the fridge turned out to contain nothing but vegetables. One of the things that he'd always liked about Helen was that, unlike ninety-five per cent of the rest of her sex, she didn't confuse food with scenery. Had she chosen this moment of all moments to go to the bad? Or had she simply written 'fridge' when she meant 'freezer'?

The latter hypothesis proved to be correct, since the freezer turned out to contain two frozen pizzas and a microwave lasagne. He decided on the lasagne, turned it out of its foil container on to a plate, and smiled at it.

Then he frowned at it, to give the melted cheese on the top that distinctive browned-under-the-grill look.

Callous? Insensitive? Just like a man? These are hard thoughts, and not really applicable. It's true that there have been heroes and men of action who've gone haring off to rescue damsels on an empty stomach, but what the epics don't tell you is that their subsequent performance was considerably hampered by indigestion and heartburn. Your class hero knows this. Hercules, for example, had a double cheeseburger with fries, coleslaw and an ambrosia shake before snatching Alcestis out of the arms of the King of Death, and Sir Lancelot always insisted on a round of cucumber sandwiches with the crusts cut off before so much as looking at a dragon.

Logic, said George to himself. A spot of logic is called for here.

Who'd want to kidnap Helen of Troy? Well, yes, that's a pretty dumb question, so let's rephrase it. Apart from every red-blooded male in the world, who'd want to kidnap Helen of Troy? Easy. Lundqvist.

By way of confirmation of this working hypothesis, there was the tape in the video camera which some untidy person had left lying about by the silage clamp, right next to the corpse. Having laughed at the bit with the sheep and been suitably impressed at the big jump into the hayloft, George wound back the tape and sat for a few minutes, his mind turning over like Mozart in his grave during a Jonathan Miller production of *Cosi fan Tutti*. Then he suddenly scowled and snapped his fingers.

Two seagulls hopped down and perched on the top of the telly, trying to eat the aluminium trim.

'Hey,' George said, 'this isn't on, you know.'

'Quark?'

'Kidnapping people,' George explained. 'My compliments to Mr Lundqvist, and ask him if there's any particular order he wants his bones broken in.'

'Quark.'

'No.'

The seagulls flapped their wings and lifted out of the window. George played the video through once more. Then he made a phone call. *How! This is a recorded spirit message. Kindly leave your name and a medium through whom you can be contacted and I'll get back to you as soon as I can.*

He shrugged and tried a different number. When it answered, his side of the conversation went like this:

'Hello? Yes, could I have Mr Bosch, please, extension 3092. Yes, thanks, I'll hold.'

The hold facility on the switchboard played you the *Dies Irae*, as interpreted by a computer synthesizer. Eventually . . .

'Bosch here.'

'Ronnie,' said George, 'how's tricks? The project coming together at last?'

'Bloody hell, George . . .' The voice changed in pitch, though not in volume, until it became a rather heavy conspiratorial hiss. 'You really have got to stop calling me at work like this. You have no idea how *embarrassing*—'

'Yes, sorry. How's the Garden of Earthly Delights coming along, by the way?'

Bosch sighed. 'Don't ask,' he said. 'Even if we make it out of foam rubber instead of expanded polystyrene, the ninety-foot-high cracked eggshell just isn't going to stay up there, I just know it, and the sprinkler system's completely up a tree. I've got seventy-six thousand purple tubular carnivorous plants out there dying of dehydration, but do they listen?'

George tutted sympathetically. 'Par for the course, it sounds to me. Look, can you do me a quick favour?'

Bosch growled darkly. 'Depends,' he said. 'I mean, there's favours and favours. I think opening wormholes in the fabric of virtual reality for you to hide your rope ladder in probably puts us all square, don't you?'

George laughed cheerfully. 'Call those wormholes, Ron?' he said. 'I'd have been better off stashing the gear under the bed only I didn't want to hurt your feelings. I would also remind you of that time back at Wittenberg when I let you borrow my red slashed fustian doublet three weeks running when you were chasing after that barmaid with the big —'

'All right,' Bosch cut him short. 'I was younger then. Dammit, I was *alive* then. What do you want this time?'

'Just a note of where Lundqvist is right now.'

'That's *all*?'

'For now, Ron.'

Meanwhile, Lundqvist was negotiating with two seagulls.

'We got the Revenue off your back like you said,' Larry croaked, 'although we couldn't do anything about your 1986 expenses claim. I mean,' he added quickly, as Lundqvist's eyes smouldered, 'putting five thousand cubic feet of cyanide gas down as entertaining potential clients *is* going a bit too far, you've got to —'

'The hell with you,' Lundqvist snapped. 'Those particular clients were pretty peculiar people. So what? You've got to be weird to need a transtemporal security consultant in the first place.'

'Okay,' said Mike. 'But do you really expect the tax guys to believe you got through thirty-seven dozen throwing knives in one fiscal quarter. Don't you *ever* re-use them?'

A shrewd thrust from a wingtip suggested to him that this was a subject best left alone. He cleared his throat, ruffled his feathers with his beak and changed tack.

'Anyway,' he said, 'they've unfrozen your bank accounts and the bailiffs have released your goods. We've kept our side of the bargain.'

'Good,' Lundqvist replied icily. 'Now we can start talking.'

The seagulls exchanged glances. 'I thought we'd been —'

'Preliminaries,' Lundqvist said. 'Now we get to the good stuff. That is, unless your man wants to play it the hard way. Because if he does, the only thing the girl's gonna be launching from now on is oil rigs.'

Larry sighed. 'Let's hear it, then,' he said.

'Fine by me,' Lundqvist said. 'I want George, I want him here, and no tricks. You got that?'

'Quark.'

'Right. Now piss off.'

The seagulls lifted their wings and flapped noisily out through the open window. Lundqvist grinned and drew the shutters.

'Actually,' said a voice from the corner of the room, 'would you mind awfully much leaving the window? It's a bit stuffy in here.'

Lundqvist snarled.

'Please.'

'Sure. You want me to leave the window. You think I was born yesterday?'

'Not really,' Helen said, smiling. 'If you had been, you'd be all pink and small and covered in fluffy down, and you'd need feeding all the time. Talking of which, I thought we'd have dinner around sevenish.'

Lundqvist scowled. 'We'll eat when I say so,' he said. 'If I say so. You got . . .?'

Helen ignored him. With a dainty flick of her slim wrists, she wriggled free of the handcuffs and drew a liberated finger along the top of the table next to where she was tied up. It left a furrow in the dust. She didn't say anything, but she tutted.

'I'll need some ingredients,' she went on. 'Four pounds of potatoes, a large cabbage, two pounds of parsnips . . .'

'We'll have corned beef and like it,' Lundqvist grunted.

'I doubt that,' replied Helen. 'Also some desiccated coconut, some ginger, sunflower oil – it's better for you, more polyunsaturates – and a pound of self-raising flour. You'll just have time to pop out before the shops shut.'

Lundqvist turned round slowly. Helen had slipped free of all her bonds by now. She was standing up and tying a pinny round her waist. There was a horrible look in her eye, and for a moment Lundqvist's heart stopped.

Far back, in the left luggage room of one of the most twisted psyches in the history of Creation, a woman's voice was calling; shrill, hard, cruel.

Kurt, it shrieked, *You come here this instant, you hear me? You want that I tell your father?*

But Mom . . .

Kurt Lundqvist, you tidy your room, you polish your shoes, you

*do your homework, you practise the violin for half an hour like
Miss Horowitz told you, then maybe you can go play with your
impaling-sticks.*

Yes, Mom . . .

The flashback faded, as swift and terrible as it had come,
leaving Lundqvist standing with his mouth open. 'You get
back in the corner,' he said, 'or I'll —'

'Nonsense,' replied Helen briskly. From somewhere – God
only knew where – she'd produced a feather duster and a can
of furniture polish. 'Off you go. Don't forget the sunflower
oil.'

Lundqvist struggled to remember. He was Kurt Lundqvist,
the biggest, meanest, most savage . . .

. . . Untidiest, scruffiest kid on the whole block. *No!* The
most savage . . .

'Sure,' he said weakly. 'I go out and as soon as my back's
turned you're outa here and . . .'

Helen smiled. 'Don't be silly,' she said. 'First, I'm going to
give this place a really good clean. Then we'll be able to see
what colour the curtains are.'

She fluttered her eyelashes cruelly.

'I mean,' she said, 'if we've got to be cooped up in this
smelly old place, we might as well make it as comfortable as
possible.'

Lessons Learned The Hard Way Number One: Don't Kidnap
Helen of Troy.

The wooden horse was basically a face-saving exercise,
something to make it all look slightly more convincing to the
outside world.

Within three months of Helen's arrival in Troy after her
abduction by Prince Paris, there wasn't a square inch of
original carpeting in the whole city. The entire workforce had
been transferred from sword-tempering and arrow-sharpen-
ing to curtain-making, and King Priam had mortgaged his

empire and taken out a personal loan from the First Achaean Bank to pay for new three-piece suites in every room in his gigantic palace. It wasn't Achilles or the wrath of the gods or the curse of Dardanus that did for Troy of the Hundred Gates; it was the sheer bloody havoc wrought on the Trojan economy by a determined home-maker with a Liberty catalogue and a Gold AmEx card.

The reason that the siege of Troy took so long was simple. Once King Menelaus had got used to being able to wipe his hands on the towels and smoke in the living-room again, it took the concentrated moral pressure of three continents ten years to persuade him to take her back.

CHAPTER ELEVEN

THERE is only one bar in Potters Creek (population 53) but the awareness of its own monopoly hasn't led its enterprising and forward-thinking management to grow complacent. Nothing is too good for the customers (especially the beer, which wouldn't be too good for an elephant, let alone a human being) and the proprietor is constantly striving to make such improvements as his means permit. Thus, last year, he put in chairs. This year, tables.

Around the smaller of the two tables, a film crew sat, staring into the suds at the bottom of their glasses, trying to shame each other into getting in the next round.

'Reminds me of that time in Afghanistan,' said the sound recordist.

'Yeah.'

'Or that time last year in Ghana.'

'That wasn't Ghana, that was Mozambique.'

'Nah,' interrupted the assistant cameraman, 'I'm not thinking of *that* time in Ghana, I'm thinking of that *other* time in Ghana.'

The sound recordist nodded. 'Yeah,' he said. 'I was reminded of that, too.'

There was a long silence, broken only by the distant

commentary of the kookaburra, and the whisper of a slight breeze in the eucalyptus.

'Let's give him till half-seven,' muttered the chief cameraman. 'Then we bugger off, right?'

His companions nodded (except the continuity girl, who'd fallen asleep). Everyone fiddled with their glasses, suddenly noticing that they were empty.

'Aidan,' said the chief cameraman at last to the junior electrician, 'go and buy the beer.' The junior electrician, who was young, poor and saving up to buy a moped, slouched to the bar.

'Sodding lousy country, this,' opined the chief cameraman. 'Bit like Paris.'

The others nodded. 'Except,' qualified the chief electrician, 'the handles on the bogs are on the left. Anyone else notice that? I did.'

'Sodding awful place, Paris,' continued the chief cameraman. 'Full of holes.'

'Yeah. Like Tangier.'

'Or Laos. Laos is full of sodding holes. Can't get a tripod level anywhere.'

Under their hands, the table moved.

Well, you know how it is with tables in bars. There are strict international specifications about precisely how much shorter one leg should be than the others. The object is to make customers spill their drinks and buy more.

'I remember we were in Cairo once,' said the chief electrician. 'Holes *and* flies. Bloody horrible place.'

'Like Valparaiso.'

'Or Genoa.'

'Venice,' said the assistant cameraman, 'is a real bog-hole. Armpit of the universe, Venice. You want to film something, a building or something, you step back to get the bugger in the frame, splash. Here, who's jogging the bloody table?'

'Not me.'

Simultaneously, the film crew lifted their elbows. The table continued to move.

'Hey,' remarked the chief electrician, breaking a nervous silence, 'this *is* like bloody Valparaiso.'

'Yeah, or Archangel.'

The table was balancing on three of its legs. With the foot of the fourth, it was pecking tentatively at the ground, like a spider at its first tap-dancing lesson. The continuity girl woke up, blinked, and went back to sleep.

Help.

'Did someone just say something?' enquired the sound recordist.

'Yeah.'

'Ah. Right.'

'The table just said Help!'

Listen, it's me. Danny Bennett. You've got to help me.

The crew looked at each other. They were, after all, a film crew, and he was a producer. Had they thought of it, they might have quoted the line about the triumph of hope over experience.

I'm dead.

The sound recordist cleared his throat.

'Not a lot we can do about that, my son,' he said. 'What you need is more like a priest or something.'

I was murdered. It was a cover-up.

The chief cameraman checked the movement of his glass to his lips and frowned.

'Jesus!' he said. 'Danny! That really *is* you, isn't it?'

It was a cover-up. I knew too much. They killed me because I knew too much.

'Too much about what?'

The table bucked like an unbroken colt, lifting all its feet off the ground and landing six inches from its original position. *I don't bloody well know, that's the whole bloody point. That's why I need help.*

The chief electrician raised an eyebrow. 'Hang about,' he said. 'If you're dead then it's all watchercallit, academic, innit? I mean, if you're dead, you're dead, doesn't matter a toss *why* . . .'

The table jumped again, landing on the chief electrician's foot.

It matters to me, Julian. Look, about seventy miles from here there's a sheep farm . . .

'So?'

Let me finish, will you? There's a sheep farm, called George's Sheep Farm. That's where I died. I want you to go and pick up a video camera, because there may be a clue . . .

'Seventy miles?'

Yes, more or less. There may be a clue . . .

The chief cameraman furrowed his brows, creating the impression of copulating hedgerows. 'You want us to go there.'

Thank you, Colin, yes. You see, there may be a clue . . .

'And we can claim the mileage?'

What?

'If we go there,' said the chief cameraman. 'We can claim the mileage, can we, off the firm?'

How the hell should I know? Look . . .

The chief cameraman looked at his colleagues. 'And it'd have to be time and a half, because by the time we get there, if it's seventy miles like you said, not to mention getting back . . .'

Look.

'It's our rest and recreation period,' the sound recordist butted in. 'If we work in R and R time, it's time and a half. Are you *sure* the firm'll pay the mileage? Mean sods, the lot of 'em, I remember once in Finland —'

I neither know nor care, you bastards. Look, I'm dead, I need your help. I always thought you were my friends . . .

The camera crew looked at each other; then they stood up

and walked over to the other table.

The other table was, of course, bolted to the ground.

After a while, the hammering noise stopped, and the crew relaxed and calmed themselves with another round.

'You know what?' said the assistant cameraman, wiping foam off his lips. 'That was bloody Szechuan all over again.'

His colleagues nodded sagely. That, they felt, put it in a nutshell.

CHAPTER
TWELVE

WE have touched lightly on the subject of friendship.

The classic definition – friendship means never having to pay the full retail price for car spares – is all right as far as it goes, but there is another, more spiritual side to friendship.

A *true* friend is someone who'll lend you his Lear jet and a full tank of petrol without asking what you want it for.

'Thanks,' George shouted, above the roar of the engine.

'Any time, George, you know that. Thanks for the tip, by the way.'

'Oh, that's all right,' George yelled back. 'It works even better if you add a thimbleful of turps.' He opened the throttle, pulled back on the stick and let her have her head.

At least finding her would be easy, he said to himself. It might get a bit tricky after that, but we'll cross that bridge when we come to it.

As soon as he'd worked out his course and pointed the plane in the right direction, he leant forward and grinned at the radio; which bleeped, crackled and homed in.

... This is Radio Dante, I'm Danny Bennett, I'm your host for this afternoon, and later on I'll be talking to Benito Mussolini in our regular Where I Went Wrong spot. But first, this.

George twiddled a knob slightly, leant back and took the

two-way control in his hand. 'Hi,' he said. 'How's tricks?'

His voice echoed over every tannoy, loudspeaker and PA in the place; and, believe it or not, there are more speakers per square metre in Hell than anywhere else in Creation. For the piped music, you see.

The Finance Director swore.

'Get him off the bloody air,' he shouted. 'Switch 'em all off or something.'

Once the nuisance had been confined to one small telephone, the Finance Director picked up the receiver and said, 'Well, what is it now?'

'I thought you said you were getting that nutcase off my back.'

'We did.'

George shook his head. 'No you didn't,' he replied. 'And he's starting to get ever so slightly up my nose. In fact, his head is wedged up my sinuses and I want something done about it. Otherwise there's going to be trouble.'

The Finance Director winced. 'We did our best,' he mumbled. 'Put our crack team on it. What more —?'

'I heard about that,' George said. 'Got stuck in an onion, the way I heard it. Try again. Helen walks by six o'clock your time, or I won't be responsible for the consequences.' He paused, and the Finance Director could just picture the nasty little grin flitting across his face. 'Well, actually I will be responsible for the whole lot of 'em, so think on. Over and out.'

Before the Finance Director could reply, the line went dead and almost immediately, every speaker in the Nine Rings started to play *Chicago*, until the Chief Technician pulled out all the wires.

The Head of Security held up both hands.

'No can do,' he said. 'If I ask those lads to go back out there again, I'll be going home tonight in a plastic bag. Can't you buy him off?'

'Lundqvist?' The Finance Director considered. 'Nah,' he

said, 'not this time. Anyway, even if I could I don't know where he is. He's not answering his carphone and his bleeper's switched off. We'll just have to let George do his worst and then blame it on someone else.'

The Head of Security frowned. 'Who?'

'I don't know,' replied the Finance Director. 'The CIA. The nuclear power people. The Milk Marketing —'

'Which reminds me . . .'

'Anyway,' continued the Finance Director, 'we'll just have to do the best we can. I wish I'd never started this whole perishing thing now,' he added.

The Head of Security shrugged his shoulders. 'Maybe we're worrying too much,' he said. 'I mean, when it comes right down to it, he can't do anything *too* terrible, can he?'

There's a time differential between Hell and the rest of the cosmos, naturally. In Hell, however, time is told not in hours and minutes but episodes, such as half past four on a Sunday afternoon when there's nothing on the television except the Olympics, or three minutes after the bar you've just walked into closes.

One minute past six in Infernal Mean Time is, therefore, the split second between the moment when you've just let go of the china ornament that's been in your employer's family since 1868 and the point in time when it hits the lino. To match this up with Greenwich, you multiply by four, divide by six and forget to turn off the gas before leaving for a fortnight's holiday.

And that was the precise moment when . . .

'Brilliant,' said the Finance Director, between gritted fangs. 'You've got to hand it to him. For sheer brilliant simplicity . . .'

'The switchboard,' reported the Marketing Director, 'has just overloaded.'

'Oh good. Now perhaps we can hear ourselves think.'

(In the clouds above New South Wales, Lucky George felt a tug on one of the tendrils of his mind. He smiled, and four hundred thousand miles of fused fibre-optic cable running through the centre of the earth took on a new lease of life . . .)

'Malcolm!' The Finance Director waved a hand vaguely at the Duty Officer. 'Get that for me, will you?' He turned to his fellow directors. 'Let's go down to the executive lavatory for a bit. There's no phones there.'

'Basically,' he went on, when the meeting had reconvened, 'the situation is that, thanks to Lucky George and his magic bloody wand, the entire human race have all gone on holiday at precisely the same moment.' He paused and tried to take a sip from his glass of water, the meniscus of which danced like a formation flamenco team. 'This has, of course, produced complete and utter havoc in every country in the world except France, where they're used to it. The tailbacks on all major roads leading to airports and coastal resorts are causing a critical mass which is threatening to send the whole works shooting off into another dimension, and the price of a pair of Bermuda shorts has now risen to approximately twice the gross national product of the United States. Now, what are we going to do about it?'

He looked up. The room was empty.

'Come back!' he roared, and flung open the door.

He was just in time to see the Production Director and the Marketing Director, in bathing trunks, heading for the car park with a plastic bucket and spade and a large rubber ball.

And there it was. Plain as the proverbial pikestaff.

A three mile tailback of articulated lorries in the middle of the Australian Outback, it is fairly safe to say, is probably a symptom of something; apart, that is, from road works. George peered down from the cockpit of the Lear, grinned and circled away.

His second pass over the traffic jam, a few hundred feet

lower, simply confirmed his diagnosis. He read the names on the sides of the lorries and that was enough. Certainty.

There were soft-furnishing lorries, DIY homecare lorries, carpet vans, lorries of all descriptions, delivering to a small, bleak wooden shed in the middle of half a million acres of wind-scoured, sand-blasted nothing. What you might call a woman's touch.

In the back yard of the shed, a team of forklifts were staggering about like exhausted dung-beetles under enormous loads of big cardboard cartons, while on the other side, a team of crack carpenters were starting work on a huge, Versailles-dwarfing extension to the shed, presumably to provide a bit of space for all the stuff to go. Two enormous industrial cement-mixers stood like hormone-stuffed dinosaurs round the back, while conveyor belts fed them unlimited supplies of cans of paint. George nodded; Helen's favourite colour, what she in her artistic way called Harvest White. Many years ago, George had made himself temporarily unpopular by pointing out that you could get exactly the same effect by painting the room in question ordinary white and smoking unfiltered cigarettes in it for twenty years.

He knew without having to look that one of the giant artics backed up out there in the desert was carrying a cargo of forty square miles of anaglypta

With a flick of a wingtip he turned the plane round and headed off. When the curvature of the Earth had hidden him from the shed, he landed the plane, got out and whistled . . .

· . . . Whereupon two seagulls drifted down out of the sky, perched on his tailplane and tried to eat it.

'Dry old place, this,' said Larry, critically. 'Gives me bad vibes, to be honest. Dunno where my next fish is coming from.'

'Yes,' George replied. 'Putting that to one side for a moment, I want you two to do something for me.'

★ ★ ★

'You're *sure* you like it?' Helen enquired. 'I mean, really *really* sure?' She observed Lundqvist carefully. 'You aren't, you know. Admit it.'

'It's fine.' Lundqvist ground the words out like flour. 'I love it. Really.'

'No.' Helen shook her head. 'You're just saying that to please me.' She leant out of the window, picked up the loudhailer and shouted, 'Excuse me!'

The wallpaper-pasting squad heard her, downed tools and signalled to the rest of the workforce, using flags and mirrors. A few minutes later, there was silence.

'Sorry to be a pest,' Helen loudspoke sweetly, 'but I'm afraid we've changed our minds again. Could we try a paleish sort of Chrysoprase White on the walls of the ballroom, please, with Crushed Eglantine on the ceilings and the Summer Caramel carpet. No, not the Axminster, the Wilton. Thank you.'

There was a moment of complete stillness; then a great deal of subvocal muttering; then an emptying and refilling of cement-mixers, a ripping-up of carpets and a cleaning of brushes, like the foreriders of a tsunami hitting the outlying coral reefs of a Pacific atoll. There was a certain practised resignation about the whole scene. Not all that surprising; it was the fifth time she'd changed her mind that morning.

'Now then,' Helen said brightly, 'if you don't like it, promise you'll say, won't you? I mean, you've got to live here too, you know.'

'Gr.'

'And, like you said, we might be here for some considerable time before George does the sensible thing and gives himself up.' She smiled warmly, like the sunrise. 'And you did very sweetly say I could tidy the place up and give it a lick of paint and so on, didn't you?'

Lundqvist nodded sadly. His 'Yeah, sure, do what you like' in this context clamoured for inclusion in the Library of Congress Index of Incredibly Unfortunate Remarks, along with such classics as 'Of course it isn't loaded,' 'Let them eat cake' and 'When I leave school, I want to be a solicitor.' However, even the meanest street punk in the barrios knows that any kidnapper who values his professional credibility doesn't welch on a deal unless he wants the word to get around that he's a two-face who can't be trusted. It was just a pity he'd also told her his AmEx Gold Card number.

'Well,' Helen said, putting her feet up on a Louis Quinze fauteuil and leafing through the colour charts, 'this is cosy, don't you think?'

'Mmm.' Lundqvist nodded as if his head had just been replaced with a large log. 'You think so?'

'It's coming along, anyway,' Helen replied. 'I mean, we're not there yet, but we're beginning to see the light at the end of the ... Oh.'

She broke off and held the colour chart up against the wall. Inside his chest, Lundqvist's heart stopped and tried to burrow its way into his intestines.

'Oh *yes*,' Helen said. 'Yes, I think I'm on to something here. What do you think?' She pointed to a small square in the middle of the page. As far as Lundqvist could tell it was exactly the same colour as the seventy-four other little boxes. 'For the ballroom, the main hall, the drawing room, the sitting room, the front stairs, the back stairs, the pantry, the scullery, the study, the loft conversion, the annexe, the loggia, the cloister, the fifth spare bedroom and the observatory? Then we can do the rest out in Orchard Haze and have the Golden Wave curtains in the back hall and the conservatory.' She paused. 'What d'you think?'

Lundqvist considered. It took him a long time.

'I think,' he said, 'it'd be very easy to escape from here right now. Very easy indeed.'

Helen raised an eyebrow. 'Oh no,' she said, 'I wouldn't *dream* of trying to escape. After all,' she added mercilessly, 'you told me not to.'

Lundqvist scowled. 'You don't want to take any notice of all that,' he said. 'That's just bluster. I mean, all you'd have to do,' he went on, pouring out a cup of coffee and passing it across the table to her, 'is, say, throw a cup of coffee in my face, run across to that door there, the one that's conveniently ajar right this very minute, and —'

'Not really,' Helen interrupted.

'Oh I think you'll find you could.'

Helen shook her head. 'Because,' she explained, 'in about thirty seconds the men are going to take that door out and make a start on the french windows.'

'French windows? In a hideout?'

'Absolutely,' Helen replied. 'Then, I thought, you'll be able to keep a good watch out to see if anybody comes up trying to rescue me. And if we put a couple of yards of old Venetian lace curtain across — I saw some in one of the catalogues, it's only ninety dollars a metre — then they couldn't see in. And of course, there's the locks.'

'Locks?'

Helen nodded. 'I told them, we want deadlocks *and* mortice locks on all the doors and windows. After all, security's the one thing you've got to have in a place like this, isn't it?'

Lundqvist choked back a whimper, with indeterminate success. Back in the second millennium BC, when the Greeks besieged Troy, things had been a whole lot different. Carpets, for example; the most expensive carpet you could get back then was little more than rush matting with ideas above its station. Velvet curtains were still over a thousand years in the future. Split-level grills and co-ordinated built-in kitchen units were nothing but a troubled oscillation in the subconscious mind of God. It had been, in other words, a very basic and primitive trial run, nothing more.

'Okay,' Lundqvist said. 'Sure, if I'm conscious it might be a bit tricky getting out of here. But if I was accidentally to slip on something and knock myself out ...' He picked up a banana from the fruit bowl and unobtrusively started to peel it.

'Unlikely,' Helen replied with a smile. 'That's why I insisted on wall-to-wall fitted carpets.'

Lundqvist abandoned the banana. 'All right,' he said, 'point taken. Something might land on my head, though. Have you thought of that?'

Helen frowned. 'Such as what?'

'Well,' Lundqvist said, looking round, 'say a big glass ashtray. Like this one here, for example.' He tested it in his hand for balance. 'Knock a guy out cold with no trouble at all, something like this.'

'Do you really think so?'

Lundqvist grinned at her, threw the ashtray up in the air and ducked under it. It landed on his head and broke cleanly in two.

'Thought not,' Helen said. 'If I were you, I'd put iodine or something on that cut.'

Muttering something under his breath about goddam cheapskate Taiwanese glassware, Lundqvist stood up and walked to the door.

'Hey,' he observed, as he reached for the doorhandle, 'my back's turned. Just thought I'd mention it.'

He went out, found the iodine, applied it liberally, counted up to a thousand, and went back. Helen was still there, her feet up on the sofa, reading a glossy magazine.

'There's a really good bit in this about ideas for brightening up drab mezzanines,' she said. 'Have a look.'

Lundqvist stood in the doorway and growled for a moment. Then he cleared his throat.

'Good lord,' he said. 'I left my gun right there on the coffee table, just where you could reach out and pick it up. How careless can you —?'

With a quick movement, Helen reached out and grabbed for the gun. Her fingers closed tight around the Pachmayr grips . . .

'Okay,' Lundqvist started to say, 'you win, I'll come – what are you *doing*?'

'Catch.'

The gun flew through the air towards him. It took a considerable effort of will to suppress the instinct to catch it. There was a thud as it hit the door.

'Butterfingers,' Helen remarked tolerantly. 'Now that door'll have to be painted again. While we're at it, actually, I thought of having all the woodwork a sort of light Drowned Violet . . .'

Lundqvist closed his mouth, which had frozen open, just as his mother had warned him it would all those years ago. Nevertheless. He was as patient as he was resourceful.

'Just come wonder,' he said, without moving. 'Lucky you don't know about the *other* gun, the one hidden under that cushion you're leaning against right now.' To reinforce the statement, he smiled; a pleading, rather endearing little smile, which Helen ignored.

'Yes,' she said, her head in a pattern book. 'Isn't it?'

CHAPTER THIRTEEN

'COME in,' said the Finance Director, 'sit down, make yourselves at home. What can I get you to drink?'

The Captain of Spectral Warriors looked suspiciously round, perched on the edge of a chair, and said that he'd quite fancy a small Babycham, if that wasn't too much trouble.

'Small Babycham coming right up,' replied the Finance Director, bustling. 'Now then, introductions. This is the Company Secretary, the Head of Security you already know, of course, and this is Harry, he's the Production Director, and Steve, who heads our Sales team. Lads, I'd like you all to meet Vince, Captain of Spectral Warriors.'

The boardroom table bobbed and sparkled with smiles and little waves. Unnerved, the Captain waved back.

'Right,' said the Finance Director. 'Here's your small, er, Babycham. Everyone else, then, the usual? Right, fine.' He clattered some bottles and whooshed a soda syphon.

'Excuse me.'

'Yes, Vince? What can we do for you? Peanuts, perhaps? Or how about an olive? Steve, get the olives.'

'Right, coming up, won't be a —'

'Excuse me,' the Captain repeated, 'but what's all this in aid of? With respect and all that, but . . .'

The various directors nodded approvingly. Here was a man, they seemed to be saying, who comes straight to the point and no mucking about.

'Well,' said the Company Secretary, folding his wings on the table in front of him, 'basically, what we wanted to do was, well, really say thank you for all you've been doing . . .'

'Greatly appreciated . . .'

'Sterling stuff, of course, absolutely sterling . . .'

'. . . And just kind of get to know you better, with possibly a view to asking you if you've ever considered – I mean if you'd *like* to – well, join the, um, board.'

'As a director,' the Production Director explained.

'One of us.'

'Absolutely.'

'Quite.'

The Captain slowly put his glass down. 'What,' he said, 'me?'

The Directors nodded. 'Why not?' said the Head of Security. 'Just the sort of bloke we're looking for.'

'Committed.'

'Dedicated.'

'One hundred per cent, twenty-four hours a day, eight days a —'

'*Seven* days . . .'

'Oh, they did bring that in after all, did they?'

'Just a moment,' said the Captain. 'Let's just get this straight. *You* want *me* to be a Director?'

The Directors nodded.

'Oh.'

'Just as soon –' The Finance Director addressed his remarks to the wall behind the Captain's head. '– just as soon as we've cleared up this little bit of nonsense we've got on at the minute, of course. Actually, you might be able to help us there, because . . .'

A forty-watt bulb started to glow in the back of the

Captain's mind. He asked, 'What little bit of nonsense?'

'This whatsisname . . .'

'Loonquest?'

'Lunkfish?'

'Lund-something. Damn, it's on the tip of —'

'No.'

The Captain stood up, his face white as a soap-ad sheet. 'Absolutely not,' he went on. 'Not after last time. Sorry, but —'

'Sit down.'

'I really don't think there's much point, because —'

'*Sit down!*'

The Captain sat down. Someone refilled his glass and the Production Director produced a bowl of cheese straws, some of which had already had the ends nibbled off. This was, after all, Hell; where all the boxes of chocolates come with the coffee creams already removed, and the detective stories in the library all have the last five pages missing.

'Obviously,' purred the Finance Director smoothly, 'a little reluctance, let's say, is only to be expected. Quite right too. Absolutely understandable, under the circumstances. We respect you for it, don't we?'

Heads nodded.

'Nevertheless.' The Finance Director slid a tumblerful of breadsticks and a plate of vol-au-vents down the table towards the Captain. 'Someone's got to do it. From each according to his abilities, and all that.'

'Very sound,' murmured the Company Secretary, and he pursed his lips judicially. 'Absolutely.'

The Captain shook his head. 'No way,' he replied, trembling slightly. 'Have you people got even the faintest notion of what it's like, three days in a damn onion? Quite apart from everything else, the smell —'

'Jolly good idea,' broke in the Production Director. 'Smashing suggestion of yours. I've ordered five tons of onions for the

Adultery Wing, by the way, and we're working on the design right now. Actually, we were thinking of changing the name to the Captain Vincent Schwartzschatte Adultery Wing, just to show our application of —'

'You're all crazy,' the Captain shouted. 'There's absolutely nothing you can do that'll make me go back in there after that lunatic, nothing at all. And as for the lads . . .'

The Finance Director held up his hand. 'Fair enough,' he said. 'Point taken, say no more, subject closed. And, like we said, we respect you for it, no doubt about it. Don't we, lads?'

'Absolutely.'

'No question.'

'Utmost respect. Utmost.'

'However.' The Finance Director leant forward on to the boardroom table and fixed the Captain with a selection of his eyes. 'That does bring us on rather neatly to what we might call –' He paused, and grinned disconcertingly. '– the consolation prize. Tell him about it, Steve.'

'The other, um portfolio, you mean?'

'That's right.'

The Sales Director ruffled some papers, took off his glasses and laid them on the table beside him. 'Yes indeed,' he said. 'The other portfolio. Right, where to start?'

Spectral warriors, being entirely made up out of solidified paranoia and racial guilt, have no hearts, or toenails, or anything else. However, years of mixing with human mortals had given the Captain a pretty shrewd idea of what a heart is, and what it does under circumstances of extreme apprehension. Accordingly, when the Sales Director said the words *the other portfolio*, his notional or imaginary heart turned to water and tried to seep quietly out through his ear.

'Pretty straightforward job,' the Sales Director went on. 'Recognised punishment for swearing, blasphemy, slanderous gossip and saying nice things about one's employers with intent to procure advancement – up to the neck in a big vat full of, ah, thing. Ordure. The smelly stuff. We get it delivered, you know, fresh every day. Well, not *fresh* exactly. New. Anyway, there's the question of quality control . . .'

'Ah.'

'Vitally important, quality control,' broke in the Production Director. 'There are rigid specifications laid down in the franchise, so we can't just go around giving the clients any old —'

'As my colleague says. Well, to cut a long story short, the post is now vacant.'

The Captain swallowed hard. Vacancies simply do not occur in an immortal and ineffable workforce. In Hell, dead men's shoes means nothing more than the pairs of leather things left outside the doors of the more expensive suites for the hall-porter to clean before morning.

'What,' he asked slowly, 'happened to the previous . . .?'

The Finance Director grinned very slightly. 'Resigned,' he said. 'Or rather, misplaced.'

'Fell in the main vat,' the Production Director explained. 'Leant over too far one morning, lost his balance, splosh. Presumably,' he added carelessly, 'the poor bugger's still in there somewhere; damn steep, slippery sides that vat's got, to stop the clients getting out, of course. Very dodgy indeed. For some reason or other, volunteers to dredge the vat to look for him were not forthcoming.'

'Fourth in six months.'

'Dirty job, but someone's got to . . .'

'Still,' repeated the Captain quietly, 'in there somewhere. With the clients. I see.'

The Production Director smiled affably. 'Sooner or later,' he said, 'the thing'll solve itself. There'll be enough of them down there – our people, I mean – to form a sort of human pyramid so they can climb out again. Some of them, anyway. Meanwhile . . .'

He left the sentence unfinished. For his part the Captain

closed his eyes and thought about it for a moment. He was not a dramatically imaginative person – you can't be if you're a spectral warrior, without having severe personality problems – but he could vaguely sort of picture . . .

It wouldn't, he decided, be the shit that'd get to him in the end. It'd be the endless bloody squabbling with all the other poor bastards stuck down there as to whose turn it was to stand on whose shoulders.

He indicated with a gesture his willingness to join the Board of Directors instead.

What Sitting Bull did best was, of course, sitting. Otherwise he'd have been called Standing Bull or Bull Leaning Non-chalantly, or even Bull Getting His Head Down.

On this occasion he was sitting in the Polo Lounge of Attila's Palace, sipping a margarita before wandering into the Casino to play a few hands of blackjack and feed some coins into the slot machines. He had, after all, suddenly come into money.

'How.'

He nearly jumped out of his skin. If that had been a question rather than a greeting, the truthful reply would, of course, have been, 'By grassing up Lucky George to Kurt Lundqvist.' He turned his head, and his jaw dropped like a badly lowered drawbridge.

'I,' said the taller of the two figures looming over him, 'am Carpet Slippers, of the Cigar Store nation. This is Changes Light Bulbs, of the Hollywood nation. You must come with us.'

'What, now?'

'Now.'

'How.'

'No, *now*. With a N.'

'You mean Hnow?'

The dialectic confusion was resolved by Changes Light

Bulbs taking hold of Sitting Bull and lifting him out of his chair, an operation that Changes Light Bulbs was able to perform with the thumb and forefinger of his left hand.

'Disciplinary tribunal,' he explained.

The tribunal met in a small, rather musty teepee at the edge of one of the back lots of the Happy Hunting Grounds. When the tribunal was not sitting, the teepee was used as a combined charnel-house and offal depository. It had ambience.

'Hear ye, hear ye, disciplinary tribunal of the Combined Amerindian Nations, His Honour Judge Five Ovenproof Dishes presiding, all stand.'

'Sitting Bull, alias Consorts With Lawyers, you are charged with breach of trust, betraying a friend of the Combined Nations to the common enemy and behaviour likely to bring the Combined Nations into disrepute, how . . .'

'How.'

'. . . do you plead, guilty or not guilty?'

'Hey, not guilty. Who are you guys, anyway?'

Five Ovenproof Dishes rapped his desk with a miniature tomahawk and frowned. The prisoner at the bar wilted slightly.

Couper Ses Gorges of the Paris Apaches, for the prosecution, presented his case quickly and succinctly, whereupon the judge turned and called upon the defence.

'Your Honour.' Carpet Slippers rose to his feet and frowned. 'I am of the Cigar Store nation. My nation do not tell lies. The scumbag is as guilty as a wigwamful of rapists.'

'Hey!'

The entire court turned and gave Sitting Bull an unpleasant stare. He sat down again.

'The sentence of this court,' said Five Ovenproof Dishes, breathing heavily, 'is that you be expelled from your nation until the wind ceases to blow and the eagle lies down with the wolf. I have spoken.'

'Ah come *on*,' shouted Sitting Bull incredulously. 'This

whole thing is getting hopelessly jejune. I demand to know by what right . . .'

Counsel for the Defence nutted him with an obsidian club and he resumed his seat. The judge scowled.

'For calling the court jejune,' he growled, 'the mandatory penalty is burial upright in an anthill. Perhaps you would care to rephrase . . .?'

'Okay, not jejune.' Sitting Bull looked around, selected a big, thick legal tome (*Giggles Incessantly on Criminal Procedure*), held it over his head umbrella-fashion and rose to a wary crouch. 'Forget jejune, sorry. But really, you guys are making one big mistake here. I'm a medium, goddammit, people ask me questions, I tell 'em. It's my job. I had no choice, okay?'

There was a pause. Counsel for both parties approached the bench, and whispering ensued.

'Prisoner states that he is a medium,' intoned the judge. 'Correct?'

Sitting Bull nodded.

'Fine. Call Marshall Macluhan.'

Witness testified that, in his expert opinion, the medium was the message. The message found to be inherently unlawful. Appeal disallowed. All stand.

Twenty minutes later, Sitting Bull's suitcases were put outside the front entrance, followed shortly and at great speed by their owner. After a pause, Sitting Bull got up, dusted himself off, shooed various members of the spectral buffalo herd away from his suit covers and slouched off into the Upper Air.

As he slouched, he considered.

It was fortunate, he said to himself, that he was a fully westernised, regenerate member of the indigenous American community, free from the absurd superstitions of his ancestors; because otherwise, he'd be firmly convinced that being slung out of the Hunting Grounds would inevitably result in his being chased six times round the Sun by the Great Wolf Spirit, bitten in half and eaten. 'Absolutely just as well,' he muttered aloud. 'Crazy bunch of goddamn savages . . .'

He hesitated. He could feel hot breath on the back of his neck, soft fur rubbing his ankles, a nose as cold as Death nuzzling his ear.

'Woof.'

He turned round. Behind him, two piercing red eyes, a pair of gnarled ears laid back against a long, thin, cruel skull, jaws like scrap car compressors holding between them a yellow and blue rubber ball.

CHAPTER
FOURTEEN

SLOWLY, with infinite pains and an almost superhuman patience, Kurt Lundqvist made his way across the main room – sorry, we must now call it the drawing-room – of the hideout, towards the corner with the loose floorboard.

They train you for this sort of thing at Ninja School, of course; crossing a dark and unfamiliar room full of hideously lethal booby-traps without waking the guards. The orthodox technique is to use the scabbard of your sword as a sort of blind man's white stick. Untold generations of Japanese silent killers have succeeded with it; or if they failed, they never came to report back. And anyway, the Japanese are a conservative people.

Lundqvist believed in progress and he had no scabbard, so he used the snapped-off aerial of the clock radio he'd received as a free gift for spending more than A$15,000 on soft furnishings with a leading Melbourne furniture warehouse. It was tricky going, and his hand was starting to shake.

Goddamnit, the place was an absolute fucking *minefield*.

Because when you buy furniture, you buy surfaces, and every major league homemaker worth her velour crowds each surface with enough breakable ornaments to fill a ceramics museum. One false move and the air would be full of needle-sharp porcelain splinters, higher velocity and more deadly than the latest generation of anti-personnel fragmentation mines (and, of course, unlocatable with a metal detector).

Ting. The tip of the aerial tapped against something cold, hard and musical. Probably the big blue pot-pourri bowl. Lundqvist froze, then reached forward with the aerial, glacier-slow and gentle as the softest breeze. Ting. Yes. Right. At least he knew where the bugger *was*. He'd been worrying about that ever since he'd millimetred his way round the standard lamp.

Thunk. The sound of metal on walnut. Bookshelves. The end wall. He flicked gingerly and tapped against the spines of big, glossy coffee-table books (*Modern Interior Design*, *This House A Home*, *Three Thousand Lounges In Full Colour* and other similar titles). He was nearly there, and nothing dislodged or smashed. Ninjas; fuck Ninjas. By this time, even the best of those black-pyjamad loons would have fallen over the footstool and be picking Wedgewood shrapnel out of his windpipe.

Delicate probing with the aerial and the fingertips located the corner of the wall, which meant that the rest would be sheer dead reckoning. The loose floorboard, under which he'd stashed the shortband radio and the spare Glock about thirty seconds before the carpet squad had turned the place into a deep-pile killing zone, was at the point of a right angle seventy centimetres out from the corner.

Lundqvist opened his big Gerber TAC II lockknife, paused and listened. He had no reason to believe that Helen wasn't still sleeping soundly, but in this game you don't last long if you confine yourself to mere existential evidence. You have to reach out and feel for the mind of the assailant, the guard, the sentry; you have to taste sleep in the air. He recognised it – the less-than-absolute stillness which means that the other person in this house isn't standing motionless behind you with a whacking great knife – and started to cut the carpet.

The Gerber is state of the art, the nearest thing to Luke

Skywalker's lightsabre ever made, but there are some materials that even Death's scythe snags on, and really expensive carpeting is one of them. As he sawed, Lundqvist could feel the exquisitely honed edge of the blade being wiped away, like spilt coffee on Formica.

His hand found the floorboard, tilted it, and burrowed, until the tip of his index finger made contact with cold, smooth plastic. Gently, quietly, he drew the package out, slit it open, and felt the radio.

'Links,' he hissed. 'Links, can you hear me? For Chrissakes, Links, this is no time for goddamn screwing around – oh, God, sorry Mrs Jotapian, is Links there, please? Links. Your *son*. Yes, sorry, *Jerome*. Thank you.'

'Hi,' crackled a voice, sounding like a PA system in an echo chamber in the quiet of the drawing-room. 'Links Jotapian here, who's this?'

'It's Lundqvist, you bastard, and keep your voice down.'

Lucky George isn't the only one who has friends, you see. Admittedly, since Crazy Mean Bernard was dragged out of a blazing chopper somewhere in Nicaragua and vanished from the face of the earth Lundqvist only has one friend, who happens to be sixteen years old and short-sighted, but it evens the score a little bit. Like, say, a single hair cast on to the balance.

'Hiya, Mr Lundqvist,' Links yelled happily. 'How ya doing? You on a job right now?'

'Yes.' Lundqvist closed his eyes and tried to find a little scrap of patience he'd overlooked previously, clinging with limpetlike tenacity to the bottom of the jar. 'That's right, Links. That's why I want you to keep your stinking voice *down*, okay?'

'Sure thing, Mr Lundqvist. Can you tell me about it, or is it a secret?'

Not for the first time, Lundqvist found himself asking why in God's name he'd allowed himself to take on a skinny, mush-brained adolescent as an apprentice. The answer was the same as always. Teenage males being, fundamentally, weirder than a lorryload of stoned ghosts, sooner or later you'll find one who's prepared to hero-worship anybody, even Kurt Lundqvist. In Jerome Jotapian, five foot eleven of virtually unfleshed bone and hideously bezitted complexion from Pittsburgh, Lundqvist had found his Robin the Boy-Wonder. And in this life, you've got to do the best with what you can get, so when a middle-aged hit-man gets a fan letter from out of the blue (*Dear Mr Lundqvist, you don't know me, I'm sixteen years old and live in Pittsburgh Pa, I really admired your last assassination and can you help me get into this line of work, I expect to get satisfactory grades in Math and English Literature and I have my own throwing knife*) he finds it hard to resist writing back.

'I finished the correspondence course stuff you sent me, by the way,' burbled Links. 'It was good. You want me to read you a bit of it now? How about the question about what plastic explosive you'd use to blow up a Roman Catholic cardinal in a small Latin American republic? I thought a lot about that, Mr Lundqvist, and finally I figured Semtex, because —'

'Not now, Links.'

'Okay, boss. Actually, Semtex isn't the answer I finally said, but you'll see when you read what —'

'Links.' Lundqvist drew a deep breath. 'I need your help.'

'Hot damn, Mr Lundqvist! Really? You mean really *help*, in a *job*?'

'Yes.' Lundqvist's face was twisted into a hideous mask of self-contempt. 'Yes, Links, and it's very important. I'm in a bit of a jam and I need you to get me out. Look, I want you to hijack me an airliner . . .'

'Wow!' The boy's whoop of joy seemed to fill the room and large parts of the surrounding outback. 'Hey, I know how to do that, it's the part you sent me the week before last, only I think that's in with the stuff Mom made me put down in the basement last week. You want to hold while I go see if I can find it?'

'No, Links, just stay where you are and keep your mouth shut for a minute.' Lundqvist stopped and herded his straggling thoughts. Talking to the boy for more than fifteen minutes was like trying to gather up a ream of A4 paper in a Force 9 gale. 'You get the plane, right? Nothing fancy, just something with enough legs to get to Australia and back. You take the thing to Australia, which is where I am now, you dump it out in the desert somewhere, you get a chopper, you come in, you get me out of here, we split. Now, do you think you can manage that?'

There was a short pause. 'I figure so, Mr Lundqvist. You'd better tell me where you are.'

Lundqvist told him.

'That's a long way away, Mr Lundqvist, do you think we can do this so that I'll still be back by half-eleven? Mom doesn't like me being out after half-eleven, you see, and —'

'You leave Mom to me,' Lundqvist interrupted, 'you just get the plane and hurry. Before that crazy bitch spends every last cent I own.'

'I beg your pardon, Mr Lundqvist?'

'Just do it, okay?'

A glider careened through the night air like a giant owl. The side door slid open, and three parachutes blossomed like inbred magnolias, drifted through the blackness and slowly folded on to the ground.

'We're here then, are we?' enquired the first spectral warrior. He was wearing a Hawaiian shirt and brightly coloured knee-length shorts and carrying a suitcase.

The Captain nodded and pulled the brim of his huge straw hat down over his eyes. 'Oh yes,' he muttered. 'We're here all right.'

'Great,' said the first spectral warrior. 'Can you let us in on the surprise yet? I mean, yes I know it's a *surprise* works outing, to make it up to us for having to go after Lundqvist and all that, but . . .'

The other spectral warrior looked around him and felt the desert sand between his toes. He sighed happily.

'Who careth?' he observed. 'Jutht tho long ath we're at the theathide, it doethn't really matter where, doeth it?'

'Exactly,' said the Captain. 'Right, we'd better be making a move before it starts getting light.'

Number Two looked at him. 'Getting light?' he said.

'Spoil the surprise,' said the Captain quickly. 'Now then, the, um, *hotel* is this way. Follow me, and, er, keep the noise down.'

'Tho ath not to wake the other gueththth, you mean?'

'Something like that.'

In the darkness some way in front of them they could just make out the outline of a long, low building, something like a cross between a garage and a cowshed, only bigger.

'Thith ith the hotel?'

'Yes, and keep your voice *down*, will you? They're very fussy about —'

'Here, skip.'

'Yes?'

'Look at all these empty packing cases. Like the sort of thing furniture comes in.' An unpleasant thought crossed Number Two's mind. 'Hey, skip, you're sure this hotel's actually *finished*? I mean, you hear stories, people turning up, hotel's still being built . . .'

The Captain made a noise in the back of his throat.

'It's not exactly a hotel, chaps,' he observed in a small voice. 'It's not, um, quite that sort of holiday.'

'It's not?'

'No.'

'How d'you mean, thkip?'

'It's more . . .' The Captain paused, choosing his words with care. 'More a sort of, well, adventure holiday really.' As he spoke he unbuttoned his jacket, drew out a .44 Super Redhawk and, from sheer force of habit, spun the cylinder.

'Cor,' said Number Two. 'It's one of those paintball things, isn't it? Where you run about with paint guns pretending to shoot people. I always wanted to try one of them.'

The Captain breathed out through his nose. 'Great stuff, Keith,' he said. 'Now's your chance.'

'Doethn't look like a paint gun to me, thkip.'

'That's all you know.'

'Yeth, but thkip, thothe paint gunth, they're much bigger and bulkier than real gunth, and that lookth like a real gun to me, don't you think . . .'

'Yeah, well.' The Captain grinned nervously. 'We want to *win*, don't we?'

'Okay, skip, if you put it that way . . .'

'I do. Vern, break the window, I'll cover you.'

'What with, thkip?'

'What do you mean, what with?'

'I'th got a blanket in my luggage, thkip, if you want to uthe that. To thtop the glath from the window. That ith what you meant, ithn't it?'

'Shut up.'

Links Jotapian had one quality that made him stand out from the crowd. Well, two; but there was still a reasonable chance that he'd grow out of one of them. The other, the useful one, was a quite disproportionate quantity of beginner's luck.

The first time he did anything, he did it well. The next time, maybe not so hot, maybe even a complete and utter disaster; but the first time, no problem.

Fortunately for all involved, this was the first time he'd ever flown a helicopter.

'Depress joystick,' he read aloud, mumbling slightly because of the torch gripped between his teeth, 'while simultaneously engaging left rudder flap.' He stared hard at the control panel for a moment – why didn't they write the names of the various controls on the panel, you'd think they'd do that, there were so many little knobs and levers. He sighed, and leafed back through the instruction manual to the diagram at the end.

'Okay,' he said aloud. 'The third from the left, just down from the cigarette lighter.' He tried it. It worked. The helicopter stopped in mid-air and hung there.

He turned to the index.

Holding the stick steady with one hand, he leafed through the manual with the other. 43, 44, 45, 46 . . .

Page 47 was missing. Or at least, it was there, in part; but there had been a coupon ('Why not enter our grand spot-the-rotor-blade competition and win the holiday of a lifetime?') on page 48 which some previous reader had clipped out and sent off. All that was left of the paragraph on landing procedure was the headline.

'Nuts,' said Links, annoyed.

He'd just have to work it out from first principles.

Lundqvist froze, one leg over the window-sill, and put his hand in front of his eyes.

'That you, Links?' he shouted, but his voice was drowned by the roar of the whirring blades and the rush of the down-draught. Blinking furiously in the glare of the chopper's landing lights, he threw out his rucksack and prepared to follow it.

'Freeze!'

He turned towards the voice, and saw a dark shape

silhouetted against the glare of the lights. The barrel of a large-calibre revolver flashed as it swung up on target.

'Hey, thkip. *Thkip!*'

'I said be *quiet*. Okay, nice and steady . . .'

'But thkip, it'th *him*. Lundqvitth. Let'th get out of here, thkip, the bathtard'th obviouthly following uth.'

'Look, for the last time, will you shut up? You, Lundqvist, nice and easy, throw down your —'

'Hey, skip.' Lundqvist could hear the anger in the voice above the scream of the blades. 'You knew, didn't you? You bleeding well set us up!'

'Yes, fine, later. Just now I'm busy, okay? Throw down your weapons, nice and . . .'

The helicopter landed.

There's beginner's luck and beginner's luck. In this case, it consisted of Links being very, very lucky indeed to be thrown clear of the chopper before it hit the deck and blew up.

A quick status check told Lundqvist that he was being hurled violently through the air by a shock-wave of hot air. That was all right by him; he'd been there before, he knew exactly how to roll with it when he landed. The good part about it was, once he landed he'd be back on even terms. And being on even terms was, in his experience, a very unfair advantage in his favour.

By contrast, the Captain of Spectral Warriors came round from a moment of temporary unconsciousness to find himself sprawled full length, still holding the revolver, on a green satin Chesterfield. Further investigation revealed a large patch of corrugated iron between him and the cushions of the sofa, the result of his having entered the house via the roof.

'Will you get off that sofa immediately,' said a cold, hard voice behind him. 'Look, you're getting blood all over it. Have you any idea how hard it is getting blood off satin?'

The second spectral warrior, for his part, came to rest halfway through a solid pine door; his head on one side, the rest of him on the other. He wriggled, tried to free himself.

'Oh *shit*,' he said.

And stopped, dumbfounded.

'Hey skip, *skip!*' he yelled. 'Hey, skip, you know what? The fall, it must have done something to me, it's cured my speech impediment, listen, I can say esses and everything . . .'

His colleague, lodged high in the shattered rafters, sighed wearily.

'That's because you're dead, idiot,' he explained.

'Oh. Hey, what a bummer, the first time in my life I can speak properly and I'm dead. You're sure I'm dead, Keith?'

'Believe me.'

'And that's what's cured my . . .?'

'Dead men don't lisp, old son. Well known fact. Don't worry about it, though, they just reincarnate us back into new bodies. Any old new bodies,' he added bitterly. 'I know. I've been there.'

'You have?'

'Sure.' He indicated his own body, what was left of it. 'You think I *chose* this?' he complained. 'Arms like bloody coat-hangers, but do they listen?'

By now, Lundqvist had landed. He opened his eyes and assessed the situation.

'Help,' he said.

There was a scuffling noise down below. 'Is that you, Mr Lundqvist?'

'Yeah. Links?'

'Right here, Mr Lundqvist.'

'Marvellous. Help me out of this tree, will you?'

'Tree?'

'Yes. This tree here.'

'The thorn tree, you mean?'

'That's the one, Links. Try hurrying, will you?'

'Coming right up, Mr Lundqvist.'

Links Jotapian scrambled to his feet and looked around.

Lesson Three had been all about using your initiative and improvising material out of unlikely objects found in the vicinity. He found the page and followed the relevant line with his finger.

Under combat conditions, he read, *a makeshift ladder may sometimes be improvised out of a broken segment of helicopter rotor blade, using only a Bowie knife and three feet of stout cord. Full instructions are given in Lesson Twelve . . .*

'Mr Lundqvist?'

'Yes?'

'You still there, Mr Lundqvist?'

'Reckon so, Links.'

'Do you think I'm ready for Lesson Twelve yet? Only I remember what you said about not taking the lessons out of sequence, because each one led naturally on from the previous, and . . .'

'Rules were made to be broken, Links. Right, listen carefully.'

Right. Fade out on Lundqvist, cut to . . .

. . . Two seagulls, black drifting shapes against a velvet sky, circling before coming in down on the glide and pitching on the remains of the roof.

'Anybody home?'

Helen of Troy stopped and looked up. She had been rubbing at the cushions of the Chesterfield, trying to get the blood out with half a lemon steeped in vinegar.

'Larry?'

'We're on the roof. Do you need rescuing?'

Helen considered for a moment. 'Not rescuing, no. I could use a little help in here, though.'

'Coming in.'

As the seagulls dropped down through the hole in the roof, the Captain of Spectral Warriors woke up. He had been sleeping peacefully ever since Helen had bashed him on the head with a copy of *Mrs Beeton's Everyday Cookery*.

'All right,' he said, staggering to his feet and levelling the

Redhawk. 'Nobody move or I'll . . .'

The barrel of the gun became suddenly heavy, its weight augmented by a perching seagull. By the time it accidentally went off, it was pointed directly at the Captain's left foot.

'Oh my God, the *carpet*!' Helen wailed. 'Look, for pity's sake, just get out of my way before you damage anything else.'

'But . . .'

'*Out!*'

The Captain wilted. It wasn't, he decided, one of his good days. Slowly and painfully he hobbled out of the room and through the front door, and was therefore just in time to be directly under the thorn tree when Links Jotapian's makeshift ladder broke.

'You all right, Mr Lundqvist?'

'Sure, Links. I think something broke my fall . . .'

(*'You knew, didn't you, skip? You knew all along, and you pretended . . .'*

'*Look, I had no choice, they threatened me . . .*'

'*I trusted him, Keith. When he said it was a holiday, I actually trusted him . . .*'

'*Hey, lads, now come on . . .*'

'*Keith, will you tell your friend that when I get reincarnated, I'm putting in for a transfer . . .*')

'Gee, that was lucky, Mr Lundqvist. I guess I didn't use enough cord where it said bind together tightly with cord, only it didn't say exactly how much cord to use, and . . .'

'Never mind.' Lundqvist pulled himself to his feet, looked round and saw Helen framed in the doorway. 'C'mon,' he hissed, 'let's get out of here before she has the whole goddamn place done out in rose damask.'

Two or three hours later, Lucky George came by with the Transit to pick them up.

'You've been enjoying yourself, haven't you?' he observed.

Helen shrugged.

'So?' she said. 'I *like* nice furniture and things, you know that. George, don't you sometimes think it'd be fun if we had a little place of our own that I could do up and make all nice and —'

'No.'

'You could have your own little study,' she said wistfully, 'for all your books and magic stuff and things, and we could —'

'No.'

'Oh.' Helen clicked her tongue. 'Never mind,' she said, 'it was only a thought.'

'Good.'

'Anyway,' she said, producing a lighter and a can of paraffin, 'I think Lundqvist's gone off the kidnapping idea. Curious,' she went on, splashing paraffin, 'how anyone could be so *dozy*...'

'You missed a bit.'

'Did I? Oh yes. I mean, kidnapping *me*. After the last time and all ...'

George nodded. 'All brains and no intelligence,' he said. 'Can I do the setting alight? You know how I love setting light to soft furnishings.'

Helen smiled fondly. 'Go on, then. Only George, the labels all said *Fire retardant* and *Specially treated for your safety and peace of mind*, do you think they'll ...?'

George grinned. 'If I say so,' he replied.

CHAPTER
FIFTEEN

THE half-life of Time is notoriously long.

Being neck-deep in boiling shit is the mother of invention, as the chronological technicians say, and some of the things they've tried have been quite staggeringly ingenious, if futile. Sealing toxic temporal waste up in lead-lined cylinders and burying it is completely passé now; recently the trend has been towards boiling it, sending it back through hairline dimensional faults in the hope of setting up a Moebius effect, or selling it to the gullible citizens of Plato's Republic in big wooden crates marked 'Tractor Spares'. These devices have taken small deposits out of circulation; however, in the time it takes to get rid of, say, 4,000 metric tonnes this way, twice as much of the loathsome stuff has built up and is leaking merrily away into the environment, poisoning the fish and causing innocent parties all over the cosmos to seduce their great-grandmothers and be late for their own funerals.

In desperation, some authorities have been illicitly shipping it out into the future, which doesn't help exactly but at least means that it becomes somebody else's problem.

Unless something is done about it pretty soon, the boffins say, the whole unhappy mess is pretty soon going to go critical and start doing horrible things to the nature of reality. Already, they report (from the relative security of their nostalgia-lined bunkers), there are rumours of the spontaneous occurrence of the dreaded isotope Overtime.

The only possible solution is recycling. Maddeningly, however, nobody has the faintest idea how to go about it.

Nobody who's been asked, anyway.

One of the few people not worried sick about the problem is Kurt Lundqvist. His own proposal for getting rid of it (loading it into canisters and dropping it from a great height on South-East Asia) having been rejected, he dismissed the matter from his mind and turned his attention to more immediate issues.

Such as nailing Lucky George. Dawn over the outer suburbs of Aspen, Colorado, found him sitting on his porch with the remains of his fifth pint of black coffee and nothing to show for his pains but a pile of screwed up bits of paper.

He'd tried direct attack. He'd tried abduction. Dammit, what else was there?

Like a dog returning to its own vomit, his mind kept coming full circle back to the idea of hostages. Kidnap one of Lucky George's friends, his instincts shouted at him, and you have Lucky George himself, because the man lives and dies by his friends. The true professional prefers to attack the enemy through his strengths rather than his weaknesses – weaknesses are carefully guarded, strengths are taken for granted – and what George really had going for him, apart from a repertoire of largely meretricious magical effects, was a quite depressingly huge network of friends and acquaintances stretching throughout space and time, but centred on the University of Wittenberg, Class of '88.

For the twelfth time that night, Lundqvist picked up that year's UOW Yearbook and flicked through, hoping that a name would catch his eye.

Martin Luther (Theology). HRH Hamlet, Prince of Denmark (Philosophy, Politics and Economics). Hieronymus

176 · Tom Holt

Bosch (Design Studies). Cristoforo Colombo (Geography). Leonardo da Vinci (Business Studies).

The sun rose on the Rocky Mountains; and suddenly Lundqvist had the answer. Simple. Of all the friends of Lucky George, who had ultimately achieved the most?

No contest.

He who achieves the most has the most to lose.

Mr Van Appin leant back in his chair and rubbed his chin. Right now, he was beginning to wish he'd never taken Lucky George on as a client in the first place.

Sure, there had been the good times. The patent applications. The intellectual property work. The trial itself, and then the appeal. There had been big money down along the line (it's not every client who pays in genuine functional bottomless purses), not to mention the prestige and the cachet and, of course, the travelling expenses. But you had to take the holistic view; and when the presence of Kurt Lundqvist in one's waiting room at nine o'clock on a Monday morning is taken into account, even a lawyer may be heard to speculate that money isn't everything.

Pure bullshit, of course. It is. But even the Pope has doubts sometimes.

Which reminded him. He flipped the intercom.

'Sonia,' he said. 'Ask John Paul if he wouldn't mind coming back at half-past, and show Mr Lundqvist in.'

In Mr Lundqvist came, like Death into the world; sat in the client's chair and put his feet up on the desk.

'Kurt,' said Van Appin with insincere cheerfulness, 'always a pleasure, how's business?'

'Slow,' Lundqvist growled. 'Listen. I need a lawyer.'

Van Appin quivered slightly. 'Delighted to help in any way I can,' he said. 'Matrimonial problems?' he hazarded.

'No,' Lundqvist replied, 'I need to borrow a lawyer. Not you, somebody else. You got any?'

Mr Van Appin looked at Lundqvist over his steepled hands. 'When would you be needing him?' he asked.

'1492.'

'I'll see who we've got available.'

He swivelled his chair and tapped a few keys on the keyboard. The screen flickered.

'Any particular sort of lawyer?'

'Property lawyer.' Lundqvist laughed, a sound like sandpaper on sharkskin. 'Little development project I got in mind.'

'In 1492?'

Lundqvist shrugged. 'Tax reasons,' he explained.

'Bit out of your usual line, isn't it?'

'It pays to diversify.'

'True.'

Lundqvist leant forward. 'One other thing,' he said. 'What we're talking here is utmost good faith stuff. I don't want anyone to know, you got that? Especially any of your other clients.'

'Hey, Kurt.' Mr Van Appin gestured his protest. 'I got my ethical position to think of.'

He hesitated. For some reason he was finding it hard to concentrate on anything apart from the muzzle of the .40 Glock that had suddenly appeared in Lundqvist's hand.

'Ethical,' he said slowly, 'schmethical. Hell, Kurt, what are friends for?'

Lundqvist considered for a while. 'Decoys,' he replied.

Imagine . . .

You can't, of course. It's impossible. Nobody in the plush suburb of History we call the twentieth century could possibly conceive of the stunning, mind-stripping shock of seeing, for the first time . . .

It is 1492. Three tiny wooden shells bob precariously on the meniscus of a blue-grey infinity. High in the rigging, a man turns, stares, opens his mouth to shout and closes it again.

There is, he decides, no tactful way to put this. But he's going to do his best, anyway.

'Hey, skip!'

On the deck below, a short, weary individual looks up from a chessboard and shouts back, 'Well?'

'Skip . . .'

'What's the matter, Hernan?'

'Skip . . .' Hernan bit his tongue. 'I spy,' he said, 'with my little eye, something beginning with A.'

'You what?'

'With A, skip. I spy it. With my, um, little eye.' Hernan drew in further supplies of air. 'It's a game, skip. You've got to guess what it is I've —'

'Have you been at the applejack again? You know it's reserved for the scurvy.'

'Go on, skip, be a sport.'

'Look . . .'

'Three guesses?'

Columbus sighed. Sixty-one days he'd been cooped up on this floating strawberry-punnet with these idiots. A lesser man, one without his inexhaustible patience, would have blown the ship up by now.

'Albatross.'

'No.'

'Aurora borealis.'

'No. Hey skip, you aren't even *trying* . . .'

'Okay, okay.' Columbus thought hard. When dealing with morons, he'd learnt the hard way, the trick is to think like a moron. This is no mean accomplishment. 'Arquebus,' he said. 'Am I right?'

Hernan lifted his eyes and gazed for two seconds at the distant coastline, the one that quite definitely wasn't India, and said to himself, Look, why me, whoever says it first is going to get lynched, they'll know soon enough without me telling them. 'You got it, skip,' he replied. 'Oh, and by the way, land ahoy.'

'What did you just say?'

'Land, skip. Ahoy. Just over there on the left.'

'What ahoy? Speak up, you're muttering.'

'Land, skip. L for laundry, A for Amer . . . I mean arquebus, N for . . .'

As Columbus jerked like a shot deer and started capering hysterically up and down the deck, Hernan leant back in the crow's nest, shrugged and found the remains of his apple. He'd been nursing it along, one nibble per day, for a fortnight, saving it for a special occasion. He looked at it and chucked it over the side.

A freak gust of wind carried up to him scraps of the conversation buzzing away below – Roderigo was saying that as soon as they got in he was going to have a roghan ghosh with spicy dall and nan bread, Diego was saying no, make mine a chicken tikka with pilau rice and spoonfuls of mango chutney. The poor fools, Hernan thought. It was going to be bad enough when the crew found out, but that was likely to be nothing compared to the embarrassment that would ensue when the news was broken to their Most Catholic Majesties back in Madrid. Well, no, ma'am, not India *as such*, in fact more like a clump of hot, scrawny little islands populated by savages with no commercially useful exports of any kind; we were thinking of calling it San Salvador.

Maybe they could just sort of hush the whole thing up. Forget about it. Pretend they got to the edge of the world, turned round and came straight back.

Nah.

Hernan shook his head sadly. Some fool would be bound to let something slip, and then where would they all be?

Anyway. Hernan leant his elbows on the rail of the crow's nest and took a long, hard look. Okay, so it wasn't up to much, but it was a new country. A new continent, maybe. And here he was, the first man ever to set eyes on it. That was something. Not much perhaps, but something.

Wrong.

Because, at the precise moment when Columbus was ordering the lads to lower a rowing boat and feverishly trying to remember the exchange rate for moidores into rupees, a small, bedraggled man in a Brooks Brothers suit and waders was dragging a rubber dinghy behind some bushes on the seashore and opening a small suitcase.

The man was one Morrie Goldman, and the suitcase contained a portable fax machine with the special digital transtemporal wave shift function.

He looked at his watch. Mr Van Appin had been very insistent that he log in the precise moment of landfall. Having dictated a note into his pocket dictaphone, he switched on the fax and started typing out the message on his laptop word processor.

Not exactly an orthodox assignment, he reflected as he typed. Whizz back through time to the late fifteenth century, go to San Salvador, arriving at such and such a time, send a fax to the Land Registry stating time of arrival, and then clear off. Not perhaps the most complex matter he'd ever handled from a legal standpoint, but the travelling expenses were going to be just out of this world.

From: Maurice Goldman, Messrs Van Appin & Co
To: The Chief Registrar, Central Land Registry
Message: Arrived 3.25 p.m. precisely. Please accept this communication as our indefeasible claim of title to the continent edged red on the plan annexed hereto and confirm registration by return of fax.

He paused for a moment. If he was discovering this place, wherever in hell it was (geography wasn't his thing), he supposed he ought to give it a name, if only to enable it to be sufficiently identified.

Newly discovered territory to be known as Goldmannia.

No. You couldn't call a country Goldmannia. It lacked that certain something.

He deleted Goldmannia and typed in Mauretania.

No. There was somewhere else called that. Try again.

He deleted Mauretania and . . .

Nice snappy name. Something that'd look good on the stamps. The United States of *something*. Life is all right in *something*. The business of *something* is business. The *something* dream. Bye bye, Miss *something* Pie.

It was on the tip of his tongue.

He typed in Lundqvistia, hit the Send button and made himself scarce.

Scroll fast forward through Time, until the monitor reads 1996, and hold. The place: the Polo Lounge, Valhalla. Christopher Columbus discovered, nursing a long, cool drink and smoking a big cigar.

Not, of course, that Valhalla's what it was. Gone are the deep leather armchairs, the inedible food, the self-effacing spectral waiters. Evening dress is no longer a prerequisite for the Carousing Hall, and people no longer glare at you if you refrain from shouting in the Fighting Room. Mead has been replaced by fiddly things in stemmed glasses in the Members Bar, and the iron-corseted Valkyrie barmaids have been quietly replaced by less statuesque, softer beings with names like Cindi, Nikki and Cheryl. Nevertheless, it still has a certain cachet, and visitors still steal the headed notepaper from the library.

'Paging Mr Columbus. Visitor for you at the front desk. Thank you.'

Columbus got up and made his languid way to the lobby, his mind still lovingly turning over the thought of next month's ground rent payment. There were those, he knew, who referred to him behind his back as the biggest slum landlord in the universe, but that was just jealousy.

'You said there was a message for me?'

'Over there, Mr Columbus, by the fountain of milk and honey.'

'Him in the mac?'

'That's him, Mr Columbus.'

'Right.'

He finished his drink, placed the empty glass on the desk and wandered over to the stranger . . .

Who served him with a Notice to Quit.

Mr Van Appin leant back in his chair and replaced the telephone.

'That was Goldman,' he said. 'Everything according to plan. Columbus should be getting the eviction papers any minute now.'

The muzzle of the .40 Glock lifted and disappeared inside Lundqvist's jacket. 'Good,' he said. 'Now then, how long'll it take to get vacant possession?'

Mr Van Appin shrugged. 'Say three to four weeks. Unless they appeal, of course. They may have grounds, I couldn't say offhand. This is pretty much a grey area so far as the law is concerned.' Perfectly safe to say that, of course; as any lawyer will tell you, the law is full of the most amazingly large and expensive grey areas, so that seen from the air it resembles nothing so much as the Confederate army camped on a shale beach on a cloudy day.

'Do it in three,' growled Lundqvist. 'I want those bastards out of there as soon as possible, you got that?'

Mr Van Appin twitched slightly. 'When you say bastards, Kurt, you mean . . .'

'The Americans,' Lundqvist replied. 'All of them.' He grinned. 'Goddamn trespassers. Get the place cleared, okay? And make sure they leave it clean and tidy when they go, because I might just have another tenant lined up.'

'Yeah?'

Lundqvist nodded. 'I was thinking,' he said, 'of going into the private prison business. Long term, violent offenders. New York. It's just a matter of putting a few extra bars on the odd window and cleaning the streets up a bit, and there we are, ready to start trading.'

Mr Van Appin made a soft, lawyerly clicking noise with his tongue. 'I don't want to sound alarmist in any way,' he said, 'but something tells me the bailiffs aren't going to find it that easy. Maybe you should just stick to raising the rent a bit. You know, gradually, a few cents per annum over say the next three hundred —'

'Vacant possession, Van Appin. And if the bailiffs have any trouble,' Lundqvist said, smiling thoughtfully, 'just let me know. I haven't done an eviction since Atlantis.'

Mr Van Appin swallowed. 'That was an eviction, huh?'

'We all have our different methods.'

'I guess so, Kurt. Only . . .'

'Just do it.'

'Okay.'

Lundqvist rose. 'A pleasure doing business with you, Van Appin,' he said, adding, 'For me, anyhow,' and left. After he'd gone, Van Appin sat quite still for well over a minute, thinking Oh shit.

His special lawyer's sixth sense was telling him that there could possibly be a bit of comeback on this one. A pity, but there it was.

Lundqvistia, he said to himself. Jesus God, what an awful name for a continent.

Not a patch, he couldn't help thinking, on Van Appin's Land, or something like that.

'George?'

'Chris! Great to hear from you. How's things?'

'Not so hot, George. In fact, I've got a bit of a problem.'

Lucky George frowned and reached for the scratch-pad that lived beside the phone. 'Fire away, Chris, tell me all about it.'

On the other end of the line, Christopher Columbus took a deep breath, said, 'Well, it's like this;' and told him. After he'd finished, George sat for a while, chewing the end of his pencil.

'You still there, George?'

'Still here, Chris. Bit awkward, isn't it?'

'Yes.'

'And the bailiffs are going in – when, did you say?'

'A week's time, George. Backed up by four million spectral warriors from the Court Office.'

'Suitcases on the pavement time, huh?'

'You could say that.'

George doodled a few wavy lines, coloured in the 'O's in *While You Were Out* and chewed his lip for a moment. Then he smiled.

'Don't worry about a thing, Chris,' he said at last. 'I think I can see what we're going to have to do, and it shouldn't be much of a problem.' He paused. 'At least, it won't be if we can get the right help.'

'Anyone I know?'

'Old friend of ours, Chris. Leave it with me, all right? It's really just a question of hydraulics.'

'*Hydraulics?*'

George nodded. 'Hydraulics, Chris. Be seeing you.'

CHAPTER
SIXTEEN

EUROBOSCH, the theme park to end all theme parks, was on its way. Five hundred thousand spectral construction workers laboured night and day to bring into being the most sensational leisure facility in the history of Time and Space. And all because one man dared to dream the impossible nightmare.

The man in question sat in the window of the site office, looking out over the muddy shambles and trying to discern any resemblance, however slight, to the vision of unalloyed nastiness he could see in his mind's eye. It wasn't easy.

Take, for example, the helter-skelter. This took the form of a seventy-foot-high hourglass, on which was seated a stomach-churning bird-headed demon, its feet improbably thrust into two wine-jars, meditatively nibbling on the leg of a woman taken in adultery. On paper, it had looked fine. Translated into three dimensions, it was quite another sort of nightmare.

The basic structure hadn't been a problem; you've got your reinforced steel joists, your basic chipboard panels, your sixty-by-thirty sheets of galvanised. You bung those in with a few girders braced crosswise for rigidity, everything fine so far. Next you put in your actual helter-skelter track, starting under the demon's armpit and exiting rather ingeniously through the raised rump of a sinner being hideously mauled by a nine-foot-high animated tree; no problem, the builders' merchants just happen to have a continuous spiral sheet of anodised aluminium long enough to do the job and going cheap owing to a cancelled order. It's then that the fun starts.

Bird-headed demons are, to put it bluntly, a pain. You can go for your injection-moulded propylene, but you can bet your life that the two halves won't fit flush, and for the price of just one moulding you could afford to panel the Crab Nebula in French walnut. On the other hand, you can opt for good old expanded polystyrene, just so long as you're prepared to put up with bits crumbling off in wet weather and the whole bloody thing threatening to take off in a high wind. Fibreglass would be too brittle because of the length of the adulteress's leg, and anything else is out because of the weight factor and/or the aggravation of getting the sonofabitch thing installed without all the pointy bits getting broken off. Finally you persuade the money men to lash out on the injection mouldings, only to find that the pattern makers are booked solid for the next three months and when they eventually can get around to doing it, they've quarrelled irrevocably with the moulding contractors and refuse to lift so much as a Stanley knife without fifty per cent of the contract price up front. Just when you've ironed all that out and sorted out the building inspectors and the fire inspectors and the little arsehole from the planning department who's always wittering on about not exceeding the overall permitted height, the quantity surveyor (who plays golf with the company accountant who wants to see the whole project called off) tells the board that there's a firm down the road he knows who'd do the whole job for forty per cent less, including road haulage and wiring up the psychedelic lights. The moulding contractors are by now threatening to sue for breach of contract, and quite possibly the aluminium strip (which hasn't had its three coats of primer because the painters are waiting until the sound system's wired in) has turned all grey and flaky and needs to be replaced from scratch. Finally, the Finance Director drops by on his monthly tour of inspection and says, yes, love the basic concept, but really don't you think we need it a bit more, well, *yukky*, how about a couple of skull-headed snakes slithering up and down the main uprights?

The phone rang. Ronnie Bosch, his eyes riveted to an outsize polystyrene eggshell just starting to work free from its anchor points on the side of the Ferris Wheel, groped with his left hand and picked it up.

'Bosch here,' he said.

'Ronnie.'

Bosch closed his eyes. 'You *again*,' he hissed. 'For crying out loud, George, this really isn't the best time for me right now...'

'Won't keep you a moment, old son. Just a little job I need some help with. Basically, all I need is ...'

With fervour, Hieronymus Bosch told Lucky George what, in his opinion, Lucky George really needed. It was pretty far-fetched, anatomically speaking, but compared with some of the feats of engineering he'd pulled off in the last few months, it would probably have been a piece of cake.

'The project getting you down, huh?'

'You could say that, George. Like, how the hell am I supposed to suspend a seven-hundred-ton plywood and fibreglass mandolin with worms crawling out of the soundbox forty feet in the air without using an overhead crane because the planners say it'd be seven feet too high for the surrounding environment?'

George laughed. 'Easy,' he said. 'Look, all I really need from you for this little job of mine is —'

'*Easy?*'

'Sure. I thought you were joking when you said you were having a problem. You built the mandolin yet?'

Bosch laughed mirthlessly. 'Not much point, really, until

I've sussed out how to fly the bastard thing.'

'Great. You don't make it out of plywood, Ron, you make it out of rubber. Aluminium tube frame, reinforced rubber skin, fill the bugger with helium and you're well away. Just make sure it's securely tethered with a few steel hawsers to stop it wandering off. As I was saying . . .'

Bosch nearly dropped the phone. 'George,' he said, 'that's bloody brilliant. Hang about, though, what about the volume-to-weight ratio on the worms, because . . .'

There followed a few minutes of technical discussion; after which, Bosch drew a deep breath and said, 'What was it you said you wanted?'

'Got a pencil?'

'Yes.'

'Right, then listen. First, I want you to drill me a hole in the bottom of the Marianas Trench.'

Bosch broke the pencil lead. 'Fine,' he said. 'I just stroll out on my day off with a snorkel and a bradawl, do I? Or shall I get the YTS lad to do it?'

'Next,' George went on, 'I'll need some nice, tough, hydraulic hose.' He specified how much. 'And a steam turbine, Ron; nothing fancy, just a good, old-fashioned piece of kit to work the pump. I expect you've got something of the sort lying about in one of the engine sheds down at your place. I seem to remember there being all sorts of useful bits and pieces quietly rusting away down there. Get some of the men to give it a rub over with a wire brush, she'll be as right as rain.'

'I'm not listening, George. I mean, thanks a lot for the tip with the balloon, I definitely owe you one, but this is —'

'I think that's about it,' George said, checking the list he'd scribbled on the back of a beer mat. 'No, sorry, I tell a lie, there's just one more major bit I need. Can you rustle me up a hydraulic ram? Hold on, I'll just give you the specifications.'

'George . . .' Bosch was just about to give notice of putting the phone down when his professional curiosity got the better of him. 'George,' he asked cautiously, 'what the hell are you planning to do with all this gear?'

George told him.

Engineers are a bit like mountain-climbers; not in the sense of having bushy beards and no toes because of frostbite, but because the one thing they really can't resist is a challenge. Ask an engineer to change the washer on a leaking tap and he'll tell you to get lost. Show him a design for making water roll uphill without pressure and drive a flywheel and ask him if he thinks it might work, and before you know it he's reaching for his Vernier calipers and his slide rule, and all you've got to do is decide whether you want the flywheel in pale fawn or avocado.

'You're kidding.'

'No I'm not,' George replied. 'It's basically a very simple design. Big but simple. Do you think you can do it?'

Hieronymus Bosch hesitated, his mind a Cemetary Ridge of conflicting emotions. On the one hand, his rational sense was telling him, No way, stay well clear of this, if they ever caught you at it then bird-headed demons would be Beatrix Potter compared with what they'd do to you. Louder and more insistent was the clamour in the genes, Man the Toolmaker whispering, Yes, and come to think of it there's that old molybdenum steel acroprop left over from the second day of the Creation, all you'd have to do is stone a couple of thou. off the edge, mill it square on the top and there's your basic material ... The temptation pounded against the sides of his better judgement; as if Eve had come sidling up to Adam with a plate of apple charlotte with double whipped cream and a glacé cherry.

'I dunno,' he said. 'I'd need to see drawings.'

'I'll fax them through now.'

'Somebody's bound to notice.'

'Just tell 'em it's for the project. Say it'll save them money.'

'You do realise it's going to be touch and go with the wall thicknesses, what with all that internal pressure.'

'Don't make me laugh, Ron. Listen . . .'

And that, of course, was that. As soon as the detailed specifications started flowing up and down the telephone lines, it was all a foregone conclusion.

'Thanks, Ron,' said Lucky George. 'Oh, one last thing, we've got a forty-eight-hour deadline. A bit tight, but you can do it.'

'George . . .'

'Anybody else, I'd be worried, Ron. Absolute confidence in you, though. I'll get those plans off to you this minute.'

'George . . .'

'Ciao.'

Having replaced the receiver, George wandered out on to the balcony and sat for a few minutes, watching the gondolas go by.

'Well?' asked Helen, joining him with the coffee. 'Any luck?'

George nodded. 'No problem,' he said. 'Ronnie's a good lad, very suggestible. Mind you,' he added, dipping his top lip in the froth, 'his end of the job's the easy bit.'

Helen frowned. 'By easy,' she said, after a moment's thought, 'you mean extremely difficult, don't you?'

'Difficult?' George shook his head. 'Piece of cake to a man with the facilities at his disposal that Ronnie's got.' He sighed. 'Good lord, if I could lay my hands on all the plant and machinery he's got to play about with, I could . . .'

Helen smiled indulgently and removed the sugar bowl, from which George had been absent-mindedly saturating his coffee for the last fifteen seconds. 'When we get married and settle down,' she said, 'I think I'll let you have a little shed, down at the bottom of the garden. You can keep all your bits and pieces in that, and then we won't have them cluttering up the house.'

Below their balcony, the olive-drab waters of the Canal Grande rubbed catlike against the piles on which the house rested. Like most houses in Venice, more or less the only thing keeping it from slithering into the lagoon was force of habit, with just a soupçon of artistic licence. George had bought it as a pied-à-eau some four hundred and sixteen years ago, and one of the many things he was looking forward to doing once this dratted Lundqvist business was out of the way was chasing up the descendants of twelve generations of tenants for quite substantial arrears of rent.

'This house you keep on about,' he said. 'It's going to be terribly inconvenient, you realise.'

'What is?'

'Having to step over my dead body every time you go through the front door.'

'Nonsense,' Helen replied. 'I'll have a little bridge built over you.'

'All right,' George said, stifling a yawn. 'If you're so dead set on having a house, what's wrong with this one?'

'What, this place?'

'Why not? It works. It does the job. It's got four walls, and I'm pretty sure I saw a roof lying about somewhere, the last time I looked.'

'Don't be silly.'

'Oh.' George shrugged. 'Anyway, that's a bit academic, really, just at the moment, what with Lundqvist still on the loose and everything. Strictly between you and me, that chap's beginning to get on my nerves.'

'You don't say.'

George nodded. 'All right, at the moment he's not posing any direct threat. Actually, I'm not particularly bothered when he is. So long as he's out in the open where I can see him, bless his little heart, I can generally deal with him without too much bother.' He frowned, and rubbed his lips with his knuckles. 'But this business of hassling my friends really isn't on.

Something's got to be done about it.'

'True.' Helen gazed out over the canal, watching a pair of slightly larger than average seagulls hovering over a gondolaful of German tourists. Every few minutes, they would suddenly dive like Stukas, come up on the gondola's blind side and pass uncalled-for remarks in German directly behind the head of a member of the party. During the diversion thereby occasioned, one of them would then bite a further chunk out of the little girl's ice-cream cone. 'Easier said than done, though, don't you think? I mean, if there was a simple way of stopping the wretched man from bothering us, we'd probably have thought of it by now. It's not exactly a new problem, is it?'

'Not a simple way, no. On the other hand, simplicity isn't everything. I'd settle for fiendishly complicated like a shot, if only I could think of something.' He lifted his cup, found it empty, smiled into it and burnt his tongue on the result, thereby conclusively demonstrating that his mind wasn't on the job. 'Anyway, in the meantime we've got to do something about this Columbus thing.'

'The difficult bit.'

George grinned. 'Comparatively difficult,' he said. 'All we really need to wrap it all up is a good, dirty presidential election.'

'Turning to item five on the agenda,' said the Finance Director, 'can we start with you, please, Steve? Any new marketing initiatives in the pipeline?'

The Sales Director picked up his pencil and revolved it slowly between his claws. 'One or two balls in the air right now,' he replied. 'Something we're very keen on at the moment is the Damn-A-Friend promotion.' He turned to face the projector screen, and picked up the remote control. 'Just to remind you of the basic thinking on this one, the idea is that if you the punter can bring about the damnation of a fellow human being between the first of February and the end of

May, you win a recurring dream holiday for two in the guilt complex of your choice. This one works particularly well as we've got very substantial stockpiles of guilt at the moment, and we don't seem to be getting through the stuff nearly as quickly as we used to.'

'I blame the psychiatrists,' interrupted the Personnel Director, waking from a light doze. 'Damn interfering little sods, always mucking up perfectly good personality disorders and stopping people murdering their fathers. Heaven's too good for 'em, if you ask me.'

'Thank you, Dennis. Anything else, Steve? Got anything lined up for the winter season?'

'Ants.'

The Finance Director looked at his colleague over the rim of his spectacles. 'Ants, Steve?'

The Sales Director nodded eagerly. 'That's it,' he said. 'It's like a sort of sequel, really, or maybe spin-off's the word I'm looking for.'

There was a brief moment of puzzled silence, broken by the Company Secretary.

'Oh I *see*, you mean as in "Lord of the". Nice idea.'

The Sales Director nodded his head in acknowledgement. 'Yeah,' he said. 'I mean, flies, all a bit passé for the Nineties. What I had in mind was, every time you break a commandment, you get a voucher thing. So many points, depending on which commandment and the level of breach. Then, when you've collected enough vouchers, you can cash them in for ants. And when you've got *x* amount of ants, you write in for your badge and become a Deputy Lord. Pretty neat scheme, I thought.'

'Sorry to interrupt,' broke in the Finance Director, 'but why ants particularly?'

'We've got a lot of 'em,' the Sales Director replied. 'Anyway, when you've collected enough vouchers, you automatically go through to the prize draw. Pretty straightforward really.'

'Gimmicky.'

'Yes, thank you, Harry.' The Sales Director glowered at his colleague from Production. 'Actually, I don't accept that it *is* gimmicky. Good, solid marketing ploy, year's duration to start with and we'll see how we go from there. And best of all, the raw materials aren't going to cost us a penny. Look, I'll run a few projected figures up on the screen and you can see for yourselves.'

When the slide-show finally ground to a halt, the Finance Director thanked his colleague and drew the attention of the meeting to the final scheduled item.

'Any suggestions?' he asked.

There was a silence as deep and awkward as a badly-flooded gutter. At last, the Personnel Director raised his hand.

'I've been thinking,' he said. 'Why don't we just parole the bastard?'

The Finance Director looked at him. 'Go on,' he said.

'Well,' continued Personnel, 'I think it's the obvious answer. There's no chance I can see of getting him back. Security's made no headway at all, Lundqvist's been a complete wash-out, and every time we even try anything, the bugger makes us all look like complete idiots. That holiday stunt . . .'

'Yes. We'll skate over that one, shall we?'

'All I'm saying is,' said Personnel, 'why not just accept the situation and put it on a regular footing by letting him out early. Formally, I mean.'

'Hang on,' said the Finance Director. 'You're not suggesting we say he's been released early on grounds of good behaviour, are you, because —'

'Quite the opposite. Since when has good behaviour been a plus mark in these parts anyway?'

The Finance Director shook his head. 'Good idea in its way, Dennis, but unfortunately not possible. Not up to us, parole. We can recommend, of course, but in the circumstances . . .'

'Oh I dunno,' interjected the Sales Director. 'Look at it this way. If the guy's basically virtuous and good and fit to be at large, naturally it stands to reason he'd want to be out of here as soon as possible. I mean, the place is simply crawling with villains, you could get into bad company. I'm all for it myself.'

'No,' said the Finance Director, 'and that's final. Well, I think that just about wraps things up ... No, just one more item. EuroBosch.'

A slight ripple of pleasure lapped round the boardroom table. It was the one project everyone approved of; very high-profile, very prestige, very image-enhancing, very Us. The Finance Director cleared his throat.

'Memo from H.B.,' he said. 'Apparently, he wants permission to –' The Finance Director squinted at the paper in front of him. '– to drill a hole in the bottom of the sea somewhere off America, install a steam turbine on Number Six furnace, and – you know, his handwriting is *abysmal* – and he says there's a bit of old metal rod he wants from out of the Bonded Stores. He doesn't say what he wants it for, but I for one wouldn't understand if he did. Any objections?'

Thick as autumnal leaves that strow the brooks in Vallombrosa, where the Etrurian shades high over-arched embower, the Directors shook their heads, until the boardroom resembled nothing so much as a display of car rear-window ornaments produced by the design team for *Alien*. If Ronnie wanted it, Ronnie could have it.

'That's fine, then,' said the Finance Director, initialling the pink chit. 'Same time next week?'

CHAPTER SEVENTEEN

'WHO, me?'

Lucky George leant forwards slightly. A persuasive enough man at the best of times, he was giving it everything he'd got. An Arab coming up against George in this frame of mind would have found himself the bewildered owner of many cubic tons of very expensive sand.

'Yes, Lenny,' he cooed, '*you*. You've got just what it takes to be a success in politics, hasn't he, Helen? I mean, you'd vote for him, wouldn't you?'

'Like a shot,' Helen replied, not looking up from her callisthenics book. She'd just got to the bit where the heroine had wrapped her left leg round her neck, with the heel sticking in her right ear; and she wanted to find out how the hell the author was going to engineer a happy ending out of that lot.

'There, you see? The women's vote tied up, just like that. C'mon, Lennie, don't be a loser all your life. Just for once . . .'

'I dunno.' Leonardo da Vinci stroked his beard, a full-time job in itself. 'To be absolutely frank with you, George, I don't think I'm really, you know, qualified to stand. Like, you know, not eligible.'

Lucky George gestured impatiently. 'Rubbish,' he said. 'What on earth gave you that impression, Len?'

'Well,' said Leonardo, counting on his fingers, 'number one, I'm Italian. I always thought that to be president of the USA you had to be American . . .'

George laughed. 'No problem,' he said. 'We get you US citizenship first, naturally. And then, of course, you've got the Italian vote sewn up before you even start.'

'Retrospectively, even,' Helen murmured. Nobody heard her.

'Also,' Leonardo went on, 'I'm dead.'

'So?'

Leonardo waved his hands feebly. 'So I guess that's not exactly going to inspire confidence in the electorate, George. I mean, *Vote for Da Vinci, he would have made a good president if only he'd lived* isn't the best sort of platform you could —'

'On the contrary,' George replied. 'Look at the Kennedys. Secret of their success, that was.'

Leonardo shrugged. 'Odd you should mention them,' he said. 'Did you know that it was really the Milk Marketing Board who were behind the —?'

'Besides,' George went on, ignoring him, 'there you are, dead, running for the White House, that's the disabled vote in the can, right from the word go. Plus, being dead, I guess that makes you a sort of minority group figure . . .'

'Being *dead*? A *minority*? You're crazy, man, there's millions of us out there.'

'Yes,' George replied, 'but not that many of you down here, that's the whole point. Being dead, you say, that really gives you an insight into the problems of the victims of bigotry. Because when you're dead, you add, every man's hand is against you. Segregation, reservations, cheap dead trash – you've got it absolutely made, Lenny, you really have. The only thing that surprises me is why you haven't stood before.'

'Better things to do with your time, probably.'

'Be quiet, Helen, you're not helping. Come on, Lenny. What have you got to lose?'

'All right.' Leonardo backed away slightly. 'But anyway, isn't it a bit academic? I mean, the election's tomorrow, there really isn't time . . .'

George smiled. 'Is that all you're worried about?' he said. 'Look. I anticipated you'd jump at the chance, so I took the precaution of registering you as a candidate . . .'

'You did what?'

'Retrospectively, of course. Easy if you know how. And before you say you haven't got time to do any campaigning, I managed to get you on the Ed Sullivan show – he's a friend of mine, it wasn't a problem – so you'll have at least fifteen minutes prime time, that ought to be enough. The trouble with most campaigns is, you see, they're too long'

'But . . .'

'Which reminds me,' said Lucky George. 'You're on air in about twenty minutes, so if I were you I'd be getting along.'

With retrospect, the pundits say, it was clear the moment the Utah results came in that it was going to be a Da Vinci landslide.

By 3.20 a.m., the results were in from fourteen states. All had voted Da Vinci.

By 5 a.m., it was all over.

Interviewed on the Johnny Carson show later that fateful day and asked to explain why the pollsters had once again got it completely wrong, the head of the Gallup organisation said in his defence that the election had turned on factors which couldn't have been foreseen at the time the polls were taken. Such factors as (among others):

(a) a personal endorsement of the Da Vinci platform by the Mona Lisa, interviewed live on NBC five minutes before voting began.

(b) the invasion of New York by hundreds of thousands of strange, unearthly gibbering fiends threatening to burn the city down if Da Vinci wasn't elected.

(c) the simultaneous withdrawal by all the other candidates, accompanied by a passionate appeal from each one to vote for Da Vinci and a better America.

And if that wasn't enough, he continued, wiping his forehead with a large red silk handkerchief, there was the intrinsic merit of the Da Vinci manifesto to consider. Admittedly, it had only been released hours before the election, but its basic inspired simplicity made that a plus rather than a minus. When a guy stands up and says, Listen, America, all we need do in order to stop inflation, restore full employment, revitalise the dollar, put the USA back in her rightful place as the leader of the free world and give those scumsucking Ayrabs a stomping they'll never forget is to link up every building from the Rockies to the Rio Grande with a network of steel scaffolding pipes, not forgetting to install at least ten heavy-duty cup-hooks on all roofs, gable-ends and porches at the same time, and there's no way you're going to lose. With a message like that, even Jimmy Carter could have got elected ...

At which point, the pollster's eyes seemed to glaze over, and he sat motionless in his chair with an expression of extreme bewilderment until the ads came and covered his embarrassment.

The only other dissentient voice to be heard that day was that of a caller to a low-rent phone-in show broadcast on a small-town radio station somewhere in the back end of Iowa. Giving his name as Danny Bennett and his address as the Burning Fiery Pit, the caller claimed that the Da Vinci victory was the result of gross electoral manipulation, using magic, necromancy and other forms of unconstitutional inducement, on the part of one Lucky George Faust, a fugitive from Hell with a colossal price on his head. The caller was in the middle of a confused tirade about international hit-men and plots against his life (rather peculiarly phrased in the past tense) when the workmen installing the steel girders to link the radio station building with the delicatessen next door dug through a telephone cable, cutting the caller off. Since ninety per cent of the calls to any local radio phone-in anywhere are comprised of this sort of material, none of the show's seven listeners took the slightest notice.

'Great,' said Lucky George, switching off the television. 'Now all we need are the balloons.'

Repossessing a country is not, perhaps, the most straightforward of operations. It ought to be, but it isn't.

In theory, the bailiff goes along to the head of state with the necessary paperwork and delivers it, and that should be that. What's then supposed to happen is that the population leave the country in question, taking with them all movable items (but no fixtures, fittings, mineral resources or growing plants or trees) by twelve noon of the day specified in the court order. Tenants' improvements are then set off against dilapidations, and any sum required to be paid to either party by way of adjustment is lodged with the court office pending a final decision by the arbitration officer.

In practice, though, there is always hassle and not infrequently trouble; sometimes even violence. That is why most repossessions these days are handled not by the everyday court bailiff but by a firm of specialist certificated bailiffs, of which there is one: Kurt Lundqvist Associates.

Once Lundqvist is on the job, things move fast. His record for clearing a country is thirty-nine seconds, although in fairness we ought to point out that it wasn't a particularly big country. Certainly not by the time he'd finished with it.

Lundqvist attributes his success in this line of work to forward planning, executive efficiency, a calm and reasonable attitude towards the resolution of difficulties and an absolutely fucking *enormous* satellite-mounted industrial laser, capable of vaporising a land mass down to bedrock level at the rate of three hundred and twenty-five thousand square miles per hour.

He calls it the Denver Blowtorch.

Maybe, he says, it makes a mess of buildings, infrastructure and, indeed, mountain ranges. On the positive side, it clears up unsightly litter deposits, disinfects unhygienic areas and leaves a pleasant glassy-smooth surface all ready for the new tenant to build what he likes on. After all, he argues, the first thing you do when you buy a house is strip off the wallpaper and take up the old carpets.

Right down at the bottom of the Marianas Trench, the deepest point in the whole of the ocean, there is no light whatsoever. The strange and uncanny creatures that grope out a nightmare existence down there at fifteen-tons-per-square-inch pressure are born, live and die without even rudimentary traces of eyes, although there are two schools of thought as to why. One says: no light, why bother? The other replies: if you'd ever seen one of those weird buggers they've got down there, the last thing you'd want any truck with ever again is vision.

When working on the bottom of the Trench, therefore, it's vitally important to remember to bring a torch.

'What, me, thkip? I haven't brought it. Thorry, I thought you'd got it.'

'I haven't got it. Keith, you got the torch?'

'Not me, skip. I thought Vernon was going to bring it.'

'Fine. I see.'

'You thure about that, thkip? I can't thee a thing.'

'I was speaking figuratively.'

The three spectral engineers (recently transferred at their own request from the Security division) trod slime for a moment, reviewing the situation.

'Bloody dark down here, skip.'

'All right, so it's a bit dimpsy. We'll just have to do the best we can.'

'We seem to do rather a lot of that, skip, if you don't mind me saying so.'

'It'th what we're betht at,' replied his colleague proudly. 'Muddling through.'

'Right. Now look, maybe we haven't exactly got off to a copybook start here, but so long as we all keep our heads and don't go all to pieces, this is going to be a piece of cake, all right? Or would you rather go back to playing seek and destroy with Kurt Lundqvist?'

There was a heavy silence.

'It's dogged as does it, skip, that's what I always say.'

'You bloody liar, Keith, what you always say is, "Oh my God, we're all going to die."'

'With good reason, skip, be fair.'

'Ekthcuthe me.'

'What?'

'Would thith help?'

The other two turned, and became conscious of a light. Not a wholesome, help-you-see-in-the-dark sort of light, more your ghastly livid green glow. It proceeded from the tail of a sort of flatfish thing; a flatfish, that is, such as Ronnie Bosch might have thought up on one of his gloomier days and then painted over because it gave him the willies.

'Stone me, Vern,' gasped the Captain, 'what the hell have you got there? It's awful.'

'It'th a fith, thkip, with a light in itth tail. I thought it might come in handy, thkip, inthtead of a torch . . .'

'All right, all right. You hold the, er, thing while we do the hole.'

In order to dig holes in the bottom of the deepest point in the ocean, you need a large cordless drill, an enormously long drill bit and a pressure hose to blast away millions of years of accumulated, undisturbed slime. And, of course, the chuck key for the drill.

'Right, Keith,' panted the Captain. 'Gimme the chuck key, and I'll just . . .'

'Now hold on a minute, skip, you know perfectly well you've got the . . .'

'Oh *shit*!'

'Ekthcuthe me again, Thkip, but would thith be any good?'

The other two engineers turned and stared.

Basically, it was a sort of depraved looking crab. With a most peculiarly shaped tail.

'This is bloody ridiculous,' muttered the Captain.

'Dead handy, though.'

'There's still no guarantee it'll *fit*,' the Captain grumbled. 'I mean, it might be a metric size or something . . .'

It wasn't. Nor, unlike your common or garden inanimate chuck key, did it slip out of your hand just when you're giving it that last half-turn and hide under the workbench. The Captain dabbed the trigger-button lightly, thereby confirming that all systems were operational.

'Lads,' he said quietly, just before setting drill to rock, 'don't you get the funny feeling that things are going a bit too well on this jōb?'

The drill screamed, and started to bite. As he guided the thing, the Captain could feel his whole body juddering and stretching as the vibrations twanged through him and out into the water all around.

'Thkip!'

'What is it?' the Captain screamed. 'You'll have to shout, I can't hear you very well because of the noise of this thing.'

'I thaid thkip!'

'Yes, I heard that bit.'

'Well, that'th all I'd thaid tho far.'

'Then carry on,' the Captain screamed above the sound of the drill, whining in the rock like a baby Tyrannosaurus with wind. 'Try and maintain the admirable standard of narrative clarity you've set yourself up till now.'

'Thorry?'

'It's all right, I was only . . .'

'It'th very hard to hear you, thkip, becauthe of the drill. Can you thpeak up a bit?'

'Yes. Get on with it.'

The spectral engineer shrugged. 'I jutht wanted to athk, thkip, why are we doing thith?'

The Captain shuddered horribly. The drill had just touched on something it couldn't cut, and the side-effects radiated out across the sea-bed, giving rise to duff seismographic readings right across the world.

'Good question,' he said, as soon as his teeth had stopped waltzing about in his mouth. 'Something to do with this EuroBosch thing, they told me. Apparently, he wants to tap into this lot for the fountains in the main courtyard.'

'I think,' said the other spectral engineer, 'it's for drains or something like that.'

The other two looked at him.

'Drains?'

'This hole we're digging. It's either drains or telephone wires, one or the other. Stands to reason,' the spectral engineer asserted confidently.

'You reckon?'

'Use your loaf, skip. Why else do people dig holes?'

The Captain paused, drill in hand, the light from the flatfish making strange shadows on the ocean floor. Why *do* people dig holes? he wondered.

Graves.

Mantraps.

Planting land mines.

Because they get told to, mostly.

And, of course, drains. He straightened his back and looked around. Nothing to be seen, except the solid walls of the darkness all around them.

'As simple as that?' he said at last.

'Yeah.'

'No hidden or ulterior motive?'

'Why should there be?'

The Captain shrugged and repositioned the drill bit in the hole. 'No reason,' he said. 'It just seems too, well, normal to me. Useful, too.'

The drill made contact, and there was a long interval of screeching metal, spine-jarring vibrations and Keith whistling (the latter audible despite the Captain jamming the drill on to full speed). Then something gave way, and before the Captain could call out 'I think we're through, lads', the water around them started to seethe and boil. Like the emptying of God's bath, it gurgled, whirlpooled and sucked. The drill, the three engineers and forty thousand tons of yucky black goo were swept up and swallowed whole.

The last two thoughts to pass through the Captain's mind, before the whirlpool got him and catapulted him back into the whole tedious rigmarole of temporary death and routine reincarnation, were:

Maybe we drilled a bit too deep.

Funny. I didn't remember seeing Lundqvist anywhere.

Water. Mother Nature's flexible jackhammer.

Billions of gallons of the stuff, enough to fill all the swimming pools in Beverley Hills, roaring and burping down a molybdenum steel drain towards the centre of the earth.

Ronnie Bosch was proud of that drain. Not because it was a miracle of engineering (walls only ninety thou. thick, but proofed to twenty-six tons per square inch; machined from solid out of one of the pillars used for thousands of years to support the sky until they discovered it stayed up there perfectly happily of its own accord); more because he'd managed to get it made and installed in twelve hours flat, and nobody had even troubled to ask him what he wanted it for. When you've been used to having to sign four pink chits and a green requisition every time you want your pencil sharpened, it comes as a bit of a shock.

Makes you think, really.

Anyway, down the water went until it emerged in the form of white high-velocity spray in an enormous cauldron arrangement, seated slap bang above Hell Holdings plc's very latest, state-of-the-art Number Six furnace.

Let nobody say that the management buy-out hasn't led to some pretty radical changes in the way Hell operates. Number Six furnace is one of the new regime's most impressive showpieces. By the simple expedient of converting it to oil-burning from sabbath-breaker burning, it has been possible to double calorific output and halve running costs, thereby saving enough to finance a whole new sabbath-breakers' wing equipped with the latest in microwave technology. Just to add to the ingenuity of it all, the electricity to power the microwaves comes from a steam turbine built into Number Six; resulting in further savings, which in turn pay for twenty-four-hour, round-the-clock canned laughter in the extremely unpleasant corner of the Hell complex set aside for game show hosts.

It was because of the steam turbine that Ronnie Bosch had routed the water down on to Number Six. A few surreptitious modifications here and there were enough to divert the steam from the boiler away from the turbines and up another molybdenum steel tube, bigger and better than the first, proofed to an incredible thirty-seven tons per square inch, running straight up through the earth's core and coming out in an expansion chamber several thousand feet under North America.

The rest of the design was basically very simple.

The rising steam powered a piston.

The piston went up.

And all across America, in the cool stillness of the early evening of the day before the bailiffs were due to move in, people out walking were tripping over enormous steel girders that hadn't been there an hour or so earlier, and wondering what on earth was going on.

Then they remembered. They remembered that, for reasons which at the time had seemed very cogent, they had voted into the White House a centuries-dead Italian inventor whose sole proposal to the electorate had been that every building in the USA be rigidly attached to its neighbour with bloody great steel rods.

America loves cleverness. In a land where inventors of better mousetraps really do have six-inch-deep ruts worn in the tarmac of their driveways, a man who can come up with an entirely practical plan for doing something previously thought to be impossible must inevitably become the hero of the hour, even if the thing he's able to do is something nobody would ever have dreamed of doing in the first place. Otherwise, how do you explain Mount Rushmore, or the space programme, or the atomic bomb?

Even the sceptics had to admit that it was a goddamn colossal achievement. To take just one example: between Las Vegas and the small but by no means indispensable township of Pahrump, Nevada, lie fifty miles of tyre-meltingly hot desert, scarcely improved in terms of habitability by having a range of twelve-thousand-foot razor-edged rocks fatuously named the Spring Mountains running slap bang through the middle. It's the sort of geographical entity that can only be fitted into the Christian world-view by accepting that somewhere around lunchtime on the third day of creation, He stopped for a breather and left a few bits for the Youth Opportunities lad to finish off.

Yet, within fifteen hours of the Da Vinci Act becoming law, Pahrump had been welded on to Vegas by a single continuous high-tensile steel link, with spurs off it at intervals to connect in the few outlying homesteads in the middle of the desert. In fact, the whole Sierra Nevada was covered with what looked from the air like silver varicose veins, glinting and twinkling in the dazzling desert sun and playing merry hell with satellite TV reception from Bakersfield to Redding.

Or take the vast single-span bridges connecting Immokalee, Florida with Clewiston, Sunnilands and Fort Myers, arrow-straight across the soggiest excesses of the Big Cypress Swamp; the massive iron beam supporting Riley, Oregon between Burns and Wagontire; the absurd lengths gone to in order to attach Wolf Point, Montana securely to its neigh-bours; or, on another plane entirely, the scintillating spider's webs of carbon steel enveloping Brooklyn, San Francisco, Chicago and similar hamlets.

A message banged out on the girders in Morse code in the northern suburbs of Seattle could, in theory, be picked up by someone with a stethoscope in San Diego or Miami or Boston, although it would probably be just as easy to telephone.

And America said to itself:

Hey, *we* did that!

Hey, *why* did we do that?

'Fine,' said Lucky George, replacing the receiver.

'Well?'

'Sounds like Lenny's side of things is tied up all right. Ronnie's part ...' He glanced at his watch, and nodded. 'If everything's running on time, Ronnie's part should already be under way. Any word yet from Larry and Mike?'

Helen nodded. 'They called in about three minutes ago. It's all ready.'

'Good.' Lucky George pulled out the original envelope on which the whole thing had been sketched out, and ran his finger down it, checklist fashion. 'And Chris is ready to cover all the legal stuff?'

'He's waiting outside the Registry right now.'

'Martin and Julius got their people in position?'

'Standing by.'

'That's all right then.' Lucky George folded up the envelope, sat down on the sofa and put his feet up. 'I could murder a coffee if you're making one.'

Helen folded her arms and frowned. 'Hold on,' she said. 'While everyone else is hard at it, what precisely are you going to do?'

George smiled. 'Nothing,' he said. 'And everything too, of course, but only after I've had my coffee. Two sugars, please, and a digestive biscuit.'

It was, needless to say, the biggest moment in all the seventeen years of Links Jotapian's life.

'Scanners,' he commanded, 'on.'

There is a convention that people who sit in front of screens giving orders have to speak funny; it's all 'Activate thruster motors' and 'Uncouple forward connecting gear' and 'Initiating docking routine'. Anybody in the least self-conscious about sounding a complete nana wouldn't last five minutes.

'Scanning,' said one of the men in white coats. 'All functions normal for phase two initiation.'

Up above the world so high, like a death ray in the sky, the Denver Blowtorch was muttering drowsily. A few lights began to flash here and there on its titanium carapace, like the jewels with which a dragon's belly is reputedly encrusted. It bleeped, twitched in its orbit and dreamed strange dreams. Radio waves crackled off it into space like the hairs of a moulting cat.

For crying out loud, it broadcast to the barren cosmos, *there's some of us trying to sleep.*

Links consulted his watch. It was a pity that his Spyderco Combat Chronometer had chosen this day of all days to fall into the bath and get all clogged up with suds, because this was just the sort of special mission he'd bought it for ($14.95 plus postage). As it was, he'd had to rummage around in his dad's bedside drawer for his spare, the one he got free with five litres of oil at the gas station. It worked fine, sure, so far as telling the time was concerned, and all that stuff; but it wasn't black parkerised steel and it didn't have a camouflage strap with a built-in compass. Sometimes, Links reflected bitterly, Life can be so *unfair*.

'Hello, Mr Lundqvist, are you receiving me? This is Links here, Mr Lundqvist. Ready when you are, Mr Lundqvist. Mr Lundqvist?'

He was just about to try again, only louder, when the reply came in through the headphones. It took the form of an urgent request for radio silence until further notice, combined with a warning as to the anatomically complex consequences of non-compliance.

'Sorry, Mr Lundqvist,' Links replied, 'I didn't mean to speak so loud. Is that any better? Gee, I hope I haven't spoiled things, I'd feel really bad if —'

'Links.'

'Yes, Mr Lundqvist, I'm here.'

'Shut up.'

'Yes, Mr Lundqvist. Am receiving you, over and out.'

Nothing to do, apparently, except wait.

Links gazed round the operations room, his eye passing over the banks of computer consoles and the white-coated boffins behind them. So far, he hadn't got to the part in the course that dealt with stealthy waiting, but he felt confident that, with his newly acquired skills, he'd be able to work it out for himself from first principles.

Waiting. Well, for a start, you obviously didn't just sit there like a sack of potatoes. Any dumb civilian could do that. Presumably you had to wait like a coiled spring, concentrating the mind's potential energy and regulating the adrenaline flow. Probably there was one of those mystic Eastern things you could do, but that was most likely somewhere around Lesson Thirty-Six. Links focused his mind and tried to imagine the sound of two hands clapping. It had said one hand in the book, but that was obviously a misprint.

Just as he was getting the hang of it (Clap. Clap. Clap.) a

light flashed on the console. Incoming message from Operative One.

. 'Operative One, this is Guadalahara Central,' he said brightly. 'Guadalahara Central receiving you, come in, Operative One, over.'

'Yeah,' said the voice. 'This is Morrie Goldman here, can I talk to Mr Lundqvist, please?'

Links frowned. 'Negative, Operative One.' He paused, trying to translate what he wanted to say into commandspeak. He gave up; too difficult. 'Mr Lundqvist isn't here right now, can I take a message?'

'What? Oh, sure. Look, this is Goldman. I'm just about to go in and serve the possession notice right now. Have your guys standing by, because I have this feeling the tenants aren't going to be too happy.'

'Receiving you, Operative One. Confirm all systems are operational, awaiting clearance to proceed, over.'

'Yeah, well.' The voice hesitated. 'Just tell him I called, okay?'

'Positive. Message received and logged. Over and out.'

Morrie Goldman hung up and looked around him.

This, he felt, was as good a place as any. He walked up to the counter.

After all, he reassured himself, the man had told him to serve the papers in Washington DC. And here he was in Washington. And besides, the whole goddamn country was going to be blown to antshit a few seconds after he'd effected service, so nobody was ever likely to know even if he did goof it up.

'Hi, my name is Cindi, can I take your order, please?'

Goldman froze. The papers were already in his hand. All he had to do was hand them to somebody, say what they were and timejump out of here; simple as that. He looked at the waitress and flexed his larynx.

'Hi,' he said, 'I'll have the double cheeseburger, the vanilla shake, regular, and, um, large fries.'

'Coming right up.'

He opened his mouth to say the next bit . . .

(*This is a sealed copy of a possession order issued out of the Sublime Court, requiring you to surrender possession of the premises known as North America. If you are in any doubt as to the effect of this order or the likely consequences of failure to comply with the terms hereof, you should immediately seek the advice of your own legal adviser.*)

. . . but the waitress had gone. She now had her back to him, and was yelling the order through to the kitchen. There was obviously more to process-serving than he'd originally anticipated.

'Hi, I'm Ayesha, are you being served?'

Goldman stared into the friendly brown eyes in front of him, closed his own, thrust the papers over the counter and said the magic words. They came out in a sort of congealed lump, like melted popcorn.

'Excuse me?' said the waitress.

The sensible thing to have done would have been to turn away quickly and run for it. Instead, Goldman made a fatal mistake. He tried to explain.

'Look,' he said, 'I'm a process-server, and . . .'

The brown eyes clouded over. 'Get outa here,' they said. 'I'm telling you, I never owned the goddamn car. I never signed *nothing*. What you come in here hassling me for?'

'No, it's not about a car,' Goldman said. 'In fact, it's not you personally, it's . . .'

'You wait there,' said the brown eyes. 'I'm gonna get the manageress.'

Goldman winced. 'No, there's no need for that,' he said. 'Look, it's perfectly in order for you to accept service, in fact service has now been effectually, um, effected, so . . .'

'Don't you give me none of that bullshit, man. I ain't signing nothing. You think I'm crazy or something?'

Meanwhile a large man in a cook's hat had materialised from somewhere out back. Was there, he enquired, some sort of a problem going on here?

'You bet there's a problem,' said the brown eyes emphatically. 'This guy here says he's a process-server, I told him, I ain't accepting no service, I ain't signing *nothing*, and he says —'

'That's all right,' said the large man. 'You just get Carla and everything's gonna be fine.'

A statement which turned out to be more accurate than he could possibly have imagined.

The building began to move . . .

It happened like this.

The water from the Marianas Trench hits the boiler over Number Six furnace, turns to steam . . .

Which passes through a series of ports into an expansion chamber in the centre of the planet, fills the chamber and starts to move upwards . . .

Bearing against the piston, which is driven with staggering force up towards the surface of the Earth, until . . .

It connects with and locates into a receiving slot on the underside of a thirteen-thousand-ton slab of kevlar-reinforced concrete directly under the biggest skyscraper in Kansas City (which is, of course, as near as makes no odds the geographical centre of the United States), whereupon . . .

The skyscraper is pushed up clear of its foundations into the air; but of course . . .

Thanks to the Da Vinci Project, it's linked with steel girders to all the neighbouring buildings, which in turn are linked to all the buildings across the entire nation, with the result that . . .

(The force being exerted on the piston is, remember, absolutely phenomenal; almost a quarter of the Pacific

Ocean's been turned to steam by now and the water's still coming; and when steam expands, it's got to go somewhere; and those steel girders they've got linking up all the houses aren't rubbish, they make the Golden Gate bridge look like a cheap Taiwanese paper-clip, so . . .)

America rises.

Or at least, the buildings do. The ground stays put. The ground, after all, now indefeasibly belongs to the Lundqvist Trust (Holdings) Corporation, and has to be surrendered in accordance with the notice to quit. On the other hand, the buildings are tenants' improvements, and may be removed at any time prior to the surrender of the premises. Ask any lawyer.

A split second after the moment of lifting, of course, the steam pressure in the cylinder blows out the gaskets; the piston goes crashing back down to the centre of the Earth in a cloud of burning steam; the network of girders crumples under the strain like gossamer and falls away . . .

But not so the buildings, because for the last thirty-six hours, all the birds in North America, under the direction of two extremely persuasive seagulls, have been feverishly occupied knotting helium-filled balloons to all the cup-hooks screwed into all the roofs of all the buildings in every state in the Union; and a micron of a second before the whole thing is due to succumb to gravity and hit the deck, the balloons take the strain, and . . .

America floats . . .

Some twenty feet or so above ground level. Fortuitously it's a pretty windless day, and the birds have also tethered the buildings together to stop them drifting too far apart. They're now zooming from building to building (a pigeon's work is never done) with rope-and-plank bridges, to take the place of the sidewalks.

It goes without saying, incidentally, that the balloons are coloured red, white and blue and have been neatly arranged to form an appropriate pattern when viewed from above. Lucky George got them cheap, as a job lot, surplus, after the recent round of party conventions.

And, as a final touch, from the roof of the United Nations building in New York, twenty thousand specially trained white doves take off and glide in perfect formation across the city and out over Long Island. As they fly, they spell out:

OKAY KURT SHE'S ALL YOURS

until, as they pass over Port Jefferson and turn north towards New Haven, they change formation and instead read:

ENJOY

Somewhere in the City of London a young stockbroker dashed into the firm's main office, tore off his coat and tucked his long knees under his computer terminal. Preoccupied with his own concerns, he failed to notice the deathly hush.

'Sorry I'm late, everyone,' he said generally. 'Update me, someone. Wall Street gone any higher since we opened?'

One of his colleagues turned his head and gave him a long, strange look.

'In a manner of speaking, yes,' he said.

Impossible.

On the following grounds:

(a) No labour force, however well-equipped or motivated, spectral or otherwise, could dig the tunnels, machine the parts, install the girders, blow up the balloons in so short a time. Nothing was ever built that quickly. Okay, the world was put together in seven days; but that's net working time. What the book of words glosses over is the three weeks between Day Two and Day Three, during which time He sat around twiddling his thumbs waiting for forty billion reinforced steel joists to be delivered from the foundry.

(b) There isn't enough water in the ocean, let alone the Marianas Trench, to provide enough steam to lift America; or . . .

(c) Alternatively, the design as specified would have produced so much force that not only would America have lifted, but Manhattan Island would have been shot out through the Earth's atmosphere and into orbit.

(d) In any event it's academic, because that much pressure would blow apart any cylinder small enough to fit inside the Earth's core in three seconds flat.

(e) Besides which, absolutely no way could you join all the buildings in the USA together like that; and if you could, it's completely out of the question that any steel framework built by Man could withstand the leverage you'd get under the Da Vinci design.

(f) Not to mention the fact that even if you could get all those houses and factories and office blocks to go up, it'd take more than a few poxy little balloons to keep them there.

Correct. Impossible.

America swayed in the slight breeze.

Gradually, her population began to come to terms with it.

True, they were hanging out of the sky from balloons; but once the rope and plank bridges were in place, they tentatively began to venture out, not looking down, trying very hard indeed not to think about it all. Within two hours, the first rope-and-plank-bridge-theatre performers were miming the man-inside-a-box routine twenty feet above Central Park.

True, there were no fields to plough, no lumber to jack; worst of all, no roads to drive on. Take away America's cars and you take away her soul. But within an hour and a half, the first Mack airship was bobbing drunkenly across Arizona airspace, country music blaring from the cockpit, the propulsive force being provided by a propeller and five thousand rubber bands.

True, with no mean streets, there was nowhere for a man to walk down; and for the first forty minutes all the cops in all the precincts in all the states of the Union suddenly found themselves with no excuse whatsoever for not catching up with the paperwork. But there are too many rooftop chase sequences in cinematographic history for the lack of streets to be a problem for terribly long.

True, nobody had the faintest idea what was going on, or what was all behind it, or whose fault it was or how long it was going to last. In other words, normality. The status quo.

Lucky George gritted his teeth and wondered whether, this time, he hadn't been just a trifle over-ambitious.

No trouble at all lifting America by sheer magical force. Keeping it there – child's play. Suspending the disbelief of the entire human race – piece of cake. Putting the idea of staying indoors into the mind of every man, woman and child in America – a doddle. And just as easy to do them simultaneously as one after the other.

Where perhaps he had over-extended himself slightly was in doing all this and trying to make it look as though it was possible. Hence the business with tunnels, furnaces, pistons and steel girders.

Essential, nevertheless. Where there are laws there are lawyers; and the lawyers who enforce the laws of physics are arguably the nastiest ornaments of a universally unsavoury profession. Goof around with relativity, or try having an action without an equal and opposite reaction, and the next thing you know is the usher telling you to speak up because the judge can't hear you.

Bearing in mind the number of times Lucky George had disregarded the simple instructions set out in the Universe's users' manual, he'd figured that breaking every single law in the book apart from parking in the Director of Gravity's reserved space, without at least some show of mechanical activity, would be pushing his luck just that smidgen too far.

Hence all the ironmongery. Right now, the site was swarming with feasibility assessors and reality surveyors, all scratching their heads over the fact that although according to the rules it couldn't possibly work, there was a hell of a lot of existential evidence that it did, and maybe the rules were in need of a little discreet revision. By the time they'd done their sums and could prove it was all physically impossible, there was a better than average chance that the mess would have been sorted out and America could be put unostentatiously back, some time in the early hours of the morning when all the inhabitants were asleep or watching the late, late film.

Fine. But it made things that bit harder, like trying to break into a hard-boiled egg with a lead-weighted feather. Instead of just keeping the houses in the air, for example, he was having to do it by means of all those countless millions of balloons. You could put your mind out, lifting something like that the wrong way.

Accordingly, George was rather preoccupied.

With the result that he didn't hear the soft splash of oars below the balcony. Or see the shadowy figure climb hand over hand up to the railings and silently hoist himself over.

The first he knew of it, in fact, was the feel of the muzzle of the .40 Glock in his ear, and Lundqvist's voice saying, 'Freeze.'

CHAPTER EIGHTEEN

IF there is more joy in Heaven over one sinner that repents, it's a wet Sunday afternoon in mid Wales compared with the ecstatic jubilation in Hell over one escaped sinner that gets his collar felt.

Not surprisingly, the denizens of the Inferno know how to party. Within twenty minutes of the news breaking, the management had declared a half-day's holiday, and five thousand years' worth of tormented souls had formed a whirling, tail-lashing conga that roared and billowed through the various Rings like a rattlesnake on amphetamines. Objectively speaking, what with the noise and the smoke and the crush of bodies, the epicentre of the party was quite markedly worse than the torments from which the revellers had temporarily been released; however, there's absolutely no limit to what the human spirit can endure when it sincerely believes it's enjoying itself.

Meanwhile, in the large conference room, the Board were taking counsel as to the reception to be accorded the returning guest.

'It's got to have manure in it somewhere,' insisted the Production Director. 'I may be old-fashioned and set in my ways, but . . .'

The Personnel Director shook his head emphatically. 'With respect, Mr Chairman,' he said, 'no offence, but my colleague is talking through his arse. You —'

The Finance Director frowned and lifted his index finger slightly to indicate that he required silence. 'Hold on,' he said, looking dispassionately at the Production Director's rather bizarre anatomy. 'Point taken, Dennis, and excuse me if I seem pedantic, but Harry always talks through his arse. It's the way he's made, you see, what with his head being in his tummy and all back to front . . .'

'My colleague,' said the Personnel Director frostily, 'is, if you prefer, talking nonsense. Dammit, this isn't the time for poncing about, we're looking at brimstone here, because —'

'Excuse me,' interrupted the Production Director, icier still, 'but perhaps my friend from Personnel would be kind enough to let me know where I'm supposed to get brimstone from, since he's so bloody keen on the stuff. In fact,' he added spitefully, 'perhaps he'd just tell us, briefly and in his own words, exactly what brimstone is, because I've been in this business three thousand years, imp and fiend, and the amount of your actual brimstone that I've seen around here you could fit into a very small egg-cup —'

'All right, Harry, thank —'

'And still have room for the egg.'

'Quiet!' The Finance Director raised his hand. 'Thank you both very much for your views, which are noted, but I think I can offer you all an alternative suggestion which does have quite a lot going for it.'

The Directors turned and looked at him. He smiled.

'Just to recap for a moment,' he said, leaning back slightly in his chair, 'so far we've had a bed of red-hot coals from Jerry, and Colin's forty-foot earthworm, and Steve's very innovative Game For A Laugh concept – far be it from me, by the way, Steve, but in my opinion there's such a thing as over the top, even for us – and of course Terry's Moebius loop of Dame

Kiri Te Kanawa Sings Country, which we're definitely going to have to use somewhere, but not here, I think. Plus, of course, Harry's shitwell and Dennis's brimstone.' He paused, and flicked though his microchip Organiser. 'While we're on the subject, Harry, from memory I think Fiends' Provident do synthetic brimstone in fifty-kilo tubs, if that's any help to you.'

He paused and took a sip of water; then went on:

'It's all good stuff, lads, but where's the money coming from? Just think about that for a moment, would you, because once we've paid Lundqvist's invoice and settled the compensation claims for all those practical jokes George pulled while still nominally in our charge and therefore our responsibility, there'll probably still be enough left in the Entertainments budget for a cup of tea and a ginger nut, but nothing else. Anybody got any thoughts on that one?'

There was silence, except for the soft fizzing of the varnish on the boardroom table where the Sales Director had breathed on it. The Finance Director nodded.

'Okay,' he said, 'here's a suggestion. I took the liberty,' he went on, standing up and walking to the back of the room, 'of bringing along a few slides to illustrate what I've got in mind. The lights please, someone.'

The lights went out, and a few seconds later the back wall was covered with an eye-catching, rather familiar image. The Finance Director pointed to it with his right index claw.

'You all should know what this is by now,' he said. 'It's the right-hand panel of the *Garden of Earthly Delights*, courtesy of our very own artist in residence, Ron Bosch. Now, as you're all well aware, Ron's using this as the central tableau for the main shopping and recreation area of the theme park. Can I have the next slide, please?'

A machine clunked softly in the background, and the image on the screen zoomed in to show a close-up of the justly celebrated centre-piece of the panel; the bird-headed demon with a cauldron on the back of its head and its feet in two

water-jugs, perched in a high-chair-cum-hourglass arrangement, daintily chewing on a human torso and legs. If Hell had
a mascot, this was it; the Guinness toucan, the Esso tiger, the
Andrex puppy, and Captain Beaky.

The Finance Director grinned. 'Get the picture?' he said.

There was a bemused silence.

'Frankly,' said the Production Director at last, 'but no, not
really. I expect I'm being really thick here, but what's Captain
Beaky got to do with getting even with Lucky George?'

'Plenty, if you agree with my proposal,' the Finance
Director replied. He motioned for the next slide. 'Here,' he
continued, 'we've got the design specs for the fibreglass model
of Beaky we're all set to order for the Park.' He tapped the
bottom left-hand corner of the screen with his pointer. 'Note
particularly,' he said, 'the price. Now please don't think I'm
advocating corner-cutting because I'm not, but that really is a
lot of bread.'

'Too bloody right,' commented the Production Director
sourly. 'I've said it before, these boys from the pattern-makers
are ripping us off, and we're doing bugger-all about it.'

The Finance Director smiled. 'Maybe,' he said, 'but in this
instance I don't think the pricings are excessive, because the
whole point about the Beaky model is that it actually works.
Moving parts, all singing, all dancing. What you do is, you put
a coin in here –' He indicated the hindquarters of a soul in
torment just below the high chair. '– and immediately Beaky
eats the sinner, with realistic noise and odour effects and piped
screams. Boschy reckons it's going to be a real moneyspinner
once it's up and running, but in the meantime there's the
capital costs to find. Bad news, gentlemen, bad news. On
present costings, it's going to be a tight squeeze.'

There was a rustle and a ripple around the boardroom table,
which the Finance Director noticed. He nodded his approval.

'I can see you're way ahead of me, gentlemen,' he said. 'I
think that with a little ingenuity, we've got the whole damn

flock with one small pebble. Just to make sure we're all on the same wavelength, however, I'll quickly run it past you and we'll see what happens. Instead of a fibreglass disposable sinner – $750 each according to the quotes, and we estimate he'll get through ten or twelve in a day – if we could substitute a flesh-and-blood, perpetually reusable organic sinner, not only would we save on parts but the whole sideshow's going to be one hell of a lot more authentic and appealing to the punters. What d'you reckon, gentlemen?'

After a short interval, the comments started to flow. Diabolic humour is to a large degree shaped by its environment; hence the Production Director's comment that it was the sort of thing he'd like to chew over for a while, the Personnel Manager's remark that it was the sort of design you could really get your teeth into, the Company Secretary's observation that Harry had taken the words right out of his mouth and the Senior Redcoat's warning that they shouldn't bite off more than they could chew. When the Finance Director had had about as much of this sort of thing as he could stand, he raised his finger for silence.

'Agreed, then,' he said cheerfully. 'I'll tell Lundqvist to deliver on site first thing in the morning. Thank you, gentlemen.'

'You planned the whole thing, didn't you?'

Lundqvist nodded. 'And you fell for it.'

'Well, yes.' Lucky George tried to nod, but the huge steel collar clamped round his neck precluded movement of more than a thousandth of an inch. 'If it's any satisfaction to you, Smiler, yes I did. Happy now?'

'Don't call me Smiler,' Lundqvist growled dangerously.

'Why not, Smiler?' George raised an eyebrow, about the only part of him above waist level capable of motion. 'It's your nickname, isn't it? I mean, yes, when we were at school together you did use to ponce around the yard telling everyone that from now on you were to be known as Captain Death the Terminator, but I thought Nick Machiavelli and I had kicked that out of you by the end of third year.'

'That'll do, George.'

'Sorry, Smiler.'

Lundqvist pulled savagely on the chain attached to the collar and made no reply. For his part, he blamed his entire collection of terminal personality disorders on the way George and his gang had spent their mutual schooldays running verbal rings round him and then beating him up, just because he was small and delicate and liked setting fire to people in their sleep. He'd waited a long time to get even, and he wasn't going to be hurried or flustered.

'Here, Kurt,' George called out after a while. 'Are you sure you know where you're going?'

'Yes. Why?'

'Fine, Kurt, fine, so long as you're sure. It's just that there's no deserts in Europe, and this is a desert we're in, and I thought I'd just mention . . .'

On either side of them, sand dunes rolled away into the fold of horizon and sky. Lundqvist snickered, and turned in his saddle. 'We're going the scenic route, George,' he said. 'I felt you might like to stretch your legs one last time.'

'That was thoughtful of you, Smiler.'

'Before they're stretched for you, of course.'

'Of course.' George grinned. 'There you go again, Smiler, pulling my leg as usual. Nice sunny day, isn't it?'

'You like it?'

'Yes.'

'That's just as well, isn't it?'

'You know me, Kurt, never one to complain.' George yawned. 'Yes, like I was saying, that was good thinking on your part, getting to me through my friends. My Achilles heel, you thought to yourself, or rather, my fatal flaw, because I expect you get Achilles heel and Achilles tendon muddled up. Sneaky, of course, and despicable, putting everybody to all that trouble, but there we are. All's fair in love and law enforcement.'

'They made me give it back.'

George looked at him. 'Sorry?'

'America,' Lundqvist said, with as much bitterness in his voice as there is vermouth in the driest of dry martinis. 'They made me give it back. Not,' he added, 'as if I really wanted it for anything. In fact they're welcome to it.'

'That's all right, then,' George said. 'Fun's fun, and nobody enjoys a good stunt better than I do, but it'd have spoilt it a little bit to think of the entire USA being carbonised just because of me. I was a little bit worried about that, actually, though I don't know why. It's not as if it was me that started all this.'

Lundqvist gave the chain another vicious tug, so that George staggered and nearly ended up on the ground. But he found his feet again and started to whistle.

'Been missing the old place?'

George looked up. 'Well, to be honest with you, no. Still, there are worse places.'

Lundqvist pulled hard on the reins and stopped his horse. 'There are?' he asked.

'Sure'. George stood on one leg and rubbed his left ankle with his right heel. 'Millions of 'em. All over the place. Honestly, Smiler, your mob have about as much idea of how to go about torturing souls as my aunt's cat. Less,' he added on reflection, and accurately. 'It was on my mind for a long time to mention it to somebody, because I'm a helpful sort of chap by nature, but then I thought, nah, why bother, nobody'll thank you for it. So . . .'

Lundqvist's skin prickled as he sensed a verbal trap, but his curiosity got the better of him. 'Go on, then,' he said.

George smiled. 'One of these days,' he said, 'do yourself a favour and get a job in an office somewhere. Any office, anyplace. The term soul-destroying's a bit of a cliché, but it's damned accurate. Two years in Accounts has the same effect on your average soul as two teaspoons of salt on a garden slug. Whoomph!'

Lundqvist frowned. 'You're winding me up,' he said.

'No I'm not,' George replied. 'You don't know because you've never tried it. Nice outdoor life, travel, killing interesting people, you don't know you're born. And as for all those so-called torments they've got down in the Basement there, we're talking summer holidays compared to being stuck on the end of a telephone all day being shouted at because the green forms at Central don't tally with the pink paying-in slips.'

'No.' Lundqvist shook his head slowly. 'You wait and see what we've got in store for you, and then tell me all about it.'

George mustered an expression of polite interest. 'Something fun?' he asked.

Lundqvist told him.

EuroBosch: a visitor's guide.

Enter through the Burning Cities at the northern end of the Park, buying your ticket from the four-legged owl-headed egg (who also retails a wide range of souvenir goods, postcards, plenary indulgences and Masses for the Dead). Each visitor or party is then assigned a personal fiend to act as escort and guide for your tour. It's very helpful if visitors can specify any preference for a particular fiend type well in advance; the spoon-headed monks in particular are in great demand, and are allocated on a first-come first-damned basis.

As you pass over the bridge embattled by armies, the first exciting and enjoyable activity you will come to will be the Ferris Ears. All you have to do is climb up the scaffolding to the gallows on the left of the Ears to get to your seat; you're then churned round and round inside the Ears, being narrowly missed by the huge pendant knife-blade, until you're hurled out, dizzy and terrified, through the slot at the front.

Next on the programme is the amazing free-to-enter Satanic Bagpipe Karaoke, situated on the flat circular platform on top of the severed head. Look closely at the illustration in the brochure and you'll see a delighted visitor being led to the microphone by a bird-headed fiend with a burning torch.

Just down from the Karaoke is the popular Refreshment Area, conveniently situated in the shattered eggshell. The Refreshment Area offers a wide range of traditional infernal hot and cold dishes, light snacks and bird-headed fiends. Patrons are requested to refrain from smoking in the Refreshment Area, although residents may of course smoulder unobtrusively.

Across the boating lake from the Refreshment Area is the family favourite Lost Souls Tortured On Musical Instruments game. For a moderate admission charge, you can be crushed in a viol, rolled in a drum, strung on a harp or crucified on a lute, and the attendant dog-, rabbit- and amphibian-headed demons will be pleased to assist you in any way they can.

You may then wish to cross back over the boating lake to enjoy the unique sensation of participating in the rollicking Knight Eaten By Dogs stall; or perhaps you will prefer to spend a quarter of an hour or so simply walking about the grounds marvelling at the many varied and different species of wild fiend to be found there before embarking on a helter-skelter dash through the Horse's Skull assault course, followed by a thrilling twenty minutes with the Manta Ray Paintball Team.

Whichever of the many colon-twistingly enjoyable activities you choose to take part in on your way round EuroBosch, you should on no account miss the high spot of any visit, the all-action non-stop Captain Beaky Extravaganza, guaranteed to haunt your nightmares with feverish intensity for whatever remains of your life.

Finally, a few Dos and Don'ts to make your visit more enjoyable:

1. Please *do not feed the fiends*, except with the specially prepared human souls obtainable from the gift shop situated in the Giant Lantern. The fiends' diet is carefully regulated for their own health and well-being, and sweets, sandwiches and gobbets of human flesh can be harmful.

2. Please do not ask to be mangled by the giant bird-headed butterflies. Their wings are extremely fragile, and you risk spoiling your own and other people's enjoyment.

3. Please take your sins home with you, or place them in the receptacles provided.

4. Only children purchased on the premises may be consumed in the Refreshment Area.

'... And after that,' Lundqvist was saying, 'they stuff you straight back into your skin and round you go again, over and over and over, for the rest of —'

'Sounds all right to me.'

Lundqvist lost his temper. 'No it *doesn't*,' he shouted, 'it's *horrible*, and you'll scream and howl and beg for mercy, but nobody will hear, and it'll be the same, every day for ever, and —'

'Except Thursdays.'

Lundqvist's head snapped round. 'What do you mean, Thursdays?' he spat.

'The park's shut Thursdays,' George said, 'for cleaning and maintenance. And I don't imagine your bosses will want to pay for the electricity if there's nobody there, do you? I expect the whole thing'll grind to a halt until opening time on Friday.'

'Look . . .'

'By the same token,' George went on implacably, 'I very much doubt whether the machines will be running every evening after all the visitors have gone, because that's when the little men with the oil-cans come round and do all the bearings. Mind you,' he added, 'if it's like any fun-fair I've ever been to, at least a third of the time the place is open the machines will have broken down or overheated or something, so the actual net being-chewed time is reduced by – what, something like . . .'

'All right,' Lundqvist thundered, 'it won't be absolutely incessant. It'll still hurt like buggery when it *is* working.'

'It would hurt,' George replied calmly, 'if I hadn't learnt advanced tantric yoga as a young man at college. Marvellous stuff, you know, means you can lie on beds of nails and prance about on red-hot coals for hours on end and not feel a thing. You should try it some time.'

Lundqvist was pulling handfuls of hair out of his horse's mane by now. 'Okay,' he said, 'so maybe it's not incessant and maybe it won't hurt as much as it should, but it'll be very, very boring. Or hadn't you considered that?'

George smiled beatifically. 'I come from a large family,' he replied, 'and we were for ever being visited by some cousin or other; usually middle-aged, with photographs. And you presume to talk to me about being bored.'

'Look . . .'

'Plus the tantric yoga helps with that, too. It's extremely hard to be bored when you're contemplating the vastness of Being through the sharp focus of Experience while standing aside from your Persona.' George grinned like a mantrap. 'It's a bit like twiddling your thumbs, only less exhausting physically.'

Lundqvist glanced down at his bald horse and got a grip on himself. 'You'll see,' he said, 'who has the last laugh.'

'Oh, I expect you will,' said George, 'Smiler.'

Although there was still a full week to go before the scheduled Grand Opening, the management had reckoned that it would be good business to have a few sneak previews. Potential advertisers, reps from the main holiday companies and other major clients in the making were therefore cringing and lurking their way round the Park when Lundqvist trotted through the main gate, remembering to duck so as to avoid leaving his head behind as he passed under the fish-headed monster perched over the lintel. It had been put there as a hat-check fiend, but old habits die hard.

A wave of his .40 Glock was enough to persuade the Egg that Lundqvist didn't need a ticket and didn't want any hand-made demonic fudge, and after Lundqvist had parked his horse in the horse park they passed through into the Burning Cities area. Once or twice Lundqvist nearly jumped out of his skin as they turned a corner to be confronted by a flute-headed badger or a nine-foot-high cowled lizard; George simply smiled and occasionally nodded in tacit salutation.

'Scared?'

'Shut up.' Lundqvist yanked hard on the chain, and George reeled heavily against a four-legged, Alsatian-sized wine jar, which staggered, slipped in a pool of its own spillage, and crashed to the ground, shattering into hundreds of razor-edged splinters. There was a howl of fury from a scaffolding tower overhead, followed by a forceful request that the two of them should look where they were going.

'Smiler.'

'Now what?'

'If I were you, I'd let me go now.'

Amazing, the way that Life can still find things to take our breath away, even when we think we've seen and heard it all. 'Are you out of your skull?' Lundqvist demanded. 'I wouldn't let you go now for all the napalm in Iraq.'

'Sure?'

Lundqvist grinned nastily. 'Absolutely positive.'

'Okay,' George said, and shrugged. 'On your head be it, then.'

And a few seconds later, it was.

It was a truck-sized expanded polystyrene turbot, dressed in a cardinal's hat and playing a harp, and it hit Lundqvist in the back of the head before landing directly on top of him. All that was visible of him was his hands and one toe.

'Told you,' said George.

Furtively, and with a face like thunder, Hieronymus Bosch climbed down from the crane and looked round.

'Right,' he hissed, 'that's it, that's the very last time I help you out of a jam. Understood?'

'Afternoon, Ron.'

'We are now,' Bosch went on, fumbling in his pocket for the diamond-edged hacksaw, 'finally and definitively quits. Got that?'

George nodded. 'Very good of you to help me out here, Ron,' he said. 'Always could rely on you in a crisis.'

'Well,' Bosch snapped back as the severed halves of the first handcuff hit the ground, 'in future you can rely on me not being here, understood?'

'You always were a pal, Ron,' said Lucky George, smiling. 'Well, I mustn't keep you. How are you getting on with those chains and things?'

'Huh!' Bosch winced sharply as he touched the blade of the hacksaw with the tip of his finger. It was hot, very hot indeed. 'Bloody things, they've gone and used carbon steel for these damned manacles. Don't they have any idea whatsoever of how much things cost?'

'Never mind.' George swung his arms and rolled his neck to suggest that it would be nice to move, if only eventually. 'Can't expect this lot to know things, Ron. Be seeing you.'

Once he was clear of the chains and the collar, George made for the giant lantern. He needed food, and a drink, and quite possibly a new pair of feet.

Well, he said to himself as he looked round. If I did want some new feet, this would be the place to come. Hundreds of them, and some with nothing attached at either end.

After the drink and the sandwich, of course, there would be the problem of getting out of the Park. As priorities go, however, it wasn't exactly holding pole position. He walked up the back of the oversize carving knife and swung open the door.

Then he remembered. No money. Damn.

He tried to conjure for some, and then remembered. Magic doesn't work here, because of interference from the tannoy system.

'Hi,' he said. 'You got any washing-up needs doing?'

Seven pairs and three trios of eyes turned and stared at him. 'You what?' said a voice from behind the bar.

'I said,' George repeated, sitting on a bar stool, 'any washing-up you want doing? In return for a cup of coffee, something like that.'

The barfiend cackled through its twisted beak. 'Listen, chum,' it said. 'This is Hell, right? No problem getting washing-up done here.'

'Fair enough.' George nodded. 'Plenty of unhelpful husbands, you mean. All right, then, will you take a cheque?'

The fiend scowled, and pointed with its wingtip at a notice over the fireplace, which said:

NO CREDIT
NO LOITERING
SERVICE NOT INCLUDED

'I think I've been here before,' George said. 'Well, sorry to have bothered you. See you around.'

The door through which he had just walked swung shut. Worse than that, it folded its arms. George sat down again and surreptitiously pulled a bowl of peanuts towards him. Before his fingers could close around any of the contents, they jumped out of the bowl and scurried for the ashtray.

'Where d'you come from, anyway?' demanded the fiend. 'Haven't seen you in here before, have I?'

'I'm with the preview tour,' George replied. 'Actually, I'm a bit lost.'

'Who isn't?'

'Good point.' With a deft flick of his wrist, George brushed a slower-than-average peanut into the palm of his hand and swallowed it quickly. 'Could you direct me to the main gate? The bus leaves in ten minutes, and . . .'

The fiend wrinkled its beak. 'I know who you are,' it said. 'You're that Lucky George character. Well, sunshine, this time you won't be so bleeding lucky, because . . .'

Out of the corner of his eye, George caught sight of something nice. Niceness, like beauty, is very much in the beholder's eye, because all he'd seen was two more bird-headed monsters. But these ones were different. They were seagull-headed.

'Here,' the barfiend was saying, 'you two. Are you from Security?'

A seagull head nodded.

'Took your bloody time, didn't you? Here he is. Now get him out of here.'

George waited till they were past the Knight Eaten By Dogs and out on to the hard ice of the pond before breaking the silence.

'Like the thing said,' he muttered. 'You two took your bloody time.'

Larry shrugged. 'It's not easy, you know,' he said. 'We had to find costumes.'

'And they had people in them, too,' Mike added. 'So we had to get rid of them, and then we had to find you. And people kept stopping us and asking where the lavs are. We did our best.'

George nodded. 'No problem,' he said, 'just so long as you can find the way out. To be honest with you, I don't like it much here. Don't let Ron know I said that, by the way.'

'It's over there,' Larry said, pointing. 'Up past that big head thing with the plate on top. Better still, there's a fire escape just below the Burning Cities. We could go through that.'

George nodded. 'Where's Helen?' he asked.

'Waiting out front with the car,' Mike answered. 'She insisted on coming.'

'Quite right too. Now then, I left Lundqvist under a fish, but he's probably on the loose again by now, so we'd better get a move on.'

As they made their way up the bank away from the pond, a rabbit-headed demon shuffled up and asked them if they wanted to go on the Man-Eating Lute. They shook their heads and walked on.

'*Freeze!*'

'Oh for pity's sake,' George muttered, clicking his tongue and dodging a bullet from the .40 Glock. 'Come on, we'd better make for that thing over there.'

'Just a minute, boss, you don't want to go there, it's the —'

'Come *on*, Larry, and don't dawdle.'

'I see,' George whispered, 'what you mean.'

Larry acknowledged the remark with a tiny dip of his head. The rest of him was frozen with terror.

'It's all right really, Larry, the worst that can happen is they'll ask you to sing. What's so terrible about . . .?'

George caught sight of the seagull's face and decided that this was a topic best left alone. He folded his arms, looked straight in front of him and set his lips in a slight smile.

Lundqvist woke up.

William Shakespeare was a great describer of sleep, referring to it as (*inter alia*) balm of hurt minds, knitter-up of the ravelled sleeve of care, great nature's second course and the season of all natures. Kurt Lundqvist, who had always taken the view that the pen may be mightier than the sword but is still no match for a twelve-gauge Remington Wingmaster with an eighteen-inch barrel loaded with Double-O buckshot, pre-ferred to think of sleep as a right bastard, particularly when induced by an outsize expanded polystyrene fish.

It didn't help matters that the first thing he saw on opening his eyes was Links Jotapian, who said, 'Are you all right, Mr Lundqvist?'

'Yes. Get this bloody thing off me and raise the alarm.'

'Straight away, Mr Lundqvist.'

'Links.'

'Yes, Mr Lundqvist?'

'Try pushing it the other way.'

'Gosh, sorry, Mr Lundqvist, I wasn't thinking. Did it hurt?'

'Not nearly as much as what I'm going to do to you if you don't get a goddamn move on.'

'I'm doing the best I can, Mr Lundqvist.'

'Yes,' Lundqvist replied bitterly, 'you probably are.'

A few minutes later, every alarm bell in the complex was howling its head off, producing a volume of noise so great that it was almost audible over the sound-effects from the various rides. On the Karaoke stall, however, it had about as much chance as a Bic disposable against Lundqvist's Remington.

'Every time I say goodbye,' Larry was singing, 'I die a little.' He didn't carry absolute conviction, because to judge strictly by appearances he was already dead; more than that, he'd been steeped for a week in formaldehyde and inexpertly stuffed.

'He's really very good, isn't he?' hissed the other seagull under his breath. 'Mind you, he gets that from his mother.'

Larry carried on singing until the rat-headed fiend in nominal charge of the proceedings eventually took the micro-phone away from him and passed it on to a circular nun with lights shining out through her ears. All right, so this was Hell; but there are limits. The nun started to sing 'My way'.

'Come on,' George hissed, 'let's get out of this. I really do fancy something to eat.'

Before he could make good his escape, however, the rat-head snatched the mike away from the nun, and jabbed it into George's hand. He smiled, as if receiving a bunch of flowers from a welcoming committee, took a deepish breath and sang.

It took the rat-head less than seven seconds to realise that he'd made a serious mistake; but by then the damage was mostly done. When he tried to take the mike away from Lucky George, all he got for his pains was an expertly placed elbow in his solar plexus. Thereafter he confined his energies to switching the whole plant off at the mains and biting through the mike cable with his teeth. The difference it made was negligible.

Finally, having assured the world at large that he'd done it his way, George handed back the mike and sighed contentedly.

'Can I have another go, please?'

The rat-head gave him a look of three parts pure terror, two parts unmitigated hatred. He shrugged.

'Pity, that,' said George. 'I was enjoying myself.'

He stepped down off the platform, weaving his way round the bodies of six or seven fiends, all curled up like woodlice with their hands clamped firmly over their ears.

'Philistines,' he remarked. 'Okay, Larry, Mike, last one to the bar gets them in.'

Three minutes or so after he'd gone, an assistant fiend with the toes and claws of a lizard crawled down the nozzle of the giant bagpipe and collapsed at rat-head's feet. He'd nearly perforated his own eardrums by sticking his claws in his ears, but that was a small price to pay.

'Stone me,' he muttered. 'That was bloody horrible, wasn't it, chief?'

'Pardon?'

'I said, that was bloody horrible, wasn't it?'

'Pardon?'

'I SAID THAT WAS BLOODY HORRIBLE, CHIEF, WASN'T IT?'

Rat-head shook himself and shuddered. 'You'll have to speak up,' he said.

Links Jotapian had found a helicopter.

We use the term loosely. What he'd in fact found was a sort of walking tree with hideous branches like dry bones and a goat's skull growing out of its left armpit; it had taken the eye of youthful enthusiasm to see that if you climbed up the thing's trunk and prodded it viciously with a penknife, it could be persuaded to whirl its branches fast enough to achieve a rotor effect. Sikorski wouldn't have approved, but no matter.

'Nothing as yet, Mr Lundqvist, over,' he reported into his two-way radio. 'Results so far are one-hundred-per-cent negative.'

'Keep looking, Links, he's down there somewhere.'

'Roger and out.' Links peered through a screen of small twigs and jabbed at the tree to go lower.

This is fun, Links said to himself, much more fun than school. I mean, compared to this, school sucks. I mean, this is, well, Life. He brushed cinders out of his eyes and lifted his feet clear to avoid the pincers of a bored-looking anthropomorphic lobster, positioned on the top of the horse's skull swimming pool area.

'Quark!'

Not, said something inside him, that it's not also a tad scary. Like, it's a very long way down, and this tree could get cramp in its branches any minute. And falling a long way is bad enough at the best of times, without taking into account some of the really weird things a guy can land on in this place.

'Quark quark!'

'Get down more, you sucker,' Links yelled into the knot-hole which he hoped was the tree's ear. 'And when you start feeling tired, for Chrissakes rustle a leaf or something.'

The tree wobbled. Links looked up, to see two seagulls roosting in the branches. They looked decidedly nauseous, as well they might.

'Shoo!' Links yelled, and waved his arms. 'Go lay an egg or something.'

'Quark.'

'You crazy dumb birds, you'll make this thing crash.'

'Quark.'

'Oh.'

His last thoughts, before he hit the frozen ice of the boating lake and disappeared in a cloud of ice-shards, spray and matchwood, were *Never mind, this is still better than school.* His first thoughts after the fiends had fished him out and pumped half a gallon of stagnant Styx water out of his lungs, were *On the other hand, there's a lot to be said for double geography.*

'And another thing,' said Machiavelli.

With a tremendous effort, the barfiend in the Hellza-Pop-Inn refreshment area ground his head round until he was facing his most regular customer. Sure thing, these were the Torments of Hell, and this was the spot reserved for married men who forsake their wives to go boozing every evening, and as a happily married fiend with a mortgage and three wonderful imps he reckoned those drunken bums deserved everything they got, even this; but, dammit, he was staff, not a customer, and he had to bear the brunt of it.

'All this acid rain,' Machiavelli was saying, 'and all these volcanoes and stuff, sodding up the weather. You aren't going to tell me that's all a coincidence, now are you?'

'Anything you say, Nick,' yawned the barfiend.

''Cos,' Machiavelli ground on, 'it's a matter of cold fact that on the day JFK was assassinated, the weather forecast for the whole of Texas was Mainly Dry, Some Light Cloud Clearing

Early. But of course, that's what they *wanted* us all to think, because ...'

The door opened, a man came in, sat down on a barstool and said, 'Hiya, Nick, what're you having?'

'And then,' Machiavelli went on, 'when you compare the records for seismic activity for the day of the Kennedy murder with the night of the Watergate break-in, you find that exactly the same level of activity was recorded in Chicopee Falls, Iowa, on both occasions, which makes you think.' He paused, as if trying to remember something he'd just heard, and then said, 'Dunnit?'

'Sure thing, Nick,' said the barfiend, polishing a glass. It just wasn't *fair*, he said to himself. All the inconsiderate husbands are out there in the back bar playing pool and getting pissed as rats, I'm stuck in here listening to the floorshow. They've gotta *do* something about this.

'Hiya, Nick,' the stranger repeated. 'Same again?'

Slowly, Machiavelli turned his head and stared.

'George?' he enquired.

'Been a long time, Nick,' replied Lucky George. 'I was very interested in what you were saying just now, by the way. I expect you were discussing that new book by that journalist bloke, the one who got himself killed not so long back. Bunnet or something, I think he was called.'

'What the hell are you doing here, George? I thought you'd —'

'I have, Nick, I have. And a Michelob and a toasted cheese sandwich for me,' he called through to the barfiend, 'when you've got a moment. So,' he said, turning back to Machiavelli, 'how's things with you?'

'Oh, all right,' Machiavelli replied, flushing slightly. 'They've made me a trusty now, actually.'

'Have they really,' George said. 'Well my goodness.'

'Yeah.' Machiavelli looked down. 'I got this job as a saloon bar bore.'

'And what's it like, Nick?'

'Boring.'

'Uh-huh. Anyway, I interrupted you. You were saying.'

'Was I?'

'Yes. About Bunnet's book.'

Machiavelli cringed slightly. 'Oh, that. His theory is,' he went on, without expression, eyes fixed on floor, 'that the Martians have been behind all the major political cover-ups of the post-war era, which they have stage-managed by clever manipulation of the climate. This also,' Machiavelli concluded wretchedly, 'accounts for deforestation, acid rain, the greenhouse effect . . .'

'I see.' George scratched his ear. 'Enjoy your work, do you?'

'Not a lot, no.'

George's beer and sandwich arrived – the latter slightly charred and served on the tines of a pitchfork – and he devoted his attention to them for a moment. Then he looked up.

'You know,' he said with his mouth full, 'funny, isn't it, the way things pan out.'

'Mmm.'

'I mean,' George said, 'think of what we were like back at school. Me the quiet, studious one. You the guy with the big ideas of everything you were going to do, big career in politics, get on the pundit circuit . . .'

Machiavelli made a noise; part agreement, part shame and part pain. Surreptitiously he bit a corner off George's sandwich.

'And yet here you are,' George went on, 'stuck in this dead-end job . . .'

'No pension to look forward to,' Machiavelli interjected.

'No fringe benefits.'

'No travel. No input into the fate of nations.'

'Bet you don't have your own reserved parking space.'

'The hours are bloody terrible, George.'

'I'll bet they are, Nick.'

Machiavelli sobbed slightly. 'It's not just the hours, George,' he snuffled, 'it's the hours and hours and *hours* of it that get me.'

'They would,' George agreed. 'I wouldn't stand for it.'

'Oh, I've got to stand,' Machiavelli replied unhappily. 'Stools are all reserved for the customers. I've worn this damn brass rail paper-thin, George, I could stick my finger through it any time I like.'

'Yes.' George blinked. 'What I meant was, I wouldn't put up with it.'

'You wouldn't?'

'Not if I were you, Nick. Not the Nick Machiavelli I used to know. By the way, seen anything of Kurt Lundqvist lately?'

Machiavelli shook his head. 'Last I heard,' he said, 'he was in business assassinating redundant gods. Good line of work to be in, I should say.'

'Yup.' George nodded. 'Good steady work.'

'Must be interesting.'

'Fascinating.'

'Lucky little sod,' said Machiavelli bitterly. 'When I think how he used to burst out blubbering every time we took his stiletto away from him.'

George sighed. 'And yet,' he said, 'look at him, and look at you. No, if I were you, Nick, I'd do something about it.'

Machiavelli looked up. There were the first ripe buds of tears sprouting at the edges of his bleared eyes. 'Yeah?' he said. 'Like what?'

George finished his sandwich and drained his glass. 'Well,' he said, 'first off, I'd start a diversion.'

'Mr Lundqvist.'

'Hi, Links.'

'He's not in here, Mr Lundqvist.'

Lundqvist looked down into the pit, narrowing his eyes. 'That so, Links?'

'I'm pretty sure of it, Mr Lundqvist.'

'You'd better come back up, then.'

Pause. 'I've got a slight problem with that, Mr Lundqvist.'

Lundqvist sighed. The term 'idiot', he decided, fitted Links Jotapian like the proverbial glove. 'I thought you might say that, Links,' he replied. 'That's why I got this rope.'

'Gee, Mr Lundqvist.'

Lundqvist unslung his rope and lowered it down into the pit. It was a very long rope, and when he'd paid it out completely and was just holding the end, he leant forward again and said, 'Got it?'

'Not yet exactly, boss.'

'Jeez, Links, how deep is this pit?'

'I think,' Links replied faintly, 'it's more sort of bottomless. Like, I am in fact still falling.'

'You are?'

'I believe so, yes, Mr Lundqvist. And Mr Lundqvist, there's all sorts of really weird things down here, like —'

'Fine.' Lundqvist stood for a moment, thinking. 'Links,' he said, 'I want you to think basic physical and mathematical theory.'

'I'm doing just that, Mr Lundqvist.'

'Okay. The universe is curved, right?'

'If you say so, skip.'

'In which case,' said Lundqvist, straightening his back and blowing the dust off his trouser knees, 'if you keep falling, then sooner or later you're gonna end up exactly where you started. The trick at that point is to grab hold of something and haul yourself clear. Is that okay with you, Links? Save me having to clamber down with ropes and things.'

'Anything you say, chief.'

'It may take some time, you realise.'

'I'm game, Mr Lundqvist.'

'Thousands of years, maybe.'

'No problem, Mr Lundqvist. I can catch up on my written

coursework while I'm down here.'

'Good lad. Well, if you do get free in the next hour or so, I'll be around here somewhere.'

'Okay, Mr Lundqvist. Message received, over and out.'

And, of course, in Links' case, down as well. We down, we gone, in fact. Lundqvist stood up, stretched his cramped muscles, and walked off in the direction of the refreshment area.

'You ready, Nick?'

Machiavelli nodded grimly. Since resolving to do this thing, he'd been bought several large brandies and a double measure of the native infernal liqueur, Evil Spirit. The result was that he was bloody, bold, resolute and quite incapable of standing up on his own. Standing up was not, however, a prerequisite for what George had in mind.

'You got everything?'

'Think so, George. In fact . . .'

'Mm?'

'Looks like I got two of everything,' Machiavelli burbled. 'Looks remarkably like, acshlky, because . . .'

'That's fine, Nick,' said George firmly, 'that means you'll have a spare. Ready, you two?'

Two hovering seagulls dipped their wingtips in acknowledgement.

'Okay.' Lundqvist straightened his back, blew into the loudspeaker a couple of times to check it was working, and took a deep breath. The fires of EuroBosch glinted off his mirror sunglasses, miraculously unbroken.

Around him, six concentric circles of apprehensive fiends crouched slightly lower and wished they were somewhere else.

'OKAY, GEORGE,' Lundqvist amplified, 'I KNOW YOU'RE IN THERE. IT GOES WITHOUT SAYING I

HAVE THE AREA SURROUNDED.'

Pause. No sound, except for the background screams, groans and hisses of hot iron on perpetually renewed flesh. You could have heard a twenty-foot molybdenum steel pin drop.

'GEORGE,' Lundqvist boomed, 'IT'S TIME TO CALL IT A DAY. COME OUT WITH YOUR HANDS ...'

A figure appeared, silhouetted against the background flames, in the doorway of the refreshment area. Its hands were above its head. Lundqvist relaxed perceptibly, until he was only as tense as a steel hawser at breaking point.

'Hi,' the figure said.

The fiends edged back slightly. Sure thing, they were fiends, fiends are incapable of fear. It's just that there's no point in being bloody daft, that's all.

Lundqvist jumped up. 'C'mon, guys,' he yelled, 'what are you waiting for? Grab the sucker.'

A fiend turned its bird's head and gave him a look. 'What, us?' it cheeped.

'Yes.'

'What do you take us for, cocker bloody spaniels?'

Lundqvist glanced round the various shoulder-ornaments around him. 'Some of you,' he said, 'yes. Now get on with it.'

With a whimper, the fiends threw themselves forward and sprang at the outline in the doorway. When they were within about ten paces ...

... The figure suddenly went *whoosh!* and burst into flame.

Screaming with frustrated rage, Lundqvist shoved his way through the throng of gibbering, terrified fiends and hurled himself at the human torch; who hit him quite hard in the stomach, winding him, and grinned.

'Hiya, Kurt,' he said. 'Long time no see.'

Lundqvist rubbed the ash from his eyelashes out of his eyes and gurgled. 'Machiavelli!' he howled. 'You'll burn in hell for this!'

Machiavelli shrugged a pair of incandescent shoulders. 'You really think so?' he said. 'We'll see.'

Meanwhile, Lucky George, who had spent the last ten minutes breaking open all the disposable cigarette lighters from the display pack behind the bar and emptying them over Machiavelli's head, grinned and slipped quietly away down the fire escape. Every permanent structure in the complex, by the way, has to have a fire escape, because of the building regulations. Where on earth the fire is supposed to escape to is anybody's guess.

A quick dash across the frozen lake brought George out at the foot of the Try-Your-Strength machine. A nice idea, this; you push hard against a huge lever shaped like a flute, which sends the marker on the dial of the machine up the calibrated scale. If you're strong enough, the marker hits a little bell, and assorted nightmarish fiends spring out of a trapdoor in the side of the machine and carry you off to everlasting torment. Serves you right for showing off.

A seagull floated down from the top of the machine, came in on the glide, turned into the slight breeze and dropped on to George's shoulder.

'Thanks,' George said.

'It waff noffing,' replied Mike through his badly singed beak. 'Pief of duff, onfe I'd got the matcheff lit.'

'Where is he now?'

The seagull turned its head. 'Ofer there by that horfe'f head fing,' he replied. 'No more idea of tracking than my granny'f cat.'

'Fine,' George said. 'Found the emergency exit yet?'

'Larry'f ftill looking. Af foon af he'f found it, we'll let you know.'

'Good stuff,' George replied. 'I'll go over there and make myself inconspicuous for a bit. Ciao.'

'Here, boff . . .' But George had gone, stepping quickly and silently across the scorched grass. The seagull shrugged.

'Big enuff and ugly enuff to look after himfelf,' he muttered, hopefully.

Over there turned out to be the activity described in the brochure as the ultimate in paintball games.

'That was good timing,' remarked the round-bodied, owl-headed gatefiend as George strolled in. 'Just in time for the next detail. You get the stuff from that shed over there, and they tell you what to do.'

'Thanks,' George replied.

You must remember this; a shed is but a shed, a hut is but a hut. The fundamental things apply, as time goes by. True, it was apparently constructed out of a giant mother-of-pearl pumpkin with a hole smashed in the side for a doorway, but inside it was pure Portakabin.

'What size?' demanded the attendant fiend.

'Dunno,' George replied. 'You're the man with the experienced eye, you tell me.'

'67D,' the fiend replied. 'You can change over there.'

He handed George a plastic carrier bag, and George retired into a sort of sub-shed, or cubicle, where he opened the bag and inspected the contents.

'Hey!' he said, with admiration in his voice. 'Now that's really something else.'

The bag contained a full-size replacement skin, with fitted scalp and all matching bits. He hoped very much that it was designed to be worn over one's existing skin. It was.

Sticking in the small of the skin's back was a dagger, driven in up to its hilt. There was no blade, fortuitously. George eased his way into the skin, settled his face as comfortably as possible into the mask, and stepped out of the cubicle.

'Okay,' said the attendant fiend. 'The rest of the detail are waiting outside.'

'Just going.'

'Hey.'

'Yes.'

'Forgotten something?'

'Have I?'

'In the rack,' said the fiend, pointing. 'Take your pick. Limit of three per competitor.'

From the rack, George selected a nine-inch stiletto, a Venetian-pattern cinquedea dagger and a short Flemish falchion. Then he stepped outside.

There were about thirty competitors, all dressed (to take them at face value, so to speak) in skins with knives stuck through them. Some of them were having a crafty last cigarette, others were fine-tuning their eyebrows, polishing their elbows, or just standing around tapping their feet. An eagle-headed fiend with talons for hands waved an umbrella in the air to attract their attention.

'Right, guys and girls,' it said. 'Just a few ground rules before we start. Now, we all want to have a good time, so the key thing to remember is, don't get carried away. Right?'

A few of the competitors nodded. The fiend continued.

'Now,' it said, 'the objective is, to stab as many of your fellow competitors repeatedly through the body and neck as you can within the allotted time without getting stabbed yourself. Now, for your comfort and convenience, we have to say No Head Wounds. The skins are perfectly safe under normal use, but in the past we have had a *few* problems with direct hits on the temples and the eyes. That still leaves you a hell of a lot of body surface to be going on with, and I'm sure you'll all agree that safe's better than sorry.'

A slight sussuration of background grumbling soon faded away, and the fiend continued:

'The only other thing we do insist on is, for obvious reasons, No Disembowelling. Now I realise that some of you here today will have perfectly genuine tribal, cultural or religious disembowelling traditions, and of course we respect that. So all of you are equipped with our very realistic plastic giblets, which fit neatly into the concealed pocket in the front of your skinsuits here –' The fiend demonstrated, pulling a yard of polythene colon out of his stomach and folding it away neatly. '– and you release those by simply pulling on the little blue ripcord which you'll find midway between the nipples on your skinsuit. Right, that's it, basically. Go out and have a bloody good time.'

The fiend blew a whistle, jumped sideways and curled up into a tight ball with its arms over its head. George hadn't been standing there for more than a twentieth of a second when the man who'd been on his immediate left threw away his cigarette, brandished a stagshorn-hilted Provençal hunting sword and jumped at him.

George sidestepped, landed a kick on his assailant's behind as he sailed by, and said, 'Boo!' Then he ran for it.

From the cover of an overturned table (in which a Florentine-pattern broadsword and two richly inlaid baselards were already embedded) he watched the game with growing fascination. After the first heady slugfest, which eliminated the duffers and the majority of the corporate entertainment crowd, the pace slowed down dramatically and the element of skill came to the fore.

Since there was sod-all natural cover, concealment and stalking were confined to pretending to be a hideously mangled corpse until your prospective victim had turned his back. That explained, George realised, the knife-hilt already inserted in the suit. The trick, apparently, was simply to count the number of hilts projecting out of each potential body. Two or more meant he was probably genuine. Once you'd got that far, approach with caution nevertheless, because a number of competitors (who'd clearly done this before) had taken the precaution of impaling themselves with one of their three permitted weapons before hitting the deck. Not, in George's opinion at least, strictly ethical, but presumably within the letter if not the spirit of the rules.

George was just bracing himself to step out from his hide and have a go when a body crumpled down over the side of his table and landed heavily in his lap. As it fell, its face-mask was pulled aside and George recognised the features of his lawyer, Mr Van Appin.

'Hello, Pete,' George said. 'What are you doing here?'

Mr Van Appin grimaced. 'I died,' he said.

George raised an eyebrow. 'I thought you had a special arrangement,' he said.

'I did,' Van Appin replied. 'I had a watertight agreement. Trouble is, I drafted it myself.'

George restrained a snigger. 'Bad move, that.'

'It was, rather,' the lawyer replied. 'Still, a fee's a fee, and when your best client comes to you and asks you to do a job, you don't turn round and say, Sorry, conflict of interests, try the guys down the road. That's not the way successful practices are built up, George.'

'Suppose not.'

Mr Van Appin shrugged. 'It's not so bad, actually,' he said. 'I've still got my, uh, other offices in the other centuries, so I can continue to service my existing client base, more or less, while being in a position to extend my operation to this exciting new catchment area down here. I mean, if you can't get business down here . . .'

'Pete,' George shook his head sadly. 'I think you're in for a bit of a shock if you think you're the only lawyer in these parts. I think you'll find there's rather a lot of them end up here. All of them, in fact, sooner or later.'

Mr Van Appin shrugged. 'So what?' he said. 'A little competition never did anybody any harm. So long, George.'

'Ciao, Pete.'

Mr Van Appin quivered and lay still, and George leant back against his table leg and watched for a few minutes. Two competitors had run each other through with Spanish rapiers at exactly the same moment and were arguing heatedly about who scored what.

'Excuse me.' George felt a light tap on his shoulder. He whirled round, saw a figure with no clothes on looming over him with some sort of poleaxe, and lunged with the cinquedea. The blade went through smoothly and out the other side.

'I think you're supposed to fall over or something,' George said.

'Actually,' replied the man, 'I'm just the linesman.'

'Oh.' George grinned awkwardly. 'Sorry about that.'

'No problem.' The linesman, who had just been transferred at his own request from the spectral engineers' corps, after a long and distinguished term of service as a captain of spectral warriors, shrugged and died. 'It happens to me all the time,' he said posthumously.

'Was there something?' George asked.

'I just wondered,' said the linesman, 'are you Lucky George Faust, by any chance?'

George nodded. 'Who wants to know?' he asked.

'It's just that Kurt Lundqvist's headed this way with a posse of heavily charred fiends,' the linesman replied. 'For reasons of my own which I won't bore you with, I don't fancy being around when he gets here. In fact,' the linesman added, 'things have worked out pretty damn near perfect, you killing me like that. I mean, stands to reason, even that vindictive little sod can't kill me if I'm dead already.'

'It was nothing.'

The linesman smiled, reached in his pocket and produced two credit cards, which he laid on his eyelids. 'It's cheaper this way if you're a regular customer,' he explained. 'Good luck.'

'Thanks.' George looked up and saw a seagull hovering overhead. It occurred to him that Larry wouldn't be able to recognise him in his skinsuit, so he stripped it off and dumped it.

'Hey,' said a competitor, who'd been stalking George for

seven minutes with a two-foot balloch knife. 'That's cheating.'

'Nuts,' George replied, and swatted him over the head with a chair. He collapsed on the ground, muttering. The seagull pitched on the edge of the table and ruffled its wing feathers with its beak.

'Sodding awful place for flying, this,' Larry remarked with his mouth full. 'Thermals in all the wrong places, because of all the fires.'

'Found it yet?'

'The emergency exit?' The seagull nodded its beak. 'Follow me.'

THERE is much esoteric argument in contract killing circles about the greatest asset a hit-man can have. Some say, the new Steyr sniper's rifle with infra-red dot sights and integral sound suppressor. Others argue for a mint condition, first-issue Sykes-Fairbairn combat knife, while a significant minority gives its vote to the .50 calibre Desert Eagle with Hydrashock +P ammo and a Kassnar 'scope.

Kurt Lundqvist begs to differ. As far as he's concerned, the assassin most likely to succeed is the one who has rather more brains than can comfortably be fitted into a matchbox, all the matches having been removed. This, he realises, rules out about ninety-seven per cent of his professional colleagues, but so what? The last person to call him a reactionary elitist is now an integral part of the foundations of New York's celebrated Flatiron Building.

His sequence of thought, once he'd realised that Lucky George had slipped past him at the Hellza-Pop-Inn, was as follows:

Lucky George has escaped.

When it comes to getting away with it, Lucky George is about the best there is.

It is, therefore, pointless to try and stop Lucky George

getting to the emergency exit. Far better to go directly to the emergency exit and wait for him there.

Slowly, with infinite labour, Links Jotapian drove the last crampon into the side of the pit and paused, dragging air into his creased lungs before hauling himself over the lip of the pit and on to solid ground.

Some escape, huh? First, he'd broken his fall by throwing his arms and legs out to their full extent, until the friction of his hands and feet against the toughened glass sides of the shaft had slowed him down and eventually stopped him.

Fair enough, but he couldn't stay wedged like that for ever; and as soon as·he moved hand or foot, down he'd continue going.

Fortunately, however, he'd got with him his Kurt Lundqvist Limited Edition Adventurer's Kit. As a matter of cold fact, the production of this piece of merchandising hadn't been sanctioned by the man himself, which may account for the fact that the merchandiser now lives at the bottom of the Hudson River and wears concrete trainers. Nevertheless, the contents of the package (which collapses down to the size of a ballpoint pen, and is made, of course, in Korea) include such useful items as suction pads for hands and feet, crampons, a folding iceaxe, two hundred yards of gossamer-thin polymer cord (breaking point six tons) and a small rectangular key thing with no discernible purpose whatsoever.

One-handed opening of Kit, extraction of suction pad, donning of same and adhesion to the wall. It was then just a case of biffing in crampons and the long hard slog uphill. Still better than school.

'Mr Lundqvist.' The walkie-talkie was dead, squatted into a jumble of springs and wires by a collision with the shaft wall. He dumped it – a month's waiting on tables at Baisbekian's Diner down the tubes, but one learns to be stoical under combat conditions – and applied his mind. Think like

Lundqvist, and you'll know where he is.

Links cast an eye over the grounds of the Park, and concentrated. Lucky George is a pro, right? Where would a pro hide? Think Lesson Six. Answer: a pro will always try and find a crowd to mingle with, because the best camouflage is people. In fact, that's really the only reason Links could possibly imagine for their existing at all.

Various crowds dotted about the place. The queue for the Ferris Ears; no, too static. A pro tries not to remain stationary for more than five seconds in a combat zone. Therefore rule out also the milling throng waiting to go on the torture by outsize musical instruments, and the Knight Torn By Dogs booth. There was quite a knot of people hanging about at the top of the campus, opposite the Ferris Ears, but that was also too conspicuous; the Toad Rides (up to the top of the sand dunes and back astride a giant red-spotted toad, conducted by a bear-headed fiend – fifty cents, children and perjurors half price) were closely supervised by fiends, and a pro doesn't go anywhere where there's too many guards looking at faces. There were a few passers-by waiting for Captain Beaky's next feed, but in the circumstances George probably wouldn't feel too comfortable hanging about round there. That left the paintball game.

Idiots rush in where demons fear to tread. Slowly and deliberately, Links checked his equipment. Night-stick; Smith & Wesson Model 686 in .357, loaded with Federal 160-grain jacketed hollow-points; handcuffs; ninja throwing-stars. Something else, but he couldn't remember what. Ah yes, that was it, and he had indeed remembered to put on clean underwear that morning. He pulled his balaclava down over his face and broke into a loping run.

Honest to God, his intention had been simply to find Lundqvist and help out. The thought of making the collar himself, alone and unassisted, wiping his mentor's eye and incidentally claiming the staggeringly huge reward, hadn't once cross his mind. But . . .

There he was, large as life, strolling hands in pockets towards the emergency exit, eating candy floss and with a seagull sitting on his shoulder. Lucky George, History's most wanted man. Hot *damn*!

With a cool smoothness born of countless hours of practice in front of the bathroom mirror, Links crouched, drew and assumed a perfect Weaver stance. Feeling for the bottom of the trigger, McGivern-style, he drew a fine bead on the side of George's head, took up the slack on the trigger and yelled, 'Freeze!'

George stopped, looked round at him and said, 'Me?'

'You.' Links half-closed his left eye, concentrating with all his being on the little strips of light either side of the foresight. 'One move and you're history, man.'

George raised an eyebrow. 'How do you mean?' he said.

The gyroscope inside Links' brain wobbled slightly. 'What?' he shouted.

'How do you mean, history? Do I become suddenly famous or something?'

'It means you get to be strictly past tense, man. Like, the late Lucky George, kinda thing. You get?'

'Late for what?'

'Your own funeral, sucker.' The foresight of the Smith wavered about; no matter how you try, you just can't combine repartee with marksmanship. Ask Oscar Wilde or anyone.

'Oh, I think they'd wait, don't you?' George replied. 'I mean, not much point having the wretched thing if there's nothing to bury. Mind you, if, for example, mine was at ten thirty and they'd got another one booked in at eleven fifteen, say, I can see there could be problems. Hearses double-parked, that sort of thing. Right, I'll bear that in mind.'

'Look . . .'

'On the other hand,' George continued through a mouthful of finely spun sugar, 'the same would go for weddings, wouldn't it, and think how many times the bride shows up late.

Never causes a problem in the long run, through, does it? I think they make allowances for that sort of thing in the scheduling.'

'*Look . . .*'

George nodded upwards. 'There's a seagull hovering over your head with a ten-pound lead weight in its claws, had you noticed?'

Links sneered. 'You think I was born yesterday?' he said contemptuously.

George considered. 'Well,' he said, 'if you were you're pretty damn precocious, that's all I can say. I take it you're not fussed about the seagull?'

'*Look . . .*'

The lead weight fell, hitting Links on the back of the head. 'Thanks, Larry,' George called out. 'Right, can we please get on? This place is starting to get on my nerves.'

The emergency exit was just behind the Helmeted Dwarf, cunningly concealed in the gaping jaws of a twelve-foot-long polystyrene dragon. Just to ram the point home, there was also a big No Entry sign just above the dragon's head, qualified by the words *Except for Access*. After a final look round, George reached for the door handle . . .

. . . But the door swung out of its own accord, to reveal Lundqvist, standing behind his trusty .40 Glock. Before George had time to move at all, Lundqvist was through the door and the pistol's ugly snout was nuzzling his ear.

'Okay, George,' Lundqvist hissed. 'Lose the gulls. Now.'

George shrugged. 'You heard the man, guys. Go for a ride on the Lucky Dipper or something. I shan't be long.'

Mike flapped his wings and opened his beak to protest; but his bird's eye, hundreds of times more perceptive than its human equivalent, saw Lundqvist's finger move maybe a thousandth of an inch on the trigger and he subsided. 'Be seeing you, then,' he gulped, and bobbed away into the breeze. Larry remained where he was.

'You too, beakface,' Lundqvist growled.

'You'll pay for this,' the gull replied. 'One day.'

Lundqvist grinned. 'You reckon?'

Larry nodded. 'Maybe not tomorrow,' he said, 'maybe not this year. But sometime, somewhere, you'll be hanging out washing or cleaning the car, and then, *splat!* You just think about it, Lundqvist, that's all.'

With long, heavy wingbeats he dragged himself into the air, and soon was nothing but a white speck. Lundqvist let his breath go.

'You and me, George,' he said.

'You and me, Kurt. How about a nice game of back-gammon?'

Lundqvist shook his head. 'Not this time, George,' he said. 'This time it's goodbye, for ever. Dead or alive, they said, remember.'

'I take it you're going for the lazy option.'

Lundqvist nodded. 'It's my back,' he said. 'Too much heavy lifting and I get shooting pains up my left side.'

George raised a quizzical eyebrow. 'Don't think dead's got a lot of significance here, Kurt,' he said, 'if you don't mind my saying so. Sort of goes with the territory, if you see what I—'

'No.' Lundqvist's grin widened. 'This thing's loaded with hollow-points filled with holy water.'

'I see,' said George. 'A water pistol.'

'Holy water,' Lundqvist repeated. 'Dead and exorcised in one shot. We call it one-stop termination. You ain't going *nowhere.*'

'How terribly clever.' George's face had on its patient, let's-humour-the-child expression, the very same one that had haunted Lundqvist's childhood nightmares. It meant, 'Kurt, I'm going to make you look an absolute plonker in front of the whole school,' and it had never once failed to deliver. Lundqvist quickly reviewed the situation in his mind and decided that for the first and last time, George was simply bluffing.

'So,' George said, 'you reckon you can just cold-bloodedly pull the trigger and blow my brains out, is that it?'

'Yup.'

The expression blossomed into a smile of tender contempt. 'Not unless you take the safety catch off first you can't,' he said.

In the split second it took Lundqvist to check, see that the safety catch was indeed off, and start squeezing off the shot, George had taken the reminder of his candy floss, stuck it up the barrel of the gun and kicked Lundqvist savagely in the nuts. With a howl that was five-per-cent pain and ninety-five-per-cent frustrated rage, Lundqvist slowly doubled up and sagged on to the ground.

'Never mind, Kurt,' said George, not unkindly, as he stepped over his fallen assailant. 'One of these days you'll get something right, just you wait and see.'

Then he stepped through the door and closed it behind him.

Thanks to his abstemious lifestyle and peak physical condition it took Lundqvist maybe a total of three minutes to recover sufficiently to haul himself up on to his feet, totter wildly and fall flat on his face, banging his forehead painfully on a sharp stone. Which only goes to show; had he ruined his health with alcohol, rich foods and dissipation he'd never have been fit enough to get beaten up in the first place.

Once he'd managed to get his legs working again, he pulled the candy-floss stick out of the muzzle of his gun, kicked open the emergency exit door, and burst through.

Circumstances alter cases. None of that hyper-cautious catlike stealth one associates with the covert operations pro – flattening oneself against walls, darting in and out of shadows and leaping round corners in a copybook FBI crouch. As soon as he was through the door, he simply ran as fast as he could down the tunnel, firing wildly into the darkness and shouting,

'You bastard, I'm gonna rip your frigging lungs out!' at the top of his voice.

Which is why he didn't notice the pillar; not, at least, until it connected with his chin.

Thirty seconds later, Lucky George emerged from behind the pillar, prodded Lundqvist's head with his foot to make sure he was indeed fast asleep, bent down, picked up the pistol and slipped it in his pocket. A more punctilious man would have written out a receipt, but George was in a hurry.

A length of parcel string and a few Boy Scout knots later, he stood up, looked both ways along the tunnel, switched on Lundqvist's torch (which the silly man had forgotten all about in his excitement) and strolled on up the tunnel, whistling.

Four hundred yards or so later, he came to a T-junction. There were helpful signs painted on the wall, thus:

> HELL →
> ←DAMNATION
> ←ADMINISTRATION

Synonyms, George thought, but never mind. He turned left.

Three hundred yards brought him to a lift. Why walk, he said to himself, when you can ride?

The trick is, not to go down.

The doors slid open, revealing the usual selection of buttons, labelled:

> PENTHOUSE
> CENTRAL ADMIN
> ACCOUNTS
> CAFETERIA
> BOILER ROOM
> MEZZANINE
> GROUND
> HELL FIRE

DAMNATION
FILE STORE

The red light was on opposite GROUND. As for the rest; CAFETERIA sounded nice, MEZZANINE was anybody's guess, and FILE STORE sent a shiver oscillating through his central nervous system. He was about to press CAFETERIA when something inside him coughed discreetly and whispered, *Try the boiler room.*

George rationalised. Well, why not? The words conjured up a picture of a big, noisy, dark jungle of pipes and machines, the sort of place you could hide in for ages with no chance of anybody finding you; a good place to pause, regroup and work out what to do next.

George wasn't convinced. What the devil do I want to go to the boiler room for? Sounds absolutely awful. He reached out to prod CAFETERIA, but his finger froze, a few thousandths of an inch away from contact.

Try the boiler room.

The philosopher Socrates, so tradition has it, played host to an inner voice, accustomed to telling him what to do in moments of indecision. History tells us that Socrates was found guilty on trumped-up charges and executed by poison, but maybe we don't have all the facts. Maybe, a nanosecond before drinking the hemlock, Socrates asked his inner voice *What the fuck have you gone and got me into, peanut-brain?* and the inner voice explained it all in words of one syllable, allowing the great philosopher to die with a huge cocky grin frozen all over his face.

Maybe there's a coffee machine in the boiler room.

He lowered his finger and pressed the appropriate button, closing the lift door.

* * *

Blessed are the pure in heart, for they shall see God.

Blessed are the jammy bastards, for they shall see God without an appointment.

It was dark in the boiler room, as he'd predicted. It was also very quiet, and very cold. All the surfaces were thick with dust. All in all, Lucky George decided, he'd been in more convivial graves. Which was, incidentally, true.

There were pipes, just as in his mental picture, and machines. Enormous machines, painted matt black enamel with heavy solid brass fittings, very old-fashioned, high quality looking. No plastic anywhere; steel, brass and the occasional glass cover, white enamel dial, engraved brass control panel. None of the machines appeared to be switched on. The place had the look of a major vintage traction engine rally five minutes after the beer tent has opened.

George had been wandering about for perhaps ten minutes or so (not that Time seemed a particularly useful concept in a place like this, like an umbrella at the bottom of the sea) when he thought he heard a tiny, distant screaming noise, like a very small, fast lathe. He walked towards it.

It was a long walk. The place was, he realised, absolutely huge, and full of these enormous, silent pieces of hardware; each one, he noticed curiously, apparently different. He hadn't the faintest idea what any of them were. Ah, but if only he could get in here with a small crane and a fleet of big lorries, there was an absolute fortune in scrap value alone.

If wishes were pantechnicons, beggars would invest heavily in offshore roll-up unit trusts. George dismissed the thought from his mind, because the light and the noise were getting closer. Still a hell of a long way away, though. George's feet were beginning to hurt.

Scree-ee-ee-eee. Pause. *Scree-ee-yoww-ee.* Unmistakable sound of cutting metal. Someone was making something.

Screee-ee-ee

Screeeeee-ee-yowwww-eee
Screee-eeeee
'Bugger!'

A minuscule voice, ever so far away. George stopped dead in his tracks and listened, but all he could hear was the sound of the lathe, like the shriek of an hysterical elf.

Blessed are the bone idle, for they shall stand and watch other people working.

George walked on towards the noise.

Had Links Jotapian been there, instead of lying on his back sleeping the sleep of the mildly concussed, he'd have witnessed a near perfect exhibition of the art of getting out of being tied up without cutting your wrists on the string.

Having woken up, assessed the position and sworn a lot, Lundqvist used his feet to back himself up against the wall. No help there; the sides were smooth as glass, so no useful rocky outcrops to saw through the rope on.

String professionally tight, so no percentage in curling the hands up small in the hope of slipping them through.

Never mind. The seasoned campaigner anticipates this sort of thing. On the back of Lundqvist's trouser belt was a thing like a big plastic button. In fact, this was a snap-on cover, easily flicked off with the fingernails, underneath which was a tiny sliver of scalpel blade fixed lengthways into the belt on a rivet. Nothing easier than to fray the rope up against that a few times and then gently ease it apart.

Cheating? In the trade, they call it materiel superiority.

A little later Lundqvist stood up, marshalled his limbs into some semblance of discipline and trudged up the corridor. He knew without being told that he was on a hiding to nothing. He was lost, unarmed, punch-drunk and thoroughly demoralised. High time he retired, made way for all those up and coming youngsters who were the hope of the profession for the years to come.

Absolutely. Just as soon as he'd found Lucky bloody George and disembowelled him with his bare hands, he'd pack the whole thing in, buy a little bungalow somewhere and grow lupins. Until then, the idea of giving up was unthinkable. It would be like going on a round-the-world cruise knowing you'd left the oven on.

In due course he came to a lift.

PENTHOUSE
CENTRAL ADMIN
ACCOUNTS
CAFETERIA
BOILER ROOM
MEZZANINE
GROUND
HELL FIRE
DAMNATION
FILE STORE

A likely story. You don't get presented with the Academy of Elite Forces' coveted Gold Silencer Award three years in succession ('First of all I'd like to thank my victims, without whom . . .') unless you can recognise a supernaturally induced hologram when you see one. If the wretched thing had had TRAP over the door in three-foot-high neon letters, it couldn't have been more obvious.

On the other hand, what the hell? He walked in, pressed a button at random, and folded his arms.

Screee-eee-eeeeee-ee-clunk.

'Anybody home?'

George waited for a moment, listening to his voice echoing around the galleries of silent ironmongery until it was soaked up in the dust-insulated vastness. If there was anybody there, they were either lying in wait, too engrossed in what they were doing to hear, or listening to something on headphones.

Well, if they were lying in wait, they'd had plenty of opportunities by now. He walked on.

Scree-eee-ee-scrinklescrinklescrinkle.

'Oh sod!'

The light suddenly vanished, blocked out by the bulk of an enormous machine. Slowly, feeling his intestines practising left-hand clove hitches, George edged round the machine, and suddenly saw . . .

A workbench, illuminated by a low, brilliant lamp, throwing out the special brand of extra white, hard light that you need if you're dealing with tolerances of fractions of a millimetre. Around the bench were racks of tools – George assumed they were tools; most of them he'd never seen anything like before, even in the sort of dreams that would have had Freud under a cold shower in three seconds flat – but he knew they were tools. They had that worn, shiny, reliable look, that says *I know what I'm doing even if you don't*. Mounted in the centre of the bench was this really weird lathe; it wasn't big, but it seemed to ooze power, as if once you'd worked out how to use it you could make absolutely anything at all on it. And, George realised, it was transparent. In fact, that was where the light was coming from, not the poxy 100-watt bulb in the anglepoise. Light was seeping out from it in all directions, as through a window or the crack under a door. Light from where, you really didn't want to know.

Behind the bench was a man; short, round, wearing a brown overall and a cap with a few wisps of untidy grey hair curling out under its brim like Russian vine, his face consisting of a nosetip and a mouth huddled in the shelter of an enormous pair of thick-lensed spectacles. In one hand, he held a Vernier caliper, while with the other he was scratching his neck, just behind the ear.

'Hullo, George,' the man said. 'You found your way here all right, then.'

George nodded. Never seen this guy before in my life, he thought. Something funny here.

He glanced down at the lathe. In the jaws of the chuck he could see a tiny, er, *thing*, a component, a bit out of something; minute, hard, shiny with the magnificent hard gleam of newly turned steel, that beautiful clarity of tone that makes polished silver look like fog. Whatever it was, it had been machined to perfection. It seemed to sing in the lathe.

'Bloody thing,' said the man.

'Problem?'

The man nodded. 'Taken too much off, haven't I? Useless. Have to start again.' He opened the chuck, lifted the thing out and tossed it contemptuously into the scrap bucket under the bench. 'Me own fault,' he said, grinning. 'In too much of a rush, as per usual.'

'Been doing it long?'

'Twenty-three years,' the man replied, 'not a big job, really.' Already, he had a new blank of material in the jaws and was winding the chuck. 'Don't suppose it'll take me much longer to turn up another one.'

'I . . .' George began, and then stopped. 'What was it?' he asked.

The man looked up from his work. 'Ratchet collar for the main inner bearing,' he replied. 'Fits on the main driveshaft, stops the auto-index from getting out of synch.'

'Ah.'

''Cos,' the man went on, smiling, 'if that gets out of sequence, your whole locator drive's up the spout, and you'll be having Wednesdays for Tuesdays and Sundays midweek.'

'Ah.'

'Yeah.' The man nodded. 'It's a good life if you don't weaken,' he added, and measured something.

'Sorry,' George said, 'am I disturbing you, because . . .'

The man shook his head. 'Glad of the company,' he replied.

'Gets a bit lonely up here, fiddlearsing about all day long. You getting on all right?'

'I suppose so. Can I hold anything, or pass you things?'

'If you like.' The man scribed a line with an invisibly thin scriber. 'Four hundred yards got to come off that,' he said. 'Should be all right so long as we go nice and steady.' He stooped down and began rummaging in a box.

'Four hundred yards.'

The man nodded. 'I know,' he said. 'Bloody fine tolerances, bugger all margin of error.'

Something clicked in George's mind. It wasn't Time that was weird here, it was Scale. Everything here was much, much bigger than it looked, but the immensity of the place created its own unique perspectives. He'd probably been standing here for five years already.

'Look at the bloody mess this place is in,' the man said, waving vaguely. 'The time I waste, looking for things. Soon as I've done this job, I've got to have a bloody good tidy-up.'

George licked his lips, which were suddenly dry. 'Excuse me asking,' he said, 'but who exactly are you?'

The men looked up. 'Me?' he said. George nodded. With a flick of his finger, the man switched on the lathe. Thousands of feet below, George just knew, the faint, scarcely perceptible noise it made was midsummer thunder.

'Well,' the man said, 'the job description is General Operative (Dilapidations).'

'I see.'

'Bit of a mouthful,' the man said.

George nodded. 'Usually abbreviated, I suppose.'

'That's the idea.'

'Right.' George took a deep breath. 'I've been wanting to meet you for a long time,' he said.

General Operative (Dilapidations), better known by the handy acronym.

* * *

Lundqvist stopped dead in his tracks. He could feel the point needle-sharp against the skin of his neck; that particularly vulnerable spot between the collar bones.

'G'day,' said the angel.

Lundqvist thought about edging backwards, but knew that the point would follow him. Angel or no angel, this guy knew his trade.

At least, Lundqvist realised, I know where I am now.

'I thought,' he said, looking down the runway of fine blued steel that ran from his neck to the angel's hand, 'you people were supposed to be equipped with flaming swords.'

The angel gave him a look. 'Stone the crows, sport,' he said. 'What d'you think this is, a flamin' letter opener?'

'Hi, God,' said Lucky George.

'Could you just pass me that file?' God replied. 'Not that one, the little Swiss job with the red handle. Ta.'

George looked down the rack, saw something like an extra-thin hair with the appropriate coloured handle, and passed it over. God pushed his glasses back up his nose, closed one eye and swept the file feather-light over the surface of the metal.

'Bugger,' he said. 'Pressed too hard. Look, bloody great graunch-marks all over the thing. Have to stone it all off and start again.' He sighed, and reached for an atom-thin whetstone. 'I must be having one of those days,' he said.

George replaced the file in the rack. 'Dilapidations?' he asked.

The man nodded. 'That means fixing things,' he said. 'It's what I mostly do these days. You made it, they said to me, you damn well fix it when it plays up. Fair enough, I suppose. Means I can put in a few mods here and there, whenever I see something I can improve.' He pointed at the component in the chuck. 'Like this, frinstance.'

George smiled weakly. 'You did say what it was,' he said, 'but I'm afraid I've forgotten.'

'Pretty simple, really,' God replied. 'Time, right? Your basic seven-day week revolves on a central spindle. Each day is indexed into position by a lifting hand driving a ratchet, and then it's locked in place by a spring-loaded pawl locating in a groove, see? Absolutely basic design.'

George nodded helplessly. Somehow or other, he understood, vaguely.

The man shook his head. 'Bloody awful,' he said. 'Makes me ashamed every time I think of it. All it needs is for the bearing the cylinder rides on to wear a bit, and the whole thing grinds to a halt.'

'And has it?'

'Bound to. This is the third one I've had to make so far, and the bloody thing's scarcely run in.'

George stared. 'You mean the World?' he said.

'The Universe,' God replied. 'Shouldn't have components like this packing up already. Should be good for another forty billion years at least, with a bit of lube and a good clean now and again, before I've got to start replacing the bearings. Must've got it wrong somewhere, don't you think?'

George remained silent. Not for him to say, he reckoned.

'So,' God continued, rubbing his nose with the back of his hand, 'this time I'm making the bugger out of sixteen-gauge chronium carbide, and I'm going to case-harden it again before it goes back in, making sure there's no soft spots where I've cut too deep. If that doesn't do it, then stuff it.'

He increased the lathe speed slightly and the cutter screee'd across the surface, throwing out tiny specks of swarf-like powdered stars.

'Leap year,' George said.

'You got it,' the man replied. 'That's only when it gets really bad, mind you, when the whole poxy year gets out of sequence. A little bit like that, you see, it can bugger up the whole sodding thing in no time at all.'

'I suppose so.'

'No suppose about it.' Screeeee, went the lathe. Tiny flecks of ground material, so small as to float in the air, drifted down, out through the air conditioning system and onwards through the galaxy, tails burning, frightening the living daylights out of superstitious princes. 'Your Time, see, that's your major motive force. If your Time goes wrong, everything goes wrong. Bits get out of place, components get all graunched and burred up, things fall apart, the centre cannot hold . . .'

'Entropy,' said George.

'Poncy name for it, yeah.' God was silent for a moment, brooding. 'This ought to do the trick. Just have to try it and see, won't we?'

He turned up the lathe speed until the component disappeared in a white blur, and scree'd for a while. From time to time, he stopped, measured, tutted, scratched his ear, started again. The surface of the Thing was so smooth it seemed to evade eyesight, like wet soap in a bath.

'Well now, George mate,' God said, miking the component up for the tenth or eleventh time, 'I suppose we ought to be getting you back to the old hot spot in a minute.' He closed one eye and squinted through his right spectacle lens at the micrometer dial. 'Another gnat's nibble still to go,' he sighed. 'Always takes longer than you think, this last bit.'

George stayed where he was, immobilised. For the first time in his life, he didn't know what to do. Not a nice feeling, but somehow it didn't hurt. This was because he knew the man would do the right thing.

'Can't have people breaking out all over the place,' God went on. 'Shocking. Got to do something about it. Just pass me that small oilcan, the one on your left. No, the other one. Thanks.'

'So,' George said (and the trumpets all sounded for him on the other side) 'you're having a problem with Time, are you?'

The man laughed. 'You can say that again,' he said. 'Bloody old stuff. Biggest blessed nuisance in the whole set-up. Here, what d'you make that? My eyes are getting so bad, it's terrible sometimes.'

George peered. He could just about make out the dial, but no calibrations whatsoever.

'I make it point three six four,' said God.

'Yup.'

'Ta. I mean,' he went on, 'this horrible old thing's the easy bit. Take out the knackered part, turn up a new one, slap it in, job done. It's what to do with all the waste stuff that's the problem.'

George nodded. He'd worked that out for himself, although by what logical route he had no idea. 'Temporal waste,' he said. 'Nasty.'

'Diabolical.' God sighed. 'Twenty-four hours more of it every day, leaking like buggery and stinking the place out. Can't burn it, can't bury it, doesn't dissolve in anything. You're stuck with it.'

'And,' George interrupted, 'it's not as if there's an endless supply of it to start with.'

God groaned. 'Don't remind me,' he said. 'Daftest thing I ever did, making the thing run on fossil fuel. Should've known better.'

'Easy mistake to make.'

'Daft mistake to make.' God switched off the lathe and lifted out the finished part. 'It's not brilliant,' he said, 'but it'll have to do. Pass me that duster, will you?'

'In other words,' George went on, 'on the one hand you've got too much waste time, and on the other, not enough raw material.' He paused, fully aware of the awesome nature of his position. 'Doesn't that suggest something to you?' he said quietly.

God looked at him.

'Like,' he forced himself to continue, 'recycling?'

God laughed. 'Sure,' he said. 'If I could. But I can't, can I?'

This is it, George old son. So go for it. 'Yes you can,' he heard himself say. 'No trouble.'

God looked at him again, and Hell was much, much better. In Hell, they only beat you up. Reflected in the lenses of God's spectacles, George could see himself; the truth, the real thing. Could have been worse, he realised, but still not a pleasant thing to happen to anybody, the sum total of your being splashed like a fly on a windscreen.

'No trouble,' he repeated. 'It works like this.'

CHAPTER TWENTY

'FREEZE!'

Bleary eyed and thoroughly narked, Lundqvist swung the door open and slouched through.

'Knock it off, Links,' he sighed wearily, 'it's me.'

'Oh.' Links Jotapian looked down at the revolver in his hand, and then at his mentor. 'You got him, then?'

'No.'

There was a moment's silence. The faint tinkling audible to the extra-perceptive ear was the sound of shattering dreams. 'You mean you *didn't* get him?'

'Mmm. Is there a bar round here, Links? I could murder a drink.'

'But.' Links stared. 'You must have got him, Mr Lundqvist. Kurt Lundqvist always gets his fiend.'

'Not this time, son. Now be a good boy and go away.'

Jotapian's lower lip quivered ominously. 'You let him escape?' A thought occurred to him. 'I get it. So's he'll lead us to where he's got the money stashed. Sorry, Mr Lundqvist, I should've guessed.'

Lundqvist gave him a cold look. 'What money, Links? There isn't any money. The little scumbag just escaped, that's all.'

'And you're just walking away?'

'You got it.'

Links pulled himself together with an effort, and stuck out his chest, what there was of it. 'No, Mr Lundqvist. He may have gotten away from you. He ain't gonna get away from me.' He jammed his hand down on the butt of his revolver, jerked his chin up high and walked resolutely through the doorway. There was a thump.

'It opens the other way, Links,' Lundqvist said. 'To open it, you pull.'

'Okay, Mr Lundqvist.' Pause. 'Mr Lundqvist?'

'Yes?'

'You *sure* you're not coming?'

'Sure, Links.' Lundqvist sat down on a rock, pulled off his left boot and massaged his foot. The lift had been out of order and it was a very, very long way down by the stairs.

'Okay, boss,' Links said. He tried not to let too much irony creep into the word 'Boss'. 'Be seeing you around, then.'

He pulled on the door, banged his nose, and was gone. For a moment Lundqvist sat motionless, thinking.

The boy was his apprentice. In his charge. His responsibility. It was hard going in there.

On the other hand ... His roving eye lit on the sign outside the Hellza-Pop-Inn; bright enough to be coming out the other side of garish, but broadly hinting that strong liquor was kept on the premises.

The boy's never going to learn for himself if you keep him wrapped up in cotton wool all the time.

But ...

He got up, put on his boot and pulled open the door.

'Links,' he yelled down the corridor.

'Yes, Mr Lundqvist?'

Kurt Lundqvist considered for a moment. 'When he hits you, try and roll with the punch. Sometimes it helps.'

He closed the door and went to the bar.

* * *

'I dunno,' said God, reaching for an old envelope and a stub of pencil. 'Could work, I suppose.'

George held his breath. Maybe Lucky George was the right name for him, and he'd been riding his luck all these years. But luck's rather like sponge cake; it's always better if you make it yourself.

'Tricky,' said God. 'I mean, you'd have to go a bit steady. One slip and, well . . .'

'I didn't say it was easy,' George interrupted. 'I said it was possible. There's a difference.'

God grinned. 'Just go through it again one more time,' he said, 'make sure I've got it straight in my mind.'

'Okay.' George took a deep breath. 'The problem with recycling Time,' he said, 'is that it's got History engraved all over it. You can't melt down Time without losing History. You lose History, nobody has the faintest idea who they are, or what's going on. Okay so far?'

God nodded.

'Well then,' said George, 'my idea is, you skim all the History off in thin sheets, using something like a very fine-bladed bandsaw. You've got something that can do the job?'

'Somewhere,' God replied. 'There's all sorts of bits and pieces out there. Like I said, one of these days I've got to have a really good tidy-up in here.'

'That's fine,' George said. 'So, you slice off the top three or four thousandths of an inch, leaving you with sort of tin foil stuff with all the History on. You can roll that up and store it in a fraction of the space you're using at the moment. The rest you melt down and use again. That's all there is to it.'

God took off his glasses and polished them on his sleeve. 'Still going to run out one day, though, isn't it?' he said. 'You're just putting off the problem, that's all.'

'Ah,' George replied. 'That's where the clever bit comes in, the new technology and all that. You set things up so that in future, the History foil is split off as soon as it's been processed, right? The rest of the stuff goes straight back in the melt. The history foil is then copied on to disc – it's absolutely amazing how much stuff you can get on a single disc these days – and then the foil can be melted down too. As and when you've got a moment, you can transfer the archives on to disc as well. Problem solved.'

'Hmm.'

George waited.

'Well,' God said at last, slowly unwrapping a peppermint, 'there are still problems. Like, suppose when I was cutting off the foil, my hand slipped or something and a great chunk of History got torn or buggered up.'

'Well . . .'

'Or what about when it's actually on the discs? Bits could get wiped. It happens.'

'Well . . .'

'Take a case in point,' God went on. 'The whole bit where you sell your soul to Them Buggers might get somehow lost. Think about it. We'd have to turn you loose, wouldn't we? Couldn't keep you banged up if what you did never happened. And if it's not in History, it never happened, did it?'

George opened both eyes wide. 'Do you know,' he said, 'that thought honestly never once crossed my mind.'

God laughed. 'I'll believe you,' he chuckled. 'Thousands wouldn't.'

Hard to gauge exactly how many years, or tens of years, passed in the world of mortal men while God crunched up his peppermint and drew faint, deft squiggles on the back of the envelope. George could feel time passing, just as you can feel lorries going by on the main road a mile away. Nothing to worry about, in context.

'It's a bit crude, though,' God said at last. 'It's not the way I'd have wanted to do it, really. In the first place, I mean.'

George shrugged. 'In the first place,' he said casually, 'was the Word, remember? You can only do your best with the materials available.'

God nodded his head slowly. 'Damn silly word it was, too,' he said. 'Took me a hell of a time just to get a good edge on it. Between me and you and these four walls,' he added confidentially, 'I've always reckoned the daft beggars must've spelt it wrong.'

'Get away.'

'Straight up.' God drew a few more squiggles, shrugged his shoulders and laid down the pencil. 'All right,' he said, 'I'll give it a go. Why not?'

'That's the spirit.'

'Yeah. And those bits of History we were talking about just now.'

'Yes?'

'Well.' God looked away, into the darkness of the boiler room. 'Trouble is, my old eyes aren't what they used to be. Could easily muck up quite a big bit before I knew what I'd done. And then where would we be?'

'Exactly.'

'In fact. I've got this horrible feeling that might just happen.'

'Just a feeling?'

'Virtual certainty.' God winked. 'On your way, George. I've enjoyed having a natter like this.'

'Me too.'

'Yeah.' God turned, picked up another envelope and sharpened his pencil. 'Mind how you go.'

In the darkness, Links froze. His hand tightened on the butt of his revolver.

There was something out there. He could smell the danger. Very slowly, he drew the gun and thumbed back the hammer.

A soft sound, like a footfall on a million years of dust. He opened his eyes wide, trying to make the most of each stray photon.

'Jerome?'

Inside him his heart turned to water. Suddenly the gun became heavy, far too heavy to hold. His arms sagged, as rigid as overcooked tagliatelli.

'You there, Jerome?'

'Yes, Mom,' Links whimpered.

'Jerome Jotapian, I've been looking all over for you. What you mean by sneaking out like that and worrying us all near to death?'

'Sorry, Mom.'

A shape loomed up in the darkness. Instinctively, Links shrank back.

'You just wait till your Pa gets home,' said Mrs Jotapian.

CHAPTER TWENTY-ONE

'FREEZE!'

'Piss off.'

'Oh.'

Helen of Troy frowned. She'd been to great trouble to acquire the small, pearl-handled automatic, more trouble still to get here, and virtually infinite pains to sneak up on Lundqvist in the bar and jam the muzzle of the gun into his ear. A girl likes to be appreciated.

'You do realise,' she said huffily, 'that this is a *gun* I'm—'

'Yeah,' Lundqvist sighed, 'sure. To be precise, it's a .25 Bauer, chrome finish, early seventies at a guess, pearl grips and machine engraving on the rear of the slide. I imagine you chose it to go with your earrings.'

Helen was impressed. 'You can tell all that from feeling it in your ear?'

'Lady,' Lundqvist replied with dignity, 'I've had more pieces shoved up my ear than you've had men. The difference is, I can tell them apart in the dark.'

'Pig.'

Helen sat down on a bar stool. 'It's still a gun,' she said, 'and if you make a move, I'll pull the trigger. Understood?'

'I was way ahead of you.'

'Fine.' With her left hand, Helen grabbed a handful of peanuts from the dish on the bar and gobbled them. Seven hours since she'd last eaten, not counting the biscuits on the plane. 'So what have you done with him?'

Lundqvist laughed bitterly. 'What have *I* done with *him*? Get outa here, will you? It's been a long day.'

Helen caught her breath. 'You mean he escaped?'

Lundqvist nodded. It takes practice to nod safely with a loaded gun in your ear, but Lundqvist had the experience. 'Yeah,' he said. 'If you're buying, mine's a very large Jack Daniels, no ice. If not, get lost.'

'You're sure he escaped?'

Lundqvist allowed himself a wry smile. 'Well,' he said, 'he escaped from *me*. What became of him after that is entirely his own problem.'

'You mean he's in danger?' Helen demanded angrily. 'And you're just sitting drinking?'

'I'm trying to drink. Idiots come and shove iron in my ears, but I guess I'll have to learn to take that sort of thing in my stride.'

'Men!'

Helen finished the peanuts, then nudged a little harder with the gun. 'If you don't find him this instant, I'll shoot you.'

A look of utter contempt flitted across Lundqvist's face, wiping its feet on his eyebrows as it passed. 'I get you,' he said. 'First you'll shoot me if I don't lay off, now you'll shoot me unless I find him. Consistency's not a big thing with you, right?'

'Just shut up and get on with it.'

'Anything you say, sister. Just one more drink, and I'll be—'

'Now.' By way of reinforcing her remarks, Helen pressed what she took to be the safety catch. The net effect was to send the magazine shooting out of the bottom of the gun into the residue of Lundqvist's Jack Daniels. He fished it out, made a vulgar noise and handed it to her.

'Does this mean you won't help me?' she said.

'Yeah.'

'Please?'

Lundqvist lifted his glass to his face, noticing the thin scum of gun oil on the meniscus just in time. He sighed, and waved to the barman.

'I think you're *mean*,' said Helen, and started to cry. Everyone in the bar turned their heads and stared.

'All *right*,' Lundqvist snapped. 'Whatever you like. Just for the love of God shut up that goddamn . . .'

'Sniff.'

'. . . Sniffling.'

'And no going arresting him when we do find him?'

Lundqvist chuckled bitterly. 'Me?' he said. 'Arrest anybody? That'll be the day.'

They stopped outside the emergency exit. 'He went in there?' Helen demanded. Lundqvist nodded, sat down on the grass and started to make a daisy chain.

'Come on,' said Helen impatiently. 'What're you waiting for?'

'Lady.' Lundqvist didn't look up. 'If you want to shoot me, first draw back the slide with your left hand, holding the pistol firmly in your right. When the slide is back against the stop, let go smoothly so as not to jam the feed, and release the safety catch, which is the small lever above the back of the grip on the left hand side. Your gun is now ready to fire. Do not pull the trigger; rather, squeeze firmly but smoothly in one continuous movement. I've been in there once and that'll do me fine.'

'Chicken.'

Lundqvist nodded, pulled up a dandelion and stuck it behind his ear.

'I'll start crying again.'

'Be my guest.'

Just then, Hieronymus Bosch hurried by clutching a portable telephone, flung open the door and shot through. Close behind him, running lopsided because of the heavy toolbox he had with him and looking rather charred round the edges, was Niccolò Machiavelli. Following him at a rather longer interval came Christopher Columbus, Hamlet Prince of Denmark, Leonardo da Vinci, William Caxton, two seagulls, Don Juan, Albrecht Dürer, Cornelius Vanderdecker, Martin Luther, Don Quixote de la Mancha wearing odd socks, Sir Thomas Malory and others too numerous to particularise. The painter Botticelli, bringing up the rear, called out, 'Wotcher, Nellie, do me another sitting sometime?' as he dashed past. All of them were carrying big dufflebags.

The door slammed.

'I take it you don't need me any more,' Lundqvist sighed. He had finished his daisy chain, and lowered it gingerly over his head. It stuck around his ears.

'No,' Helen replied distantly. 'Thanks.'

'Glad to be of service,' said Lundqvist, and returned to the bar.

The Marketing Director of Hell Holdings plc stood back, admiring his handiwork and sucking his thumb where he'd hit it with the hammer. The notice wasn't quite straight, but nailing bits of plywood to polystyrene trees wasn't exactly his thing. Not bad for a beginner.

GALA NIGHT!!!

There is no universally accepted definition of a gala night, except that it costs more to go in. He ran his eye down the list of advertised attractions and nodded his head contentedly.

BIRD-HEADED FIENDS!!

TORMENTS OF THE DAMNED!!!
UNIMAGINABLE HORRORS!!!!
OX-ROAST AND MAMMOTH CAR BOOT SALE!!!!!

He hesitated for a moment. At the time it had seemed pretty neat, but now he actually saw it in place, perhaps it lacked a certain culminating zing. Taking a thick-nibbed marker pen from his pocket, he wrote in:

CONGA!!!!!!

at the bottom, grinned and turned to depart. Just then the tree caught fire. It burned without being consumed, predictably enough. Not so the notice, which vanished in a curl of ash.

Why couldn't the old fool use the phone like everybody else?

Imagine Time.

There is no way you possibly could; but try and picture in your mind's eye an enormous machine, with a hopper at one end and conveyer belt at the other.

Into a hopper go phenomenal quantities of the raw material. It's invisible and intangible, naturally, so they use special harmless dyes to make it easier to perceive and handle. These are burnt off in the processing.

That's us.

So if some cleverdick philosopher comes up to you and tries to tell you that Man is the measure of all things and we're working towards an ultimate purpose, take no notice. The role of humanity in the Great Design is somewhere between permitted food colouring and bar codes.

Time is a convenient if misleading term used to describe the potential energy of the impending future. It burns, and the gases produced by its combustion compress a piston in the cylinder of physics, producing the power needed to turn the year on its axis and drive the barrel-organ of the spheres. Like most internal combustion engines, its burn is depressingly inefficient; Time burns at about one-per-cent efficiency, because the future is so impure with alternative sequences of events that only a minute part of each load of raw material actually oxidises on ignition. The rest might have burnt if only things had been different.

The waste material comes out the back end, is loaded on tipper trucks and taken away for the neighbours to complain about. And boy, do they complain.

CHAPTER TWENTY-TWO

OVER the years there have been many attempts to describe Hell, some more felicitous than others. Jean-Paul Sartre, for example, would have you believe that Hell is other people.

Now, then; no disrespect whatsoever to the late Mr Sartre, as fine a writer as ever honed a subordinate clause and by all accounts a very competent amateur pianist. But no. To be disagreeably pedantic, Hell isn't other people at all. Other people are never worse than bloody aggravating. Hell is *hell*.

It's a very hot, noisy, unpleasant place full of inhuman tortures and bird-headed fiends; and the moonlight walking tours, souvenir sweatshirts and conference weekends introduced by the new management have, if anything, added to the efficiency of an already superbly effective eternity-spoiling unit. Any attempt at description which omits these basic elements is inaccurate.

And EuroBosch is to Hell as Picadilly Circus is to England; more picturesque, perhaps, if you like that sort of thing, but definitely an integral part. The same rules apply; and one of the rules is that all stories in Hell have to have an unhappy ending.

The emergency exit opened.

Helen looked up, catching her breath. For a moment she couldn't see anything. Then ...

... Then she cast her mind back, involuntarily, to a moment some years ago (though it seemed like only yesterday).

'Hi,' he'd said. 'My name's George. You must be Helen.'

This strange voice, coming at her from incredibly far off. A nice voice, she remembered thinking as the particles of matter and soul that had once comprised her being were suddenly scooped back from the four corners of creation for a totally unexpected reunion. A calm, wry voice, slightly cynical but not bitter. The sort of voice ...

Just a cotton-picking minute, she remembered thinking, I'm dead. Life and I were very adult about it all and went our separate ways long ago, no recriminations, death is never having to say you're sorry.

'Pleased to meet you,' said the voice. 'I've heard *so* much about you, and ...'

Goddamnit, she'd got her legs back. And *her* legs, too; the long, perfectly proportioned honey-coloured ones she'd had as a girl, not the varicose travesties they'd fobbed her off with in her declining years. And her arms, too, and her ears, and her lips and *everything*; the whole ensemble, in fact, all in perfect working order. No scent of mothballs, no corners chewed off by earth-dwelling invertebrates. Her hair was even combed, her nails varnished. Cerise, which wasn't really her colour, but ...

'Yippee!' she said.

'Do you mind?' retorted the voice called George. 'Only, my head is a wee bit sensitive this morning. Would you just sign here, please?'

She'd opened her eyes, and seen – well, a big piece of paper, with black squiggles all over it. They'd had paper in her day, back around 1450 BC, but not black squiggles.

'It's just a receipt,' the voice called George had told her, 'for Mephisto here. Just to say you've got your body back and it works okay. Mephisto's a good lad, for a foul fiend, but he does love his admin. Go on, just do a squiggle or something.'

She'd found a feather in her hand, with something black and wet on the end; some sort of paint, presumably. 'You want me to paint something on the paper with this feather?'

'Yes, please.'

'All right.' She splodged, and the pen and the paper vanished. And there she was. In this sort of place, sitting on what she could only presume was a chair, looking at something which might almost have been a table. On the table was a wine bottle, wrapped in straw, with a candle shoved in its neck.

'I think I'll have the sole in butter,' said the voice called George, 'followed by the stroganoff. What about you?' The voice, she noticed, was coming out of the mouth of this man sitting opposite her. He looked nice.

'To eat,' he explained. Yes, she'd thought, definitely nice. Priorities absolutely right and everything.

Over lunch he'd explained. How he'd always wanted to meet her, Helen of Troy, and how, since he'd sold his soul to the devil for an effectively blank cheque, her having been dead for well over three thousand years wasn't the insuperable problem it might have been, and how here they were with a ticket to ride throughout Time and Space, expense no object, if she felt like coming along.

'This,' he'd said, gesturing at the environment and nearly knocking a bowl of soup out of the hands of a passing waiter, 'is the twentieth century AD. Not the best of times, in my opinion, except for the food. I come here for lunch most days, in fact.'

'This place?'

'This century. It's worth the effort just for the pasta.'

'Ah.'

'But not the wine.' He'd frowned. 'Phylloxera, in the early

part of the century. Killed off all the best varieties of grape.'

In actual fact she hadn't really taken to him all that much, not at first; he seemed a bit arrogant, seen and done everything, met everyone, been everywhere. The fact that he *had* seen and done everything, met everyone and been everywhere only made it worse. There was also the fact that he'd brought her back to life from the grave, and gratitude is always a truly poisonous start to any relationship.

On the other hand, a choice between going about with a suave, accomplished, amusing, handsome man-about-Time-and-Space who has virtually infinite magic powers, and being dead, isn't exactly something you agonise over in the small hours of the morning. And after a relatively short while, she realised that being aggravating was only one facet of the man's multiplex persona. A significant facet, to be sure; but only one. Besides, George Faustus being aggravating had a lot to recommend it, particularly when he was being aggravating to somebody else. The Pope, for instance, or Napoleon, or the head waiter at Maxim's.

She'd become quite fond of him, in fact.

Which was why, the first time he'd been foreclosed upon and dragged away to Hell by bird-headed fiends, she'd been really rather upset. She had no great desire to see it happen a second time.

Accordingly, she turned her head and looked away.

Therefore she didn't see a howling, lurching nightmare of demons, beast-, bird-, and fish-headed, loathsome random assemblies from the spares box of evolution, whooping and brandishing toasting forks, kicking and dancing their way in a phantasmagorical conga against a background of leaping red flames; and, hoisted on their shoulders, the small, motionless figure of Lucky George.

Imagine ... There isn't enough cheese in the world, Wesleydale, Stilton and Brie, to make up a bedtime snack capable of giving rise to the sort of bad dream you'd need to picture it in your mind's bloodshot eye. A riot of tentacles, pincers and talons. A maelstrom of pitchforks, meathooks, carving knives and corkscrews. Teeth beyond the wildest opium vision of dentistry, claws beyond even Satan's chiropody. Enough scaled hides to make handbags for all the witches in eternity. Enough plastic red noses . . .

Plastic red noses? Wait a minute . . .

Kurt Lundqvist, well and truly into the bourbon and branchwater, hold the branchwater, looked up and grinned. Thanks to enough alcohol to poison Chicago, he could now see clearly that he'd in fact succeeded, and the inevitable happy ending was chiming in nicely on cue. After all, he reasoned, as another billion brain cells fizzed into mucous slime, the fact that a bunch of penny-a-day fiends made the actual collar is neither here nor there. If he hadn't chased George into the one place on the whole campus where there was no possibility whatsoever of escape, there'd have been no collar at all.

'Drinks all round,' he snarled. 'C'mon, move it.'

The barfiend favoured him with a look of pure hatred.

'It's a quarter to three,' he said. 'Unhappy hour,' he explained. 'There's no-one in the place 'cept you and—'

'Okay,' Lundqvist replied. 'So I'll have another.'

As we mentioned a moment ago, the demons danced. And as they danced, they sang:

For he's a jolly good fellow
For he's a jolly good fellow
For he's a jolly good fellow –
And so say all of us.

All stories in Hell have an unhappy ending. Unhappy for whom is at the discretion of the management.

* * *

'Three cheers,' yelled the lead demon, pulling off his rubber mask, 'for Lucky George. *Hip hip* . . .'

'Hooray!' bellowed Cornelius Vanderdecker, Sir Thomas More, Hieronymus Bosch and Leonardo da Vinci, through their latex mouthpieces.

'Hip hip . . .'

'Hooray!' answered Niccolò Machiavelli, Christopher Columbus, Pieter Breughel the Elder, William Caxton, two seagulls, Lorenzo de' Medici, Sir Thomas Malory, Pol de Limbourg and Andrea del Sarto.

'Hip hip . . .'

'Hooray!' shouted the rest of the friends of Lucky George, raising their burden, pink with embarrassment and smiling foolishly, shoulder-high.

The barfiend turned and scowled meaningfully.

'Hooray,' muttered Kurt Lundqvist into his glass. 'Satisfied?'

All stories in Hell have an unhappy ending. The trick is therefore to keep going, so that there can be no ending.

The procession halted, dumped their rubber masks and stood. No prizes for guessing what was expected to happen next. Nevertheless, Lenny da Vinci, master of the unnecessary remark, shouted, 'Speech!'

Lucky George looked down, smiled, and scratched his ear.

'Thanks,' he said. 'I owe you all one.'

'Any time,' chorused the friends of Lucky George; and, for the first time, Helen guessed exactly why they called him Lucky.

The procession stayed halted and continued to stand. It's at times like this that inevitably somebody says, 'First of all I want to thank my agent.'

It is to George's eternal credit that he didn't. Instead, he made a vague gesture with his left hand and smiled . . .

. . . Whereupon the biggest, shiniest yellow brick road you ever saw materialised under everyone's feet. Straight as an arrow it ran, right across the middle of the theme park, due north. It was at this point that the Production Director, who'd been watching gobsmacked from the Bridge Embattled by Armies, leant over the parapet and threw up.

'Well, quite,' said the Marketing Director, standing next to him. 'On the other hand . . .'

His colleague looked up, hurriedly wiping his face with his sleeve. 'You can't be serious,' he gasped.

The Marketing Director shrugged. 'Okay,' he said, 'integrity counts for something in this game, but we've got shareholders to consider. And what it all boils down to in the final analysis is bums on seats.'

'Not seats,' insisted the Production Director. 'Spikes.'

'Whatever.' The Marketing Director stood for a moment, his head tilted slightly to one side, visualising. 'All right, maybe it's not our idea of Hell, yours and mine. But so what? We have,' he added ingenuously, 'a duty to the public. Elitism's a thing of the past, you know. You've got to go with the mood, right?'

'No.'

'That's your final word, then, is it?'

'Yes.'

'The hell with you then,' replied the Marketing Director affably, pushing his colleague off the bridge into the leaping flames below. Then he straightened his tie, and marched purposefully away in search of Walt Disney.

'George,' said Helen.

'Mmmm?'

'Where exactly are we going?'

George looked down. Under his feet, still yellow bricks, although the procession had now diminished down to two, plus a pair of seagulls circling high overhead.

'Does it matter?'

Helen snuggled closer. 'Not really, I suppose,' she replied. 'Just so long as when we get there, there's going to be fitted carpets.'

'Maybe, love.'

'And matching curtains. Say there's going to be matching curtains, George, go on please.'

'All right,' said George, 'there'll be matching curtains. Somewhere.'

'Where?'

George thought for a moment. 'Would "over the rainbow" be sufficiently precise, do you think?'

'No.'

'Oh.' He sucked his lower lip. 'Do they really have to match?' he asked.

'Yes.'

'Couldn't they clash even slightly?'

Helen shook her head. 'George,' she said, 'I've waited for you over three thousand years, I've lied for you, stolen for you, been kidnapped for you, followed you to Hell and back, don't you think I've *earned* matching curtains?'

'Well ...' George considered. 'Just so long as they're not pink,' he said.

'What I had in mind was more a sort of pinky peach,' Helen replied, 'to go with the loose covers, which I thought of as being something like pale apricot, with perhaps just a hint of—'

'And a shed,' he added. 'I really must insist on a shed. Somewhere I can work on the magic and that sort of thing.'

Helen laughed musically. 'If there's time,' she said. 'I shall need a lot of shelves putting up.'

The sun chose that moment to glint on Helen's hair, as golden as ripe corn; or, as George couldn't help thinking, more a sort of light honey with just a soupçon of goldy fawn.

'All right,' said George, meekly. 'Anything you say.'

Somewhere in the Sublime, God looked up from his lathe and laughed.

OVERTIME

Tom Holt

Only in a Tom Holt novel can you discover the relationship between the Inland Revenue, the Second Crusade and God's great plan to build starter planets for first time life forms . . .

It all started for Guy Goodlet somewhere over Caen. One moment he was heading for the relative safety of the coast, aware that fuel was low and the Mosquito had more than a few bullet holes in it. The next, his co-pilot was asking to be dropped off. This would have been odd if Peter had still been alive. Since he was dead, it was downright worrying.

But not quite as worrying as when Guy found himself somewhere in the High Middle Ages – rather than in 1943 – in the company of one John de Nesle. Unsurprisingly, Guy's first thought was to get out and home sharpish. But then he saw John's sister, Isoud, and somehow found himself agreeing to help John, also known as Blondel, in his quest to find Richard Coeur de Lion . . .

Overtime is another riotously funny novel from the acclaimed author of *Ye Gods!* and *Flying Dutch*.

AN ORBIT BOOK
FANTASY

HERE COMES THE SUN

Tom Holt

All is not well with the universe – entropy and the
cutbacks have taken their toll, and the sun is dirty and
late, thanks to being 30,000,000,000,000 miles overdue on
its next service. And you just can't seem to get the
personnel these days, what with all the older workers
retiring rather than face the problems of another round of
financial constraint. And none of the committees can
agree on anything. Extreme measures seem to be
called for.

But there's extreme, and there's recruiting mortals to help
run things. The Chief of Staff is uneasy when the dapper
Mr Ganger suggests it as a solution. But he's not half as
uneasy as Jane, who, after a momentary fall from grace
with three cream doughnuts, finds herself sitting next to a
daemon offering her a very strange job, which involves
tidying up after a certain carelessness with earthquakes
and tidal waves, and responding to crises, such as when
joyriders decide to try their luck with one of the more
important heavenly bodies.

AN ORBIT BOOK
FANTASY

GRAILBLAZERS

Tom Holt

THE HOLY GRAIL AND THE WHOLLY INEPT

Fifteen hundred years have passed and the Grail is still missing, presumed ineffable; the Knights have dumped the Quest and now deliver pizzas; the sinister financial services industry of the lost kingdom of Atlantis threatens the universe with fiscal Armageddon; while in the background lurks the dark, brooding, red-caped presence of Father Christmas.

In other words, Grailmate. Has Prince Boamund of Northgales (Snotty to friends) woken from his enchanted sleep in time to snatch back the Apron of Invincibility, overthrow the dark power of the Lord of the Reindeer and find out exactly what a Grail is? And just who did do the washing-up after the Last Supper?

Take a thrilling Grailhound bus ride into the wildly improbable with Tom Holt.

AN ORBIT BOOK
FANTASY

☐	Expecting Someone Taller	Tom Holt	£4.99
☐	Who's Afraid of Beowulf?	Tom Holt	£4.99
☐	Flying Dutch	Tom Holt	£4.99
☐	Ye Gods!	Tom Holt	£4.99
☐	Overtime	Tom Holt	£4.99
☐	Here Comes the Sun	Tom Holt	£4.99
☐	Grailblazers	Tom Holt	£4.99
☐	Odds and Gods	Tom Holt	£14.99

Orbit now offers an exciting range of quality titles by both established and new authors. All of the books in this series are available from:

Little, Brown and Company (UK),
P.O. Box 11,
Falmouth,
Cornwall TR10 9EN.

Alternatively you may fax your order to the above address. Fax No. 0326 376423.

Payments can be made as follows: cheque, postal order (payable to Little, Brown and Company) or by credit cards, Visa/Access. Do not send cash or currency. UK customers and B.F.P.O. please allow £1.00 for postage and packing for the first book, plus 50p for the second book, plus 30p for each additional book up to a maximum charge of £3.00 (7 books plus).

Overseas customers including Ireland, please allow £2.00 for the first book plus £1.00 for the second book, plus 50p for each additional book.

NAME (Block Letters) ....

....

ADDRESS ....

....

....

☐ I enclose my remittance for _____

☐ I wish to pay by Access/Visa Card

Number ☐☐☐☐☐☐☐☐☐☐☐☐☐☐☐☐

Card Expiry Date ☐☐☐☐